The Conjuror's Apprentice

Best wishes

G Williams

The
Conjuror's
Apprentice

The first book in Tudor Rose Murders series

G J Williams

Red Door

A RedDoor book
Published by Ember Press 2022
www.emberpress.co.uk

© 2022 G J Williams

ISBN 978-1-9997701-2-9

A CIP catalogue record for this book is available from the British
Library

Cover design: Kari Brownlie

Typesetting: Jen Parker, Fuzzy Flamingo
www.fuzzyflamingo.co.uk

Printed in the UK by CPI Group (UK), Croydon

To my dear friends

Conjuror

One that practises magic arts

Doctor John Dee, born in 1527, was described as the Arch Conjuror of England. The reference incensed both him and his supporters. Until this slur he had been seen as the most learned man in England – a scholar whose studies had taken him from Cambridge to Louvain and the other great courts and universities of Europe to work with the most brilliant minds of his time. His studies covered mathematics, astronomy, religion, geography, the great tides of the world, alchemy, and he even drafted the first paper on the English Empire.

But this was not enough for Dee. He craved higher knowledge through magic, the spirit world, communing with angels and the power of crystals and artefacts. It was this wisdom which made him both a favourite of Elizabeth I and yet a dangerous man with whom to be too closely associated. Today his brilliance is clouded in mystique – was he a conjuror of the dark arts or simply a man centuries ahead of his time?

CAST OF CHARACTERS

The Constable household

John Dee – scholar, astronomer, theologian, physician, conjuror
Margaretta Morgan – his apprentice disguised as a maid
Master Constable – merchant
Katherine Constable – his wife
Mam – Margaretta's mother
Huw – Margaretta's brother

The Cecil household

William Cecil – lawyer, politician and advisor/friend to Princess
    Elizabeth
Mildred Cecil – his wife and one of England's most educated
    women
Goodwife Barker – housekeeper
Lottie – housemaid
Father Thomas – priest and family friend

The wherrymen

Sam – young wherryman and apprentice
Master Tovey – Sam's master

Other characters

Robert Meldrew – Architect of the Savoy as it is renovated

Lord Englefield, Thomas Prideaux, George Ferrers – Men of rank at court

Lord Herbert of Pembroke – Courtier, politician, soldier and advisor to monarchs

Susan McFadden – sister to Margaretta, wife to Angus and mother of little Jack

PROLOGUE

They dragged the bundle from the small waves lapping detritus at the north shore of the Thames. Robert Meldrew rolled it over and retched. The others ran. In the bloody pulp that had once been a young boy's face, the broken lips moved with an urgent whisper, but the wind carried the words away.

His finder took a deep breath and bent closer. 'Say it again, lad.'

The words made no sense, but he could write them later. Behind him, footsteps clattered along the path and then the cry of a nun muffled by the hands she clasped over her face. Meldrew shouted at her to fetch the priest. Then he looked out across the river and screamed, 'You spleen of Satan! Do not bring your evil here!' But the wherry was already gone.

CHAPTER ONE

May 1555

The screaming started when the flames licked at their feet. Then the smell of burning flesh. One of the poor wretches screamed to his God to douse the fire. But for these three souls, no one was listening.

Margaretta Morgan turned and ran away; pushing up the thronging street so as not to witness the writhing and begging for mercy, covering her ears to shut out the baying of the crowd and the frightened cries of children. She prayed for the merciful explosion – the sign that someone had the goodness to fill their clothes with gunpowder and blast them to God's care. It never came. The wretched wailing of burning Protestants still filled the air three streets away. Her head swam with anguish.

Oh God, why did Doctor Dee send me here? He says I am an old soul who may have been on this earth many times. That I have seen too much but that every birth wipes out memory. So I know much and yet recall nothing but this life. So says he. But does being his hidden apprentice make me deserve such lessons?

She bent to be sick in a gutter outside a tavern. Wiping her mouth, there was relief to see a goodwife staring from the battered door. Might she give a little kindness? No. With a screech the tavern woman rushed across the cobbles with a twig broom, yelling that her custom did not want to tread through a weakling's mess. Margaretta ran. When tears turned to anger she stamped home to the lodging house of Doctor John Dee to tell him that witnessing the horrors of Queen Mary's venom was no education. It was a cruelty.

As usual the Constables' house in the parish of St Dunstan's was in darkness, save a lone candle in her master's window. John Dee – astronomer, alchemist, mathematician, scryer, all-round optimist in regaining his rank at court and, today, a cruel tutor. She pushed the door and escaped the smell of the foetid River Thames which flowed behind the banking only a patch of grass away from the front wall. One of the mangy hounds ran to her for food. All was quiet. Master Constable would be propped up in a tavern somewhere; Doctor Dee locked in his office preoccupied with numbers, stars and magic; Mam would be sulking in her bed and her brother, Huw, probably still on the riverbank counting wherries. As for Mistress Constable, she never deigned to enter the kitchen since Margaretta, Mam and Huw had arrived, as payment in lieu of Doctor Dee's lodging rent. 'As if we were his chattels to lend and loan as he likes,' she hissed, the horror of the burnings now conflagrating to a general anger with the world.

Margaretta lit a taper from the bread oven cinders and went to the door of John Dee's room at the top of the stairs. She would speak her mind and say his education was folly, before the passing of the night took the edge off her indignation.

'Doctor John?'

No answer. He must be sleeping on his desk again. She pushed the door and peeped in. He was bent over, a magnifying glass held close to a paper, his face etched with worry. Fury deserted her.

'Do you want food, Doctor?'

He grunted and crooked a finger. The desk was a tumult

of papers, candles, his measuring implements and a few plates smeared with butter and uneaten breadcrumbs. Manuscripts papered the floor; shelves bowed under books and the room glinted with the objects he had brought from his travels to Louvain, Paris and elsewhere – Mercator's globes, his treasured magical sigil, brass implements for measuring the stars, all things of magic which still meant little to Margaretta. It smelled of tallow candles and the dried lavender he kept in a silver dish on his mantel. Apparently, angels like sweet smells and will turn their faces from stench. The parchment under inspection was a map of the Thames. He tapped on a bend in the river with the word Savoy next to it.

'They found him here.'

'Who, doctor?'

'A young lad called Jonas Warren. The boatmen pulled him from the water thinking he was a dead seal. Face battered to a pulp. Body broken to pieces.'

Margaretta grimaced. 'How do you know?'

'Lord Cecil's messenger came here this afternoon. He wants me...us...to investigate.' A pause. 'Claims an advisor suggested my name.' The voice was low and bitter. He narrowed his eyes. 'This might be the chance I have been waiting for.'

'Chance?'

'Back to court. Through Cecil.'

'I don't understand.'

Dee rolled his eyes, as he often did when others did not follow the convolutions of his mind. 'William Cecil lies low, having escaped the axe when Queen Mary forgave him for signing the paper putting Lady Jane Grey on the throne instead of her.' He made a cynical laugh. 'But he is building favour with the queen's half-sister, the Lady Elizabeth. When she ascends the throne, he will be back on his path to power at court. If I help him, he must help me.'

Margaretta looked nervously at the door. 'How can you speak of Lady Elizabeth being queen? We have a queen in Mary.'

Dee gave a self-satisfied smile. 'My horoscope shows Elizabeth will be queen.' Dee shifted in his chair and looked away. 'I did not tell you. A month ago I was called to Woodstock by Blanche ap Harri, my cousin and Elizabeth's confidant.' He emphasised the words 'my cousin'. 'She asked me to draw up the horoscopes of Elizabeth and Mary. Also Mary's husband, Philip of Spain.' He frowned. 'I did not need your gifts. It is only mathematics and calculing.'

Margaretta stared, gulped and shook her head. 'Only mathematics? It's conjuring the dark arts…and its treason.'

Dee wagged his hands as if batting away her words. 'But it was Cecil who advised Blanche to consult me. He dare not risk offending court. So I will be protected.'

It was Margaretta's turn to roll her eyes. 'What has this to do with investigating the death of a river boy? He probably wronged the boatmen. You know what a rabble they are.'

John Dee raised his hand. 'He was a groom at Lord Cecil's house. His tongue stabbed – the sign that they were stopping him speaking. But he spluttered something before his soul departed.'

'What?'

'Cecil believes it might have been a name.' John Dee looked up at Margaretta, his eyes red with reading for hours. 'Maybe the name of the person who threatens Cecil. Find that and we find the killer; then Cecil can pay me and go back under his stone.'

Margaretta gave a little shudder and stared at the map. The doctor pulled at his beard. 'And there is something else.'

He leaned over and opened a pewter box. Inside, a deck of cards nestled in a bed of blue silk, each one richly painted with images and symbols and people. He kept this box well hidden behind books and Margaretta had not yet been schooled in their meaning. The doctor deftly pulled out the top card and laid it on the map.

'This was the first card I pulled.' It depicted a woman sitting on a throne. Each hand holding a sword held vertical.

Margaretta looked at her master, her face puzzled, and then turned again to look over her shoulder at the door. 'Do the Constables know you have these?'

He ignored her concern and tapped the card. 'The queen of swords. The card speaks of a clever, independent and practical woman. She sits alone but has power and influence. One who will fight and defend her right to her place in life.'

'Your admirer, doctor?' Margaretta winked, trying to lighten the atmosphere.

'No,' he growled. 'And do not use that term for Mistress Constable. She is the good wife of my late father's business associate.' Then he nodded back at the cards. 'Listen on, Margaretta, and take your mind off foolish prattle.'

He turned over the next card: a young man below an angry sky holding the swords of other men who are fleeing in sadness. 'The five of swords. They tell of terrible conflict driven by cruel ambition. A man who will go to any length to gain the power he craves. He brings the fury of the heavens to earth in pursuit of his desire for dominance.'

Margaretta jumped as the candle sputtered next to her. The doctor kept staring and then turned a third card. It was the image of a skeleton, holding a scythe. The numbers XIII – thirteen; and only two words – 'La Mort'.

Margaretta shuddered. 'What does it mean?'

The doctor's voice dropped to a whisper. 'It is a major arcana card whose message binds the other two.' He paused. 'Endings, beginnings, transitions, change. It means life will be in flux. One phase will die and another will rise.' He winced. 'But the rising of another phase will be a time of despair and demise.' Another frown. 'But whose demise? Usually there are several affected.'

Margaretta waited in tense silence.

He tapped a long finger on the queen card. 'This, I believe, is Princess Elizabeth.' Then he tapped the five of swords. 'This shows the man or people who seek to harm her.' The third card was tapped. 'And this will be the storm of their ambition.'

He turned to look Margaretta straight in the eye. 'We face terrible times, my dear, just as my horoscope foretold. And the death of the boy heralds the beginning.'

Chapter Two

It was a chill morning for May. The dull kitchen smelled of damp and unbaked dough. Margaretta rubbed her eyes after a troubled, dream-filled night.

'Come, Huw. You cannot talk to the dogs all the time. If you are going to learn a trade and be a man you have to know your letters. To the table now.'

Margaretta's brother took no notice and continued to sit cross-legged on the floor, rhythmically petting and then sniffing the hound. He muttered a rhyme in his mother tongue of Welsh over and over, rocking gently with the rhythm of the words.

Margaretta stamped over and bent to take his face in her hands. 'Listen to me. Stop this and get to the table for your letter study.'

In an instant the boy twisted away, letting out a wail of frustration. She clasped his cheeks and forced his head back to centre, staring directly into his eyes. When he shut them closed she shook him.

'Look at me, Huw. If you don't move to the table, I'll hold you here.' Then she tightened further to stop him writhing. 'Look at me. You are fourteen years next birthday. Soon a man. You will need your letters in this hard world.'

Slowly, reluctantly, he focused on her green eyes. His were crumpled with a frown and his mouth turned down in frustration. 'Bad letters, good letters, bad letters, good letters.'

'Doctor John has made you a wooden alphabet of letters and your daily task is to make up as many words as you can.'

'Good letters, bad letters, good letters, bad letters.'

'Doctor John says they are all good. Now do your lesson.'

Another frown, but his legs moved. This was Margaretta's sign to release his face and hope he was obedient. Lord knew she needed to make him more useful around this house before Doctor John's rental agreement began to wane in value. Mistress Constable's initial delight at having three servants to order around had soon dulled when she realised that two of the three were of limited use. The boy sloped off towards the table and stared at his oaken letters, before carefully arranging himself on the chair, checking that he sat exactly in the centre. Then the scraping as the seat was adjusted over and over to be exactly square with the table and the right distance away. Eventually his hands went into a blur of movement as letters were arranged into the alphabet, each one exactly the width of a finger apart. Then he pulled out the bad letters – K, Q, X and Z – and hurled them in the direction of the fire. They bounced on the stone floor, falling shy of the flames. Though he had, no doubt, intended that. Those letters were not in his mother tongue.

'No, Huw.'

He ignored his sister and began compiling words. Faster and faster he made the combinations. Every time he had used all his letters, they were gathered into a pile and he started again, making more words or repeating those he liked. This would occupy him for hours and so Margaretta could turn her attention to the pottage. She was already behind and the mistress would be calling soon for her morning honey tea.

A few minutes later a small bent figure shuffled through the door. Margaretta tried a smile. 'Good morning, Mam. Did you sleep well?'

A shake of the head and a mournful look as ever. 'Not I. Cold. I think my bones will never warm again.' Then she looked at Huw, still muttering every word he created, faster and faster as his excitement grew. 'God help us for the trials he sends.'

Her daughter rolled her eyes to heaven and let out an exasperated sigh. 'Blessed Lord, Mam. Compared to the poor wretches I saw yesterday, we have no trials.'

Her mother shook her head slowly, looking back into the fire as she pulled a knitted shawl across her thin shoulders. Everything about her was grey – her dress, her wrap, her hair, her skin. Even her eyes were grey. 'Look at me. No husband. No strength. A moonstruck son. No hope. No future.'

Margaretta hit the ladle on the cauldron to signal her anger, making both her mother and brother jump. 'We have a roof, a bed, food in our bellies and a master who lets us all stay under his protection. Most men would turn us out on the road for being too much trouble.'

'I think his landlady will do just that.'

'Stop this, Mam. Be glad that we have what we do.'

'It's only your gifts which keep us here. Only the fact that the doctor has been honing them. That is why he brought us from our home. What if they leave you?'

'They are God-given. If I say my prayers and do my best, why would He take them from me?'

Dear God, Mam. All I feel from you is anger and resentment. Do you ever think of me? Do you ever wonder if I regret telling John Dee that I could sense the thoughts and feelings of others? Regret agreeing to be his experiment? What did he call it? An apprentice of angelmancy. Maybe I was better off as laundry girl to his cousin in Wales. But life changed the day John Dee visited. I felt the dread his companion was feeling and asked why. The doctor's eyes lit up and my fate was sealed. Four months later here we are – far from the beauty of our home in Brecon and working for our food in this filthy city of London. If only I could bring Dada back.

Mother Morgan did not see her daughter looking at her sadly, but stared into the flames in a determined ploy to remain miserable. Thankfully another voice entered the kitchen, hailing from the central hall. It was Mistress Constable.

'Margaretta, bring tea. Then the doctor wants you to travel with him. Hurry now.' The tone was shrill with her perpetual disappointment.

Doctor John must have stayed in his office all the night rather than give his landlady, and evident admirer, the attention she liked while her husband was out doing business in the taverns of the London Quays. She craved John Dee's company every night in her sitting chamber after spending the whole day doing nothing but play with her kitten and sew pretty linens.

Huw giggled at the table and Margaretta saw he had made a new word of his letters. *Bobaloyne.* His sister quickly disarrayed them, glaring at her brother. 'Don't make bad words of others, Huw. You will have us in rags the way you're going.'

The boy growled and started to rock. But there was no time to calm him now. There was honey tea to be made, pottage to be stirred and a murder to be investigated. John Dee had previously created their tactics in the investigation of a dead farmer in Wales. A simple case but he had proved his formula and now he would apply it again. She would walk in her master's shadow, using her gifts to go amongst the people, watching, listening, investigating and feeling their thoughts and fears. As a woman she could be invisible and bring back the snippets, talk and evidence which they would compile into a picture in his office. Her ancient gifts of insight would meld with his brilliance of mind and they would uncover the story behind the murder, reveal the killer and their motive. Then Doctor John Dee would present his conclusions and attain the applause he so craved and which he hoped would get him back to the status and courtly standing his father had so spectacularly lost. But she was a hidden apprentice, for a woman with gifts would only be branded a witch in these times. Margaretta shuddered at the memory of the burnings and vowed to thank her God for keeping her one of John Dee's many secrets.

Today her apprenticeship would start her on a journey to unravel the mystery of a boy in the river with a cut tongue.

CHAPTER THREE

The coach rattled out of St Dunstan's onto Eastcheap and headed west. The night's rain had made the road a mess of mud and small stones. Every few minutes, a large divot would make their vehicle lurch to the side. Margaretta clung to the window frame and stared out to stop herself getting sick in her stomach. Doctor John, dressed in his favourite coat of blue and his head well covered by his cap, was reading a document, apparently oblivious to the rolling and clattering. He had taken care to wash his beard this morning so it shone like a dark waterfall from his chin to his chest. His face, prematurely lined but kind, was golden as the early sun shone through from the East.

Margaretta studied him. She had calculated he was only twenty-seven years old yet his face seemed to hold the history of a hundred men – though this was not so surprising. In his life he had already been a scholar in both England and in foreign lands, a tutor, a maker of fantastical models, a mathematician, an astrologer, and advisor to King Edward, the poor child. Even the great warrior knight, Sir Herbert of Pembroke, had trusted him in his household. John Dee had been born the son of an immensely rich wool-tax collector, favoured by King Henry. But now he was poor and ignored by Henry's daughter, Mary Tudor, though he was ever seeking a route back to the riches of court, recognition and the resumption of the family fortunes.

In John Dee's lap was a parchment covered in circles within

a divided square. Words were carefully entered into a panel at the side while numbers littered the circles. Periodically, he would sigh and shake his head.

'What is the document?' asked Margaretta, bored with the silence now.

'Another horoscope divined using my new method of measurement,' came the vague answer.

'Is it not foolish to carry such things out of the house, doctor? Anything but the words of the Pope is beckoning accusation these days and you...'

John Dee batted away the end of her sentence with an irritated wagging of his hand. 'I need to check my calculations. If this is true then the tarot underestimated the future. This portends many enemies surrounding the Lady Elizabeth. I saw it last month when I conjured her first horoscope. But it worsens.'

Margaretta pushed her head out of the window to see if the coachman could hear them. Thank the Lord he was singing to himself and so taking no notice. She turned to warn Dee anyway but he was deep in contemplation again.

Margaretta stared out. The streets thronged with animals and people all busying their way through the detritus of the road. Hawkers screeched their wares, delivery boys shouted for a clear path to save dropping the huge packages on their back, well-dressed women held up nosegays and looked away from the beggars and children who held out hopeful hands. But not a single face held a smile. Yet only a few short weeks ago, the streets had been full of rejoicing, hailing of glad tidings; Te Deums were sung in every church. Priests thanked the Lord for the safe delivery of a son to Queen Mary and in the streets people danced as if this child was the second coming, here to save them from a terrible fate – being ruled by Mary's husband, the very Spanish King Philip.

Then the rumours started. There was no cry of a newborn. Some said the queen had lied, others spoke behind their hands of Lord North trying to buy the babes of women who had birthed the child of a Spaniard; pamphlets shouted that the queen was dead. Court went quiet and London waited while criers claimed the doctors had simply miscalculated the birthing day. Sullen silence. Then the screams from the pyres started again.

As if he could read her thoughts, John Dee suddenly looked up. 'You have not told me about your lesson yesterday.'

Margaretta swallowed hard. Recalling the flames and the screams would only raise the bile already collecting in her throat. 'Cruel,' she snapped, not looking at him.

'Come, Margaretta. If you are going to hone your gifts you have to understand the full spectrum of men's feelings, fears and fallacious thoughts. The good, the evil, the kind, the cruel, the intelligent and the witless. It is all part of our soul and you need to see them all.'

Margaretta turned bright, green eyes on her master. 'I can feel evil without having to see its result, Doctor John. I'll never forget those cries. Terrible it was.' She sat back with a self-righteous huff.

Abruptly, her travelling companion looked out of the window, his face setting into a grim glare. 'They will be with their maker now, Margaretta. There will be peace for them.'

'But not for the poor souls sitting in a cell condemned to such an end...nor their kin who have to watch.'

'That is enough, Margaretta.'

'Then I have had *enough* learning for this week, doctor.'

John Dee sighed and stared down at his parchment.

Margaretta gazed at him. *Strange. He is the only one I cannot read, cannot feel. I cannot sense the spirit below the skin. It's as if he is able to block me. What thoughts fill that great head, other than dreams of getting to court and recreating his family's position in the palace?*

The carriage pulled to a halt. A few hundred feet inland was the Savoy Hospital, dark and imposing, more like a prison than a place of healing. On the other side of their coach, the great river was flowing fast. Out on the water were the comings and goings of vessels large and small, moving goods, people and rubbish along the glistening highway. Doctor John moved quickly, pushing the horoscope into his pocket and jumping down. Margaretta followed and, as she moved from the lee of the vehicle, a breeze hit her face.

'Oh, dear God. What is that stench?' She clasped her hands to her face.

'Dead flesh,' Doctor John answered, pointing to a rough wooden shed at the side of the water. 'Come, Margaretta. We have a body to inspect.'

She pulled back, shaking her head. 'You can tell me what you see. I'll wait here.'

'Do not be weak. You dealt with the death of the murdered farmer earlier this year. Our first case – where we honed our magic craft.'

Margaretta's hands flew to her hips and she halted. 'Yes, but the body was buried before you sent me to feel the malice. I did not have to look on death.'

He did not look back but simply called over his shoulder. 'Come, girl. You have to experience everything if you are to be useful to me.'

Panic set in. 'Maybe I do not want to be…'

This time he turned with a growl, his blue eyes seeming to go black and his usually kind mouth setting into a line. 'Do you expect me to walk to Lord Cecil and say we have failed because we never even started? Will you let us fall further into the realms of oblivion? Poverty? Will you keep me from my rightful place in court, girl?'

She swallowed. 'No, sir.'

He smiled. 'Good.' He turned and stepped forward with determined strides. 'Come, Margaretta. Let us begin your next lesson – reading the story of death in a body.'

It was hot, dark and rank inside the shed. The only sound was the buzzing of flies.

'Open your eyes.'

'I cannot.'

'Open them. It is only a body. The soul is gone to the angels. Do not be feeble, girl.' He tutted. 'You must learn.'

Margaretta swallowed. The stink grew worse by the second. She obeyed and struggled not to scream. Who on God's earth could do that to a child?

CHAPTER FOUR

'Beaten a few hours before he was found here, I would say.' John Dee was leaning over the body, a linen clasped over his nose and mouth. 'See how the bruising has started to develop?' He pulled the linen tighter. 'Then the heat of this shed for a few days has quickened his decaying.'

The body lay on a board straddling two wooden carpentry horses. Around the shed were bits of wood, a few tools and a good layer of sawdust. A carpenter's shed. Margaretta looked back at the body. The lad would have been thirteen, if that. His mousy-brown hair was plastered to his head and tangled with green weed, making him look like the drawings of sea creatures she had seen in Doctor Dee's library books. Flies buzzed and landed on his face, clustering in the dull eyes. Clothing was the simple attire of a groom – brown tunic, a white collar and good hose. If it was not for the terrible mess of his face he would look peaceful.

'Beaten with fists,' muttered her master. 'No cuts. Just bruises and broken cheek bones. See this.' He picked up a stick of wood from the floor and pushed the side of the boy's face.

Under the swollen, grey flesh, she could see the structure of the face move. Then the doctor prised open the mouth and peered in. 'Yes. They were right. Look at this.' Getting no response he glanced sideways. 'I said, look.'

Margaretta stepped forward, holding her breath. The mouth was grey inside and the tongue swollen to a hideous bulb made more awful by a gaping wound.

The Conjuror's Apprentice

'Stuck right through with a dagger,' mumbled Dee.

Horrified, Margaretta looked away. As she turned her head, something caught her eye. 'What is that?'

It was a small ribbon made of yellow wool, carefully tied into a bow on the boy's cuff button. Hanging from it was a ball of the same wool tied in the middle with four strands hanging down. They both stared at it and then at each other. Doctor Dee checked the other cuff. Nothing. 'Why would a boy make such a strange decoration on his tunic?' He turned it in his long white fingers. 'It looks almost like an animal with four legs,' he muttered. 'What do you think?'

Margaretta shrugged and then shivered. The doctor looked at her sharply. 'Do you feel something?'

She shook her head. 'I think this awful sight would make anyone's gut churn, doctor.'

'Yes, but do you feel what he felt?'

'No. I can only feel my own feelings.'

The doctor tutted and turned back to the body.

'Doctor Dee. Can I speak with you?' The voice was from outside and rang high and urgent, startling both of them. Dee nodded to the door and they made their way out into the light and the blessed breeze. Their summoner was standing some way from the hut, his hand across his nose and mouth, eyes wide and skin so white it appeared as green as a sick sailor. He was a thin man. Blonde, wispy hair fluttered in the wind, which was making his long black coat flap like a raven. He beckoned for them to walk to him.

'Who calls us?' asked Dee.

'My name is Robert Meldrew, architect of the Savoy Hospital restoration,' he answered, his voice muffled by fingers clasped across his mouth and nose. With his free hand he gestured over his shoulder to the building. 'I wanted to talk to you about this terrible find.' Then he beckoned and turned quickly to walk away.

The hospital architect held open a door for them. 'Please, come in. I will get us some refreshment and a bowl of herbs to help our noses.' He led them along a long narrow corridor, lined with dark wood and lit with candles set high on the wall. Every few panels were decorated with portraits of men, all stern and old. Below each one was a name plaque of a 'master'.

'And will you also be master here, Goodman Meldrew?' asked Dee.

'Me? No. I am appointed architect by Lord Englefield's office and, when I am done, I will be glad to be away. A man called Ralph Jackson has been appointed master. He arrives at year-end.'

The office was simple but well appointed. A large desk dominated the space, covered in ledgers and pens. Behind it a high-backed chair and to the side two more chairs well upholstered in brown leather. The walls were lined with shelves all packed with books. In an instant, Doctor Dee was inspecting them and ignoring the hospitality of his host, who was pouring small beer from a jug into three cups.

'What volumes do you own on the spirit?'

Robert Meldrew looked perplexed. 'I really cannot say. We found them collecting dust in one of the wards.'

John Dee pulled down a volume, swiped off the dust and opened the cover. 'May I borrow this?'

'Well, yes, I suppose.' Meldrew looked a little abashed. 'It is really not my decision. Lord Englefield, as a favoured privy councillor, makes all decisions about the queen's property – even the smallest of assets.'

John Dee wafted a hand in feigned disinterest. 'I know Lord Englefield well. A good friend. He would want me to read them.'

My God, John Dee, you will lie like truth when your paws are on a book. You are not a friend of Lord Englefield or any other powerful man in Queen Mary's Privy Council. It may be your heart's desire, but you could not be further from it.

Margaretta supressed a tut and smiled at Meldrew, who gave Dee a worried look as he started to read intently. 'Can we talk of the dead boy, Jonas Warren, rather than books?'

Doctor Dee seemed to jump back to his senses. 'Yes, yes. Tell us what happened.'

Robert looked at Margaretta, his questions about her position and role evident, but he was too polite to ask. So she assumed her disguise of servant, sat still, looked away and only listened.

'I was alerted by a wherryman at the door. He said he and a few others noticed something in the water. They thought it was a dead seal, such was the shape. But when they rowed closer, they could see it was a boy. My God, what hell did that child go through?' Robert sat down heavily in his chair and stared at the table.

Dee leaned forward. 'Go on.'

'I ran to help, but there was nothing to be done so called for the hospital priest. Thank the good Lord, Jonas survived long enough to hear the last rites. So his soul will go in peace.'

'Lord Cecil's letter said he uttered a word, maybe a name,' urged Dee.

'Yes, indeed. I wrote it down.' Robert Meldrew opened the drawer of his desk with a scrape and pulled out a paper, handing it across with a trembling hand. On the parchment were written two words, BRAD WIR. 'The second word was hard to understand. Maybe he had an accent which made the words sound harsh. It was like the first syllable of Wirral.'

Margaretta supressed a gasp.

John Dee snatched up the paper and then looked hard at

Meldrew. 'This is not a name. If the letter I was changed to a Y then this is the word for traitors in Welsh. And the pronouncing of it would sound hard to an English man.'

Robert Meldrew gulped and opened his mouth to speak but no words came out. The room seemed to go cold. Little wonder. In these days of plot, intrigue and inquisition, everybody lived in fear. Margaretta looked up at him. Then the feelings started.

Your gut is tight and your heart pounds. The small beer cannot slake the dryness in your mouth. Deep inside a dark feeling grows and your mind keeps flitting to Cecil. It's dread. You feel the dread of being pulled into this. Or is it dread of something else? Now you think of your master. The one you call Englefield. But another face, darker. And a woman, children. Suddenly your mood shifts to panic. You think of another word. There is another note in your drawer. But the doctor has his back to me.

She cleared her throat and began to sing lightly, '*Mae'n ofnus iawn ac yn meddwl am air arall.*' He is full of fear and thinking of another word. She knew John Dee had enough of his mother tongue to understand.

Meldrew turned to her and frowned. But it melted to sympathy as John Dee turned to him and stated: 'Ignore her. She is a little simple with no sense of grace.' Then he turned to Margaretta and commanded her to be silent and a good servant.

Simple and no sense of grace! Damn you, Dee.

Dee was already sitting forward. 'What else did he say?'

Robert Meldrew looked uncomfortable. 'Not a word I understood. But he said it three or four times. He pulled a second scrap of paper from the drawer. 'The first part of the word was "bren". Then…well I cannot tell what he meant.'

'Just say the sound,' snapped Dee.

'Well, it sounded like "heenus".'

John Dee gave a small yelp. 'Queen. He was saying queen in Welsh.'

Robert Meldrew seemed to sink like a stone and groaned. 'May the Lord save our souls.' He looked up at Dee, his eyes wide with fear. 'I will need to inform Lord Englefield. He will be most unhappy.'

'I could attend court to tell him,' insisted Dee, his eagerness barely covered.

This time it was Meldrew's turn to bat away the words. 'No need. My brother-in-law works in his office.'

Dee sniffed his disappointment and turned to other questions. 'How did you know the boy was of the Cecil household?' asked Dee.

Robert reached back into his drawer and pulled out a seal tied to a ribbon. 'This was around his neck. I sent notice to Lord Cecil.'

Doctor Dee frowned. 'But that boy must have been in the shed a few days. Why did it take so long?'

Margaretta watched closely. The sides of Meldrew's face flinched and he swallowed. Usually this heralded a lie, but it could also be fear. 'I did not recognise the seal. I had to make enquiries.' He sniffed and his eyes looked to the side. 'As soon as I knew the household I sent word.'

'So who identified the boy?'

'Cecil's stable master came. He told me the boy's name was Jonas Warren.'

'Why did he not take that back?' demanded Dee, jabbing a finger at the seal.

'The man was much distressed, as if Jonas were his own son. He left quickly and, I must be honest, I forgot to hand it over. Then I had Lord Cecil's note asking me to keep the body in a place it would not been seen until you arrived today.'

'So that is why the poor lad is in a carpenter's shed and not a chapel.'

'Indeed, Doctor Dee.' Then the architect of the Savoy

insisted there was nothing more he had seen or heard and rose to signal the end of the meeting.

Back in the shed, Margaretta set down the four books Doctor Dee had borrowed with a cheery insistence that they would be returned within the month. The old scut. His growing library was full of promised returns. She put them carefully in the corner, hoping the putrid air would not invade their covers.

Doctor Dee was already back next to the body. 'It makes no sense.'

She approached slowly, not wanting to look again but knowing he would only get irritated. 'You mean that a stable boy was carrying a seal?'

'Exactly, Margaretta.' With that the doctor picked up the stick again and started prodding. 'Maybe there is something else.'

'His hands are tight clasped. Check them.'

The right hand was bare, but when the left was prised open they were both drawn to the wound in the centre of his palm. Three small holes and, in the middle, a bruise. 'A fourth hole and it would make the shape of a Christian cross,' muttered Dee. 'Strange.'

He pulled the horoscope from his pocket and a pencil, then made a sketch of the wound. 'Might lead us to something.'

Margaretta stared the length of the body. Inside her head she spoke to the boy. *Come, child. Tell us what happened to you. Help us find your killers.* 'Look in the pocket.'

Dee moved quickly, pushing the arm aside and tugging the cloth. Sure enough, he pulled out a folded paper and carefully flattened it. The writing was almost washed away by the water and impossible to read in this light. But he pointed to the very bottom where a signature was visible.

Elizabeth.

He looked up at Margaretta, eyes darkening. 'Oh, God. The cards were correct. She is central to this. It is starting.'

Chapter Five

There were just a few embers glowing in the range when Margaretta pushed open the back door. Doctor Dee had gone to the front, resuming their pretence of being master and servant. The one time they slipped, an indignant Mistress Constable had scolded Margaretta for forgetting her place. John Dee had brought her a kitten which had mollified her but had also fired her ardour. She had named the kitten DeeDee in his honour.

'Mam? Huw? Where are you?' The tone was exasperated.

A creak of a door heralded her mother's grey face. 'Thank God you are back. Cold it has been all day.'

'So why didn't you put more wood on the fire?'

In an instant the hand went to her mother's back and a look of feigned pain to her face. 'Not with my back.'

'So, where is Huw? He can lift wood for you.'

'Your sister Susan did visit this afternoon and has taken him for his meal at her house.'

'Well, good for her.' Margaretta held back the urge to spit on the fire. 'I hope you've given Mistress Constable some food and drink.'

Mam shrugged. 'She went out only an hour after you. Have been on my own all this time.'

'Well, thank God there is not a hungry household about to bark at me.' Margaretta raked at the coals, clanging the poker against the iron range to vent her frustration, then stamped out to the yard to fill the wicker basket with fuel.

Back inside, she used smaller logs to coax back the flames and busied herself, pulling out pots and a pan to cook the evening meal. All the time her mother watched, pulling the grey shawl closer and making a point of shivering. The silence between them stretched on until Mam could no longer hold her tongue. 'Susan was looking very pretty. Brought little Jack with her.'

'Good. I hope she made the brat walk a little.'

'She doesn't like him to get his feet close to any midden. Angus says the boy is to be kept well away from any ill humours. That's why Susan stays out in their house by St James's Park. She says the green of the grass makes for sweeter air and will help little Jack grow strong.'

Margaretta rolled her eyes. 'Lord above, Mam. The child was swaddled too long and now he is carried like a piglet to market. He is a child, not a little king.'

'But Angus says...'

'Angus says...' mimicked her daughter. 'My brother-in-law is a fool. That handsome face of his covers a head full of feathers.'

'Well he keeps your sister in a good house and with money in her pocket. She gave me some pennies this afternoon.'

'No, Mam. His father provides the good house. Merchant McFadden has done a fine job in building a fortune buying good wine from Burgundy and selling it to the rich of London. He owns nearly every warehouse in the Vintry.'

'And Angus works with him.'

'No. Angus sits around making pretty talk with the men of France and sampling the wine. My sister had better lower her ambitions when her father-in-law is no longer around.'

Mam, as ever when given information not to her liking, turned away with a snort, stared at the now blazing fire, then shivered again for good measure. The atmosphere was broken by the sound of the front door opening and a call from the hallway. Mistress Constable was home and demanding attention.

Margaretta moved quickly and forced a smile onto her face. 'Good evening, Mistress. Have you had a good day?'

'Purchasing cloth for a new gown,' was the dull reply. 'Lord knows I need a little colour for spring.'

Katherine Constable turned to look in the mirror and press down her hair. She was, no doubt, once a pretty woman, but now, well into her fourth decade, she was like a fading flower. Wisps of white hair showed below her coif and her once slender hips and waist were squeezed into her bodice. An ample bosom exploded from the top and seemed to be ever more on show with every day of John Dee's residence in her husband's house. Poor Master Constable was always too thick-headed with port wine to notice his wife's constant trilling and delight in the company of their young lodger. But this coquette would swap her ageing husband with a wink of John Dee's eye.

She looked around. 'Where is DeeDee?'

'The kitten? I don't know, Mistress. But usually it can be found sleeping in its basket.'

Katherine Constable turned away, then twisted back, eyes narrow. 'Where were you with the doctor?'

Damn this. Doctor Dee had not told her what to say. Then the feeling. *Your face is angry, but the eyebrows are up – not down as with the feeling of fury. No. Worry. You worry about me.* 'I really don't know, Mistress. I was just there to carry some books.'

A small flicker of a smile passed over the older woman's face. *Relief.* 'I will go and visit with him when I have found DeeDee. He will be in want of conversation. I will have warm wine to take away the chill. Bring it to the doctor's library.' She turned in search of the kitten.

Margaretta bobbed a curtsey before she ran to Doctor Dee and told him to say she had only been carrying books. When he frowned she told him it was not a lie. She had carried all the books he had pretended to borrow. She glanced up. They were already high on his shelves.

John Dee looked at the door before speaking in a conspiratorial whisper. 'I have some thoughts on our investigation, Margaretta. We will discuss it this evening after our meal.'

'But the mistress is seeking your company. Tonight is the usual evening for Master Constable to play cards. She is just finding the kitten and will come with intelligent conversation, she tells me.'

He growled and shook his head. 'Another evening of fluttering and cooing at my tales of Louvain will surely test my patience.' Then he looked at his assistant with a wink. 'Can you be liberal with the wine?'

Margaretta sighed. 'Your mother lives but a few miles away. Why don't you live –'

'No,' came the curt interruption. 'I've told you. She makes your mother look like a ray of sunshine.' He softened his face. 'We share the same curse, Margaretta. We remind our mothers of our fathers...and so their loss.' He pointed to the door. 'Liberal wine and no more talk of my mother.'

It was after the clock had struck eight before the meal was cleared and the kitchen put to rights. A platter was placed in the warm oven for Master Constable when he rolled through the front door, his belly full of wine and pockets emptied of money. He was an amiable man and had been generous in giving John Dee a room in his house for no rent and only the use of Margaretta and her family. He had said it was 'only the right and goodly action' to help the son of an old friend and business colleague. Then he had blushed and fallen quiet rather than mention Roland Dee's fall from grace and favour, taking with him the whole Dee family.

Margaretta saw her mother to bed, held her tongue at the usual moaning about the cold of the room and the stiffness of the bed, then blew out the candle knowing it would bring on the usual whine about the terror of the dark. She shut the door against Mam's complaining and said a prayer that she would be sound asleep before Margaretta came back to slip into the trestle-bed in the corner. For a brief moment she worried about Huw being out still, but this was ridiculous. Susan would have him stay and then tomorrow make a fuss about how difficult he was and how good she was to have him in her care.

The office was warm, heated by a small grate crackling with heather and logs. Doctor Dee beckoned her over. 'You did well with the victuals. Mistress Katherine had to retire early.' Then he looked sideways. 'Yet she had only one glass of wine.'

'I thought a little fortifying with Spanish brandy would warm her. The bottle slipped.'

For the first time that day, Dee laughed. He pulled a large paper across the desk and came round to sit next to her. They were master and apprentice again. As ever his work was a mass of words, symbols and numbers. He was such a scribbler. 'This is what we know so far.' He pointed to a waving line at the top of the parchment. 'This is the bend in the Thames. I have checked my calculations of the tides and also the likely weight of Jonas Warren's body to calculate how far he drifted. I am sure he was thrown in here, at Southwark. What was a lad from such a good household doing in those stews?'

'Well, from the state of his tongue and the letter, he was either talking to someone or taking messages...or both. But how long was he missing?'

Dee nodded. 'You are getting good at your questioning.

From the state of his corpse, I reckon the boy was in the water a full tide. But why did the body reach the Savoy before it was seen when the river throngs with wherries?' He made another scribble on his parchment. 'And then there are the days in the carpenter's shed after he died.'

'So, he had been missing from Lord Cecil's house since Sunday or Monday?'

'Good thinking. You are learning. But this might be a false assumption. Cecil's note did not give any details. So our first question is, "When did Jonas disappear?" Our second is, "Who was he going to see?"'

Margaretta huffed. 'Now you are making an assumption. Maybe he was taken.'

Silence. Then a grumbling agreement.

'There was also the strange bow and bauble of yellow wool, the injury on his hand and the letter. The words traitor and queen. There must be a link,' murmured Margaretta.

'All logged here and none of the clues seem to link...at least not yet.'

'What does the letter say?'

John Dee raised his hands. 'Not so fast, girl. For that I need the light of the morning and some clever way of re-creating the ink.' Dee tapped further down the page. 'The stable master is distressed, which means he either liked the lad or feels guilt.'

'Or fear. The architect of the Savoy felt fear. I felt it.'

Dee turned to look at Margaretta. 'Are you quite sure it is not horror at the death?'

'No. Fear. But I cannot tell you if it's of death or the man Englefield he spoke about. Though maybe it was Cecil.'

'Lord Cecil. You must use his full title when you speak to him.'

'Speak to him?'

Dee gave the type of tight smile that people use when they

they give bad news. 'Yes. You are to join his household. I wrote this afternoon when we returned and expect no disagreement.'

'What? Why? I don't...'

Dee frowned and raised a finger to silence his pupil. 'If a servant of Lord Cecil is found with a slit tongue and strange symbols, then a message is being given. Maybe to Cecil. If so, then the genesis of this mystery may be within his house.' He raised his brow. 'I need a spy to tell me what they think, feel and know.' He leaned back. 'And Cecil will want everything kept under the floor rushes...no dust. He will not want his household carrying messages. So I can present you as the solution – a trusted messenger bringing information to me, his secret detective.' The doctor clapped his hands in satisfaction.

'I don't understand.'

Dee shut his eyes in frustration. 'It is simple. You are to arrive as a new maid in the house of Cecil and work as my spy. You will come here by wherry on alternate evenings or whatever is required and report your findings. Cecil himself will see you as a simple messenger.' He raised a finger. 'And before you ask, Mistress Constable has agreed, as long as you fill the larder and clean on your days here. Your mother and Huw must manage.'

Mam and Huw manage? Was he mad? Margaretta stood abruptly. 'I will not go.'

The only response was a grim smile. 'Would you stand between me and the chance of great office, Margaretta? The chance of payment to take me out of penury? Is that how you repay my kindness to you and your...family?'

'You...you...' But she held her tongue, hoping her face would speak all the fury she felt. It was useless.

'You will journey to the Cecil house in Canon Row at midday tomorrow. But before you go, I need more insight and questions for you to feel our way through.' He pushed a small note, folded into perfect squares and sealed with red wax, across the desk. 'Take this to the house of my pupil – Christopher Careye. You should take your brother with you. These streets are not a place for a young girl to wander alone.'

'Huw is away with my sister, Susan.'

John Dee rolled his eyes heavenwards and let out a long sigh. 'Then you will have to be very careful and ready to run.' He returned his gaze to Margaretta. 'And no, the morrow is too late.'

'But where does he live? I have only met him the few times he has been here for tutoring.'

He has lodgings at seven Fynkes Lane.' John Dee leaned forward. 'Keep to the back streets and avoid the watchmen. Put the letter only into his hands and tell him we meet here tomorrow at rise of light.'

'Why the secrecy? I don't...' But another interruption. This time by a plaintive call from the top of the stairs. It was Katherine calling in a childlike voice that she was disturbed by the talking.

John Dee stood up, rolled his parchment and, with a sigh, stated, 'I must away and do my duty of a few soft words with my good landlady and ensure we keep a roof over our head.' He emphasised the words *my duty* as if punching the idea into Margaretta.

With that he walked out, leaving her in the mess of his room. She looked around at the books, the globes, the wooden animals he had made move as if by magic, the dusty papers covered in numbers and symbols, the notebooks full of his scribbles and writing. All this she had grown to love. It was a safe place of madness where she learned quietly and secretly every day. It was the place she would listen and absorb his mutterings, knowing that her wisdom expanded as words floated from his tongue into her mind. But tonight she must run the gauntlet of the dark streets and tomorrow be placed in a house of ill feeling and danger – a place from where a child, only half a decade younger than she, had been murdered.

'Damn you, Doctor John Dee.'

CHAPTER SIX

A fine soaking drizzle was wetting the paths as she slipped out of the back door, pulling her cloak close. Good. Most vagabonds prefer to keep their heads dry. Her footfall was muffled by the cloth rags she had tied around her shoes, so she passed like a ghost through the shadows until she reached the alleyway to the back of Leadenhall Market. The air was heavy with the smell of rotting food that had fallen from the stallholders' tables. All was deserted but for two dogs growling over a fish head in the far corner. Into Cornhill Street and a glance around to see if the watchman was abroad. Nothing. She ran on.

The house of Christopher Careye was in darkness and Fynkes Lane quiet except for a tom cat yowling for a mate. She tapped on the door. No answer. A louder knock, then she rapped hard. Minutes later an irritable voice called from behind the wood, 'Who's there?'

'I bring a message for Christopher Careye,' answered Margaretta in a loud whisper, glancing behind to make sure no one was in the street.

'Who are you?'

Damn this. She did not dare give away John Dee's name. 'A messenger.'

There was the noise of a key being turned, a bar lifted and the door cracked open. 'I know you're a damn messenger. Who are you?' The bright eye glared out, the brow showing irritation.

'Please, sir. Let me in. I'll only be a minute handing over this note and will be away.'

'Where you from? You 'ave an accent.'

'Wales, sir.'

There was a growl followed quickly by a snarl. 'Don't trust you people. Like my wife says, there are two things you should never put in a house. Sheep and the Welsh who tend them.' The door banged shut.

'And the pox on you and your damned wife.' Margaretta pounded on the door. 'I want to speak with Christopher Careye.'

There was no response. Somewhere along the lane the cat yowled again. Then footsteps. Margaretta pressed against the door. The footsteps came closer, then the voice.

'What goes on here?'

She held her breath. The steps kept coming. Only a few feet and the man would see her. Visions of being hauled into the clink across the river, accused of thieving or worse, whoring, raced through her mind. She pressed harder against the wood.

Then behind her the sound of a key. Seconds later she was falling back, landing hard on a stone floor. The door closed, and she was in blackness.

'Wh…what are you doing here?' was the whisper out of the dark. 'Wh…who sent you?' The man's voice was soft, kind, even hesitant. He tried to gulp back his stammer.

'Doctor John Dee.'

'Ah. Only D…Doctor Dee would create such a drama in the middle of the night. Good thing my room is in the front and I heard you at the door. W…w…wait here.' Footsteps passed by her and moved towards the back of the room. Seconds later there was the glow of a taper candle and she could see his face looking down at her. 'You're Margaretta, are you not? I have seen you when I visit Doctor Dee.' He held out his hand. 'Let me help you up.'

Brushing down her skirts, Margaretta pointed to the back of the house. 'Who was the old scut who left me out there... and said I was like a sheep?'

'M...Master Turnbull. G...good landlord but no diplomat.' The man smiled, and pushed hands through fair, tousled hair. He was barefoot and wearing only a night shirt. 'Forgive my appearance. I was abed early tonight.' He nodded at her. 'W... why the hell is John Dee sending you out with messages at this time of the night?'

Margaretta pulled the message from her purse and handed it over. 'I am asked to give you this and tell you to meet at rise of sun at Doctor Dee's room in St Dunstan's.'

Christopher Careye pulled open the note and held the taper close to read it. He frowned and looked up at Margaretta. 'Investigating a death? What has happened?'

'A young lad found in the Thames. The stable boy of Lord Cecil.'

Christopher flinched and put his hands through his hair again. 'Jesu. I hope there is no connection.' He glanced up. 'Did he say if this is linked to the Woodstock conjuring?'

Margaretta shrugged. 'All I know is that I have to get this note to you.'

The man groaned. 'You should not be out alone at night. What is Dee thinking of?' He put his finger to his lips as sign to be quiet. 'Wait here while I get my coat and shoes.'

Half an hour later Christopher Careye bid Margaretta a shy goodnight at the back door of the Constables' house. She had learned much as they scuttled along shadowy alleys, peeping round corners to check for watchmen. Christopher seemed to know every back lane in London. He was also shy and not used to walking out with pretty girls. His nerves loosened his stuttering tongue and she now knew every detail of the Woodstock House conjuring. At the abode of the Lady Elizabeth, Dee had conjured two horoscopes – one for her and one for her sister, the queen, and Prince Philip. They had done their work in the presence of a man called Thomas Benger and Blanche ap Harri. And there was the connection, for Blanche was called cousin by both Lord Cecil and John Dee. It had all been very secret and hushed, for conjuring the horoscope of a queen and her unborn child was dangerous, even treasonous. Christopher had become more and more nervous as he spoke and anxiety quickened his tongue.

As Margaretta bid him thanks and a goodnight she thought what a nice man he was – and how he leaked faster than a cracked barrel.

CHAPTER SEVEN

Margaretta had been up for hours trying to get everything in order before leaving. Christopher had arrived before break of day and Dee had insisted he was fed with bread, cheese and small beer. When she had returned with a tray full of food and drink, they were already well into their conjuring. The desk was strewn with the picture cards that Dee called tarot, crystals had been placed in a pattern between them and Christopher was standing at the window holding up a convex glass waiting for the first rays of sun to shine through. He now blushed every time he looked at her and suggested to Doctor Dee that they should keep their practices from Margaretta to protect her. He was given short shrift and told that she had 'the gift'. Hence, she had stayed for over half of an hour listening and watching their work. As the rays came in the crystals had started to glow. Doctor Dee, as ever, scribbled on parchment, drew symbols and etched the lines of light which flowed from stone to stone.

To Margaretta's frustration, a call from Katherine Constable asking why there were voices in her home at such an hour forced her to leave her lesson and attend to her chores, starting with honey tea.

Now she glared at her mam who was shambling around the kitchen, clutching the grey shawl and mouthing her misery at her daughter's departure to the house of Cecil.

'Dear Lord, Mam. All you have to do is daily pottage and

make the beds. I'll be back every few nights to make pies and cook meat.'

'Too old and weak. I cannot lift a finger, let alone a pot.'

'And how would you know, Mam? You've not tried to lift that finger in years.'

No response, just a sulky stare into the flames of the range.

'Is Huw back from Susan's house?'

'I heard him talking to himself in the yard earlier. Probably down by the river he is. Moonstruck as every day.'

'So, dear Susan threw him out before the sun was up.' Margaretta banged the pan of pottage onto the range and gave her mam a sharp command to move it when the boiling started. Then she made for the door, ignoring the whining claim that it would be too heavy for an old arm. She had to find Huw and try to make him understand his chores. If this household fell apart then they would all be on the streets. 'Should have left you in the hills,' she muttered to herself. Then she turned to glance at her mother. *But for all my fury, I could not leave you and Huw behind in Brecon when the doctor offered me an escape from the laundry. I told him you were my responsibility, my family…my burden. I had promised Dada I would always care for you both – for we both knew Susan would not. So that was the bargain. All three or not one. Sometimes I wonder what I have done.*

The sun was inches over the horizon. For just a moment Margaretta stopped to take in the beauty of the early light. The only sound was the gentle rustle of a dawn breeze in the apple tree whose fruits were just showing as clusters of green promise bobbing in the branches. 'More precious than any bauble on a rich man,' she said to the tree, then patted its rough bark. She looked across the path which sloped down to the river. There he was, just the crown of his head showing at the top of the riverbank, nodding rhythmically.

Margaretta ran across calling his name. Only when she sat next to him did he show any response and then only a grunt and a shunt sideways on his backside so that she would not touch him. 'Did you have a nice time at Susan's house?'

'Sugna diputs. Sugna diputs, Sugna diputs.'

'Huw, don't be annoying. What are you trying to say?'

The boy grinned and pulled a cloth bag, tied at the top, from under his coat. His wooden letters. Like a squirrel seeking hidden nuts he bent over it, pulled the cord and started scrabbling at the contents. One by one letters were laid on the ground, making the words he had spoken. Then he jumped up and started walking backwards, all the time laughing.

Then it made sense. 'Stupid Angus. You're talking backwards again.' She groaned. 'Tell me you didn't say that to Susan's husband. Did you, Huw?'

The boy's face clouded. 'Would not let me wherry count.'

'Oh, for goodness' sake, Huw. You can't spend every day counting the riverboats, the men who ride them and all their goods.'

'Doctor told me could be a rich man. Be a wool man like his father. Look after you and Mam. Said must count.' By now the boy was shaking his head from side to side and moving from one foot to the other.

'All right, calm yourself, Huw. It's good to count and learn your letters, but not every hour of the day. You have to do other work as well.'

'Must be wool man. Look after you and Mam.'

Margaretta stood up and moved towards her brother, her voice dropping from anger to softness. He began to twist away, his head shaking more rapidly.

'I'll not touch you, Huw. But you need to listen.' She waited for the head to stop shaking and give a little nod. 'I am going to work in another house for a little while. I'll be back every few nights but I need you to keep the doctor, the Constables and Mam happy…warm. Can you do that?'

Huw frowned. His usually expressionless face pinched in anxiety as he stared at the ground.

Margaretta bent over to try and look into his eyes but he only flinched away. She continued in her soft voice. 'I need you to make the fire every morning and keep it burning all day until all are in bed and then you bank it down.'

'No.'

'What if I said you need to count every stick and log you use. Then you pretend each one is worth a penny. You can practise being a wool tax man.'

'Different sizes. Different weights.'

'Good boy. You're right. Let's say half a penny for each stick, a penny for a small log and two pennies for a large log.'

Margaretta was rewarded with a grin and nodding. Without another word, Huw was scampering towards the house. She just had to hope that this new interest could be maintained as long as she was with Lord Cecil's household.

Doctor Dee was alone in his office by the time the morning pottage was served. Christopher Careye had slipped away before the streets were full, looking stern and gloomy. Mistress Katherine was in the front room making the kitten dance to a piece of string. She was in a sullen mood and had sent her honey tea back twice for reheating. Her pottage was barely touched.

Master Constable was wandering the rooms like a lost goat, rubbing his head and grumbling to himself. It was ever the same on a Saturday morning after a Friday night of gaming and port-wine. His eyes were even redder than his face and the smell of stale liquor clung to his clothes. He kept picking up his purse and then putting it down quickly, evidently too worried to look inside and see how much he had passed across the gaming table. His wife refused to speak to him and tutted every time he ventured towards the door of her room. He retreated and pressed his hands against his temples as if he could squeeze out the throbbing pain. Margaretta gave him watered beer and a lump of bread to settle his stomach. He just stared at it in misery and walked again. Escaping the tension, Margaretta packed a canvas bag and prayed Mam and Huw would not cause havoc. Or would they all be begging a ride on a wagon and heading home to Wales?

As the clock chimed nine, she heard a hand bell clanging from Doctor Dee's office. Her signal to attend. He was at the window holding something up against the cracked pane.

'Come and see this.'

He held the letter pulled from the pocket of the drowned boy. Most of it was blank, the ink washed away in the water. It was browner than the previous day. But here and there were line and scrawls which looked white.

'Can you read it, doctor?'

'Very little, but look here.' He pointed at the centre of the parchment, where the marks were more pronounced. 'The writer pressed more firmly here. So I was able to put the juice of a lemon on the paper and warm it in front of the fire. The places which were pressed harder remained white.'

'Clever,' murmured Margaretta. She was rewarded with a self-satisfied grunt from her master. She stepped closer to better see the marks. There was no complete line, but words could be read. 'Protestant...path...palace...sister...Philip...die...crown... sister...death...glory...rightful queen...sorcery...magick...in the stars.' Then, at the bottom, the name Elizabeth, which they had seen yesterday. She turned to Dee. 'This seems to me to be a dangerous document. Such strange words.'

Her companion nodded, still staring at the letter. 'Strange

indeed. But another lesson for you. Look for differences, strangeness. Do you see? Peculiar that in a letter over three hundred words long, we can only see…the dangerous words.'

'These letters were pressed harder. Either the person felt their heart heavy as they wrote them or they meant them to be found. And why was it in the pocket of a stable boy?'

John Dee let out a long, audible breath. 'And why a stable boy from Cecil's household?' He turned to Margaretta, his face pale. 'These words chime with Jonas's words. I fear Jonas died because he knew something too big to let him live. Treachery which leads all the way to court.'

'I don't understand.'

Dee carried the paper to his desk, where he sat with a groan. 'My Lord Cecil is close to the Lady Elizabeth, the queen's half-sister. He has always sworn allegiance and stands by her side no matter how weak her position.' He shuffled the debris of his desk as if it would order his thoughts, then looked to the window, his face twitching with small frowns. 'Someone is making great mischief. Our scrying this morning proved it.'

'What did you find?'

'Just confirmation.' He glanced at the door and nodded at her to shut it tight. Hardly had it clicked when he continued, 'As I said, I made some calculations last month.'

Margaretta did not tell him that she knew the whole dangerous story from the nervous Christopher Careye.

Dee continued. 'The crystals this morning confirmed my fears. All lines of light converged on the queen of swords, the card I am convinced is Lady Elizabeth. No line of light fell on the five of swords, the card which depicts her enemy. It told us he is well hidden or at least, out of sight.' Dee slumped back in his chair. 'There is much mischief being brewed.'

Margaretta sat on the chair next to his desk. 'What kind of mischief?'

Suddenly his eyes were bright and he leaned forward, lowering his voice to a whisper. 'Cecil is the cleverest politician in the country. He would never allow such a letter to reach the hands of a groom. In fact, he would ensure such words were never penned by Elizabeth.' John Dee tapped his head. 'He keeps all knowledge up here.'

'So who wrote it?'

'Someone who wants to blacken her name. As you said, to speak of the queen's death is treachery – but to plot your position after her death is high treason. Elizabeth has already been held in suspicion after the rebellion by Wyatt last year. This letter is written by someone who would see Elizabeth back in the Tower facing the axeman and taking with her the Tudor dynasty.' He sighed. 'And with that goes all our hope.' He bent forward to pen a note. 'I will do the tarot under moonlight this evening to try and find her pursuer.'

'But why will a letter make things worse? All the pamphlets say she seeks to be queen if this prince does not arrive. That she already has a secret babe to carry the line. And…' Margaretta's words trailed off as her master's shoulders rose in tension.

'You are prattling gossip from a tavern floor. Do not bring it into my office.'

'I have never been in a tavern!'

'Then do not speak like a *wanton* who does,' he spat back at her. He jerked open the drawer of his desk and pulled out the seal given him by Robert Meldrew. It was banged down on the desk with a curt, 'Put this in your bag and hand it to Lord Cecil as proof of your identity.'

Margaretta started to ask questions but he spoke over her with instructions.

'Ensure you make a good impression on the household and then watch and listen. Say nothing of Christopher coming here this morning. Ask only innocent questions. Let no one know your gifts or that you spy for me. Uncover everything, but be very sure to ascertain when Jonas went missing and anything you can find out about him. The first question is if he would have carried a seal. Then I want a list of people in the household and their feelings.' Then he turned his back, just snipping over his shoulder: 'A wherry will be here for you in the half hour. I expect you to report back to me on Sunday evening.'

Margaretta stepped forward, her hand raised in placation. But it was useless. When would she learn to button her mouth? She slipped from the room, swiping away tears, more angry with herself than him. This was a bad start.

Chapter Eight

'So where's a pretty girl like you going with her bags all packed?' The wherry boy had been grinning at her since she'd stepped into his boat.

'I've already told you. Freny Bredge steps by Westminster,' answered Margaretta, conscious of his gaze going up and down her. He was her age, fair faced, had a voice from the West Country and, evidently, like all young men, had little on his mind but maids. When she refused to look at him he was bolder and leaned forward to tap her knee. 'So where are you going once there, missy?'

Slowly she turned to glare at him and decided haughtiness was her best defence. 'To the household of my master's friend. What's it to you?'

'Don't your master want you any more?'

The question made her flinch, taking her back to their last exchange. 'Of course he does. His friend needs help for a few weeks.'

The wherry boy raised his eyebrows and went into a broad grin. 'So you is out on loan.'

Margaretta blushed. 'No. I am not "on loan". I'm a housekeeper not a...slave.' With a huff she turned away to show she had no interest in talking.

The wherry boy chuckled and pulled at the oars, each stroke making the muscles in his forearm taut. Seeing her glance at them he pushed at her toe with his boot to make her turn to him. She was given a wink.

'These strong arms would be better with a pretty maid on them. Maybe I can pass by and take you a walking some evening. I likes a maid with copper hair. Especially when it curls like yours.' He pointed at the curl that always escaped her coif. 'And those green eyes...'

She could feel her face reddening. 'I'll have no time. I need to go back to St Dunstan's every other evening or so. It depends on where I am wanted.'

Another wink. 'So you will be coming aback tomorrow on the Sabbath evening?'

'I suppose.'

He gave another pull. 'So I'll be here to take you back-away. Let us say six o'clock. You'll hear the bell of St Margaret's calling people to evening Mass.'

With that he heaved on the left oar and made for the bank where a set of steep, stone steps, green with river weed, rose to the road. Deftly he lashed the boat to a hook in the wall and with one movement picked up her bag and jumped out onto the bottom step. Margaretta had little choice but to take his hand to stop herself falling as she scrambled out. Then a slip on the weed gave him opportunity to clasp her waist. He held her a little too long and repeated his intention to be here at six o'clock on Sunday. Without another word, Margaretta grabbed at her bag and ran up the steps, furious when she slipped again halfway and looked down to see him salute and wink.

'My name is Sam to save you asking.'

Damn the boy. She was not going to be the fancy of a wherryman.

Even this part of London was like a cauldron of smell and noise. The stench of rotting vegetables came up from the river, putrefying the air. The road was a slurry of mud, animal dung

and detritus of every kind. A dead rat lay stiff against the curb.
A barrow man passed close in front, shouting the value of his
mutton pies.

'Pie-man. Do you know the way to Canon Row?'

'Aye. For the cost of a pie.'

'I go to the house of Lord Cecil. He will not be pleased you
did delay me.'

The man's face shifted from hopeful to fearful and he
pointed up a road to the right. 'Up there and Canon Row will
be on the right. If you cannot read the signs then…'

'I can well read. Thank you.'

Margaretta lifted her skirts and picked through the muck.
Halfway across the street she had to stop to let a cart pass and
looked down to see several pamphlets half buried in the dirt.
One announced that Prince Philip of Spain was planning to
celebrate the birth of a prince with the burning of a hundred
Protestant souls. Another proclaimed the birthing of a Spanish
demon to the queen and that all good souls should beg on their
knees for the crowning of Elizabeth. Margaretta shuddered
as she picked up the tension in every hawker, merchant and
beggar around her.

There was no mistaking Lord Cecil's house. It was the
finest on the street and the windows were glazed. A sign told
servants and merchants to go to the back so she followed the
path to an oak door, heavily strengthened with ironwork. A
huge knocker made enough noise to raise the dead and in
seconds the door was pulled open.

The girl who peered out was like a doll and a good head
shorter than Margaretta. Golden hair, blue button eyes, pink
cheeks and a mouth as round and rosebud-like as a suckling
child. She smiled. 'Yes, miss?'

'My name is Margaretta. I have been sent here to work for
Lord Cecil.'

The blue eyes lit up. 'They said there was a new maid arriving. I am glad you are my age. Well, you look my age. Have you been maiding long?' Her excitement grew and she opened her mouth to start another barrage of questions.

'Can I come in? This bag is heavy.'

The girl looked a little abashed. 'Sorry, miss. It's just so nice to see someone I might talk with. So how old is you?'

'This is my nineteenth year.' *But I feel as if I have been on this earth for centuries. The doctor did my cards the day he found me and they told him I am an old soul. In the religion of our ancestors, they would believe I had been born many times and had walked this earth before in numerous guises. But we dare not speak of such things these days for fear of being called heretic, conjuror, magician, witch...* *all the names which strike fear into the soul in Queen Mary's terrible reign.* 'How old are you?'

'I think I am in my fourteenth year. My name is Lottie. We can be friends. Come. I'll take you to the housekeeper.'

Without waiting for a reply, Lottie took Margaretta's hand in her own reddened and rough little fingers and led her down a corridor. The sound of clanging pots and the smell of baking bread increased as they walked along. Lottie pushed open the door and pulled Margaretta after her. The kitchen was large, steamy and dotted with people. In the centre a large oak table was set with plates of bread and cheeses, along with jugs and beakers. Two men, one in black, his face hidden under a wide brimmed hat, and the other in a brown tunic, sat eating their food, only glancing up for a moment to see who was coming in. Margaretta was startled by the man in black for his face was painted red, like a rusty nail, and one eye covered with a leather patch. He looked away quickly, maybe to avoid the surprise in her face. At the range, a woman, heavy-set, stirred food in the cauldrons bubbling over a strong fire. In the far corner another woman, sitting at a desk, quill-pen in hand and a sheaf of papers before her, turned sharply as the two girls entered.

'This is the new maid. We are going to be friends,' chirruped the younger girl. Then she turned, her blue eyes narrowing as she frowned. 'What did you say your name was?'

The woman at the desk rose. Her face was thin, severe and her mouth seemed just a crack across her face. Raised eyebrows gave her a look of surprised disdain. She might have been any age from twenty to fifty. Lottie started to talk again and was cut short by a bark from the woman, who then looked at Margaretta.

'So you must be the maid I did not request. What is your name, girl?'

'Margaretta Morgan, madam.'

'Difficult and too grand for a maid. Use the name Maggie?'

'No. My name is Margaretta.' The room fell silent and the heavy-set cook turned round, her eyes wide. Lottie gave a tiny squeak. The men at the table looked from one to another.

'I am Goodwife Barker. I run this house…and you will answer to the name Maggie.'

'I will not. It is not my name.'

The older woman seemed to grow an inch as she pulled back her shoulders. Her face hardened as nostrils pinched and her mouth gave a tiny twitch. 'What did you say, girl?' The voice was a hiss.

So what are you feeling, madam? It's in the pit of your stomach. A hard feeling. Anger…just a little…but something else. Hurt. You feel hurt. Is it because of me? Or has life brought pain to your heart? There is sadness in you. Your anger covers it. You've been left behind. I feel thoughts of a soldier. 'Please don't think me rude, madam. It's just that my dada gave me that name. He was a fighting man and so I lost him many years ago. I feel the name brings him back just a little.'

Goodwife Barker inhaled loudly through her nose as if hit

by the words, then turned away to look at her desk. 'Then, as a kindness, I will allow you to use your name.' She pulled a linen from her sleeve and dabbed at her nose. 'Lottie, take… Margaretta…to her room. Then bring her back for instructions.'

Lottie grabbed Margaretta's hand and yanked her back through the door, shutting it fast behind them. 'Ooh, you are brave indeed. Goodwife Barker does not like anyone talking back. "Yes, Goodwife", is all we are allowed to say in this house. The men servants call her Dogwife Barker.' The girl smiled and looked hopeful that she was understood. 'They are using her name, you see. A dog barks and she is called Barker.'

'Yes, I understand the joke, Lottie.'

The girl looked crestfallen, but only for a moment. Then another grin and her voice went up a pitch. 'If we are friends we can go out walking on our time off. Watch the world go by. Shall we do that Mar…gar…etta?' She grinned like a small child who had learned a new word.

Loneliness. You are lonely, child.

'Yes, Lottie. But for now you can really be my friend by showing me my room and telling me all about the house and the people here.'

She was rewarded by a delighted smile and a hand taking hers to pull her towards a set of stairs as the chatter started. By the time the two had reached the third floor, where small rooms were neatly set with trestle beds for the servants, Margaretta knew that this was only a temporary house for Lord Cecil and his family while they were building a great house in Berkshire. Oh, and there was the lovely manor in Wimbledon, where the Lord's son, Tommy, lived, though there was much concern that the return last November of the queen's favourite cardinal, a priest called Reginald Pole, would see them asked to leave that house. Cecil was a kind master, but his wife could be frightening in her piety. Goodwife Barker ruled the servants with a harsh voice and threat of punishment. No one had ever seen her smile. Lottie was an under-maid and only here because Lord Cecil had brought her from the country when her parents died of the chin cough a year ago. The cook was called Betty and really only talked to her food. She liked to hum as she peeled vegetables, but Goodwife Barker did not approve. Outside, the stables were run by Luke who had managed horses since he was just walking. At this point Lottie went quiet and sat heavily on a bed, panting a little from talking non-stop up three flights of stairs. She stared at the floor, biting her lip.

Sadness. And a little fear. Then that gnawing loneliness again.

'Why so quiet and sad all of a sudden, Lottie?'

The blue eyes looked up and the button mouth pulled tight. Lottie looked to the door and leaned forward as if to tell a secret. 'There was a boy who worked with Luke. Drowned he did…in the river. We are all so shocked…and saddened.'

'Lord mercy. What happened?'

'We don't rightly know. He was found in the river and Luke was called to say it was truly Jonas. Came back wailing and beating his chest, he did. It was pitiful to see.' Lottie shook her head, eyes wide. 'I heard Luke say that "no child should die so badly". Terrible it was.' She pressed her mouth into a line in a display of fear. 'Lord Cecil has said we must not speak of it. Not a word.' She raised her finger to her lips, though Margaretta noticed her eyes were wide and damp with supressed tears.

'Well, I won't tell. We should be getting back to Dogwife.' Margaretta winked and Lottie cheered in an instant.

CHAPTER NINE

Margaretta left the kitchen with a sigh of relief. It had taken over half an hour for Goodwife Barker to give all her instructions. She was to rise every morning at daybreak to pull in the fire logs, make sure all pans were ready for cook, then go to the first floor to clean the grates and set new fires. She could eat at seven – oatmeal only, no honey – then clean bedrooms. The rest of the day was to be spent doing the bidding of Lord and Lady Cecil and also the bidding of the goodwife. After every instruction, Margaretta had been required to repeat it to ensure she understood. The feeling of bitterness grew. Not hers but that of the older woman. When Margaretta pointed out that she was to return to St Dunstan's Parish every other night or so, it moved to derision. The last instruction had been delivered like the crack of a whip. 'Your first task is to attend Lord Cecil's office. For some reason, he wishes to speak to you.'

The servants' stairs to the first floor were narrow and winding, emerging behind a grander staircase into a square and spacious hallway, lined with dark wood. The air was thick with the smell of beeswax and everything gleamed like the inside of a church. A great table was heavily set with silver candlesticks, a bowl for wine and a clock. Margaretta stopped to admire it, tracing her finger around the glass face from number to number. If Doctor Dee were here, he would already be turning it round to open the back and see how it worked. But these wonders were for the rich and he was no longer rich. Careful not to dally too long, she found the door to the office as described by Goodwife Barker and knocked. A precise, clipped voice bid her enter.

'So, you are the young woman my friend Dee so recommends as a messenger and maid.'

Margaretta bobbed a curtsey. 'Yes, sir. Goodwife Barker said you want to speak with me.'

Cecil smiled and gestured for her to sit. He was not as she expected. Welshness was evident in his face with its strong nose, soft cheeks and the skin smooth excepting three moles. The slightly bulging, grey eyes were bright, inquisitive and intense, looking straight into hers. He sat behind an immense oak desk covered in papers neatly piled, each pile weighted down with a carved ball of wood. The room brimmed with signs of industry – polished oak, paper, ink, and soot recently swept from the grate. Brightness flooded in from the high window and from outside came the usual din of a London street. Clopping hooves, shouts of wagon drivers, hopeful cries of sellers. He leaned forward and winked with a wry smile. 'I hear they call her "Dogwife".'

Margaretta laughed and then stopped herself with a 'Sorry, sir.'

Cecil batted away her apology with a chuckle and pulled a paper from one of the piles. 'John's letter tells me you are to be trusted and will serve as both a maid and a messenger; that I can give you any information in good faith, that it will be held only by you and passed only to him.' The bright eyes darted back up to meet hers and the voice sharpened. 'Do you give me your word to hold my trust?'

'Yes, sir.' She dug into her pocket and pulled out the seal. 'Doctor Dee told me to hand this to you as proof of who I am. It was found on the boy's body. He asks whether a stable boy would normally carry a seal.'

Cecil looked up, eyes as eager as a rook. 'No. He certainly would not.'

'Do you know how it was in his possession, sir?'

There was a pause. Cecil reached to his right and opened a drawer. He took out a seal and placed it on the table. 'This is my seal. Safe in my desk as ever.'

'Do you have more than one?'

He was quiet. Then, 'No. Worrying.' He sat back fingering the seal found on Jonas, turning it in the light. 'What has John found so far?'

'He thinks the boy was thrown in the water at Southwark and was in the water for hours. He wonders how he drifted so far without being seen. The tongue was stabbed and he had an injury on one hand as if he had grasped something hard. Also, he had a letter on him which appears to have certain dangerous words written hard so they would still show when the ink was washed away.'

Margaretta stopped as Cecil picked up a pen and started to write down the facts. His eyes narrowed. 'What were those words?'

Margaretta leaned forward and lowered her voice. 'Words such as magick, rightful queen, Protestant, path, palace, death, glory. The letter appears signed by the Lady Elizabeth.'

Cecil let out a sharp cry and rose from his seat before banging a fist on the table. Margaretta pulled back and fell silent. All that could be heard in the room was his heavy breathing and the clatter from the street outside.

'Where is it?'

'In my master's office, sir. I am sure he did not think it wise to be carried in public.'

Slowly, Cecil calmed his breathing and sat back down, raising his eyes to look directly into hers. 'Good. Sensible. John Dee holds a death sentence in his hand if this comes to light. Not just Elizabeth – but a whole dynasty and our only hope for a future free of Spain. It must be destroyed.'

'Yes, sir.'

'Anything else? Luke insisted he had repeated a name.'

'It was not a name. He said two words. 'Bradwyr' and 'Brenhynes'. The architect of the Savoy confirmed it.'

Cecil paled and stared hard. 'I am not fluent in the language of my forefathers, but I think those words are worrisome.'

Margaretta nodded. 'They mean traitor and queen, my lord.'

Cecil put down the pen, leaned back against the back of his leather chair, and placed both hands over his eyes as he groaned.

'Was Jonas from Wales?'

'Yes, indeed.' Lord Cecil leaned forward and tapped a long finger on the oak table as he spoke through his thoughts. '"Traitor" and "queen". Only one word is more terrifying when uttered in connection with our queen.'

'Sir?'

'Heretic.' The man lowered his hands and looked at Margaretta. 'Just a whisper can put you before the wrath of Bishop Bonner – that great man of God who has guided our queen to sooten our skies with the smoke and flames of burning Protestants. There is no exit door from his court. Only a set of steps to the top of a pyre and a dreadful end.'

'How would Jonas know of traitors?'

The eyes glistened like a hawk. 'If I knew that, I would be less concerned.' He sat forward. 'I have spoken to Luke, our stable master, but gleaned little. He was much distressed as he treated Jonas like a son. I am told Jonas was a hard worker and not a bad lad, even though he was punished a month ago for using his charm to get sweet pies from cook only then to sell them two streets away.' Cecil chuckled. 'He was only caught because Father Thomas passed by and found him hawking.'

'Father Thomas?'

'A preacher recently arrived from the Marches of Wales. Sought my counsel as we share...ideas.'

'Ideas?'

Cecil frowned. 'I do not yet know you well enough to converse about ideas or beliefs, Margaretta.' The girl pulled back, surprised by the sudden sharpness in his voice.

Immediately, he softened with a smile. 'Father Thomas convinced me that harsh punishment was unnecessary and it was better to bring the boy to understanding right and wrong through the Bible. So he took the lad under his wing for a few lessons and no more was said. I have heard nothing about it since.'

'There was one more thing, sir.'

He was already halfway across the floor. 'Yes, what?'

'Jonas had a bow of yellow wool on one sleeve with the end formed into a bauble. Is that to denote this household?'

Cecil turned, only confusion on his face. 'No. I am a good master and fair, but I do not dress my stable lads in yellow fancies.' With that, he turned and started to walk again. Then he stopped at the door. 'I think Dogwife... No, I must not speak ill... Goodwife Barker would disapprove, don't you?' He smiled but it quickly melted away into a frown. 'We must take it as something to investigate for now.'

Without another word, he left.

Chapter Ten

'**Y**ou said your father was a fighting man.' Goodwife Barker was standing over Margaretta, who had been set on a low stool to peel carrots for cook. She stared down at the girl, her face hard.

'Yes.'

'You are to call me Goodwife Barker.'

'Yes, Goodwife.' Margaretta held her face down to hide her irritation. 'My father fought for King Harry in France.'

The other woman took in a sharp breath and the voice softened, even tremored a little. 'Did he ever speak of a man called Daniel of Hertford?'

Margaretta looked up. Goodwife Barker was looking almost bereft, her eyes bright with hope or maybe anxiety. 'I am sorry, Goodwife Barker. I was too young. All I recall is him swinging me around and showing me lambs in the field. I remember him –'

The older woman stood up straight and made another sniff through her nose. 'I have no time for chattering, girl. Attend to your work.' Her voice was back to hard.

What happened with you, Goodwife? You feel pain. Terrible hurt and longing for someone or something. And regret.

A clatter at the door heralded Lottie, her small arms weighed down with logs for the fire. After dropping them in the wicker basket she sat next to Margaretta with a smile and whispered: 'There. The logs are done. We have time to talk.' She looked round towards Goodwife Barker, who was back at her desk, writing in the ledger. 'Until she barks again.' The girl grinned, picked up a carrot and pulled at the tops.

'Tell me about Jonas. What was he like?' whispered Margaretta.

In an instant, Lottie's face fell and her eyes pooled. 'He was nice. Always helping me carry logs and all.' She looked away as if remembering him. 'Yes. A good boy.'

Sadness. Terrible sadness…and regret again. But something else. You feel fear.

'I think you were a little sweet on him.'

Lottie leaned towards Margaretta so she could whisper even lower. 'He did say he would take me walking when he was old enough. But then Father Thomas caught us.'

'Caught you?'

'It was only a little kiss.' She reddened and shrugged her shoulders. 'I wouldn't have let him lift my skirt…honest.' Then she looked worried. 'You won't tell Dogwife, will you?'

'No, Lottie. Of course not. You must be very sad he is gone.'

The child bit her lip and leaned in closer. 'I'm afeared.' She gulped. 'He knew something. He was going to take me walking in the evening on Sunday and tell me a secret.'

'So when did you see him last?'

'Why, Sunday morning at church. He was going to sit with me, but Luke said he was to sit with him instead.'

There was a sudden bark from Goodwife Barker. 'You girls are not paid to chatter like old women over a washing bowl. Lottie, go and see if Lady Cecil is ready to give instructions to Margaretta. For some reason, she wants to speak with her.' She dropped her voice to an almost inaudible mutter. 'In all my twenty-seven years, I have never known the like.'

Lottie jumped up like a frightened deer and ran to the door.

A few minutes later she appeared. 'Lady Cecil is ready to speak with you, Mar…garetta.' She grinned at her better pronouncing.

The door was open a crack. Margaretta could hear a woman's voice full of concern. 'This is not good, husband. For nearly a year now we have lived safely away from the sight of court and now a boy of our house dies speaking of treachery and the queen, an incriminating letter from the Lady Elizabeth in his pocket. It makes my heart go cold.'

Then the voice of Cecil. 'It is a false letter. Elizabeth is too careful, too intelligent to ever commit her ambitions to paper.'

'But what about those who have ambition on her behalf? The prize of power makes fools of many men.'

'I hope you do not think of me, Mildred.' Cecil sounded tetchy and indignant.

'Your clever tongue saved your life when you supported another young woman with ambitions to take the throne from Mary Tudor and I was nearly a widow. Have you forgotten how close you were to the Tower, Husband?'

A long silence, then: 'I am innocent of falsity. It has been accepted by Queen Mary.'

The woman's voice reduced to a hiss. 'No, husband. You put your ambitions behind Jane Seymour – a young woman who threatened a rightful queen. Now, you do the same with Lady Elizabeth who is still tainted with suspicion after Wyatt's rebellion called for her to be queen instead of Mary. You have led us into danger yet again.'

A scrape of a chair indicated that Cecil was readying to leave. Margaretta made two loud footsteps as if she had just arrived on the landing and knocked on the door. Lord Cecil opened it, frowned, then walked out without a word.

Lady Mildred Cecil was in the window seat. She smiled but the anxiety remained around her eyes. 'You must be Margaretta.

Come in, child. I thought we should speak if you are to be maid to me.' The voice was low, kind. She quickly put something down on the seat.

Margaretta stepped across the floor and gave a small curtsey. Her eye caught two tiny booties, knitted from soft cream wool. The size you could only ever use for a newborn. Seeing Margaretta look at them, Lady Cecil pushed them under her skirt and gave a weak smile.

Strange, I feel warmth from you. Not the usual coldness which people have for servants. You are kind. You are anxious. But oh, there is a terrible sadness underneath. A pain so deep in your soul you think it will never leave you. I hear the name Francisca. You weep for her. A baby. You still hear her cry. You cry with her. Margaretta sat on the stool and smiled, waiting for a question.

'My husband tells me you work for Doctor John Dee. What is your position there?'

'Housekeeper, my lady. Oh, and I help in his office as well. Keeping his papers and books in order...well, as best I can.'

Lady Cecil laughed. 'If his desk is as full as his mind, you will have a singular task there.' Then the smile slipped from her face and the voice lowered. 'I know you are here really as a messenger for Doctor Dee as he investigates this terrible deed. That poor boy.' She pressed down her skirt as if the smoothing would relieve the fear. 'You must say nothing to the other servants. Do you understand?'

'Yes, my lady. I am only to remember instructions or write messages and take them back to Doctor Dee.'

Lady Cecil looked surprised. 'You can write?'

'Oh, yes. My father said I was to read and write and I have learned much from Doctor Dee. I can add numbers too.'

Mildred Cecil looked confused. 'What family are you born to?'

'No great family, my lady. My father was a soldier and was taught his letters by a priest so that he could keep records for the commanders. When he came home he passed it to me as we knew I would have to keep my mother and brother. I recall him saying – but in our tongue – that "a woman who can scrive will always thrive".'

The older woman smiled, and gave a sly wink. 'My father said the very same.' She leaned forward conspiratorially. 'The mind of a woman is as good as any man, my dear. And I think you and I will get along very well.'

A knock at the door made them both rise. On command, the person entered. Margaretta recognised him as the man with the painted face who'd been sitting at the table when she'd arrived. She could see him better now. His face was round, with a strong jaw. Chestnut brown hair escaped from under his hat. The black coat reached the floor and had no decoration. But his face would frighten even the boldest child. It was red with paint of lead and under that the terrible scars of smallpox. God knew how he had survived. One eye was deep brown but the other was covered by a black patch that hid half his face. The mouth turned down as if it could only speak misery.

Lady Cecil stood up. 'Father Thomas. How goes it with you today?'

The man bowed then looked at Margaretta. The singular eye just stared. He looked back to Lady Cecil. 'It goes well, my lady. May I speak with you in private?'

'Of course. But first meet Margaretta, my new maid of the chamber.' She lowered her voice to a conspiratorial whisper. 'And also Lord Cecil's messenger between him and John Dee.'

The man gave a cursory nod and then stood waiting for his audience. In an instant, Margaretta was asked to leave and he made a smile that did not reach his eye.

Concern. You feel concern. Is it about me, what I am here to do, or what you have to say to the lady?

There was no time to feel more. Silence hung like a blanket as they waited for her to depart. She stayed a second by the door to see if there was anything to be heard. Nothing. The oak was too thick and so their conversation would be in secret as he wished.

Lottie was back to peeling carrots, her small hands red raw in the cold water. She shifted along on the bench to let Margaretta sit with her and they set to peeling the last few of the vegetables. 'Lady Cecil seems very kind,' whispered Margaretta.

'She is. She let me look at the baby as I had told her how I missed my little sister.' Lottie's eyes welled with tears and her bottom lip quivered. 'Little Francisca. She was with us only a day before her little soul went to heaven. I thought the weeping would never stop. All of us wailed. Even Goodwife shed tears at the sadness of it.' She sniffed and wiped a sleeve across her nose. 'Lady Cecil still cries each morning. I hear her when I light the fires.'

'The poor lady. It seems this house has seen much trouble. Tell me more about Jonas. I heard he was punished for hawking cook's pies.'

Lottie gave a little snigger, her mind quickly leaving the tragedy of baby Francisca. 'It was my fault really. I said I wanted a ribbon for my hair. Said I would not give him another kiss until I had one.' The girl bit her lip, eyes looking down. 'Was only a jest. I didn't think he would do wrong to please me.'

Margaretta patted her arm. 'It was not a big sin. Was he punished?'

The younger girl glanced round at Goodwife Barker and lowered her voice even further. 'Not with a beating, thanks to Father Thomas.' She tipped her head to the goodwife. 'She was all for throwing him out on the street. Made a terrible fuss and bother she did.'

'So, Father Thomas is a good man? His face surely frightened me.'

Lottie pushed Margaretta in a tease. 'Oh, it's paint of lead to help the healing of his scars. Lucky to survive the smallpox he was. He said God left him to live and spread the word and only took his eye as a reminder of His power.' Lottie put a hand over her eye. 'That's why he wears a patch.'

'Where did he come from?'

Lottie frowned. She seemed to be getting bored of the subject. 'All I do know is that he comes from Wales and is very…I don't know the word. He doesn't stand over us. He always eats with us here in the kitchen rather than with the lord and lady. Says it keeps him close to the common man. Also, it means he can be kind to Luke.'

'The stable master?'

The girl nodded, her eyes widening. 'We thought Luke would surely lose his mind when Jonas was found. Beating his chest he was. Saying all kind of strange things.' The girl leaned in closer. 'He said Jonas had been killed by "the Shepherd".'

'Who's the Shepherd?'

Lottie shrugged and glanced back at Barker. 'I don't know. He was so wild with grief that Father Thomas took him to the stables to settle him and speak of God. He has said not a word since.'

At the far end of the kitchen, Goodwife Barker rose from her seat. The time for questions was soon to be gone. 'Tell me about the ribbon Jonas had promised you. Was it a red one for love?'

The other girl shook her head. 'No. It was going to be golden-yellow with a bauble and would match the one he had been given for inside his sleeve.' She stared into the middle distance, bit her lip and looked suddenly bereft.

'What kind of bauble?'

'Made of yellow wool. Round with four dangles...like a little animal.'

'Where did he get it?'

She shrugged. 'From his new friends. He called them "the Flock".'

The Flock? Luke spoke of the Shepherd. Why would a shepherd kill one of a flock?

'That is a strange name for friends. Who were they?'

Lottie glanced back at Goodwife, who was walking towards them. 'I think he was going to tell me the day he disappeared.'

There was no time to probe. Goodwife was standing over them, glaring her disapproval. 'No more gossiping. Silence.'

CHAPTER ELEVEN

Margaretta was throwing peelings into the midden when she heard the heavy footsteps. The man walked past, shoulders slumped, head down, eyes swollen and red. He slammed the stable door open with his fist before slipping inside, letting it close behind him. There was no doubting. That man was Luke, the grieving stable master. She followed.

The stable was dark and the air thick with hay dust. The recently brushed floor was a sign of the stable man's diligence but the mound of dung at the door, waiting to be cleared, still gave off a sharp tang. The only sounds were the rhythmic chomp of a contented horse and, from the back, soft weeping.

She found him sitting on a stack of hay, head in hands, shoulders shaking with despair. She made a sound with her feet to alert him to her presence, but he was too lost in grief. 'Please, mister. I wanted to introduce myself.'

He gave a startled, rasping shout and looked up, his face pulled down at the corners of his mouth. 'What the…?'

'Sorry, mister. I saw you in the kitchen when I arrived. I am the new maid and wanted to give you my name.'

He looked down. 'It's Margaretta. You made it very plain to Goodwife Barker.' He attempted a thin smile. 'That was brave of you.'

Margaretta smiled back. 'More foolish than brave.' She sat on a small stool against the stable wall. 'I'm very sorry for the loss of the stable boy.'

The man's head jerked up. 'Who told you about that? We are ordered not to say anything. Lottie?' He shook his head. 'That child sees no danger in anything.'

'She meant no harm. I think she was upset. Lottie said Jonas was a good lad.'

Luke's face creased in pain again and he turned his head away. He was a big man, about forty years, square in every way. Even his huge hands were the shape of shovels. The physique of a man you expected to be as hard as a rock. A broad face, deep-set eyes, and a neck the width of a bull's. But, as he sat there, his face streaked with tears, he had the look of a child.

'We are not meant to speak of it.'

Margaretta looked around. 'I think the horses are to be trusted.' She smiled. 'I can see you feel his loss very badly.'

Grief. Terrible gnawing grief. That is what you feel. Memories flood in of the past, bringing back all the pain you've locked away for years. You recall a small child, a woman of fair face, and an older woman.

Luke gave a small groan and leaned forward as if trying to cover his face. 'Do you believe in evil, girl?'

'Yes, mister.'

'Then stay away from the Southwark Shepherd, my girl.'

The voice from behind them was sharp and loud. 'Luke. Remember what Lord Cecil has said.'

Margaretta and Luke reeled round. It was Father Thomas, stepping out of the shadows. He smiled and his voice mellowed to a kindly tone. 'Come, my good man. Remember that we are all asked to keep our silence. You can speak to me, but do not bother Margaretta with your troubles.'

Luke bent his head and nodded.

Father Thomas turned to Margaretta, his tone hardening. 'I know you mean well, but keep to the kitchen and your messages. Luke needs the Lord right now.' She noticed that his voice was flat – not the lilting of her tongue. Strange.

Concern again. You feel concern. For Luke? For me? For you? You are a strange one.

As Margaretta retreated through the stables, she passed a stall with the name Jonas carved into the cross beam. Inside was a truckle bed, neatly covered with a blanket and, on the floor, a leather bag. She banged the stable door closed without stepping out. It was only five quiet steps back to Jonas's bed space, where she huddled down in the black of the shadows.

The voice of Father Thomas started in a rhythm of prayer and blessing.

Then Luke, his voice strained and urgent, like all men who are trying to stop their emotions spilling out of their mouths. 'I cannot just sit here and do nothing, Father. Jonas was like a son to me…and…'

The priest's response was low and firm. 'Luke. We have spoken of this before. Lord Cecil will not let this rest until the killer has been found.'

'Killers. Jonas was a strong lad. It would take more than one to hold him down and do those things to him.' Luke's voice was tinged with anxiety now, like a child whose pleading is being dismissed. 'Have you told Lord Cecil what I told you? Did you tell him that Jonas spoke of someone called the Shepherd? Did you tell him that Jonas said he was in a flock?'

Then banging followed by a whimper. It was Luke beating his fists on the timbers of the stable. The priest was telling him to calm himself, that there was nothing he could do.

Luke almost shouted: 'Jonas was afeared the night before he disappeared. In church that morning he was praying like he had never done before. Flock be damned. He was a lamb to the slaughter.'

'Did he say who he feared?'

'No. But he had a bruise on his cheek a few days before.

When I asked him who did it he claimed a few street boys battered him...that a woman called...called...something I cannot recall...had helped. That she was good no matter what others said.'

The priest snapped. 'What woman? You did not tell me of this before.'

Luke's intake of breath was audible. 'Tell truth, father. My mind has been full of witnessing the lad's body. Memories are sneaking back.'

'You must tell me everything, Luke. How can I pass the information to Lord Cecil if you do not? Now, what was the woman's name?'

'I cannot recall.'

'You must.' The voice was hard now, like a teacher with an errant child. 'I will return in half of an hour for the name.' There was a rustle as the priest turned, his long black coat sweeping hay along the floor. His tread was heavy, determined as he made towards the stable door. Then he stopped. From the shadow on the floor it was obvious he was looking into Jonas's sleeping area. Margaretta held her breath. The cleric muttered something low under his breath as he peered into the gloom. It was not English. He stepped forward. Then a shout from outside. 'Father. Are you here?'

With a grunt, he turned for the door and walked away. The only sound was the chomping of the horse in the stable opposite and the moaning from Luke. She was listening to a heart break.

Slowly, silently she crept to the door and slipped out into the light. As if answering a prayer, Lottie came out of a shed at the back of the yard, carrying a large jug, over full and dripping small beer on the ground.

'Lottie. Come here. Do you have a beaker?'

The maid nodded and gave a delighted smile. 'I keep one

secreted in the shed so I can sneak a little for myself without Dogwife finding me.' Then her face fell and alarm set in. 'Oh, you won't say anything. Please?'

Margaretta patted the girl's arm and bent over as if speaking with a child. 'No, Lottie. We are friends. But I need to borrow your beaker. Poor Luke is breaking his heart. It would be kind to give him some beer to replace the tears he's weeping.' Margaretta raised her finger. 'Our secret. Don't tell Dogwife.'

Lottie gave a delighted squeak and handed the jug to Margaretta so that she could run back from where she came. In seconds, she emerged with a chipped beaker and held it out to be filled.

The distress was still in full flow when Margaretta stepped back into the gloom of the stable. 'Mister Luke. Will you take some small beer?'

Luke looked up slowly, his eyes puffed with emotion. 'You again? Father Thomas told you to scurry back to the kitchens.'

'I saw him leave. Then I saw Lottie carrying this and thought it would be nice to give you some.' Margaretta held out the beaker and, thank the Lord, he grasped it with a smile. 'You look worried, Mister Luke.'

The man shrugged. 'My memory is not serving me well. It's the shock I think.'

Margaretta sat down quickly, noticing but ignoring the concern that flicked across Luke's face. 'I say the letters of the alphabet until the word or idea comes back.' She smiled encouragement. 'Would that help?'

Luke rolled his eyes to the ceiling. 'And how is a man of the stable going to know the fucking...sorry, miss.' He shifted in embarrassment. 'How is a stable man going to know his letters?'

Margaretta ignored the cursing and sat forward. 'My dada taught me letters. Is it a name or a word you seek?'

He frowned. 'A woman's name, missy.'

'We start with A, or the sound "ah". Ann, Amy, Annette… Annabelle?'

Luke frowned and shook his head.

'B. So Beatrice, Betty?'

Another shake. Margaretta kept going. She reached H. 'It sounds like "huh" or "hah". So Henrietta…'

Immediately, Luke was on his feet, beginning to pace. He kept wagging his finger at her and repeating, 'hah, hah', showing the name was on the tip of his tongue. Then it came. 'Harriet. He used the name Harriet.' With a sigh, he sat down and leaned back on the hay. 'Thank the Lord. If I can find this girl Harriet, maybe I can find out what happened to my lad.' He looked at Margaretta. 'You're a good girl to help me, missy.'

'But maybe don't tell the priest I came back. I'll surely be in trouble.'

Luke winked and tapped the side of his nose. 'Not a word.' With that, he jumped up. 'I must away and tell Father Thomas.'

In seconds, Margaretta was alone in the stable. Could there be clues in here? The obvious place was Jonas's sleeping area. But there was a shout from outside. It was Lottie. The little maid opened the door.

'Come quick. Lord Cecil is seeking you and Dogwife is furious.'

Chapter Twelve

'Shirking your duties already.' Goodwife Barker was at the kitchen door, arms folded and her head back making her chin wrinkle into thin, taut angry lines. When Margaretta went to speak she put up her hand, one finger raised. 'Not a word from you, girl. Lord Cecil will hear of this.' She turned away, spitting over her shoulder. 'Always the same when I do not choose my own servants. Scum. I get scum.'

Margaretta followed inside. She waited quietly for a few seconds before venturing to ask: 'Lottie said Lord Cecil wanted to speak with me. Should I go now?'

'You will go when I bid you. Do not be trying to do my work.'

'Yes, Goodwife, but –'

The woman turned with a screech. 'Only one day in this place and you think you are a friend of my Lord Cecil. You are just a maid. Nothing more. Do you hear?'

Margaretta bit her lip. Even Mam was softer than this. Then Goodwife snapped at her to attend Lord Cecil's office and she ran with relief. But, as she left, that feeling again.

Anger and pain. Anger and pain.

Cecil was behind his desk, slumped back, staring at something in his fingers. When Margaretta entered he looked up briefly and gestured to the chair. As she sat he placed the seal on the table between them. 'This is false. A poor copy.' He tapped on the carved side of the seal. 'My seal is a simplified version of the Cecil coat of arms. A modest hat above a belt that circles a shield with six sections. In my coat of arms, the hat has four silver orbs. Same in the seal. Look here.' With that he leaned back and rummaged in a drawer, pulling out another seal. 'Look, can you see the four dints on the hat?'

'Yes. They are very clear.'

'Now look at the seal you gave me.'

He pushed it across the oak desk to Margaretta. Sure enough, there were five dints which, when pressed in wax would look like five orbs around the hat.

She looked up at him. 'Could a fake be made without handling the real seal?'

'Difficult. Unless you go to my maker of seals and use his mould. It would be hard to get the exact size and dimensions from a wax pressing.'

'But you said you had only one seal and it was safe in your desk, sir?'

Cecil gave a slow nod. 'You are a clever girl for a maid, Margaretta.' He fell sullen. 'But skulduggery has been going on in my household and kept from me.'

'Sir?'

'I am now told a servant took my seal last month, was caught with it and dismissed. But was I informed? No.' He rose with a growl and walked to the door then yelled up the stairs. 'Mildred.' Getting no reply he shouted louder. 'Mildred.' There was a reply from upstairs and Cecil came back into the room, sitting heavily behind his desk. 'When I left you earlier to attend my wife, I mentioned the seal. Only then I find out.' He raised his hands in mock despair.

Margaretta heard a footstep and turned to curtsey to Lady Cecil.

'Hello, Margaretta. I hope my husband does not alarm you

by bellowing like a bull.' She crossed the room to Cecil and planted a kiss on his head. 'Now husband, what makes you fret so?' Her voice was like cream, her earlier anger with her husband subsided.

In an instant, Lord Cecil calmed and gave a small laugh. 'Having to tell a new maid that I have scant knowledge of my household.' He gave another small growl and then looked up at his wife like an adoring youth.

Mildred sat down and turned to Margaretta. 'This must be about the maid and the seal? She seemed a sweet girl at first. I was disappointed in her. Yes, she should have been handed to the Justice of the Peace, but I was convinced to show mercy and send her back to her family.'

'Did she explain herself?'

'I did indeed ask her. But she wailed and beat her breast so hard it was impossible to get any sense from her. I sent her away only for a little peace in the house.'

'And did not tell me,' chided Cecil, his face scowling again.

But it did not last as his wife leaned over to pat his arm and explain. 'It seemed of no significance until this morning.'

Cecil softened again, then shrugged and snatched at the two seals. One was put in the drawer and the fake handed back to Margaretta. 'Take this to John. It might be useful.'

Such a muddle of feelings, it's hard to pull one from another. You think of a woman...of Elizabeth. But this is not the feeling of a friend. It is more of a father. You fear as if for a child. But a greater fear rises in you. You fear for the future...for all of us.

Cecil shook his head again, his eyes gazing at the window as the shadow of evening fell into the room. 'I will have a letter for you tomorrow to be delivered to John. Of critical importance is that he destroys that communication as soon as it is read.' He waved a hand. 'You may return to the kitchen now.'

Mildred smiled. 'Fare you well, Margaretta.'

Having served dinner upstairs, the servants were able to eat. Father Thomas kept in conversation with Luke, occasionally putting a hand on his shoulder as if comforting a child. Their low tones were hard to hear, though Margaretta caught the words 'caution' and 'Southwark'. It was impossible to hear more as Goodwife Barker was giving them her judgement. Today, Lottie was deemed a good worker. Betty had cooked well. Then the hard gaze fell on Margaretta and the tone changed.

'You have much to learn, miss. Do not think above your station.'

Margaretta nodded and held her tongue. Under the table, Lottie reached over and patted her leg. Then silence fell and there was only the clink of spoons on pewter. Minutes passed with nothing said.

Margaretta took a risk and leaned towards the priest. 'Father Thomas, Lottie tells me you hail from Wales.'

The man looked up, his eye giving away some surprise. 'Yes.'

'*Ydy ch'yn siarad cymraeg?*' Do you speak Welsh?

Before he could answer, Goodwife Barker snapped from the end of the table, 'Do not bring that robber's tongue into this house.' She raised a finger and pointed at Margaretta. 'I have warned you. You live by *my* rules. Do you hear?'

'Yes, Goodwife.'

Margaretta turned back to Father Thomas. For a second she had seen alarm in that brown eye. Or was it something else? He was not looking at her now.

Concern. I feel concern again. Stronger than before. Is it that you will have the disapproval of Goodwife? Or do you not want me speaking of your past? You hide something.

Hours later, Lottie and Margaretta were pulling off their work dresses and climbing into cold beds. The candle made their shadows flicker on the wall and Lottie shuddered.

'I do hate the dark, don't you, Margaretta?'

'Talking takes away fear, Lottie. Tell me more about the household. There must have been other servants before me. Maybe someone who was bad.'

Immediately, Lottie was sitting upright, her voice rising to a squeak. 'Oh, yes. I haven't told you about the bad girl. I'd forgotten her.'

Margaretta crossed the room, pushed in beside her friend and pulled the covers up to their necks as she used a girlish voice. 'What happened?'

'She did steal a…a something…from Lord Cecil. Terrible it was. Goodwife Barker inspected all our bags and pockets for a week after…every day.'

'Who found out?'

'Father Thomas,' whispered Lottie, nodding as she remembered. 'He did find it in her pocket.' Then she turned to Margaretta with a frown. 'But I didn't like her anyway.'

'Why?'

'She was from Spain. She didn't talk with me like you do.' With that, she patted Margaretta's arm and gave a little laugh. 'Goodwife Barker was all for calling the…the…man who sends you to prison. But Father Thomas said, "Prison makes you regret, prayer makes you repent." Yes, those are the words he used.'

'And Goodwife agreed?'

'Oh, no. But Father Thomas went to Lady Cecil and the maid was let go that very hour. Though she did shout and wail something terrible so she did.'

'So, Father Thomas has saved two servants from punishment.'

Lottie nodded enthusiastically. 'Yes. He's a good man.'

'Time to sleep, Lottie.'

The candle was doused and darkness fell. Lottie pressed her head on Margaretta's shoulder and was soon breathing deep. But Margaretta could not sleep.

I feel fear. This house is full of fear. Unspoken fear and no one says what afears them.

CHAPTER THIRTEEN

Sunday morning and the church bells called people to early Mass. Margaretta untangled herself from Lottie, who was curled up and refusing to open her eyes. She tiptoed across the room, picked the sleep from her eyes, emptied the water jug into the washing bowl and splashed her face. Then with a cloth cleaned under her arms and between her legs, giving a yelp as the cold shocked her. This pulled her roommate from her slumber and she sat up in bed, scratching her scalp and declaring, 'Sunday is meant to be a day of rest.'

'That's right, Lottie. But only for those who can afford to rest. We can't.'

With a grumble, the younger girl swung her legs over the side of the bed and pulled on her work clothes.

'Are you going to wash, Lottie? It's Sunday, so water rather than a linen scrub today.'

The child turned round with a frown. 'No. We're going to church. The priest said we go to church to be cleansed. I'll be too clean. They did say it was too much washing in cold water made my parents get the chin cough.'

Margaretta laughed and then stopped abruptly. Lottie was not joking. Instead, the child's face had become forlorn and her eyes pooled.

'I'm sorry, Lottie. I didn't mean any cruelty.'

But the tears began to flow and the girl sat heavily, her thin shoulders heaving with sobs. 'They did die so badly with their chests making that terrible whooping.'

Margaretta sat next to her and put a comforting arm around her back. 'Try not to be too sad.'

'But now I'm all alone. No one to love or care for me. Only Goodwife and she…she has no love for anyone.'

It took a few minutes of soft words and many hugs before Lottie stemmed her tears and sniffed loudly to dry her nose. Then, she perked up and squeaked, 'We could go walking today, couldn't we?' In seconds, she was cheered and chattering about how they could get all their chores completed before midday meal, even though they had an hour at church. She did not wait for a reply before she ran down the stairs, calling back that she would get the brushes ready.

The kitchen was already steaming with pottage pans over the range. Betty was stirring and singing. Lottie winked at Margaretta and whispered, 'The one day she is allowed for she does only sing psalms on the Holy Day.'

In the corner, Goodwife Barker was at her desk, hunched over and scribing into a ledger. Momentarily she glanced up with a scowl and her gaze fell on Lottie. 'Why are your eyes red? Have you two been up chattering all night?'

'No, Goodwife,' was the meek reply. 'I was telling Margaretta about my parents and how they did die and…'

Goodwife looked down at her book again and hissed: 'We all lose people we care for. The Lord's decision and not for us to question. You should just forget them.'

The cruelty of her words silenced the kitchen. Even Betty went quiet, though she did not turn from her pans. Nobody moved. Lottie stared, wide-eyed, her bottom lip beginning to quiver. Goodwife was like a statue, staring at her paper. Then her face changed with a frown and her lips pressed in.

Pain. Sadness. You've lost someone you love. I see a soldier. You were once a woman of great hope and love. You cover a great hurt. You feel shame at your words but pride keeps you locked in your cruelty.

Margaretta reached out and patted Lottie's shoulder. 'I think Goodwife was saying that if we work hard today we can go for a walk and forget any sadness. Let's start with the fires.'

Goodwife gave a start and turned to snap at them. But seeing Lottie, head bent, she stopped herself.

You feel guilt. Trapped inside you is an old softness. But the thought of releasing it into tears frightens you. For if you do, the weeping may never stop.

Goodwife turned away with a sniff. Lottie was taken by the hand and they disappeared up the servants' stairs, dragging brushes and soot bags behind them.

By nine o'clock all chores were completed and they were sent to brush their hair and wash their hands before church. At exactly ten past the hour, all staff assembled at the rear of the house to be inspected by Goodwife. Her eyes were pink-rimmed.

The walk to St Margaret's church was short and silent. Beside them on the road, Lord Cecil and Lady Mildred rode in a carriage. At the church door, Father Thomas was waiting for them and, after greeting the Cecils, he stepped into the servants' line next to Luke. Above them, the great bells pealed. Suddenly, Margaretta felt a tap on her shoulder. Twisting round she came face to face with the wherry boy.

He winked. 'You is looking very pretty, missy. Come to make your soul as fair as your face, have you?'

'What are you doing here?'

'Don't be a hissy, missy. I'm not following you. This is my employer's church. I come along on account of his leg.' He nodded towards a man, well dressed but leaning on a heavy crutch of carved oak wood. His lower leg was also wood, but of rich, dark, polished teak. 'He's reached the middle aisles now.'

'Well, I am very pleased you can sit closer to God than us.'

The lad chuckled, winked, and cocked his head sideways. 'See you at six bells. I'll be awaiting at the steps.' With that, he turned and walked quickly to his employer who leaned on his shoulder as he manoeuvred into a pew halfway down the church.

Margaretta felt another tug on her sleeve. It was Lottie, all eyes and wonderment. 'Who was that?'

'It was just Sam. He wherried me down the river when I came here.'

'Ooh, he does look a fine boy. And you have a boy after only two days in the city.'

'He is not my boy, Lottie.'

'But he did wink at you like Jonas used to do with me.'

'Lots of boys wink. Now come and sit at the back.'

Lottie followed but nearly stumbled as she looked over her shoulder at Sam. They were in the last but three pews and Luke was already bent in prayer. One side of him sat Father Thomas, who was staring up at the ceiling. The other side was Goodwife, head down, hands clasped.

Suddenly, Luke hissed to the priest, 'I'll away to Southwark and find the bastards who did this.'

Margaretta kept her eyes forward and pretended to hear nothing but she certainly heard the priest's response. 'You do not want to end up another corpse at the Savoy. Stay away.'

Someone is concerned. Anxious. It's not the anxiety of a grieving father. More the anxiety of a protector. Fear of consequence. But this could be anyone here. I could be feeling Lottie, Goodwife, Luke or Father Thomas. It is him. Father Thomas feels out of control.

But the feeling went as the congregation started a prayer for the safe delivery of a prince to Queen Mary to assure another English monarch. *Cynicism. Everyone here does not believe a prince will be born. But someone close feels anger. Someone thinks of a king.*

The service over, the church emptied from the front pew back. The wherry boy moved down the aisle, his shoulder close to his employer, carrying a book of prayers. His employer was a man of about forty years, with a scar down one side of his broad face, blue eyes and a strong nose. He had a heavy limp, though he kept a steady gait with the carved crutch. Sam's eyes searched the pews until he found Margaretta and gave a wink as he mouthed, 'six bells'. Then he spotted Lottie and winked again. *The scut.*

Back at the house, the midday meal was served upstairs and then the servants were allowed to gather at the table for a dinner of boiled chicken, dark bread and spring cabbage. As it was Sunday, each was given a pat of butter for their greens, though Father Thomas pushed his back, saying he would prefer his food as plain as the Lord provided it.

The talk was easy. Even Goodwife seemed less at ill with the world.

Margaretta leaned forward to try again with the priest. 'From what part of Wales do you hail, father?'

Immediately, he frowned and the atmosphere tensed. 'Why do you ask?'

'I just wondered if we came from near villages, father.'

'Unlikely.' That flat accent again.

'But, I thought…'

'That is enough of your questioning, Margaretta.' Goodwife Barker was glaring the length of the table. 'You have no business asking Father Thomas about his circumstances.'

Margaretta bit her lip and fell into the silence of a good servant, as instructed by Doctor Dee. But there was no reduction in tension as the priest glared down the table at her, one dark eye fixed on hers as if warning her to hold her tongue. Then the slight pull-down of his mouth, signalling contempt. She looked back, refusing to break his stare until he shook his head and turned to Luke.

Anger. You feel deep anger. What do you hide in your past, priest? Whatever it is, you feel concern if asked where you come from. Your past is uncomfortable. Do you hide a bad family? A past life? A wife?

Only a few minutes later there was a call from the top of the servants' stairs. It was Lord Cecil calling for Father Thomas, who left his half-finished plate and went immediately, though, as he left, he gripped Luke's arm and told him to stay in the stable. As soon as he had departed the room, Luke muttered something about needing to be away and rose also. Goodwife Barker instructed Lottie and Margaretta to clear the table, wash the dishes and then take their allotted time for a Sunday walk. With that, she rose and walked to the far end of the room to open a cupboard and pull out a cloak. 'I will return in two hours and expect you both to be back before me.'

Betty mumbled something about rest and went to sit in a seat by the fire. In seconds she was breathing deeply and making little snores.

Lottie was suddenly excited. 'Let's clean quickly and go a-walking.' She began to clatter the dishes into her arms. 'Perhaps we can find your wherry boy. Maybe he has a friend.'

'We will but I must do something first. Where is the rest of the household?'

'Lord Cecil and Father Thomas will be studying the Bible. Lady Cecil will be in her library. She always reads on a Sunday afternoon.' Lottie frowned again, bewildered by the interrogation.

'I need the privy and hate to be disturbed.' *Lord forgive me for deceiving you.* 'Watch Betty to make sure she doesn't crash in.'

The other girl sniggered in delight, nodded and went to sit in front of Betty, staring intently at her face to see if there were signs of stirring.

Margaretta went outside. It took only seconds to reach the stable and slip through the door.

'Luke. Are you here?'

Silence. She stepped through to the back. There was a smell of fresh dung. The horse boxes had not been cleaned for the past hour. No sign of a coat on the hook. So he had ignored Father Thomas and gone. He was in trouble, she could feel it. She ducked under the beam into Jonas's sleeping place. The thin light was enough to see the bed, blanketed and stuffed with clean straw. On a hook to the left was a pair of breeches and folded on a shelf below it a tunic. She moved them both and felt along the seams. No pockets. Surely there must be something here to tell her about Jonas.

She peered under the bed, which smelled of dust and damp. There was a pair of shoes and a box. Also the leather bag.

The bag was empty. Then the scrape of the wooden box on the floor made her pause for a second. Only the scutter of a mouse could be heard. The box opened easily. Inside she found a good coat, hat and breeches, no doubt for riding on the carriage. Under these were a few pennies. Jonas had been saving his money – or were these the pennies from hawking pies which he was going to use to buy ribbons for Lottie? Nothing else. Just bare wood. *Damn it.*

Margaretta shook the box. No sound. Then she looked again at the clothes. The breeches had no pockets and shaking them gave out only dust. She slid her hands down the front of the coat. One side felt different and there was a faint crackle. Inside she found a tiny inner pocket holding a parchment, folded many times. Taking it, she quickly put the coat back into the box, and slid it back under the bed, taking care to smooth the hay sprigs and dust to hide the fact that anything had been moved.

Opening the stable door let in a beam of summer light. She gasped when she realised that the parchment was tied by a bow of yellow wool.

So, young Jonas. It seems you were a messenger, secreting letters to be delivered. But where and to whom? This is no time to be reading. Better to take this to Doctor Dee.

She pushed the paper into her bodice, stepped out into the sunshine and on to the kitchen.

'I think the wherry boys will be taking a Sunday rest, Lottie. But let us walk anyway.'

Chapter Fourteen

'L ord Cecil says he wants to see you before you return to your real master,' sniffed Goodwife Barker as she slammed her ledger closed. 'Strange business if you ask me – having a servant who has to maid elsewhere.'

In his study, Cecil was folding a parchment. 'Ah, Margaretta. Come in.' He looked her in the eye. 'I have a letter here for John. It sets out everything I know and also my concerns. This letter is to be burned as soon as it is read. Is that clear?'

'Yes, sir.'

Cecil narrowed his eyes and leaned forward. 'My wife says you can read. So how do I know you will not read this?'

'I suggest you seal it with wax twice, sir. And put a single hair between the seals.'

He nodded slowly. 'Good. You are a girl of some intelligence. Little wonder Lady Mildred has taken to you.' He leaned forward and picked up the wax stick to hold over the candle. He flicked his finger. 'Pull a hair from your head.'

The seals and hair thread completed, he handed the letter to Margaretta. She took it and asked if there was anything else.

'No. But is there anything else you want to tell *me*?'

Damn this. How can I tell you I have found a letter closed with yellow wool under the bed of your murdered stable boy? The doctor told me to be a simple servant. A lady's maid would not dare investigate. Damn you, John Dee, you are making a liar of me. And lying is a danger around here.

'I have surely enjoyed working for Lady Cecil.'

She bobbed a curtsey and started to turn. 'Oh, one thing, sir. Was Jonas able to read and write?'

The man's face fell into a look of concern. 'No. The priest taught him to scribe his name, but nothing more. Why?'

Fear. Worry. As if I have jabbed a knife in your chest. Suspicion. You wonder if you had an informer in your midst. That fatherly feeling again. You think of a girl. Elizabeth.

'So he would have understood nothing of the letter found in his pocket.'

Relief. Your fear subsides.

Margaretta bobbed another curtsey and turned.

'Wait.' He pointed at the letter. 'How will you hide that?'

The girl turned her back, stuffed the letter into her bodice, and spun back, her hands empty.

Cecil laughed. 'Oh, the cunning of women. Be gone and travel well.'

In the kitchen, Goodwife instructed Margaretta to be back by break of fast on Monday. Lottie was skulking by the back door. 'I could walk with you to the river and wave you goodbye'

Margaretta gave a wry smile and put a hand on her hip for emphasis. 'Or wave hello to the wherry boy?' Lottie gave a little squeak of protest, but the pinking of her face gave her away. No matter, her arm was taken. 'Come along. But don't say a word to Goodwife.'

As they passed through the yard, Margaretta asked, 'Do you know where Luke is?'

'Before we went to church, I heard him say he was going to find someone,' offered Lottie. 'But Father Thomas told him to "stop his foolery". Yes. Those were his words.'

A twinge in my gut. Something makes me fearful.

Chapter Fifteen

The bells of St Margaret's sent ripples through the air. The streets thronged with people scurrying to and fro, some carrying baskets, others prayer books. A few hawkers tried to empty their trays of the last few miserable pies. Lottie clung to Margaretta's arm, eyes wide. They weaved through the crowd, sidestepping various piles of rotting vegetables, horse dung and other filth. Discarded pamphlets with their talk of doom and dark deeds fluttered along in the breeze. One stopped as it went into the gutter. It was a cruel picture of Prince Philip, a crown on his head and his face blazing a smile while he stood over a woman and babe, both with closed eyes. Dead.

They reached the steps and found Sam waiting. Immediately, Lottie started to twist from the waist in a small coquettish dance. It worked.

'So would you missies like a row around before I take you home?' he called.

Margaretta did not have time to refuse before Lottie skipped down the stairs with an eager call that she had, 'never been on a ship'.

'Take Lottie. I'll wait here with my bags.'

He gave a resigned shrug and helped a squealing Lottie into the wherry, cast off and was soon doing everything he could to impress by making circles, rowing fast, making the boat heel. With each new feat, his reward was another yelp as his passenger launched herself forward to grab his knees. *Well, you're quick to shift your interest, are you not?*

It was another twenty minutes before Margaretta was passing a delighted Lottie on the steps and throwing her bag in the stern. As before, the lad made a great show of helping her on and catching her waist to steady her step. She waved goodbye to her new friend who was looking doe-eyed at the boy.

It was only ten strokes of the oars before he was back to flirting. 'Still don't know your name, missy.'

'It's Margaretta, if you must know.'

A wink. 'As pretty as your face. And tell me about the other missy? Does she have a sweetheart to take her on the river?'

'I don't know.'

'Why are you so spiky today?' He leaned forward with a grin. 'Don't you want me liking your friend?'

'I have little care for who you like.'

He laughed and winked. 'Well, maybe I like you better anyway. It's those green eyes of yours. Like emeralds, they are.'

Oh, Lord. You are thinking of much more than walking with me. Damn. I wish I could stop this gift at times. I feel my face reddening. It's time to shift your thoughts. 'How did you get to be a wherryman?'

'I followed my master. He did first set up in Bristol after his fighting days. Then one day he did say, "Sam, it be time we made for the lights of London where all the money is." And so we did just that. A month later he had set up a workshop in Southwark and I was rowing the first wherry within four weeks.'

'What does he do?'

'Boat-builder. Learned the craft as a boy, then became a soldier, went back to his skills when the fighting was done. He builds boats and wherries for selling and has five of us as regular wherrymen.'

'Where did he fight?'

'France for old King Harry. Talks about it all the time, he does.' Then he pointed to the bank. 'You's almost home, missy.' He heaved on the oar and made for the bank.

Margaretta turned to see Huw waiting for her. He was waving and calling. As they neared he became more excited. Sam nodded towards him and raised his eyebrows only to be rewarded with a hard glare from his passenger.

When they hit the bank, her brother was jumping with excitement. 'I have lifted over two pounds of wood.'

'That's good, Huw. So, is the fire well lit for me to do my cooking tonight?'

He nodded and then ran back up the bank satisfied. Margaretta clambered out, ignoring the predictable grab at her waist. It was agreed he would be back at six in the morning to take her back up the river. As he pulled away, Margaretta called after him. 'Sam, would you ask your master if he remembers a soldier from Hertford, called Daniel?'

'Who's asking?'

'He's remembered by one of Lord Cecil's household. That's all.'

The wherry boy raised a hand and was soon a speck on the water.

The kitchen was warm. It was also in a clutter of used dishes, bits of torn bread, evidence of mice, and wine-stained beakers. Not a thing had been washed since she left. Mam was huddled by the fire, giving only a scowl as her daughter walked in. 'We have had a terrible time since you left us alone.'

'Oh, dear Lord. What has happened? Is everyone fed?'

'The fishwife has been making a terrible noise about nothing.'

Margaretta spun round to see if anyone was listening. 'Stop

your mouth, Mam. We cannot afford to upset Mistress Katherine.'

Her grey mother shrugged. 'At least we have been warm. Your brother has not stopped feeding the fire.' She pointed to the table. Sure enough, there was a parchment with a perfect ledger of logs, their size and their value. He had even calculated the running total. 'The log-pile must be almost empty.'

With a groan, Margaretta went to the door and shouted at Huw to start cutting logs, because 'a good wool merchant makes sure he has plenty of stock'. The boy was raising the axe in seconds, muttering, 'Wool stock, wool stock, wool stock.'

With the stew a-boil, Margaretta went to see John Dee. As ever, he was behind his desk, a pile of books and manuscripts making havoc of his working space. The room was smoky from a few twigs burning in the grate and smelled of damp wood. She was surprised to find Christopher Careye also at the desk, his hands full of parchments. He blushed and stuttered a greeting to Margaretta.

Dee broke into a grin as she stepped through the door, the harsh words of their last meeting forgotten. 'Ah, at last.' He turned to Christopher. 'That is sufficient study for the day.'

His pupil looked disappointed. 'May I not stay a while and show my learning to Margaretta?'

Dee scowled. 'No, Christopher.'

Slowly the pupil put his papers in a bag, rose and went to the door, bowing to Margaretta and saying he hoped very much to see her soon.

Dee waited for the door to close. 'No need to further involve the innocent. What news from the house of Cecil?'

'I have a letter for you. Lord Cecil will say little to me for he thinks me just a servant who takes messages.' She turned and tugged the parchments from her bodice and put Cecil's letter on the desk. 'Here it is. Sealed with his mark. Though he also sent this.' She took the false seal from her pocket and set it on the desk.

The doctor frowned. 'Why send the seal back?'

'It's false.' She turned over the letter to show the wax mark sealing the paper. 'See here. You can see that the imprint of the hat has four dints just as does the Cecil coat of arms. Count the dints on the seal.'

He pulled the candle close and narrowed his eyes. 'Five.' He turned to look at her. 'Do we know how it was made?'

'All that is known is that the true seal was found in the pocket of a Spanish maid a month ago. She was sent from the house for stealing.'

Dee looked back to the object, turning it in his fingers. 'But the question is whether this is a mistake by the maker or a warning by those who put it on the body. And who made it?'

'I had not thought of that.'

Dee tapped his head. 'Sometimes you need distance to appraise the truth. But another lesson for you...always ask, "Why?" Now, what else?'

Margaretta put the second letter down. 'I found this in Jonas's carriage coat.'

Dee picked it up and stared. 'Another yellow bow.' He pulled at the thread and carefully unfolded the parchment. He looked up at Margaretta. 'Have you seen this?' She shook her head and he stared back at it. 'It is written in Spanish.' He placed it carefully back on the desk, frowned, then pointed to his bag in the corner. 'Pull out the letter we found on the body.'

He spread it out on the desk next to the Spanish letter and grunted.

Margaretta looked over his shoulder. 'It's the same hand.'

'Indeed. So the writer speaks both Spanish and English.' He leaned back. 'Before I read Cecil's letter, tell me what you have learned of the servants and the family. Start with the stable boy.'

'Jonas was well liked. A good worker but recently in trouble for begging pies from the cook and hawking them to buy a ribbon for the kitchen girl, Lottie, who is as innocent as a daisy and talks too much…which is a gift to us. She wanted a yellow ribbon like the one on his arm. She described the bauble, though he hid it inside his sleeve at Cecil's house. She says he had it from friends he called "the Flock". Also, Jonas was going to tell her a secret…but he died before he could.'

Dee picked up a pen and started to scratch his notes.

Margaretta went on, 'Jonas had been visiting Southwark, and had mentioned a woman called Harriet, "the Flock" and "the Shepherd" to Luke the stable manager.'

'It was Luke who identified Jonas. Tell me of him.'

'He is surely distressed by the death because he remembers losing others – I felt a woman and a child and another – I think his mother. And I think he has gone to Southwark.'

'Hmm. Who is Harriet?'

'A woman kind to Jonas when he was in trouble in the stews but Luke remembered her only yesterday, which made the priest angry.'

John Dee cocked his head sideways, his face puzzled. 'There's a priest in the house?'

'Father Thomas has become attached to the household in the past six months. He does much to comfort Luke; he convinced Lord Cecil not to throw Jonas in the gutter for hawking the pies and he also protected the maid caught with the seal.'

'Very protective. What do you feel of him?'

'Concern, lack of control, but maybe that is natural when a stable boy under his guidance is found dead.'

Dee scribbled more, not keeping to lines, but placing thoughts on different parts of the page. He connected the patches of writing with lines. Tapping the name Father Thomas, he looked at Margaretta. 'Is he trusted by Cecil?'

'Yes – and by Lady Cecil. There is something else about him.'

'Go on.'

'He is Welsh. Yet when I spoke our tongue he looked away. His voice has none of my accent.'

'He may be from the north of our lands.'

'No. His voice is flat – as if of no country. When I asked from where he hailed, he just glared. Also, when we meet our own there is usually warmth…and understanding. With him there is nothing.'

John Dee looked at her, his brow creasing with thought. 'Tell me more.'

'The staff think he is humble. He has survived the smallpox. It took one eye, which is covered with a patch, and he tries to heal his scars with red lead paint. Would frighten a child. Lord Cecil says he is from the Welsh Marches and they share ideas. I think they mean Protestantism.'

Dee picked up the paper knife and slit the seal open, unfolded the letter and spread it across the table, pushing books aside to make room. He read, slowly, making notes as he progressed. Then he passed it to Margaretta. 'Read and see what you feel.'

The letter only repeated what Margaretta had discovered and added that the letter in Jonas's pocket was false, designed to blacken the name of Elizabeth, and must be destroyed both for her safety and for the future of England.

'Well, at least we know the priest is telling Lord Cecil everything.' Dee leaned forward. 'I think you do not like him.'

'He shoos me away all the time.'

Dee waved his hands in irritation. 'Oh, do not be proud, Margaretta. That is our game. You pretend to be a simple servant and I put together everything you gather. My mind, your gut.'

But his mouth snapped shut as Katherine Constable arrived at the door, her irritation making her voice tight. 'To the kitchen please, Margaretta. And DeeDee has been crying. She needs meat and butter.'

Why on God's earth did Doctor Dee think it was a good idea to lodge with this woman and her swithering husband? His mother is but a few miles away in Mortlake. Hell fire on that damn cat too. 'Yes Mistress.' *But now I feel your disappointment as John Dee turns back to his books. You had so hoped for a few kind words. Poor, lonely woman.*

In the kitchen, Huw was stacking logs against the hearth in piles of size. Mam was hunched by the fire, watching the pot, the sour smell of burning evidence that she had not stirred it.

'God's teeth, Mam. Can you not even raise a ladle?'

'Too heavy.'

Margaretta snatched at the implement and pulled the pot from the fire before she started stirring angrily, making the iron spoon clang on the sides of the cooking vessel.

Her mother leaned forward. 'Susan came again today. She did say you were wrong to leave me and the boy alone to fend for ourselves. "Cruel", she did say it was.'

'Oh, did she? And did she soil her pretty hands by making food? Did she bake you a loaf and pat the butter? Did she sweep the floor to prevent the rats from coming in for their dinner? Did she?'

Huw started to step from foot to foot, disturbed by his sister's anger.

Mam Morgan just shrugged. 'She had a pretty new dress. Angus would not like her toiling in finery.'

'Well, I hope she fell in the mud on her way home.' She turned on her brother. 'Enough logging, Huw. To the yard shed with you for a sack of flour. Bring eggs and then draw water from the barrel. We have a night of baking to get through.'

He did not move until the ladle just missed his ear.

Chapter Sixteen

Dawn broke with a soft falling of rain. A drip, drip, drip on her bed pulled Margaretta from her dreams. Every part of her ached. She pulled back the rough blanket and stepped across to her mother, bending over her to inspect the sleeping face in the half-light. 'Still breathing, then. No doubt to spite us.' She gently touched her mother's cheek and pulled it away as the woman stirred.

Katherine Constable snatched the honey tea and pointed at the floor. 'DeeDee is unwell.' There was a small pile of undigested meat on the floor.

Margaretta turned to hide the roll of her eyes and said she would return with a cloth, but her mistress called her back.

'The doctor seeks you.' She emphasised 'you' and then stared out of the window.

You poor lonely woman.

Dee was by his window, elbows on the sill and forehead pressed against the pane. 'I am tired.'

'Maybe beef stew and wine give Mistress Constable too much ability to talk?'

He turned with a scowl, though in seconds it dissolved into a wry smile. 'She was still twittering at half after midnight. Maybe you should slip again with the brandy next time you are back.' He gestured to the desk. 'Come. Sit. I have been thinking.'

As they sat down, side by side, he spread out a parchment full of scribbles, some circled, and lines. 'This is all our evidence so far. A dead boy, laden with a false letter and a false seal. Another letter, this one in Spanish secreted in the pocket of his carriage coat. Same hand. A priest who tried to educate him. A stable master and sweetheart who heard him speak of "a shepherd" and "a flock", and a woman in the stews who helped him. A master – Cecil – who fears ill will to Lady Elizabeth. All of this could end a dynasty. There is both much and nothing.' He tapped on the circled words. 'These are the gaps. Who is the woman Harriet? Who made the seal? Why was Jonas going to the stews when he already had a kitchen girl sweet on him? Who in the stews knew who he was – because, whoever killed him planted the seal knowing that the threat would go to the heart of Cecil's household? And what kind of shepherd kills one of his flock?'

Margaretta stared at the paper and groaned. 'I have to go to the stews, don't I? Well that will certainly be a lesson.'

There was no time for an answer. Suddenly the house was resounding with the sound of hammering on the front door. Margaretta ran. She was confronted by a messenger, hot with exertion and holding out a letter. 'I have rowed the river against the tide to deliver this. It's for the hand of Doctor Dee from Lord Cecil.'

'Come in.'

Inside, the lad followed her to the study. John Dee took the letter and flicked open the seal, 'Cecil'. He read and sat down heavily before looking up at Margaretta.

'We have to return to the Savoy. Another body. Dressed like Jonas. Body broken.'

CHAPTER SEVENTEEN

Margaretta leaned out of the coach window. 'Huw. Look at me for one second.'

He shook his head and scraped his foot on the ground, like a pony trying to escape. 'Huw good merchant.'

'And a good merchant keeps all customers happy, so build a fire for Mistress Katherine, too.'

It worked and he looked up, eyes bright, but looking at the top of his sister's head, and turned to go.

'Not just yet, Huw. Wool men pass messages.' A wherry boy, called Sam, will arrive at seven. Tell him I had to leave early but will be waiting same time tomorrow evening at the Freny Bredge steps.' She looked at him intently. 'Can you remember all that?'

'You left early. See him tomorrow. Same time at Freny Bredge steps.' He wagged his hand at her. 'Huw not stupid.'

She started to tell him that she knew this to be true, but Doctor Dee was tutting his impatience. The horses started. Within minutes, Dee was rehearsing his investigation. 'We need to ask the time he washed up on the shore. If he was also alive when he was found. And what will you look for, Margaretta?'

'I'll look to see if it is Luke. Then, I'll turn away.'

Dee growled. 'You must learn to overcome this tickle-stomach of yours. You are Welsh. Your ancestors would have been out on the battlefield with their men, dispatching any poor sot still breathing and looting his body for spoils.' He leaned back in his seat and smiled. 'We are a warrior race. Born to battle and strength. I can trace my ancestry back to the greatest warrior of all times – Arthur.'

Margaretta refrained from showing mockery. She had heard this claim many times in the months she had been his apprentice. 'So who do you think I might descend from, Doctor Dee?'

He wrinkled his brow and feigned contemplation, even raising his forefinger to his temple. 'Let me see.' Then he looked at her, eyebrows raised. 'Of course. Morgan le Fay. Sister of Arthur. A sorceress with special powers and a unique understanding of men's thoughts.' Dee made a smile. 'You see, our fate and destiny just roll on down the ages.'

Margaretta bristled. 'I am not a sorceress.' Then she narrowed her eyes. 'But I think Mistress Katherine would be your Guinevere?'

Dee grimaced. 'Well *you* be grateful that *your* duty only amounts to honey tea and a puking kitten. I have to endure the thrusting paps.'

For a few seconds, they were bonded by laughter. But as quickly as he dissolved into gaiety, he swung back to his solemnity and pulled a parchment from his bag.

'I pulled a card again this morning when you were getting your bag. It was the nine of swords. The card of fear. Everything about it confirmed my concerns.'

Seeing Margaretta confused, he started to sketch on his paper, describing his scribbles as he worked. 'This is a woman sitting in bed, her face in her hands. Behind her, nine swords hang on the wall, over her knees a blanket decorated with roses.'

'What does it mean?'

'A nightmare coming true and bringing fear and threat. A woman in despair. And no mistaking who this woman is.'

'How so?'

Dee tapped on the drawing of the blanket. 'You must learn to look into the cards. It will be an on-going lesson. These are roses. What is the main symbol of Elizabeth's family?'

Margaretta gulped. 'The Tudor Rose.'

The carriage fell silent save the clopping of the horses' hooves outside and the occasional creak of the chassis as they went over another hole in the road. Doctor Dee stared out of the window, pulling at his beard.

Master Robert Meldrew was waiting on the steps of the Savoy, hands clasped in anxiety. He was pale, strained, and constantly rolled his lips together in fear. 'Thank you for coming,' he muttered as he opened the carriage door. 'Another dreadful affair has darkened this place.'

Fear. Gnawing fear. The images will not leave your mind. You want it all to stop. What if it's you next time? What if you were seen?

As if he felt her looking at him, Robert Meldrew turned to look at Margaretta. 'Your servant again. She always travels with you?'

'No, no,' dismissed Dee, stepping out. 'Margaretta is simply in the carriage as I will take her to where she will work for the next few days.' He gave money to the carriage man. 'Though we will continue by wherry. Not paying for a man to sit and wait.' With that he turned, ignoring the carriage driver's scowl. 'Come, master. We need to know what has happened here.'

Sitting in the office, Dee looked greedily at the books, scanning the shelves for another to borrow. Robert poured small beer but this time his hands trembled. Margaretta sat quietly, watching, listening, feeling.

Dee started the interrogation. 'So, tell me in detail. What has happened?'

'Just as before. A body in the water.'

'Found by the wherrymen?'

'No. By me. I walk early in the evening. I saw a shape on the shore which was not a stone and went to look at it. That is when I saw… Oh, God.' He put his hand to his mouth and closed his eyes as if trying to stop himself from being sick.

Lying. You are lying. Every time you speak the muscles in your jaw flinch. You are withholding or hiding something. You feel horror. You have seen something, heard something. I see an image. Something dark. Then a person. You are thinking of words.

'Was he alive, like Jonas?'

'No. Dead. Horribly beaten.'

'So how did you know to alert Lord Cecil?'

With this, Robert opened his desk and pulled out a small object, and placed it on the desk. It was another seal. 'Just as before. Around his neck.'

Dee picked up the seal and ran his finger over the indented metal, counting the dents. Margaretta could see there were five. Another fake. Dee put it in his bag and looked up. 'What else have you found on the body?'

Robert shuddered and picked up his beer to take a shaky sip. 'Nothing. Nor have I looked. I followed previous orders and had the body put out of sight. It is in the carpenter's shed.'

More fear. The image again. You see a body being thrown in water. Then a voice.

Robert looked at John Dee. 'Will you inspect it now?'

The doctor rose and turned. But before he reached the door he turned back to the shelves. 'Can I beg you to lend me one more book? I have noticed your volume on angels.'

Margaretta shot a look at him. *You old scut. You always 'borrow' for your growing library. But they never go back, do they? You have a magpie in your soul.*

Robert gave a distracted agreement and opened his desk for

a key, not noticing his visitor take three books and hand them to Margaretta with a nod to his bag.

Robert unlocked the shed door and stepped back. 'I will leave you here to do your work, doctor. Please come to my office if I can help further.' He turned back to the hospital, almost running up the path.

Inside, the shaft of light from the door beamed directly onto the body. Like Jonas, It was prone on a board between two trestles. Margaretta hung back only to receive a sharp command from Dee to enter and do her work. She stepped forward, holding her breath, and forced herself to look at the face.

'Oh, God. Oh, God. Who would do such a thing?'

It was Luke. His face was blue from beating. But worse. His mouth was sewn shut with a bow of yellow wool. From the bow hung the same strange, animal-like bauble.

CHAPTER EIGHTEEN

John Dee stared at the grotesque work. 'We need to check his tongue.'

Margaretta was rooted to the spot. John Dee carefully undid the bow and then picked up a stick to open the mouth. 'And the same warning sign. Look at this.'

Reluctantly, Margaretta stepped forward. Sure enough, the tongue was stabbed through. Out of the mouth wafted the smell of decay. She looked away and covered her nose.

'For goodness' sake, Margaretta. Just a bad tooth. The body is only a day killed. Why do you think it is so stiff?' Dee picked up Luke's hands and started pulling at the fingers to open them. There was a sickening crack as they let go their grip. The left hand had marks in the palm but less vivid than seen on Jonas. 'The same pattern, I think. But these hands are toil-hardened. We cannot say it is the same scarring.'

Dee checked the pockets of Luke's tunic. No letter this time. He turned to Margaretta. 'What have you picked up?'

'The master of the Savoy saw and heard something he fears you knowing. I saw the image of a boat and a person. He heard a voice. He is sick with terror.'

Dee raised his hands in exasperation. 'Why did you not say when we were with him?'

Margaretta's hands went straight to her hips. 'Because I am just a humble servant, sir. With no sense of grace. Do you remember?'

Immediately, Doctor Dee looked away, grumbling that maybe she was right. 'But you could have said a little sooner, girl.' He looked her in the eye. 'Maybe not. Come along.'

Dee knocked on the office door but did not wait for the order to enter. Margaretta slipped in and looked around as if bored. The architect of the Savoy was at his desk, eyes flicking sideways, betraying alarm.

'Can I help you, Doctor Dee?' His voice had a slight tremble.

'Yes. I need more detail about how you came to find the body. You mentioned going for an evening walk. What time was that?'

'Six in the evening, as always. Why is that important?'

Fear again. You feel it acutely. You remember water. A boat. Someone shouting.

Dee sat down and leaned forward to ensure he had Robert in his direct line of vision. 'Tell me exactly what you saw.'

'I saw a shape. As I said, I thought it a stone at first.'

'But surely, sir, if you walk the bank every evening you know the location of stones.'

The other man gulped. 'I was contemplating. Not really thinking.'

'Go on.'

'I walked over and saw it was a man. I put a hand on his neck to see if there was life. Nothing. Then I saw the seal. I called for a few wherrymen to come in and help me carry the body to the shed. They came quickly. One was wearing a coat, the other just a tunic. I recall one had flaxen hair. They were much distressed and said they wanted away. Then I shut and locked the shed.'

Too much detail. You are making this up. The image again. The boat. The person.

'So the body was on the bank.'

'Er, no. It was floating down the river.'

'And from which direction?'

'From Southwark.'

Panic. You have said too much.

'Well, the direction of Southwark. I don't know from where it came. How could I?'

Dee leaned back and peered at the jittery man, deliberately holding silence between them. Robert licked his lips and swallowed. Dee cocked his head as if contemplating, though Margaretta knew he was feigning. She had seen it before.

'That is interesting. You see the tide was going out of the Thames at six in the evening. The body should have been going the other way.'

Robert visibly flinched; that flick of the eyes again. Then the swallow making his Adam's apple bob like a float over a pike-fish. He made balls of his hands and then a smile that did not reach his eyes. 'Maybe I saw a boat. Close by the shore. Yes. Now that I think, there was a boat.'

'What kind of boat?'

'Wherry. No. Maybe not…just a boat.' He flinched again.

The images are coming thick and fast now. A wherry close to shore. The wherryman shouting for you to come closer. The shape going into the water. They row it towards you. The face. Dark, brown eyes. Pointing at you.

Margaretta leaned forward and spoke low. '*Siaradodd e â'r dyn ar y cwch.*' He spoke to the man in the boat. '*Roedd e'n ofnus.*' He was frightened.

Robert pointed at Margaretta. 'What does she say?'

Dee leaned forward again. 'She is worried about being late to work. Ignore her. Who was in the boat? Did they speak to you?'

'No. Well, they may have hailed me.'

'Either they did or they did not. Which is it?'

The hands balled again and the tell-tale gulp before he spoke. 'They did not.'

'Are you sure?'

'Yes. I may have seen a boat. Then I saw the shape. All I recall is walking along and finding that poor man. That is all I have to say, Doctor Dee. There is nothing more I can tell you. Is that understood?' He rose and pointed to the door. 'I am called away on business at Lord Englefield's office this morning. I must depart.' He put his hands to his brow. 'He will be most displeased.'

'Why would he blame you?' Dee was frowning.

'Two bodies in a week? Both murdered. Both deaths almost ritualistic and linked to Cecil?' Meldrew's voice was high pitched and loud as if he could not keep the agitation inside. 'Jesus. I came here to build walls, not pick up the debris of other men's plotting.'

Dee rose to his feet. 'Plotting?'

Meldrew just stared and shook his head.

Panic. You've said too much. That dark face again. Now anger. Resentment. You think of a castle. You think of the queen. Terror.

Suddenly, Meldrew turned away. 'I did not mean plot. I meant evil. I can tell you no more. I will say...nothing more.'

Dee paused, like a cat waiting for the mouse to move. 'Did you see a wherry when you found Jonas, sir? Is that how he arrived unseen while floating a full tide?'

Meldrew froze, though a small mew escaped his mouth. 'I will say no more...nothing.'

Dee gave a short bow. 'Of course, and my gratitude for your assistance. I will speak to Lord Cecil about burying the body.'

Robert just clenched his trembling hands and sat heavily as Doctor Dee and Margaretta walked through the door. As the door shut, Margaretta heard a deep sigh and the words 'God save me from this.'

CHAPTER NINETEEN

They were only a few seconds on the bank when a wherryman waved from the middle of the river. 'Well at least we will not be waiting in this dire place,' muttered Dee.

They climbed aboard and Margaretta settled herself in the bow, behind her master who took the main bench. 'The Freny Bredge steps,' commanded Dee. In an instant, it was apparent that the boat man was not of the same tongue. He frowned and raised his hands to heaven. Then smiled showing a mouth of dark, crooked teeth. Around his neck, though partly hidden under a filthy scarf, was a huge silver crucifix.

'Do you speak English?' barked Dee.

'No English, señor. Español.'

Dee twisted in his seat to look at Margaretta. 'We will have to pray he can understand signs.' He turned back and pointed down the river. 'That way.' Then he held up one finger. 'One league.' Then he crooked his finger. 'Around the bend of the river.'

The wherryman smiled, turned the boat downstream and heaved on the oars.

Once they were mid-stream, Dee shuffled round to speak to Margaretta, lifting his legs over his seat so that he was facing forward. 'Was the architect of the Savoy telling the truth?'

Margaretta frowned and nodded towards the wherryman but her concern was batted away by Doctor Dee, who insisted, 'He doesn't understand us.'

'Partly. He saw more than he spoke. Also, someone spoke to him. He was a-feared of them.' She stared out over the water, accessing the feelings she had sensed. 'He saw the body being put into the water. The person in the boat spoke to him. He is terrified.'

'And he spoke of a plot. What did you feel then?'

'Even more fear. The memory of a dark-faced man and then he thought of...' She glanced over Dee's shoulder at the oarsman, but he was staring out across the water.

'Go on,' snapped Dee.

'I think he thought of a castle, a dark face, the queen. He felt sick. Threatened.'

'Good,' said Dee. 'That means we can make him speak. I will push Lord Cecil to take charge of extracting what he knows.' He leaned back with a satisfied look on his face and pointed at Margaretta. 'Was I not right? These murders stem from the dark and dangerous corridors of court. They threaten Elizabeth through her closest supporter – Cecil.'

'Be careful, doctor.' Margaretta nodded over his shoulder at the wherryman.

'Do not fret so, Margaretta. He is a rough Spaniard. Understands not a word.' He grinned. 'Think of the satisfaction of telling Lord Cecil that we are already uncovering the mystery.' He rubbed his hands together. 'And demanding an interim payment for our success.'

'Are you coming to Lord Cecil's house?'

'Absolutely. We need his insights into his servants and to decipher this Spanish letter.'

'But how do we explain I was searching in his stable block?'

John Dee's face clouded. 'I will tell him you are trained to bring everything to the investigator first.'

They spent the rest of the journey talking through their next moves. Dee insisted that Margaretta needed to visit

Southwark and find the doxy named by Jonas.

Margaretta shuddered as the feeling came. *At last I feel your thoughts. Not hidden from me as usual. Excitement. You feel excitement. No doubt because your busy mind has a problem to solve. Every time you come up with another instruction, it grows. What a strange one you are. Do you not feel the danger we might be in? What if you are found with your lips sewn with yellow wool?*

'Why are you shivering, girl?'

'Just imagining the worst, doctor. I don't feel your excitement.'

He frowned but was distracted by the wherryman making a pull on his oar to turn them to the bank. 'Ah, here we are, Margaretta.' Dee turned to the wherryman. 'Here you are, my man. A whole penny for your work.'

They parted at the corner so that Margaretta could act the servant and run to the back door, leaving Dee to announce himself at the grand main entrance.

Goodwife Barker was waiting at the staff entrance, looking severe. 'You are late.' With that, the bell on the front door sounded and she turned on her heel, muttering that it was rudely early for guests to be calling.

There was a warmer welcome from Lottie, who whooped her delight at seeing her friend. She grasped Margaretta's hand and leaned in close. 'I'm so glad you're back.' A tiny nod towards Goodwife Barker. 'She's been wicked since last night. Luke didn't come home and she thinks he's been drinking all night. That's why she waits at the entrance. Ready to give him a tongue-whipping, she is.'

Margaretta gave a weak smile. The poor child might as well hold to her belief for a while. All too soon she would be filled with fear again.

Before they could speak further, Goodwife Barker clattered

down the stairs. 'So your real master came with you. Why did you not say?'

'I did not…' She stopped herself. There was no point in antagonising. 'I was not fast enough, Goodwife. He is normally a slow walker. I am sorry.'

'Well, my Lord Cecil is none too happy to have him over the threshold.' The older woman sniffed and turned away, snapping over her shoulder. 'And for some reason, Lord Cecil has instructed that you join them.' She stopped and turned, her eyes narrowing. 'Make it quick. You are well behind with your chores. So no walking with Lottie today.'

Inside the office, John Dee was pulling various bits of parchment from his bag. Cecil was looking irritated. He nodded towards Margaretta. 'Are you insistent that your maid attend? If you and I are conversing, there can be no messages for her.'

'She stays,' was the indignant reply, and then a shift to a more conciliatory tone. 'Better Margaretta has the information so that she can keep her ears and eyes open for any titbit which could assist.'

Cecil gave a small sniff and nodded.

Oblivious to the other man's sensitivity, John Dee spread out three parchments on Cecil's desk with squares crossed through to make sections, each filled with symbols and numbers. After a second of staring, Cecil was on his feet. 'What in God's name are these doing here?' His tone mixed alarm and anger.

Shock. You feel the room move, such is your fear. Suddenly John Dee has moved from helper to danger. You feel your stomach lurch. You pull your hands together to quell the tremor.

John Dee ignored the tone and tapped on the first two parchments. 'These are the horoscopes completed for the Lady Elizabeth and Her Majesty last month, as you know.'

But Cecil cut across like a sword through silk, his voice

down to a harsh hiss. 'I asked what they are doing here – not what they are.'

John Dee looked up, his eyebrows arching in indignation. 'Well you requested them, did you not? You made the arrangements for me to go to Woodstock and conjure with Master Benger and Blanche...'

Cecil slammed his hand down on the desk and growled his next sentence. 'I simply told our cousin, Blanche ap Harri, that you might advise Lady Elizabeth, should we face the terrible news of her sister dying in childbirth.' He leaned back and sighed. 'God's teeth, John. I want no part of your conjuring. Especially with Englefield commissioned to investigate such deeds. Danger is rising. I just want to know who killed my servants and why.'

'Lord Englefield? Interesting. He is the man to whom Robert Meldrew reports.' Dee frowned. 'Investigating conjuring?' He shrugged. 'But anyway, Cousin Blanche clearly stated that you –'

Another slam of that long-fingered hand on the oak. Then the snarl. 'I care nothing for the wittering of Blanche. There is no communication from this house for anyone to see. You cannot link me to any dark arts around the queen's horoscope.' He leaned forward and stared into John Dee's wide-open eyes. 'Which you know to be a treason.' The words were spoken low and slow.

John Dee gulped, but Margaretta could not feel his thoughts. Though, by his movement, it was apparent he was beginning to bristle. 'Yet my work was acceptable when you introduced me to King Edward four short years ago. Good enough to earn me a pension in accordance with my knowledge. Good enough to recommend me to Lord Pembroke as a tutor to his children, and also Northumberland. It was good enough –'

'Enough, John.' The voice was raised now. 'Those were different times. Safer times. We did not live under the terrible eye of Bishop Bonner and his venom towards anything un-papist. We did not live in the stench of his pyres. We did not live in times when Spanish princes and emperors wait like eagles for the carrion of our queen and her child in the birthing chamber.'

'Which is why we need additional help,' insisted John Dee, pointing up as if to heaven. 'All my work tells me there is plotting, there is a danger to the Lady Elizabeth, the danger comes from a hidden person, driven by great ambition. There is much for concern in the cards and the nativities.' He made a small huff. 'And if we do not uncover the plot then England may fall.'

Cecil sighed and closed his eyes. 'That is true. We both fear what is afoot.' His eyes snapped open. 'So, we must act quickly and on the basis of facts. Facts and evidence.' He looked to Dee. 'So what are the facts?'

'Your stableman had the same false seal around his neck and his tongue was stabbed before his mouth sewn shut with a bow of yellow wool. You were being sent the same message, my friend.' Dee reached for his leather bag again. Pulling out the seals and putting them on the desk, he continued. 'We have few clues. But we do have consistency. Both bodies are linked back to you by these seals. Both tongue-stabbed as a warning sign. Both with ribbons of yellow wool decorated with a strange symbol. The wool is made into a round with four strands coming from it. Like an animal. Both went to Southwark. Both were found at the Savoy. And there is our first question.'

'What?'

'The master claims both bodies washed up on the shore. But my tide calculations defy his claims that Luke drifted there. Also, Margaretta…I mean we…sensed him lying. I think the body…no, the bodies…were delivered there. More than that, he slipped and spoke of a plot. Do you have any connection to Robert Meldrew?'

'None at all.' Cecil's eyes narrowed. 'What did he say about a plot?'

'He shut up like a clam. I think you will need to use your influence to make him speak. But that we can decide later. For now, it just confirms my thinking.'

Cecil sighed. 'Go on.'

'Then there is Southwark. Jonas was going there and told the maid...' Dee turned to Margaretta. 'What is her name?'

'Lottie.'

'He told Lottie that he had a secret. He was also fearful.' Dee pulled the folded note from his bag. 'Margaretta found this in the stable. It is the same hand as the letter incriminating Elizabeth, but a different tongue. My Spanish is not good enough to interpret. I was hoping you could help.'

Cecil undid the yellow bow and unfolded the parchment. He studied it for a few seconds and then sat back, his eyes going between master and maid. 'Why was I not given this first?'

John Dee bridled. 'Because I am the investigator, Margaretta knows to bring all to me.'

Those grey eyes flashed at Margaretta. 'So you are more than a maid.'

'I do help, sir.' She looked down. 'I am sorry.'

'No need for *you* to apologise.' He emphasised 'you' and glared at John Dee, who just pointed at the paper. Cecil growled and continued: 'I have no Spanish. But I know who can help.' He stood and went to the door, then called up the stairs from the hall. 'Mildred. I need your company, my dear.'

Mildred Cecil entered the room in a dress of blue velvet. A waft of rosewater sweetened the air. She smiled and then clapped her hands together when John Dee turned round and stood to greet her. 'John Dee. How good it is to see you. How do you fare these days?'

'Well, my lady, thank you.'

He blushed a little as she took his hand in both of hers and stood back to survey him. 'Handsome as ever, I see.'

Cecil bid his wife sit. 'We need your knowledge, my dearest.' He handed her the note. 'This was found in Jonas's carriage coat. We cannot decipher the words.'

Mildred Cecil took the letter to the window for better light, read for a minute and looked back at her husband. All colour had drained from her face. 'Our concerns are well founded, husband. This note puts you amidst high treason.'

CHAPTER TWENTY

John Dee stared at the letter, then at Cecil. 'The letter must have been penned by someone who has sight of this household – and the same person who planted the letter on Jonas.'

The master of the house nodded and put his head in his hands, propelling Mildred to cross the room and put her hand on his shoulder. He glanced up and patted her fingers. 'Are you quite sure what you read, my dear?'

'Yes. You heard the words yourself. The letter is to someone who wants testimony of your movements. The scrivener speaks of your visits to Lady Elizabeth. Each one is listed. They even know you are due to visit her again this week.' Her lips pinched together in anxiety. 'They state that you hide a book of Elizabeth's treachery to protect her.' Mildred looked at John Dee. 'Why would they make up such stories of us?'

But next to her, Cecil did not move. He kept staring at the wood of his desk, his brow crinkled in thought. A slight flush spread across his cheeks.

Margaretta shifted in her seat, the feelings rising inside her. *Dread. Something you've done. A secret. You imagine being arrested. You are hiding something.* She leaned forward, touched John Dee's sleeve, and whispered '*Mae e'n cuddio rhywbeth.*' He hides something.

Cecil's eyes darted to her. 'I do not speak my forefathers' tongue with ease. What did you say?'

Thank the Lord, John Dee stepped in. 'She says she must away to the kitchen and her chores soon.' He leaned forward and dropped his voice to a cajoling purr. 'Is there anything you have secreted, my friend? Better we know.'

Cecil sat up straight and cleared his throat. His wife's fingers tightened on his shoulder as she looked down, beginning to frown. Her husband looked at the window as if searching for the right words. 'I…I…hold a book belonging to the Lady Elizabeth. Nothing treasonous. Just her thoughts.' He swallowed and looked to Dee, a faint beseeching in his eyes. The room was silent.

Panic. Confusion. It is you, Lady Mildred. Anger.

John Dee leaned forward again, keeping the low, calm voice. 'Where is this book?'

'Mildred's library. Well hidden among the religious texts.'

At this, Lady Cecil gave a short, sharp cry and snatched her hand away from her husband. She walked to the window and put her hands on the glass. They could see her kirtle move with her fearful breathing. Then she turned and faced him, her face pale and fixed in fury. 'You brought secrets here and put us all in danger? Have your senses left you, husband?' Her voice was slow and cold.

In an instant he was on his feet, rebutting her challenge with indignation. 'No, Mildred. I was showing loyalty to a fragile girl wracked with fears. She is under constant suspicion. So, when she was summoned to court to attend her sister's birthing, she dared not take it with her, nor leave it behind. I am the only one she trusts. What could I do? Abandon her?'

'And what is in this book, William?' asked Dee.

'Her thoughts on regency. She speaks of a fair rule; of religious tolerance rather than the burning we live with today; of making this land great again and not a puppet of Spain.' Cecil dropped his head forward and his voice fell to a murmur.

'She speaks of a golden age in which men thrive, not fear life.'

Dee sighed. 'So, she speaks of being queen.' He waited until Cecil nodded. 'So, with Mary expecting her own son to succeed her, it is a tome of treason.' He gave a small laugh. 'Making my conjuring look pale in comparison.'

Cecil bristled. 'No. It is a volume of hope. The only treason lies with those who would put a Spanish prince as our ruler.' He gave a low growl. 'For the love of God, they circle court like hawks awaiting the death of Mary and her babe so they can grasp power while England mourns.'

John Dee opened his palms in question. 'Mary herself made Philip King of England. Not a prince. Not her consort. A king.'

Cecil wheeled round. 'Elizabeth is the rightful heir to the throne. Not a Spanish puppet of the Catholic Pope. A woman of the true faith…Protestantism.'

'So, if Elizabeth aspires to be queen, she is the single threat to the supporters of Philip.' John Dee pointed an accusing finger. 'And that book sets out her ambition.' He paused. 'That book will take her to the Tower and her death for treason… and someone in your household knows of it. They also know your involvement.'

From the window, Lady Cecil spoke. 'And her treasonous book is in this house. And somebody knows it.' She turned to look through the glass onto the bustling street below. 'May God save us.'

'It has been moved.' Cecil was pointing at the third shelf of his wife's library wall. 'I put it here between the book on St Thomas Aquinas and the book of St Peter's writings. But now…look. It is to the left of the book of St Peter.'

'Why did you put it there?' asked Dee.

Cecil turned with a small smile. These books are bound one in red, the other green. Elizabeth's book is bound in white calf skin. In my mind, the three colours make up the white-centred Tudor rose. So it was easy to find again.' His smile faded when behind him Lady Mildred sighed deeply.

John Dee was already fixated on the book. He pulled it from the shelf and opened the front cover, his eyes glinting like a man looking over a woman he desired. 'Her writing is surely neat and well laid out.' He was silent for a minute before looking up at Cecil. 'And her words are dangerous from the first page.'

Cecil nodded. 'But I took care. I secreted it under the carriage boy's seat and brought it inside after dark.' He faltered and looked away.

'So Jonas knew about the book,' hissed Dee.

Lady Cecil slammed her hands against the front of her kirtle. 'Dear God, husband.'

Dee pulled a notebook of rough paper from his bag and moved to the desk to pick up a pen. 'Who has access to this room?'

'Everybody,' spoke Lady Cecil for her husband. 'We are not a household to treat servants as spies.'

John Dee raised an eyebrow. 'You mentioned a Spanish maid who was dismissed for stealing the seal. Did she enter this room?'

There was a long silence before Mildred answered slowly, in a low voice. 'Yes.'

CHAPTER TWENTY-ONE

In the kitchen, Goodwife Barker was at her desk. She did not look up as Margaretta approached, even when she stood at the side of her desk. 'I am surprised you consider yourself low enough to come to the kitchen.'

'Please, Goodwife.'

'I am not pleased.' The voice was hissing bitterness.

'Lord Cecil would like your help. He awaits you in Lady Mildred's library.'

In an instant the woman was on her feet, pushing past Margaretta and snapping that she should not have been so long in telling her. As she slammed the kitchen door behind her, Lottie looked up, wide-eyed. 'Is there trouble?' She gave a little shudder. 'I feel afeared. It's just like the morning Jonas did not return home.'

'Try not to fear, Lottie. Just keep to your chores and I'll be back in a little while.'

Her small friend bent back to washing the pots, though she gave a sigh only the despairing should sound.

Cecil was seated at his desk. Behind him stood Lady Mildred, her hand on his shoulder. John Dee was in the window. Goodwife turned and glowered at Margaretta as she entered and then looked back at Cecil. 'Should the maid not be sent to the kitchen, sir?'

Cecil leaned forward. 'Not just yet, Goodwife. We have reason to think that this house has been entered by someone spying rather than working. Now…'

Goodwife gave a little cry. 'Please God, sir. I would never betray…'

Cecil growled. 'Lord above, Goodwife. We do not suspect you.' Behind him, Mildred gave a reassuring nod. 'Just answer my questions. There was a Spanish maid. Tell me about her.'

Goodwife sniffed. 'A bad one, sir. Went by the name of Maria. I knew the day she started she would be no good to man or beast. And I was surely right. Only ten days…ten days in which she was of little help… Father Thomas came and told me she was to be dismissed for pilfering.'

She was about to launch into another wave of indignation but Cecil quietened her by raising his hand. 'If you knew she was of a bad nature, why on earth did you employ her, Goodwife?'

Barker's face creased into confusion. 'But I did not, sir. She arrived at the door, just like this one.' An accusing finger pointed at Margaretta. 'She said she had been appointed by you, Lord Cecil. As we had recently lost a maid, I thought you had been most helpful, sir, and…' Her voice trailed to nothing as Cecil and his wife looked back, their faces showing bewilderment.

Mildred broke the silence. 'While we were assuming you had been most helpful in finding her so quickly, Goodwife.'

At this, John Dee looked up. 'What did you learn of her background, madam?'

Barker was blushing her discomfort. 'Little…nothing, sir. She said not a word until the day the father and I dismissed her. Then all we had was a-wailing and weeping in her own language.'

Dee frowned. 'Did she understand the instructions you gave her?' Goodwife nodded. 'But yet she could not speak our tongue.' Another uncomfortable silence descended.

Then Goodwife straightened and looked back to Mildred.

'She shared a room with Lottie. That child chatters like a sparrow. If anyone talked to her, it is she.'

Cecil nodded. 'We will ask Lottie up presently. Now, tell us about Luke. When did you last see him?'

Goodwife sniffed. 'At midday meal yesterday.' Her voice was harsh again. 'Much maudlin he was. Said he was going to Southwark.' She pursed her lips. 'I was very clear that filling his belly with beer and his head with slatterns was not going to bring Jonas back.' She sniffed loudly. 'But he would not listen to good sense.'

John Dee leaned forward. 'Did he say who he was going to see?'

'No. Just mumbled something about a shepherd. No doubt that is a new term for the men who sell doxies.' Her voice was brittle with contempt.

John Dee and Cecil exchanged glances. Dee looked to Margaretta. 'Go and get the girl, Lottie.'

The child clung to Margaretta's hand as she entered the library. Wide-eyed and trembling, she was pushed forward to stand before the desk. It was Mildred, seeing her fear, who took over the questioning.

'Be not afeared, Lottie. We simply need your help.' She pointed to a chair but Lottie shook her head and looked alarmed. 'Very well, child. There was a Spanish maid here some weeks ago. You shared a room with her. Did you make friends?'

A shake of the head.

'Did you speak with her?'

Another shake, the lower lip trembling now.

'Did she tell you anything at all?'

At this Lottie started to weep and her anxiety tumbled out in a stream of protest. 'I knew not a thing, my lady. She said nothing...not a word. Wouldn't answer no matter how many questions I asked or how friendly I tried to be. I didn't know she'd taken anything. Only when Father Thomas said she'd stolen did I know she was a bad one.'

Such was Lottie's distress that she did not hear Father Thomas slip in through the door and nod a greeting to Cecil and his wife before making a small bow to John Dee with a fleeting look of discomfort.

Alarm. That feeling again. You are concerned about what is happening here. Also irritation. You feel you need control.

Margaretta turned to look at Father Thomas but he ignored her and kept his eyes on Lottie. By now the child was speaking in a high-pitched squeak that she was a good girl and only wanted to do her best and have a home. Mildred was looking at her with concern as the child took no heed of her attempts to calm her.

Margaretta stepped forward and took Lottie's shoulders. 'Quiet, Lottie. Lady Cecil has said you are not accused. Now stop your weeping.'

The child took a deep, shuddering breath and fell silent.

John Dee stood. 'Lottie, I am Margaretta's master. She has spoken very well of you.' He was rewarded by a weak smile. 'She says you are a gentle girl with a liking for others.' A nod. 'When you tried to speak to the maid Maria…when you tried to be friends…did you feel she understood you?'

There was a pause while Lottie thought. 'Why, yes, sir. She always nodded and then put up her hands like this to say she did not understand.' Lottie turned her palms to the ceiling and raised her hands. 'I did say to her one day that I thought she could understand. But she walked away.' The girl frowned. 'There was no friendship to be found in her.'

'So, she said nothing at all?'

'Only her prayers, every morning and every night in her own tongue. Rocking and swaying to her rosary, she was, for hours. Four times on Sunday, sir.'

Dee raised his hand to stem another flow of words. 'And what did you say to her, Lottie? Did you tell her about the household?'

Lottie went quiet. Then murmured, 'No.'

'Tell the truth, Lottie,' demanded Dee, his voice moving to that of a stern father.

'Well, I did try to tell her about how to get along with people. To be obedient to Goodwife Barker, to always curtsey to Lord and Lady Cecil, to keep away from the stables, to be listening well when Father Thomas speaks, to be careful –'

'I am glad you think me of good words, Lottie,' cut in the priest.

Lottie gave a little yelp and looked round at the priest. He smiled and nodded. 'I am sorry to frighten you, Lottie. You are good to tell the truth.' Then he turned to Cecil. 'I came immediately I heard the news, my lord.'

He was rewarded with a nod and the priest continued, 'May I speak with you alone?'

Without waiting, Father Thomas turned to Goodwife and Lottie and gestured to the door. They rose. But John Dee cut in. 'I think Lottie had more to say.'

The girl looked to the priest, then to John Dee, and back again before whispering, 'No.'

Worry. A little fear. You curl your lips in and widen your eyes. Do you fear the priest or what you have not said?

By the window, John Dee was frowning his frustration. As Goodwife and the maid reached the door, he called out. 'One more question, Mistress Barker.'

The woman turned, saying nothing, though her face indicated her annoyance and the regular sniff sounding it.

'You said the girl Maria told you she was sent, yet she did not speak English.'

Goodwife reddened a little. 'Forgive me. She handed me a note of introduction.'

'Do you have that note?'

'Yes. It is in my ledger.'

'I would see that, please.'

As the door closed behind the two women, Margaretta stepped back into the shadow.

Father Thomas bowed to John Dee. 'I am pleased to meet you, Doctor Dee. I knew you could assist.' But rather than engage in conversation, he turned to Cecil. 'A few words alone, sir?' He glanced at John Dee, who glowered back.

Cecil shifted in his discomfort. 'You may speak freely in front of John.' He smiled at John.

You feel anger, Father. Or is it irritation? Then that fleeting loss of control. Is it because you want to be the favoured advisor? Why does the presence of Doctor Dee make you burn with bad feeling?

The priest stood stock still. Silent. Staring at Cecil. Discomfort grew. After a few long seconds, Cecil stood and walked to the door. 'We may speak in the hall, father.' The door clicked closed and John Dee growled.

Mildred Cecil joined him at the window and spoke, her voice soothing and low. 'Come, John, the clergy know not who they can trust or who will trust them. Father Thomas holds our views on religion, but he does not know you well enough.'

'Hmmm.' John Dee looked out of the window, his face like a petulant child.

There was a knock at the door. Goodwife Barker crossed the floor and handed a square of parchment to John Dee. 'The note of introduction. You will see it is well written. Nothing to alert me to any wrongs.' The voice was hard, clipped.

Anxiety. You feel you are being accused. Involved in something of which you have no understanding. You fear others thinking ill of you. What will you do if this place is not your home? You've lost so much. So very much.

Mildred smiled and reached out to pat the other woman on her arm. 'There is no question over your loyalty, Goodwife Barker.'

A tiny sigh gave away Barker's relief.

John Dee was staring at the paper and looked up at Mildred. 'Please can you give me the letter you read earlier, my lady?' Moments later he spread both parchments on the table under the window. 'These were written by the same hand – so now three letters.' He turned to look at Lady Mildred. 'Your maid was a planted spy.'

CHAPTER TWENTY-TWO

L ord Cecil and Father Thomas came through the door looking worried. Cecil sat heavily. When informed by John Dee that the maid was connected to whoever had written the Spanish note, he put his head in his hands.

Father Thomas strode across the floor. He stared at the letter for a minute, then turned to Lady Mildred. 'I cannot read this, my lady. But your husband tells me it implicates this household in treachery…untrue as that is.' He shook his head slowly from side to side to show his disbelief. Then, in a sudden shift from his usually mellow voice, said: 'Damn these Spanish papists. All of London mutters about their ambitions for our crown, our land and our church. They would swallow us into the Holy Roman Empire and make us not more than a dot on Emperor Charles's map.'

Mildred nodded then turned to John Dee. 'But, as you suggested, if ever there is a learned mind to uncover the evil which lies beneath these deeds, it is John's.'

Oh, you clever woman. You know how to light the doctor's candle.

Dee beamed his delight. Margaretta watched from the shadow of the library shelves and then the feeling again.

You are troubled, priest. Deep concern. Even anger. Resentment. You look at my master with an eye that has no smile, even though you smile with your mouth. But the lips curl down at the corner. Contempt. You feel it strongly. So why did you recommend him?

Cecil lifted his head and addressed the room. We must inform the staff of the latest news. He looked at Barker. 'Goodwife, please ask your staff to attend here.'

The woman nodded, her fear evident. The white hands were clasped tight in front of her and her face was fixed as if in wax, eyes bright with anxiety. Behind her, Margaretta shuddered with the dread she emitted.

Minutes later, Barker re-entered, followed by all the house staff. Lottie was first, her baby-pink mouth trembling and eyes wide. Then the cook, who yawed like an overladen boat. Behind her walked in the gardener, with a look of complete confusion. Then the rest. They lined up in front of Cecil's desk and bowed at Barker's command.

'I have terrible news,' started Cecil, but was stayed by a squeak from Lottie, who covered her face with her hands. Barker tried to pull them away but, like a child, she held them fast. Cecil cleared his throat and started again. 'I am sorry to tell you…' He looked at Mildred for guidance.

Father Thomas stepped forward. 'We must all pray for the soul of Luke.' He ignored the gasp from Barker and the wail from Lottie, who started to sob. 'He was taken from us in a grievous way. Like Jonas.' Cook clasped her hands in prayer and the priest smiled at her. 'As before, we must not speak of this outside this house.' They all nodded.

Margaretta stepped across the room and put her arm around Lottie, who was crying and wiping her nose on her sleeve. The girl looked up. 'What will happen next, Margaretta? Will we all die? One by one?'

Terror. You poor child. You've seen so much death and feel so alone. Everyone dear to you has been taken away. Like a child in the wilderness, you cry in fear.

Margaretta put both her arms around the girl and spoke

soothing words. As she did, she looked up into Barker's face. For a second – just a second – it was full of concern. She reached out a hand to put on Lottie's shoulder but pulled it back before the touch and, instead, hissed at her to be quiet.

Father Thomas started the prayer for Luke's soul, and all joined in. Then silence fell. He repeated: 'You will say nothing of these terrible deeds. Do you understand?'

As they started to leave, John Dee called to Barker. 'Forgive me, but I need Margaretta to do an errand for me tomorrow morning.' He smiled at her glowering and continued with a warm voice. 'I need her to stay here for instructions.'

Goodwife nodded and snapped at Margaretta that she would need to work through her evening rest time.

Father Thomas turned to speak to John Dee. 'How may I assist you in uncovering this terrible killer, Doctor Dee? We are both, I think, committed to protecting Elizabeth.'

John Dee responded with a wary, 'Yes.'

Cecil leaned forward. 'Father Thomas is one of us, John. We are all as one in our thoughts on religion, the crown and the rightful succession to the throne. You may speak freely.'

'But only in these walls,' cut in the priest. 'Outside is a cauldron of rumour and intrigue.'

'Did Jonas tell you why he went to Southwark?' asked Dee.

Father Thomas shook his head, looked down and sighed. 'I warned him of the dangers. But young men see drink and doxies as entertainment until the reality strikes.' He looked up and slammed a fist into his other hand. 'Whatever attracted him also terrified him.'

John Dee spoke slowly. 'Well, you cannot investigate in that garb. Too conspicuous.' He turned to Margaretta. 'But you are not.'

Someone here feels relief. The feeling is so strong. It's in all of you. But not me. I am being asked to walk into a den of sin where a child and now a man have lost their lives. Oh, God help me. I feel the sickness of fear.

CHAPTER TWENTY-THREE

The instructions had been simple: 'Go to Southwark, find the woman Harriet, make a friend of her, then seek all information on Jonas and Luke. And see if you can find a seal maker.' Cecil had turned those cold grey eyes on Dee and lowered the eyebrows for added effect. 'Go home, John, and do your work. Margaretta can go in the morning and move quickly if you have need of word from me.' He turned to Margaretta. 'You come directly to me after Southwark. No more secreting.' Then the half-smile which spat contempt, before he rose and ushered them all from the room, John Dee bridling and complaining. Only Father Thomas remained, a small smile on his face. Margaretta had felt relief.

John Dee then walked – no, stamped – to the wherry steps all the way, muttering his fury with Lord Cecil, who had insisted he leave and, worse, through the back door. Margaretta walked with him.

There were no boats by the wall but as Dee looked around there was a shout from the water and a wherry started towards them from the middle of the river. Something glinted in the early evening sun.

'I will take this one, Margaretta. You send message for your young man to collect you early tomorrow to go to Southwark.'

'He is not my "young man". He's from Southwark and just might help me find this woman.'

Dee huffed at her irritation and descended the steps. She

heard him shout, 'That way, that way.' So he must have been in a wherry with another poor sot who did not speak his tongue.

The following day, Margaretta waited in the early morning light, having been berated by Goodwife for being of little use if she was to be wandering every day. The stink of the river was high today. Margaretta looked down into the flotsam of old vegetables, dead fish and what looked like a drowned cat. She held her hand over her nose to try to stop the acrid smells making her stomach heave. It felt like an eternity before she saw Sam pulling at the oars, his linen shirt wet with sweat.

He looked up with a grin. 'I hear you want my company, missy?'

'I want a ride to Southwark, not company.'

Sam pointed to the seat. 'Then you had better climb aboard.' He grinned and winked. 'Though keep your tongue in your mouth, missy. Sharp things are not good on boats. I even keep my knife in my boot.'

Margaretta stamped down the stairs and stepped into the wherry. She tried to ignore the proffered hand but the wherry tilted and she had to grab Sam's shoulder before she sat and fumed.

Strong. So rarely do I touch another. It feels strange. Nice.

'So where are we going, missy? There are three sets of steps in Southwark. Is your business bear-baiting, praying in the church of St Mary Overy or drinking in the stews?' He leaned forward to look into her eyes. 'Not the kind of place I would expect you to visit.'

'I have business there.'

He chortled as he pulled on the oar to turn the boat. 'Do you know what that means in Southwark? I wouldn't be saying that too loud, missy.'

She felt her face run red and she snapped, 'I did not mean

that type of business.' Then she crossed her arms in indignation.

Sam fell serious. 'Really, missy. It's not a place for a young lady to wander in...unless you know where you're going.' He nodded up the river. 'I'll take you to the safer steps and wait for you.'

After a mumbled thanks, Margaretta started her questions.

'Is there a maker of seals in Southwark?'

Sam frowned. 'Seals are the tools of the rich. Not much call in Southwark.'

'What if it were a false seal?'

He cocked his head to one side. 'I hope you are not getting into bad company, missy.'

'I don't want one. Just to know if one has been asked for. I am asking for my master.'

'Try Sniffer Simeon. He has a shop at the end of Pepper Alley, behind the Dolphin Inn. He will deny everything but they call him Sniffer because he sniffs when he's worried.' Seeing Margaretta's face crease in disbelief, he offered a wager. 'A kiss if I'm right.'

'Indeed, no. I'll wager just a smile. Now, another question. Have you ever come across a woman called Harriet?'

The oarsman's eyebrows rose. 'Harriet? Yes. But I cannot think you've business with her.' He emphasised the word business and chortled again. 'She's the best-known doxy in Foul Street.' Then he frowned. 'What do you want with her?'

'No matter. How will I know her?'

'That sharp tongue again.' He shrugged. 'Just ask any passer-by. Most of them will be able to point her out.'

'I want no attention.'

'Then look for a dark-haired woman dragging a small child with her. The little one is called Tilly. You will know Harriet by her hare lip.' He paused. 'She is often by the Tabard Inn, but don't venture in there, missy.'

You worry. I am not used to feeling kindness from others. This warmth feels strange to me, yet good. Like a voice from long ago. Dada's voice.

Margaretta looked out over the water to stop the conversation. But Sam tapped her on the knee. 'You asked if my master knew Daniel of Hertford. Well, he certainly did. As brave on the battlefield as a dog of war. A good soldier, he said.'

In an instant, Margaretta was alert. 'Do you think your master would speak with Goodwife Barker at Lord Cecil's house? I think Daniel was her husband. She grieves sorely for him and it makes her harsh.'

'So you have a heart, missy. I'll surely ask for you.' The boy leaned forward. 'Is this Goodwife marriage material? Lord knows my master needs a good woman to end his loneliness.'

'I don't think I would wish that on any man. But he would be doing a kindness. What is the name of your master?'

'Master George Tovey. Boat-builder and organiser of wherries,' announced Sam with a grin. Then he looked serious. 'And a very good man, I must say.' With that, he nodded at the bank. 'Here we are.' He pulled the wherry into the wall. I'll await here for you…make sure you get back safe.'

He was rewarded with a small smile. Margaretta climbed the stairs, then stepped into the stews of Southwark. It was like hell on earth.

Chapter Twenty-Four

'How much are you asking?'
    'For what?'
    The man leered, revealing a row of black teeth and grabbed his crotch.
    'Go to hell.'
    The leer dissolved to a snarl. 'My money's as good as any man's. I'll make it quick. You redheads are always hasty.'
    'I said go to hell,' Margaretta snapped. But if this man used women, he might help her. 'Where's the Tabard Inn?'
    'So you prefer Spanish men,' was the bitter reply. 'Fuck you.' He turned away, pointing down a filthy lane. 'You'll get business down there.'
    Margaretta picked up her skirt and stepped forward. The street was swilling with all kinds of muck, human and animal. The acrid smell of piss mixed with the stink of rotting meat, which skinny dogs growled over. Men pushed through the throng with carts while women, bent under heavy sacks, used their elbows to get past. All around was the din of people arguing, hawkers calling their wares and children yelling to each other. As she moved further down the alley, the light dimmed as linens strung on ropes between upper-floor windows blocked the sun. Side alleys were crammed with rubbish and men pissing against walls. In one, an old man was rutting a girl who was protesting he had used his penny-worth.
    At the end of the street, the way divided. A young girl with

an ample chest was leaning against a wall, her face young and the eyes old.

'Can you direct me to the Tabard Inn?' asked Margaretta.

The girl frowned. 'You don't look like you're the type to be going there.'

'I'm looking for Harriet.'

The girl jabbed her thumb to the right. 'That way. If she's not on the corner, just wait. She'll be back after her business.'

The Tabard Inn was a dismal place. Sitting on the intersection of four alleyways, it was two storeys high and painted black. The sign creaked as it swung over the door. Looking up, Margaretta gave a little gasp. It depicted a young man in a red tabard. He was holding a lamb. Shouting and loud talk came from inside. Every few minutes the door swung open and a man would stumble out, the smell of stale beer and sweat following him. One fell on his knees and vomited.

With no sign of a woman or child, Margaretta stepped into a shadow and looked at the ground in the hope it would show she was not for approaching. It largely worked and only two drunks tried to buy.

It was a good twenty minutes before she was startled by a loud protest. 'Hey. What you doing on my patch? Sling your hook.' The woman was no more than her early twenties and, was it not for the lip, a beauty. A china-pale face was framed with dark chestnut hair. Her eyes, as large as saucers, were deep violet. A blue dress showed a body that would be the envy of many women.

'Are you Harriet?'

The woman's hands flew to her hips and the face darkened. 'Never mind being friendly, love. This is my patch. Now piss off.' Before Margaretta could reply, a small child ran out of a doorway and across the road, her arms up in a request to be lifted. The woman scooped her up and hugged her tight. 'Good girl, Tilly. Did you wait quietly for Mammie?'

Like her mother, the little girl was a picture. A doll-like face with pink cheeks and a perfect, round mouth smiled under a tumble of dark curls. She nestled into her mother and chattered about playing with a puppy. Then she looked up and pointed at Margaretta with a smile. 'Who's that?'

Maybe the child was the way to this woman. Margaretta smiled and dropped her voice to a kindly hum. 'Hello, Tilly. Sam the wherryman said you were as pretty as a princess.' The girl giggled and hugged her mother harder.

Harriet frowned. 'Why were you talking to Sam about us?' The voice was heavy with suspicion. 'He wouldn't send someone to take my patch, though he gives me no business.'

'Harriet, I'm not here to take any patch.' Margaretta tried a friendly smile to break the hostility but got none in return. 'I came to thank you for helping my friend Jonas.'

Tilly was put down quickly and told to go and find the puppy. As she scampered away, Harriet strode over to Margaretta and stood close, lowering her voice to a growling hiss. 'Look, I don't know who you are, lady. But don't be sniffing around here.'

'But you did help Jonas, didn't you?'

Harriet quickly looked around. 'Why are you asking? Who are you, anyway?'

'I work in the same house as Jonas.'

'You mean where he used to work. Don't pretend the poor little bastard is still with us.'

'What happened, Harriet?'

The woman bit her lip and hesitated. 'What you don't know won't hurt you. Now get your backside out of here.'

'But, I need to know what happened to Jonas. And Luke, too. I only want –'

Before she could finish, Harriet grabbed Margaretta's arm and shoved her backwards. 'You're a muddle-head if you think there's anything to learn around here. Especially from me. I know how the land lies. Now go.'

Gut-churning fear. What do you know? You are thinking of men. Many of them. A face, dark. Black eyes. Someone threatens you. Then your child's face. Terror. You've seen and know too much.

'You're frightened for your little girl, aren't you?'

Harriet stiffened, her eyes bright with anxiety. 'Tilly will be safe with me. Anyway, we'll soon be out of here. Another few months and I'll have saved enough to take her to Essex. Safe. We'll turn our backs on this hell-hole. And I'll be back to being Mistress Harriet Hern. My Tilly will be Matilda.' Behind her, little Tilly peeped out of the doorway, standing still, just listening.

Margaretta tried kindness. 'Harriet, I can see you are frightened. Tell me what happened to Jonas and Luke. I can help you if you help me.'

Harriet shook her head. 'They got caught up with the wrong ones. Jonas was a little fool. It was the end of him.' She made a cutting action across her throat. 'Then the old fool came here shouting that he would kill whoever hurt his Jonas.' She made the cutting action again.

'Who are the bad ones, Harriet?'

Harriet shook her head, then pointed down the street. 'Go. Go before you are seen.' Then she stood in silence, her face defiant. It was an impasse.

Tilly trotted back to take her mother's hand. 'Are you talking about the bad Spanish wherrymen and their turn-face shepherd, Mammie?'

Harriet rounded on her, shouting that she was 'not to ever speak of them.' Then she bent down in her panic and grabbed the child's arm to shake her. 'Go back to the puppy and never speak of anything. Do you understand?'

Tilly crumpled into tears and ran back to where she had been playing.

Terror. You've said too much. That face again. Someone dark has frightened you. Threatened you.

Harriet turned on Margaretta. 'Go.'

The Dolphin Inn was in uproar. A fight was spilling out into the street. Young men threw punches, often into thin air as the drink addled their sight. Then the smack of a fist on flesh and the furious yowl of the victim. A few lay in the gutter, trying to stop the blood spurting from their noses. Margaretta stepped over one and asked the way to Pepper Alley. He snarled and pointed to the back of the inn.

The alley stank. There were no cobbles to cover the road, only mud which reeked of the dog mess everywhere. One scabby mongrel eyed her warily and then sloped off when she shooed it away. A small boy walked towards her, barefoot, carrying a basket of cabbages. 'Where will I find Simeon?'

In a second a little hand shot forward. 'Give us a farthing and I might tell.'

My, I should clip your ear for such cheek. But look at you. No more than four years of age and a face already old. Is that hope in your eyes or desperation? 'Promise to tell and I'll give you a ha'penny.'

The child nodded and grasped at the proffered coin. He turned to point at a shabby door. The white lime was grey and the bottom of the wood was rotten with whole chunks falling away. From behind it was barking.

Margaretta banged on the door as the boy scampered away, calling, 'Shame Sniffer can't sniff his animals.' The door opened and the words made sense.

'Oh, God.' Margaretta put her hand over her nose trying to avoid the stench of dog piss and mess which wafted out.

She could see many canine faces looking at her, most barking a warning not to come in. Among them was an old man, back bent and a face that appeared to be falling off his skull. The eyelids drooped so low his eyes remained half-closed. He said nothing. Just stared. 'Are you Master Simeon?'

'Who's asking?'

'Me. I understand you can make a seal.'

'For who?'

God's teeth. I have not thought this through. I feel your suspicion. You drag a filthy sleeve across your nose. Was that a sniff? I need a reason. A person. 'The Shepherd.'

Sniff. Silence. Another sniff. 'Why the change of mind?' Sniff. 'He promised no more. Only five. Told me to break the mould.' Sniff. Sniff. Then the hooded eyes widened. Sniff. 'You ain't sent by the Shepherd are you?'

She was not quick enough. The old man called over his shoulder 'Demon. Attack.' There was a growl and a snarl and one of the dogs moved, teeth bared and muzzle pulled back. No time for another question, Margaretta turned on her heel and ran, not caring about the filth which splattered up her skirts. She careered round the corner towards the front of the Dolphin Inn and barrelled into the man who had given directions. A scream as her forehead hit his broken nose and then a slap across her face making her fall back in the dirt. He cursed at her and went to kick but she was on her feet running towards the river, the sound of men laughing in her ears.

Chapter Twenty-Five

'So is it back to Canon Row or just across the river to your St Dunstan's residence, my lady?' But Sam's face fell as she reached the bottom of the steps. 'What the hell have you been doing?'

'Simeon set a dog on me. I had to run and I fell.'

Sam shook his head. 'I told you to be careful.' Then the smile. 'Did he sniff first?' Seeing the pursed lips, he made a play of turning his cheek and pointing out where to kiss.

She took his chin and swivelled his face back to hers. 'I wagered a smile.' She made a caricature smile and sat heavily in the stern.

The boy feigned disappointment, smiled and declared all women to be contrary creatures as he reached for the oars.

Maybe you are not such a bad lad. But not for me. Though I have an idea. 'Canon Row this time.' Margaretta pulled her skirts up a little to stop the water in the bottom staining her hems as Sam's pushing off the wall made it slosh around her feet. 'Tell me about Harriet.'

Sam shrugged. 'She has her way of making money and who are we to condemn her if that is her only means?' He narrowed his eyes and leaned forward. 'I suppose a lady like you looks down on the likes of her.' His tone had moved from jocular to jibing.

Margaretta held up her hand. 'Not true. It's none of my business how she gets through life and feeds her child. I just have a feeling she is frightened.'

The wherryman made a sarcastic laugh. 'Any woman should be frightened in the stews of Southwark.' He nodded his head back down the river. 'A girl is killed every month in there. Usually found down an alley with her throat slit and her purse strings too.'

Margaretta shuddered. 'Does Harriet have anyone to protect her?'

'No. But she is one of the more wily girls. Gets along by being friendly to all and keeping her secrets close to her heart.'

'The little girl, Tilly, mentioned bad wherrymen and a turn-face shepherd. Do you know who she was speaking about?'

'Not me. I'm not –'

The hand went up again. 'I did not mean you, Sam. But there are many wherrymen, are there not? Is there a bad lot?'

He shrugged. 'Can't say I know. I only do this to get a few pennies to save up. My master has me back in the workshop learning my craft every day and he would frown upon me going to the Tabard Inn. It's where the authorities never venture.' Then he looked back at Margaretta. 'As I said, stay away from that devil's place.'

Your eyes are full of warmth and care. And I know who needs care.

Chapter Twenty-Six

The smell of burning filled the kitchen. Cook was pleading with Goodwife Barker. 'It was only a small pot,' whined the woman, shifting from one to the other of her bloated legs. 'The honey just burned. I was only –'

'You were only trying to burn us to the ground,' snapped Goodwife as she turned on her heel with a dismissive bat of her hand towards the older woman. The sight of Margaretta filled her face with more fury. 'Apparently, Lord Cecil awaits…a long while, too.' She glared. 'And wipe down your skirts. We don't want stew muck in here.'

Margaretta nodded just as Lottie entered. The child ran to her friend and clutched at her hands. 'Oh, Margaretta. I am so afeared. Where have you been?' In an instant, the lower lip began to quiver and her eyes pooled. Her voice dropped to a whisper. 'Will they come for me?'

Margaretta bent down to look into her eyes. 'All you did was talk to Jonas of a ribbon.'

'But I did let him hold my hand. And he spoke to me of the Shepherd.' Her voice was trembling now.

'Calm yourself, Lottie. Stay in these walls and nothing can hurt you.' She squeezed the child's arm. 'We'll talk later.'

Lottie gulped and nodded, though her eyes betrayed her fear.

Goodwife barked across the room, 'Margaretta Morgan, are you so grand that you can let a lord of England wait for the honour of your presence?'

Everybody jumped at the harshness of her voice. Her victim turned. 'No, Goodwife.'

Envy. I feel envy. You are concerned that I'll take your place with Lord Cecil. Then fear. What would you be without this household? There is no one out there for you. You are alone and fearful.

Margaretta walked across to the seething woman, dropping her voice. 'I was going to tell you after seeing Lord Cecil but, in case I forget, the wherryman who takes me to my master's house is apprenticed to a former soldier of King Harry. A Master George Tovey. I hope you don't mind, Goodwife, but I enquired if he might recall Daniel of Hertford.'

Barker gasped and reached out to the table.

Margaretta continued, too quiet for others to hear. 'He does remember a man of that name. "A true soldier" he says. A lion on the battlefield.'

Goodwife clasped her hands and stared, saying nothing, though her neck began to mottle and her cheeks flushed.

My how your feelings change. Shock mixed with regret, pride, warmth. You feel joy at hearing the name and deep sadness. Daniel of Hertford has died and left you alone. You grieve with a sadness deeper than a mine. You purse your lips so not to cry out.

'Master Tovey attends your church, Goodwife. I hope I have not done wrong by asking if he might speak with you.'

Goodwife just nodded and then looked at the door, her eyes glassy. As Margaretta turned to leave, she heard a whispered, 'Thank you, child.'

The clock was chiming three as Margaretta knocked on the door. Inside, Lord Cecil was seated behind his desk. On the other side was Father Thomas, who turned to stare at Margaretta.

'Come in, Margaretta. Tell us what you have learned.' Cecil smiled and gestured to a chair. Then he lifted a finger to signify a thought. 'I should call Lady Cecil.' He went to the door and shouted.

Margaretta glanced at Father Thomas.

Annoyance. You feel irritation with me. Is it because I have the ear of Lord Cecil or is it something else? You will not look at me. You want me to feel uncomfortable.

Cecil walked quickly back to his seat. 'Mildred is coming down. Sit, Margaretta.' He must have seen her looking at Father Thomas, a frown developing. 'What is the matter, child?'

'I thought I might speak in confidence, sir.'

At this, Father Thomas turned to look at her, his one dark eye narrowing and the paint glinting in the window-light. Lord Cecil looked first confused, then smiled. 'Good Lord, child. You are as bad as your master for seeing Abaddon in everything. Father Thomas is a trusted friend.' The priest smiled.

Before Margaretta had a chance to raise her concern, Lady Cecil entered. She was pale, her face anxious and the smile weak. She bowed her head to her husband and greeted Father Thomas as a friend. Turning to Margaretta, her voice dropped to that of a mother. 'I was concerned. Southwark is no place for a young woman.'

'I was careful, my lady.'

Cecil was impatient. 'And what did you learn?'

Margaretta faltered, looking again at the priest. But he smiled and leaned forward. 'Margaretta, forgive me. I am oft reserved until I know someone.' He gestured to his hosts. 'I have only the safety of this household in mind.'

Concern again. Maybe you pick up my wariness of you? Or do you think that I'll bring more problems to your friends? Maybe you think a woman can add nothing to this mystery. Like all men of religion, you no doubt think of my sex as that of an animal. Or are you concerned that I have insights? Whatever it is, you feel less than comfortable with me.

Lord Cecil sat forward and barked, 'Did you uncover anything of interest?'

'I found the woman, Harriet, mentioned by Jonas. Also the old man they call Sniffer Simeon, who may have known about the false seals.'

'You have done well. Go on.'

'Harriet is a woman of…of…the streets but seems honest.'

Anger. Now I feel anger. Whose is it?

Father Thomas rose from his seat and strode towards the window, smacking a fist into the palm of the other hand. 'Whores. Their vile work blackens the souls of men. They are a pestilence born of Eve.' He turned, eye dark. 'What would a whore have to do with any person of this house?'

Lord Cecil looked uncomfortable and glanced at Lady Mildred. She spoke softly. 'We understand your morals, father. But all we know is that Jonas spoke her name.'

Calming. Someone is calming in here. Strange, though. You react with fury about the doxies here, yet you were philosophical with Doctor Dee when you spoke of Jonas going to Southwark.

Lady Cecil leaned over and touched Margaretta's arm. 'Continue.'

'There is not much to tell, my lady. Harriet would say nothing.'

Calming further.

'But her little girl mentioned a turn-face shepherd and bad wherrymen. It made Harriet angry and she sent me away. So I could not find out who this Shepherd is. They gather in the Tabard Inn, which has the sign of a man holding a sheep.'

Alarm. Sudden worry. What have I said?

Lord Cecil frowned. 'Shepherd? Did she mean a priest?'

Before Margaretta could answer, Father Thomas came back to his seat. 'Did she say the wherrymen were Spanish or this Shepherd?'

'The men, yes,' answered Margaretta. 'She did not say if the Shepherd is…'

Lord Cecil cut in. 'It helps us little. There are many of them since King Philip arrived with a retinue of three thousand staff. He created a new business – Spanish wherrymen for the Spanish. Our own would either refuse them or cheat them.' He pulled his hand down over his face with a sigh. 'But why would Jonas be involved with them?'

Father Thomas turned to Margaretta. 'Did Harriet say where to find these people? Did she describe the Shepherd?'

Worry mixed with anger. It's growing. But which of you am I feeling? I don't feel safe to speak.

'Harriet told me nothing at all. She told me to leave Southwark and not come back. That there was nothing to be told.'

'But the child spoke.'

'Yes. But she is just a very young child. There may be no connection.'

Cecil took his hands away from his face. 'Margaretta is right. A child mentioning rough wherrymen and a shepherd is no evidence at all. Southwark is full of such villains. All we know is that Jonas and Luke mentioned the name Shepherd. We are no further forward.'

Relief. Slight relief but still the anger.

'What about this old man? What did you call him?' asked Mildred.

'Sniffer Simeon. Called that because he sniffs when alarmed. I tried to trick him into confirming he made the seals. All he said was, "only five", then set his hound on me.' Lady Mildred let out a little cry and patted her arm. Margaretta continued. 'I am sorry, Lord Cecil. I could not fight off a dog. Anyway, he will say nothing.'

Lord Cecil banged his hand down on the desk, making

Lady Cecil wince. 'Damn this. My household and my name are being threatened and there is no solid evidence, no clues, no path to reason. All knowledge has gone with the killed. We are no further forward and have no idea where to look for answers.'

Mildred Cecil leaned forward and took her husband's arm. 'Quieten yourself, husband. Maybe it is better to walk away from evil than seek its reason. We can move the whole household to our manor in Wimbledon, out of the city and away from trouble.'

Lord Cecil knotted his brows together while he thought. But before he could answer there was a sharp knock at the door. It was Goodwife Barker.

'I am sorry to interrupt, sir. But a woman has arrived at the door in some distress. She insists on seeing you in person. She is a nurse from the Savoy and alarmed.'

Cecil blanched and glanced at his wife before instructing, 'Send her up.'

The nurse almost ran through the door. Lord Cecil beckoned her forward. 'What is your name, madam?'

'Fran Hopper, my lord. Nurse of the Savoy.' She gulped and looked again from face to face, her breathing shallow and anxious. 'I have been sent to tell you of a terrible deed.' The atmosphere tensed. Every person went still as sweat beaded on her brow. 'Master Robert Meldrew has been dreadfully attacked, sir. Beaten and broken. His eyes gouged. We are not sure he will live.' She pulled at her skirt and plunged a hand into her pocket. 'This was put about his neck. The last thing he uttered was to bring it to you.' She held out her hand and stepped forward to put an object on Cecil's desk. It was a seal.

Lord Cecil snatched it up and turned it in the light. 'Another fake. Another message.'

Chapter Twenty-Seven

'Go fast now. And only ask Sam. I don't want any other wherryman.' Margaretta pressed a coin into the boy's palm and leaned over the river wall to watch the bustling while she waited.

Just a yard away from her, two elderly women bent their heads together. 'They says she lies dead,' insisted one. 'The babe still inside her.' She shook her head. 'They says in the market that we'll have blood in the streets before the mayflower wilts.' Her companion grumbled about things being better under old Harry. The first woman continued, wagging her finger for emphasis. 'They say the Lady Elizabeth has been ordered to court to keep her under the king's watch. It will be the Tower for her next and a Spaniard on the throne, mark my words.' Then they looked around to see if anyone was listening, glared at Margaretta and scuttled away.

She looked back over the water. In the middle of the river, she saw the wherryman's arm raised to catch her eye and a gesture to come over. There was a flash of light by his neck as something glinted in the sun. She waved back to say 'no', to which he responded with an exaggerated shrug.

Her ears were still ringing from Goodwife Barker's tongue-lashing after being told Margaretta was to return to St Dunstan's. Gone was the fleeting softness shown when hearing of Sam's master. Lottie had tried to make things better by squeezing her hand as she left, her big button eyes showing sympathy as she whispered: 'Don't be upset, Margaretta. I think she's much affected by the news of Luke. She was never so harsh on him as the rest of us so maybe there was a little liking there.' Suddenly, Goodwife's fury at the thought of Luke staying in the stews made sense. And maybe little Lottie was not such a muddle head.

The shout from the water made her jump from her thoughts. 'Second time in one day, missy. I am beginning to think maybe you do like me just a little.'

She looked down to see Sam grinning up at her, his brown curls falling over his face. She sniffed her feigned disagreement and called down, 'It's your arms I seek, not your mouth or your mind.'

He made no reply but just pointed at the waiting seat.

I have hurt you. All you sought was to help and protect. That is why you warned me of the Tabard Inn earlier. Now you feel foolish.

She scrambled into the boat. He did not try to catch her waist but pushed off the wall, saying nothing.

'I'm sorry, Sam. Goodwife Barker shouted at me again. It made my mood bad and my tongue harsh.'

In an instant, he cheered. 'No matter, missy.' Then he frowned. 'Is that the woman you want my master to meet?'

'Yes. The very one.'

'I am not sure my master wants to meet a sharp-tongue. He is a good man full of gentle manners.'

'I think, if your master can speak kind words about Daniel of Hertford, he will help us all. I feel she is bitter with grief rather than by nature.'

Sam grinned and tapped her knee. 'Then I'll beg my master to make his visit very soon and make your life better.' He pulled on the oars. 'So why are you going home so soon, missy? Have you not done your work well?'

Oh, how it would be a comfort to tell you everything. But the fewer tongues to wag the better. 'I've been sent back with a message. My real master has to visit somewhere. If you can wait while I get him, there's a journey back to the Savoy for the taking.'

'Then I'll wait.'

Sam was about to launch into another line of chatter when he narrowed his eyes and looked over her shoulder. 'For a minute, I thought that wherry was following us.'

His passenger spun round. There were at least ten wherries. 'Which one?'

'Three from port-side…the left side.'

Margaretta shielded her eyes from the low evening sun to better see. He was too far away to see his face but there was a glint from his neck. He changed direction and made for the bank.

'Just my imagination,' said Sam. But he pulled hard on the oars and picked up the pace. They fell into conversation about the business of the river, the terrible news of more deaths from the great cold, the pamphlets found in the street saying that the queen was not with child but planned to buy a baby from a gentlewoman. They were searching for a babe with Spanish looks. But he kept glancing over her shoulder.

It seemed no time at all before he was pulling into the bank. Huw was waiting. He took Margaretta's bag and helped her out of the wherry.

'Doctor very angry. Shouted since he came back. Says Cecil is a bastard.' He began to step from foot to foot. 'Snip tongue shouting too. Kitten peed in her shoes. She says it's because of your stew.'

Sam snorted behind them and called up the bank. 'So you're no cook, missy.'

She reeled around, ready to snap. But she remembered the feeling earlier and smiled. 'I'll be back soon with my master… and I'll bring you no stew as a kindness.'

John Dee was biting at the side of his fingernails. His index finger was already red and raw and so he had moved to the thumb. Next to him was a worried-looking Christopher Careye.

Dee beckoned her in. 'Christopher was followed. Threatened.'

'By whom?'

'A swarthy man wearing a large crucifix,' answered the pupil, blushing as he nodded to Margaretta.

'Like the wherryman?'

'Hmm. But many Spaniards wear their religion on their chest.' Dee turned to Christopher. 'You must have been seen coming here when we did our scrying.' He frowned. 'But how did anyone know? It was but a day after I saw the body.' He shrugged and looked up at Margaretta. 'What news from Southwark?'

'Little, but we have more urgent news. There has been another attack. The architect of the Savoy Hospital.'

Dee jumped up, slamming a hand down on the oak and making the candlestick topple. 'Meldrew is dead?'

'Nearly. The messenger-nurse said he was so beaten he would not rise again.' She pointed towards the door. 'I have a wherry waiting.'

'We must go immediately. Get my coat and put more paper in my bag.'

Christopher stepped forward. 'Doctor, I do not think Margaretta should be –'

But he was ignored. 'Come, girl. Do not dally.' Then Dee called over his shoulder: 'Home, Christopher. And do not use the usual streets.'

Margaretta grabbed the leather satchel, stuffed in four pieces of rough paper and picked up the coat. She nodded to an alarmed Christopher and trotted after Dee.

Katherine Constable stepped out as they passed through the hallway. 'The kitten has ruined my good shoes,' she whined.

Dee turned with a growl. 'Then make mittens of the damn kitten, madam.' He was through the door and racing for the river and so did not hear her howl of indignation.

Sam was waiting in the wherry, idly knotting green reeds. Dee ignored the introduction and just stepped in, commanding Sam to row as fast as his arms could muster. In seconds they were making pace, Dee firing questions at Margaretta.

'Did they see the attacker?'

'The nurse didn't say. But they found a seal – another false seal – around his neck.' She saw Sam look up at her, his face concerned.

Dee was oblivious to him. 'Ah, the sign. Anything else?'

'No. The woman was too agitated to get much from her. Father Thomas took her to the kitchen for a posset.'

John Dee was quiet for a second. Then he leaned forward and spoke low to prevent Sam from listening. 'What do you feel of the priest? You said before you were not sure of him.'

'Concern. But is that not expected?'

John Dee gave a dismissive snort. 'I think he is only concerned about getting close to Cecil...and keeping others away.' He shrugged. 'Though he says he wants to help me.'

The wherry slowed as Sam stopped rowing and twisted in his seat.

'Why are you stopping, boy? There is a way to go yet,' snapped Dee.

Sam turned back. 'Sorry, sir. Thought I saw something... someone.'

Suspicion with a twinge of fear. You've seen something you are not sure about. It's on the river. But I look out and see only the normal traffic and bustle. But you feel a threat. 'What did you see, Sam?'

The boy shrugged. 'The same one I thought was watching when I was taking you downriver. He was going back-a-long from where we came. Don't like the Spanish. They try to muscle in with a lower fare.'

Margaretta smiled. 'Well, the fare will stay yours, Sam.'

Sam grinned, pulled harder and flushed just a little. The feeling of threat went.

'Yes, we have been expecting you, Doctor Dee.' The nun stepped aside to allow the doctor to enter and gestured along a dark corridor. 'We have made Master Meldrew as comfortable as possible.'

'We can talk as we walk, sister.'

As they strode down the corridor the nun was interrogated. Robert Meldrew had been found on the riverbank that morning. When he did not return for an arranged meeting with the senior nurse, a nun went out to seek him. It had taken five of them to carry him back to the Savoy. A physician was called immediately but he had little hope of Meldrew recovering.

'His injuries?'

'It's as if a herd of bulls had attacked him. Many bones are broken and, the physician says, his innards made a pulp. Now he has lost all ability to speak. He is barely conscious.' She shuddered. 'Oh, and his eyes…'

'Did Robert say anything at all?'

'Nothing we understood. Except for the name Cecil when we pulled the wool from his mouth.'

Dee stopped short. 'Wool?'

She shuddered. 'It was dreadful, sir. They had stuffed his mouth with wool.'

Chapter Twenty-Eight

The room was dark and the air heavy with burning sage. Two nuns in nursing aprons stood either side of the bed, one gently dabbing Robert Meldrew's face with a damp linen. John Dee went straight to the end of the bed and leaned over to look at the man. Even he flinched at the sight.

Meldrew's face was swelling like a fruit that is about to burst, blood running from under his eyelids. One side of his jaw seemed higher than the other and the slit lips bulged blue over broken teeth. His broken body was blanket-covered but it was easy to see that the breathing was rapid and shallow. Every now and again a pained grunt would escape as if each breath was agony.

Dee went to the side of the bed and kneeled on the floor to get close to Robert's face. He beckoned to Margaretta to come closer. Reluctantly she stepped forward for another lesson. Dee pointed to the forehead. 'Do you recognise that pattern?'

She leaned in a little closer. 'Three distinct cuts into the skin. The same pattern as on Jonas's palm.'

Dee nodded. 'Get paper and make a drawing of it.' As Margaretta turned, he put his mouth close to Meldrew's ear. 'Can you hear me, master? This is John Dee.'

It was a few seconds before a tiny, high sound came out and Robert made a minuscule turn of his battered head.

'Did you see your attackers?'

Only just, but a definite nod.

'Did you know them?'

Another nod.

'The name. I need the name, Robert.'

The lips seemed to twitch, but no sound.

The nun stepped forward to object but Dee dismissed her with a flick of his hand. 'Use all your strength, man. Try to say the name.' The lips moved again and Dee put his ear close to Robert's mouth. His face creased into a frown. 'Flock?' His eyes flicked to Margaretta. 'That word again.'

He bent to the architect. 'Who is in the flock, Robert? We must know.' But it was too late. Robert Meldrew's head lolled to the side. He was gone. One of the nuns began to cry. Another pulled the sheet over his face.

Dee pulled himself up. 'Show me the wool.'

The older nurse frowned. 'But we threw it in the river, sir. It was covered in blood and mud.'

Dee threw up his hands in disbelief. 'God's teeth, woman. That is evidence.'

The woman bridled and complained she was a nurse and not a coroner. Anyway, the doctor should have more respect than to shout in the death chamber.

The horror of it. You screamed when you saw it. Who would do such a thing? Oh, God. If your master was so hurt, will they come back? Fear. Rising fear. The colour. 'Can you describe the wool, sister?

The woman nodded and looked at Margaretta. 'It was a ball of fleece tied with spun wool in the middle and four twists made as if to hang down. Then another had been balled. It looked like a dead animal.' She shuddered. 'It was dyed bright yellow.'

CHAPTER TWENTY-NINE

Sam had waited as asked but rowed in silence. Margaretta was not able to get the terrible sight of Robert Meldrew out of her mind. She recalled the fear he felt when he last talked to John Dee, how she had picked up an image of a man in a boat, a voice calling, something being thrown in the river. She had picked up nothing this time. The man's pain had masked all emotion.

Sam started to pull in from the centre of the river. 'That doesn't look like your brother, missy.'

Margaretta spun round. 'It's Mam. There's something wrong.'

Mam Morgan was on the steps, hands to her face, then reaching one out as if begging for help.

'What's happened?' called Margaretta, scrambling out of the wherry and up the stairs.

Mam was weeping. 'My poor boy. Why did they do that?'

Margaretta grabbed her mother by the shoulders and shook her. 'Huw? What's happened?'

'They beat him. Nothing has he done. Just sitting and counting. Innocent he is.'

John Dee was now at their side. 'Tell us, Mother Morgan.'

'A man in a boat. Half killed him.'

Margaretta ran to the house, leaving Dee to take her mother's arm and steady her as she walked back.

'Huw?' Silence. She screamed harder making the hounds whimper as they picked up the fear.

Then a rattling in the courtyard as the wooden wheels of a carriage halted. Katherine Constable stepped out. Gone was the usual despairing twist of her mouth. 'I have taken Huw to your sister. He was much frightened and needed care. I thought it was best he was with her as you were not here...I...' She made a small smile as if looking for approval, then added, 'I hope I have done the right thing.'

Her maid just nodded. 'Is he badly hurt?'

'He is cruelly beaten. But he is young and strong.' Katherine offered another smile. 'I think he has your strength, so do not weep.' Then she pointed over her shoulder to the carriage. 'You should go to him. I have paid the carriage man. Go talk to your sister.' Another sympathetic smile.

Sympathy. You really do have kinder feelings than suspicion of me. But you feel horror...for Huw.

Margaretta nodded her thanks and made for the carriage. Then the questions came. 'Did you see who beat him?'

The other woman shook her head. 'I was in the sitting chamber when I heard your mother scream. The boy had crawled back to the kitchen and was on the floor. He is speaking your tongue.' She looked towards the carriage. 'You should go I think.'

The wind began to rise as soon as the carriage reached the main road and the clouds blackened. In minutes, rain began to spill out of the evening skies, liquefying the mud around them. The driver stopped to pull a heavy oilskin over his shoulders and then urged the reluctant horse forward. Time seemed to creak, it went so slowly.

Susan's home near St James's Park was a three-storey symbol of success, with manicured grass and pretty trees softening the lines of the grounds. Margaretta jumped down and went ankle-deep into a muddy rut, then ran to the main door, ignoring the growling hunting hound. She clattered the iron knocker. At last, there was a clunk and the round fleshy face of the housekeeper looked out.

'Yes?'

'I've come to see my brother. I think he's here with Susan?'

She made a little sniff. 'Well, I suppose you had better come in.' She looked down. 'Maybe you could lift your hems, miss, and keep the mud off my mistress's carpets.'

Damn. I am still spattered in Southwark muck. Ah, well. A gift for Susan. And also for her damned servants who think they may look down on me.

The housekeeper opened the door at the top of the stairs. 'In here, miss.'

The room was warmed by a log fire in full blaze. Huw was in the bed, bundled in blankets like a swaddled child, Susan bending over him offering a drink while murmuring mother-like encouragement. As she looked up, her face shifted from concern to fury. 'What in the Lord's name goes on to bring Huw to me like this?'

'I don't know what happened, Susan. How is he?' Margaretta's voice was taut.

Susan rose to her full height, slammed down the beaker and clamped hands to her hips. 'Beaten to a pulp.' She looked down at him. 'You're not looking after him.'

By now, Margaretta was on the other side of the bed. Huw stayed silent, bruised eyes darting between the two women. He pulled further into his blanket.

'I don't look after him? Who was it who chased the boys away when he was little? Who stopped them from throwing stones and sticks? I look after Mam and Huw every day of my life while you parade your fancy clothes and deny our existence.'

Susan huffed and rolled her eyes to heaven. 'My

responsibilities are as a wife and mother.' She locked her eyes onto her younger sister. 'Your responsibilities are to look after Mam and Huw.'

There was a moment of icy silence before Susan hissed through her teeth: 'What will people say if they hear about this carry-on? This is a respectable household. We are rising.' Then she raised her voice to a singsong sneer. 'But I'll protect Huw if you cannot.'

Susan smoothed a lock of chestnut hair that had fallen from under her coif. She scratched at a dark spot on her partlet, then gave a loud sigh, realising it was dried blood from her brother's wounds.

'You would not protect a butterfly if it did not advantage you. Why did Dada teach me all the words and letters when you only ever learned to skip a pretty dance?'

'Dada, Dada, Dada,' was the mocking reply. 'Dada's little pet. He gave you letters because he knew no one like Angus would even look at you. He did you a charity.' Susan squealed as Margaretta's palm reddened her cheek and, from the bed, Huw shouted his distress.

'Damn you, Susan. Your head has always been bigger than your heart.'

The older sister smirked. 'But that pretty head catches the eyes of men, little sister. And the catching of men's eyes makes a lady.' She sniffed and looked down at Margaretta's muddy dress. 'So you will never be a lady.' She ducked as the hand was raised again and ran to the door. In seconds the room was in silence.

Damn you, Susan. You were born on the same farm as I and walked in the same cow-shit and pig-shit as I. You went as hungry as I when Dada was away fighting and was as cold as I in the bed we shared. The only difference between us was that Dada taught me and Mam cooed at you. The other difference was that I pulled Huw after

me every minute of every day and you ran away from him. You were
vile then and you are more so now. How are we so different from the
same womb? You think Angus has made you a lady. He has made
you a demon.

Huw had pulled the blanket over his face and was as still as
a corpse. His sister touched the round of his head gently, raising
a small groan. *'Dere nawr, frawd bach. Dim ond ti a fi yw e.'* Come
now, little brother. It's only you and me.

Slowly the blanket was pulled down and Huw's bruised
eyes peered at her, then were quickly averted to stare at the
ceiling. His breathing was shallow and short.

Margaretta spoke low in their mother tongue, asking where
he hurt, if he was thirsty, if Susan had been kind to him. Tiny
nods. Then she asked the question she knew would change his
manner. 'What happened, Huw?'

At first, he was silent, then the shivering. Small grunts as
he tried to mouth the words, but distress mashed his response.
Tears wetted his eyes and he shook his head as if trying to shake
the memories out. He said only three words. *'Y llythrennau drwg.'*
The bad letters.

Without his letters she needed paper and a pen. But there
were no writing tools here – just a linen chest in the corner
with a candlestick and a mirror on top. Damn this. She would
have to ask Susan.

The kitchen made the Constables' kitchen look like a pauper's
den. All this while the poor went hungry in the face of yet
another bad harvest and harsh winter. Damn her pretty sister
and her pretty man and her pretty baby.

'What do you want?' It was the round-faced woman who
had opened the door earlier. She was the shape of a barrel and
only a little taller. Her face was like the loaves – round and soft.
Two small eyes seemed to struggle from under heavy, puffy lids

and the mouth like a strawberry in dough. Podgy hands went to her hips and the head cocked sideways in a display of irritation.

'I need a paper and a pen for writing. My brother finds it easier to speak through written letters.'

The woman sniffed loudly and pulled back her head to look down the short, upturned nose. 'Only Goodman McFadden has paper and he is not yet home. Wait here.' She walked away.

It was not long before a boy ran in announcing the arrival of Goodman McFadden and Angus, who were calling for hot wine to warm them. There was a flurry of activity to find large beakers, warm a poker in the coals and cut oranges. In a minute there were two large beakers of brew being carried by a young kitchen girl.

Damn this. Susan lives like a queen and would happily bury the rest of her family like dirty secrets. No doubt she has lied to these poor sots about her illustrious beginnings. Well…

'I'll take that to the goodman. Susan and I are well used to serving others,' offered Margaretta, stepping forward, revelling in the girl's surprise. 'Oh, did Susan not tell you of our humble roots?' Raised eyebrows. 'Yes, indeed. Not a shoe between us. Ran in the pig-shit we did.' The girl was open-mouthed and wide-eyed. 'Yes, she was a bad-tempered, vile vixen then, too.' With a smile, Margaretta held out her hand and the beakers were released to her in stunned silence.

The men were seated on either side of the fire, hats off and shoes cast aside. Angus turned, his hand already out for the wine. 'What the…what are you doing here, Margaretta?' His eyes immediately went to her breasts.

The older man turned and rose, his face breaking into a broad smile. 'My dear child. How goes it with you and that mad master of yours?'

She curtsied and then nodded to Angus, who was running his eyes up and down her body. 'The house is well, thank you, sir. But my brother has been hurt. He was brought here to stay with Susan –'

Angus cut in with a sound of exasperation then slurred: 'The dog boy? Here in the house? That cannot be permitted –'

His father raised a hand to silence him and looked back to Margaretta. 'What happened?'

'He has been beaten, sir. I need paper and a pen. Then Huw can tell me why by pointing at letters. Please, may I…'

'Of course.' Goodman McFadden crossed the room. 'Wait here, child.' The door clicked closed.

'So,' leered Angus. 'How is my wife's little sister?'

'As I said, I am well, Angus.'

He stood, a little unsteadily, and stepped towards her. He was a handsome man, if a little pretty. Milky skin, hazel eyes, a good head of hair that was brown but shone a tinge red. As ever, his clothes were extravagant: a heavy damask doublet augmented with lace; a ruff too large; hose like two huge balloons. He took the curl that always escaped her coif between long fingers. 'So will you stay tonight, little sister?' His breath was like the base of a barrel.

Margaretta stood like a statue, refusing to meet his eye. 'I'll go home to St Dunstan's.'

He leaned in, so close his breath wetted her cheek. 'Such a shame. Two sisters under one roof.' He gave a tug of her hair. 'Our bed could do with a little more warmth.'

She shoved him in the chest, making him grunt as the breath shot out. 'Damn you, Angus. Don't you dare wrong my sister with your dirty thoughts. You are a husband and a father…not a dog in the stews.'

He was about to retort, his face furious. But the door opened and Susan floated in, carrying their child. As ever, it was swaddled like a pudding. The greeting smile slipped from her face. 'What are you doing here, Margaretta?' The tone was accusing.

Worry. You feel a twist of worry. Was he looking at me? Was he doing what he has done before? Are you being shamed again? So many questions run through your mind. Now anger. Hurt.

'Angus was telling me how he prays his thanks every day for having you and little Jack to come home to.' She turned to Angus with a smile and raised eyebrows.

'Indeed, I was,' he chimed in, and crossed the room to kiss Susan and the baby. 'I am the luckiest man in London.'

Then relief as Goodman McFadden entered with a handful of paper, an inkpot and pen. 'Here, Margaretta. See what you can learn.'

'*Gad lonydd i fi.*' Leave me alone. The angry voice was muffled through the blanket.

She tugged back the covering. '*Symuda.*' Move yourself.

'*Cer o 'ma.*' Go away.

As ever, he twisted his head away from her and closed his eyes as if the lack of seeing would make everything go away.

She softened her voice and spoke in their mother tongue as if to a small child. 'Come now, Huw. I'll not ask you to look at me. Just point at letters.'

A tiny nod gave her hope. She wrote the alphabet on one sheet of paper. It was the English alphabet, for Huw had mentioned 'bad letters'. She coaxed him to pull an arm from under the heavy blanket, which made him wince and moan. Then she held the paper in front of him. 'Can you point?' On his nod, she handed him the pen.

'Did you know the person who beat you?'

Shake of the head.

'How many were there?'

Huw tapped the pen once.

'Where did he come from?'

Huw reached out a bloodied hand with a small groan and pointed to A V O N.

'The river. A wherryman?'

Another nod confirmed.

'Good boy. Did he speak?' She waited for the nod. 'What did he say to you?'

At this, Huw began to twist and his face contorted as if the memory was causing more pain. Soothing words coaxed him to reach out again and tap D O N D E E S T A D H U. He winced and tapped further Q U E E S E L.

Margaretta took the pen from him, dipped it in ink and wrote the words on another paper. 'Spanish. Have you ever seen him before?' Another nod then moving his head from side to side. 'When you count the wherries. You've seen him going past. How many times, Huw?'

Two taps of the pen. Then he pointed to letters. D D O E – yesterday.

'You are doing well, Huw. I know this hurts but a few more questions and you can sleep. Did he say anything else?'

Huw bit his lip and winced before reaching out again. L O C A Z O. Then he began to shake his head in distress. L O M A T A R.

Again, Margaretta penned the words. No wonder Huw had said bad letters. The man had used Q U and Z – all of them bad in his mind as they did not exist in his first tongue. She peered at them helplessly. But downstairs were two men who traded on the river. Would they know?

Susan was waiting at the bottom of the stairs, holding her tight-swaddled child, who glowered at his aunt. 'Why are you bothering Huw? He needs care, not you nagging him.'

'*Cae de ceg, Susan.*' Shut up, Susan.

There was an imperious laugh. 'Do you still use the common tongue, sister?'

'Common?' Margaretta raised her hands as if imploring heaven. 'It's the old tongue of this whole land. I would also remind you it's in the blood of our royals.'

Susan made a dismissive flick of her hand. 'Court...our queen...has no truck with her Welsh blood. It has brought her nothing but pain.' A sickly smile. 'I think you will find, sister, that the future is Spanish. King Philip will lead us forward when the Tudor line dies. Everyone talks of it.'

'The Tudors have Welsh blood in their veins, Susan.' Margaretta made a false smile. 'If our queen dies, then another *Welsh* woman will be on the throne and the doing of it will make a traitor of you – to both the crown and to the courage of women.'

Margaretta ignored her sister's high-pitched protest and made for the room where she had last seen the goodman.

He was dozing in front of the fire. Thank the Lord, Angus was not to be seen. A slight press of his elbow and he looked up through bleary eyes. 'Did you get what you were seeking?'

'I think the words are Spanish.' Margaretta put the paper in his hand. 'I wondered if you could read them through your trading in the Vintry.'

Goodman McFadden turned it to the fire for light and frowned. 'Well, the first line is "Where is…something." The letters mean nothing in Spanish.' Then he gave a small grunt of concern and took his gaze back to the next line. 'This is asking, "Who is he?" The next line, "I am hunting him", but…' Goodman McFadden looked up bewildered. 'You would normally use "*Lo Cazo*" when talking of an animal hunt.'

Margaretta gulped. 'What about the third, sir?'

He looked at Margaretta, his face paling. 'I will kill him.'

Concern. Real concern. You are worried I'll be hurt. A twinge of regret. Oh, Lord. You wish Angus had married me. You don't know of your son's weaknesses? No. Another feeling. Disappointment. You do.

'Could you keep Huw a day or so?'

'No need to ask, child. A family must stand together when there is need.' But as Margaretta walked to the door he called after her, 'Tell John Dee that he may have danger coming to his door.'

CHAPTER THIRTY-ONE

Mam was standing at the back door, hands clutching and unclutching, her mouth drawn in a line of pure misery. 'How is my boy?'

'Badly bruised and frightened, but Goodman McFadden has said he can stay a day or two to mend his wounds.'

Mam relaxed. 'With Susan. That is best for him. Such a gentle girl.'

'Since when was a snake "gentle", Mam?'

The older woman scowled, then whined: 'Don't tongue-lash your sister so. Never gave me the trouble you did.'

'That's because she never did anything,' snapped her daughter as she strode through the door and towards Dee's office.

'What did you learn?' Dee was on his feet in a trice when the door opened. 'Quickly, girl. Is it linked to our investigation?'

'Huw was beaten by a wherry-Spaniard.' Spreading the paper on his desk, Margaretta pointed at the first line. 'Goodman McFadden helped me with the translation. 'The first line says "Where is", but we don't understand DHU.'

Dee went pale. Slowly he raised his eyes to his companion. 'You need to think more deeply, girl. Huw was writing in Welsh. The sound is Dee.' He pointed to the next lines.

'They say "What is he? I hunt him" and then "I will kill him",' answered Margaretta.

Dee gave nothing away save a small twitch of his face. 'Go to the kitchen and bring wine.'

Mistress Constable was in the hallway coaxing the kitten to jump for a feather on a string. She was fretting. 'DeeDee is still sick. She does not jump.' Then a look of shame. 'Your brother?'

'He will heal. Most gentlewomen would not have bothered with a mere servant. I am truly in your debt.'

Katherine was silent for a second, and then a small smile. 'In Essex we…we help the…afflicted and…'

Sadness. You remember someone. Suddenly there is great pain in your heart. A child. I feel a dark room and the sound of wailing. I feel the fear of a child as a woman weeps in a chair. Confusion. Helplessness.

'…my little brother. He could not speak or walk.'

Now a searing pain in your heart. Your lips press together as the eyebrows rise. Suddenly your eyes are wide and glassy. You've lost someone. 'But I am sure you are a good sister to him.'

A tear spilled from her eye. 'He died a little boy.' She looked away to the window. She shrugged and, in a hoarse whisper, said: 'People say it is good to have all the love…but no. To be alone is…' She stopped.

'I am sorry.' Margaretta bent to scoop up the kitten. 'Let me feed this little one to make sure nothing happens to her.'

Katherine Constable just nodded and kept looking through the window.

The wine flagon filled and the kitten in a box with warm milk, Margaretta returned to the office. Dee was hunched over papers, scribbling and drawing. He did not look up until she put the beaker on the desk close to his cheek. 'Christopher's pursuer. Could be Spanish. Maybe the same man who hurt Huw.'

'And Sam spotted a Spanish wherryman watching us earlier.

He was concerned. And he saw him going back where we had been. Little Tilly spoke of the bad wherrymen.'

'Good. You are making connections girl. Now, tell me about Huw's injuries.'

'He was so bruised and in pain, I didn't look. Anyway, Susan had him swaddled in blankets.'

Dee glared from under his eyebrows, then shouted in irritation: 'For the love of angels, Margaretta. You have had this lesson many times. The key to murder is a pattern. We have to find it.' He jabbed at the paper. 'See this. It is all our evidence and there is little of it. Cecil will be getting angry. I need to know if Huw had similar injuries to Jonas, Luke and Robert. Was there any wool left with him?'

Margaretta shrugged and bit her lip. 'I'm sorry.'

Dee pulled on cotton gloves, went to the shelves at the back of his office and picked up a large white crystal that glistened in the light coming through the window. He carried it as a priest holds a chalice and set it down on the paper he had been scribbling on. 'We will see if this can help us.'

'What is it?' Margaretta leaned over it and reached out her hand.

'Do not touch,' he snapped. Then, softer: 'It is a scrying stone. I bathed it in moonlight last night to cleanse all humours. I have not yet taught you about these tools. Touch will transfer your thoughts and feelings.' He carefully rotated the crystal until satisfied with the direction of its edges. Then he went back to the shelves to pick up a round of convex glass, evidently heavy from the small grunt he made as he lifted it onto the window sill. Suddenly the moonlight shone through the convex, directly onto the crystal, and beams of sharp light shot out in all directions. 'Hah. We have it.' He looked over to Margaretta. 'Come here quickly. Hold this exactly as I have it. Keep the beams alive. We only have minutes.'

With Margaretta holding the mirror exactly as he wanted it, Dee darted to the desk. 'Just look at that.'

'What do you see, doctor?'

'I see the messages of the universe. It brings the purity of light and beams the path to truth.'

'I thought the Bible did that.'

Another growl. 'Why does every chalice and cross in the Roman church glisten with jewels and stones?' His eyes went back to the beams and his voice dropped to a whisper. 'Because the stones are the secret to knowledge, energy and wisdom of the earth just as books hold the energy of men's minds.' A smile drifted across his face. 'And I can unlock that energy.' But a cloud went across the sky and the crystal went dark.

Margaretta stood next to Dee. The paper on the desk was covered in circles, letters and lines. Some lines were drawn thicker than others. 'What are the circles?'

'Each one represents a person who is part of the mystery. See, I have put their initials in the circle.' He pointed to each one. 'Cecil, Lady Mildred, the Princess Elizabeth, Jonas, Luke, Robert, that priest, Harriet, the Spanish maid.'

'And what about the empty circle?'

'These are the people we do not yet know. The people who plot, who killed a boy and his master, who may have killed Robert Meldrew, who beat your brother. The people behind all this who threaten Elizabeth.'

'But why attack Lord Cecil's house?'

Dee was quiet for a while and then spoke slowly. 'I do not know. But the strongest beam connected his circle with the princess.' He looked sideways at Margaretta. If they are bonded then he is a direct route to Elizabeth. To put fear into Cecil is to put fear into the princess. Maybe the warnings are for her. Or do the murderers seek to blacken her name?'

'But why?'

'Think, girl. She has Tudor blood. She is King Harry's third and rightful heir and the only one who can wrench the throne from Philip of Spain if…when…her sister dies.'

'Why are some lines thick?'

'The thicker the line the stronger the connection. See the connection between the priest and this empty circle?' Dee tutted. 'But who is in that circle?' Then he frowned. 'There was also a connection between the priest and Jonas, Luke and the maid. But not strong. No stronger than between Cecil and those people.'

'Do you think the priest is involved?'

A moment's hesitation. 'Cecil trusts him, and why would a Protestant-leaning priest from Wales harm Elizabeth?' Dee rubbed his chin. 'But he may be an unwitting helper.' With this, he picked up another piece of paper and started writing notes.

Margaretta was still staring at the circles. 'Why is there a thick line between Harriet and the empty circles? And why is there a line between Huw and the empty circle?'

Dee sighed. 'He may have seen more than we know.' He paused. 'We need to know who beat him.' With that, he picked up the crystal and nodded to the door. 'We are going to your sister's house. You can tell me what you learned in Southwark on the way.'

Chapter Thirty-Two

The round-faced house-keeper opened the door. 'Back again, miss? So late?' She looked Doctor Dee up and down. Evidently, he looked as if he deserved respect because she bobbed a small curtsey and asked who she might announce. As ever, Dee went into his convivial voice and asked her to tell Goodman McFadden that Doctor John Dee begged entry to his beautiful house.

A scowling Susan came into view behind the maid. 'What are you doing back here? I told you...' Then she saw Doctor Dee and quickly slid into her milky voice. 'Ah, good doctor. We are so pleased to see you. Though it's late for visiting.'

That's right, Susan. Put on your charm for the man whose money keeps us from under your skirts. But you feel some alarm. Most people do when they find Dee on their doorstep. A man who has been everywhere from the courts of England to the universities of foreign lands can be a daunting prospect. Especially to a featherhead like you.

Dee bowed and was granted access in a flurry of affected welcomes. As he stepped in, Susan shot a look of fury at Margaretta and whispered: 'We were almost abed. Angus will be annoyed.'

'We have come to see Huw. No need to bother your husband.'

Another strained laugh, and then the lie through clenched teeth. 'Oh, Angus will be delighted to see you.'

No. He will be delighted to stare at my bosom and feed his dark thoughts. You poor girl. If I liked you, I would feel a little sorry for you. 'May I go and make Huw a posset? It calms him.'

The voice was higher pitched now as Susan tried to cover her annoyance. 'Yes. There should be fresh milk in the dairy. Ask cook for good wine.'

'Wine?' said Dee, looking round. 'Of course, Goodman McFadden is a merchant of that elixir.'

'And bring a good beaker for the doctor,' trilled Susan through even tighter clenched teeth.

In the kitchen, the young maid sidled up. 'Shall I get milk for you, miss?' Then she paused, looking round to see if anyone was listening, and whispered, 'Did Mistress Susan really walk in the mire, miss?'

'Oh, yes. Up to her knees, she was.'

With a giggle, the maid ran for milk. She was back in a minute and hovered.

Margaretta dipped the beaker into the pail. 'But she was no use in the dairy, you know.' The temptation was too great. 'So stupid she couldn't tell the head from the udder. She used to pull their ears and expect a beaker like this to come out.'

The girl snorted with laughter, so loud that the cook barked across the kitchen. Margaretta winked and asked for wine.

Huw was pretending to sleep. He was clever enough to slow and deepen his breathing if he did not want to be disturbed.

Margaretta stood back in the shadows, watching as Dee lowered his voice to a soothing lilt and talked softly, kindly to the boy. 'Come, Huw?' A gentle touch on his arm. 'Let me see you.'

There was no response, but Dee did not give in. He went to the end of the bed where Huw would know he could not touch him. 'I know you've been much hurt. Let me help you so you can go back and look after your mam and Margaretta.'

It worked, and the bundle of blankets moved a little. Huw lifted his head and peered through swollen eyelids at John Dee. 'Cannot speak,' was the response, muffled by bruised lips.

'I know, boy. But we will speak through letters.' Dee held up the alphabet. 'But first I want to see how badly you have been hurt.'

Huw shrank back into his blankets but Dee was undeterred. Slowly, gently, he peeled back the layers. Huw was rigid with discomfort, his face turned away to the wall.

'Show me your hands.' Then, seconds later, 'Margaretta, come look at this.'

She stepped forward and cried out. In the middle of Huw's right hand was the same pattern of cuts. 'The same person who attacked the others.'

'Indeed.' Dee pulled the blankets up to Huw's chest. 'Now we will talk, boy.' He put down the paper of letters. 'First, just yes or no questions. Are you quite sure the man knew my name?'

Huw nodded. 'Yes. Did not tell where.'

'You are a good boy, Huw. I am proud of you.' Dee paused and went on. 'We will do the letters now.' Huw gave a little groan and shook his head. Dee pushed a pen into his hand and held up the paper of letters, but first turned to Margaretta, his eyes concerned. 'What does he feel?'

She stepped forward and put her hand on her brother's shoulder, though it made him pull away. Dee stood back.

What happened to you, cariad? Yes, I feel it. You first heard shouting. Then a dark face. He ran up the bank. Then the fist in your cheek. Damn him. You were down in the mud. Pushing, fighting, trying to stop the pain. The words made no sense. A terrible pain. The man has your hand. Something silver. Crushing your hand. You see blood and scream. He shouts again and kicks. You cannot breathe.

Your mouth is full. You pull away. Running. You run. It goes quiet.

Margaretta shuddered and took a breath, turning to Dee as she fought back the tears. 'One man, shouting, kicking. He crushed Huw's hand on something silver.' She turned back. 'What did he press into your hand, Huw?'

The boy winced and started to point. I E S U G R I S T.

Margaretta shook her head. 'No, Huw. He cannot have pushed Jesus in your hand. Think again.'

'Oh, yes he did,' said Dee from the shadows. He pulled open his bag and pulled out the papers, shuffling through to find the right one. 'Look at this. See? There are three puncture marks and a fourth indent.' He leaned over Huw. 'It was a crucifix, wasn't it? And around his neck.'

Another nod. 'Yes.'

Dee sighed and walked across the room to sit heavily on a chair by the fire. He looked up at Margaretta. 'Where have you seen a large, ornate crucifix in the past few days?'

'The wherryman who brought us from the Savoy to Lord Cecil's.'

'Yes. And the same man was waiting on the river when I returned. I assumed he was just waiting at the steps for another customer. More likely he was waiting for me.' Dee put his hand to his temples. 'But I asked him to stop before the house. Said I needed a walk. So he would not know our house.'

Margaretta clutched her arms across her chest. 'I think he has been following us. Sam was worried about a Spaniard following. When I looked around, all I saw was the flash of metal in the sun. It was from his neck. He would have seen Huw on the bank when I was dropped off.' She looked at Dee wide-eyed. 'And Christopher was followed by a man wearing a crucifix.'

Dee leaned forward and looked into the fire. 'So we have an attacker who is Spanish and devoutly Catholic. But do we have proof he is connected to the deaths?' In an instant, he was on his feet and over to Huw. 'One more question, boy. Did he have yellow wool?'

The boy nodded and started pushing out his tongue.

Margaretta hissed her fury. 'The man put it in his mouth. Huw couldn't breathe. I felt it. He must have spat it out. Did you see what it looked like, Huw?'

He pointed again. D E F A I D M E L Y N. A yellow sheep.

Chapter Thirty-Three

Early morning at St Dunstan's and Dee was in a bleak mood. He beckoned Margaretta over. 'Come and look at what the message is now.'

On his desk was spread an arc of cards, face down. Only one in the middle was turned over. In the centre of the arc a red stone, this one smooth and polished, unlike the scrying crystal. The doctor tapped it. 'Garnet. Said to be the most powerful stone for deducing relationships. It is also a stone of protection.'

Next to the stone was a ball of yellow wool, muddied and wet. It was just like the other symbols.

'The yellow sheep which Huw spoke about?' whispered Margaretta.

'Yes. I went to the river at dawn. It was caught at the side of the steps. Now we have the pattern. Every victim is marked by the crucifix and decorated with a yellow sheep. The symbolism of that is key. Then we have the message in the injuries.'

'What do you mean?'

'Jonas and Luke stabbed in the tongue for talking, Meldrew's eyes gauged for seeing and his mouth stuffed for speaking.' He leaned back. 'Huw was a warning. Left alive but his mouth stuffed. They were telling us to be silent.'

Margaretta let out a little cry but Dee was engrossed in the cards. 'But the wherryman must have a master.' He picked up the card. It depicted a knight riding high on a charging horse, in his hand a sword, unsheathed and ready to bear down on anything in his way. Dee tapped it. 'Determination, energy, a mission. At the extreme, a blind mission to achieve the goal, no matter what the consequences to the self or others. The knight of swords is a good soldier and a terrible enemy.'

'Well, if he is the knight, then he works for a king. Who is the king?'

Dee's blue eyes glanced up and he smiled. 'Now you are thinking, Margaretta.'

He took a taper, lit it in the candle and put it on the garnet. A line of light went direct to the card in the centre of the arc.

Slowly he pulled the card out, turned it over and exhaled loudly. 'Dear God. It is the emperor. And look at the base of his throne.'

'Sheep heads.' Margaretta looked sideways at Dee, who was staring at the card. 'What is the meaning?'

'It is the card of a ruler – the authority who demands to be heard and obeyed.' Dee shuffled in his chair. 'And the queen's love of her cousin, the emperor, is well known. She is also married to his son. The House of Hapsburg. Hence the Spanish connection – the letters, the maid, the attacker.' Dee laid a finger on the sheep heads. 'The card says all.'

Margaretta peered at the card. 'Sheep make wool.'

'Exactly. So the yellow wool links to a great authority.' He took a deep breath. 'Court.' Dee lit another taper and muttered, 'Tell us who they seek.' The red line shifted to the far right. He turned the card. It was the queen again. 'I am right. Elizabeth.'

Margaretta went cold. 'What kind of danger do we face, sir?'

'Terrible danger. But we don't have time to wallow in alarm. You will go to the house of Cecil and say nothing of my speaking in front of the wherryman. We cannot be seen as the cause of trouble. First, you must question the priest about speaking to others. Second, see if Cecil has any connection with a yellow sheep.'

CHAPTER THIRTY-FOUR

Lottie opened the back door and squealed in delight. 'You is back, Margaretta. Oh, I did miss you. Did Sam wherry you?' She frowned. 'You do look afeared.'

'No Sam today. Is Dogwife after my blood? It's midday.' Margaretta smiled to cover her worry.

The girl sighed and shook her head. 'A man did come to the door asking to speak with her. She's been out in the rose garden for over two hours now.' Lottie nodded towards the garden. 'Not even the cold rain has brought her in. They moved to shelter under the canopy.'

'Did he have a wooden leg?'

The big blue eyes widened. 'Yes. Clop, step, clop, step, clop, step he went.'

From the garden came the sound of Goodwife Barker laughing like a tinkling bell.

Margaretta nodded to Lottie. 'Let's go in and start the vegetables. I've been here for two hours. Understood?'

'Yes,' squeaked Lottie. 'I'll do carrots. You do cabbage.'

They scurried inside and pulled vegetables from the basket. Lottie ran for the paring knives as Margaretta pulled up the small stools and took down two large boiling pans. In seconds they were cutting, peeling and paring. Outside the kitchen door, footsteps heralded the return of Goodwife, but she did not come through the door. Instead, they could hear her talking, her voice quite soft. She laughed again.

It makes me think of childhood when my mam was happy.

The door cracked open. Then a deep voice. 'May we talk again, Goodwife Barker? I have so enjoyed...'

'Why yes, sir.' A trill of a laugh. 'We have much in common, I think.'

The door was pushed open and Goodwife walked past and went to her desk. For a few seconds, she simply sat and smiled. Then she saw Margaretta and the frown came back. 'When did you arrive, girl?'

Lottie answered. 'She arrived just after you welcomed your visitor, didn't you Margaretta?'

'Yes,' came the lie.

It worked. Goodwife sniffed and turned away. 'That was still very late, girl.' But the smile returned.

'Please may I report to Lord Cecil when I have cut the vegetables, Goodwife Barker?' She tried a smile. 'My master has sent a message with me.'

There was a sharp glance and the face began to return to its former granite hardness.

'I hope Master Tovey was able to give you information.'

A small wave of her hand. 'Go. Give your message and come straight back to help Lottie.'

Lord and Lady Cecil were together in the office. The tension was palpable. 'Ah, Margaretta. What news about the architect of the Savoy?' asked Lady Mildred. 'Will he live?'

'No, madam. He lasted but a few minutes after Doctor Dee arrived.' Margaretta looked down. 'My brother is also hurt, my lady. Beaten badly, though he will live.' She gulped down her distress. 'Doctor Dee says it was a warning.'

Both Cecil and his wife put their hands to their faces and Mildred gave a little cry.

'It's the same person who hurt Jonas and Luke, madam. The pattern is the same.'

The Conjuror's Apprentice

There was a tense silence. Then Cecil leaned forward. 'What does Dee know?'

'The attacker is Spanish and marks his victims with a crucifix. The injuries give a message – stabbed tongue for talking; gauged eyes for seeing. Then there is the bauble fashioned from yellow wool. It was on Jonas and Luke. Robert Meldrew had his mouth filled with the same and so did my brother. Doctor Dee says it symbolises a yellow sheep.' She paused. 'But he does not know what this sheep means.'

Cecil shuddered and frowned. 'Nor do I.'

So what are you feeling? Deep worry. Even fear. You recall dark grey walls. The crunch of an axe in a spine. I hear the word tower. Your dread returns. You think of the sheep. Your mind searching for anything. Something pricks at your memory. But you cannot place it.

Cecil looked to his wife. 'Do you have any ideas?'

She shook her head.

There was a knock at the door. Cecil showed his surprise. 'Father Thomas. We did not expect your company before this evening.'

The priest bowed low. 'I was passing and thought to see if you had news of the poor man at the Savoy.'

Mildred Cecil pointed towards Margaretta. 'Gone to God, and her brother almost sent after him.'

Father Thomas tutted and shook his head. The red paint on his face seemed shinier than usual, as if just painted.

A sudden twist in your gut. That concern again. Worry. Is this the normal worry of a man of the cloth for injury to humankind?

Father Thomas sat heavily and pulled at the patch as if it itched. 'May God save Meldrew's soul. Did he manage to tell your master any useful information?'

At this, Cecil cut across. 'Dee is making connections. Apparently, they have all been left with a symbol made of wool. Margaretta's brother has also been attacked and left with the

– 182 –

same symbol.' He turned to Margaretta. 'A yellow sheep, you say? What else has John deduced?'

Margaretta looked at the priest and halted her words. 'Father Thomas is a trusted friend,' soothed Cecil.

'Doctor Dee says there is a Spanish link to everything. We think the man who dumped Jonas was Spanish; my brother's attacker was Spanish; a letter is in Spanish; the thief of your seal was also from that land.'

Cecil groaned and looked to his wife.

Margaretta continued. 'Doctor Dee believes there is some Spanish plot against the Lady Elizabeth which goes back to court.' *But I'll say nothing of the cards and stones.*

Sweat beaded on Cecil's forehead as he pinched the bridge of his nose, his eyes squeezed shut. 'So why implicate me? I have no business at court.'

Lady Mildred slammed her hand on the desk, making her husband jump. 'But you have made business at Elizabeth's court.' She gave an exasperated sigh. 'You had a lucky escape when the queen sent you into the political wilderness rather than to the block, husband.' She turned to glare at him. 'But you could not restrain your need for mingling with power.'

Cecil was cowed and the atmosphere chilled as Lady Mildred stamped over to the window and stared out, arms clasped across her breast.

Father Thomas rose from his chair and started to pace. 'Damn these papist bastards.' His hosts turned in alarm. 'They bring a plague of Spanish papery upon us and will stop at nothing to scourge the true religion from the land. Even a rightful heir will face their flames.' There was a heavy silence and the priest sat heavily. 'Forgive me. Sometimes my fury bursts out.' He looked to Lord Cecil. 'Stay away from the Lady Elizabeth, sir. If she has no contact, she is isolated from danger and implication.'

Cecil looked fretful. 'But she will be much afeared. She has few close friends at court.'

Father Thomas said nothing. Just stared.

Margaretta turned to the priest. 'Please don't be offended but Doctor Dee has asked if there is a chance you may have spoken to anyone outside this house? As you are new to London it would be easy to be innocent of –'

But Cecil cut across her. 'Certainly not.' He nodded at Father Thomas. 'He is a most cautious man. It is he who tells us to speak to no one.' He wagged his finger at Margaretta. 'Tell John Dee there is no person of malice or foolery in this house.' Then the voice was lowered to a growl. 'Go back to St Dunstan's and tell John Dee he needs to work harder and faster. This has to end and quickly.'

Alarm. All around me. But who is feeling it most? Fear is rising here.

Margaretta was dismissed with a flick of Cecil's hand. As she rose to leave, Lady Mildred called from the window, where she still stared through the glass. 'Come to my library in half of an hour, Margaretta.'

As the door closed a heavy silence hung between the couple and their priest.

Chapter Thirty-Five

Margaretta slipped up the stairs and into the hallway on the way to Lady Cecil's rooms, Goodwife Barker's snapping still ringing in her ears. The sweetening effect of Master Tovey had been short-lived. But at least she understood this now. Barker was not nasty by nature but from fear. She had nothing left in the world and no one to care for her.

'So, your master thinks I leak, Margaretta.'

The girl yelped and spun around to see Father Thomas in the shadows of the hallway. 'You startled me, father.'

'I am sorry, my dear.' He stepped forward and his voice dropped to a milky wash. 'Tell the good doctor that as a priest I have heard the worst of all things through the grid of a confession box and never a word has left my lips.'

That smile again. It does not reach your eye. Anger. But also worry. You fear losing the trust of Lord Cecil. Almost desperate.

The priest stepped closer so that he could whisper. 'We Welshmen must work together.' He smiled. 'I have already set him on a path back to court. His conjuring for the Lady Elizabeth?' He tapped his chest. 'My idea. And also this investigation. Success will bring him a good reputation.'

Margaretta bobbed a curtsey. '*Buddaf y siwr oddweud wrtho, fe, Tad.*' I will surely tell him, father.

That hard stare again. The smile that did not reach his eye. 'I do not speak our tongue, Margaretta. Being the son of a merchant, I spent my youth travelling many lands.'

'That does explain your lack of a lilt.'

Just a nod and the paint glistening.

Margaretta pointed up the stairs to the upper floor. 'I must go to Lady Mildred.' She could feel the priest watching her every step of the way until she reached the next landing and turned out of his sight.

Lady Mildred was sitting in the window seat. Her hands were twisting and turning the baby shoes in an anxious rhythm.

Fear. You are wracked with it. Also anger. He is in deeper than he says. He will risk everything for a princess who may never be queen. You look down and fear moves to deep sadness. Tears build behind your eyes.

'You look much saddened, my lady.'

A tear escaped Lady Cecil's eye, which she dabbed at quickly. 'I sometimes wonder if the pain of loss ever dulls.' She looked down at the little shoes.

Oh, you poor, poor woman. All this wealth and yet you feel a deep black hole of grief. Your tiny little girl. Too small to thrive. You held her close; smelled her hair, suckled her as best you could. You called her Francisca...Franny. The nurse did all she could until that terrible hour when you were pulled from your bed, still aching from the birthing, to hold your little girl as her breathing slowed...and slowed...and stopped.

'I am so sorry, my lady.' As the other woman looked up, Margaretta nodded towards the booties. 'They will be worn again. I feel it.'

Mildred Cecil gave a weak smile. 'But the pain will never end.'

'No, madam. But the sound of a child will dull it.'

Lady Cecil stood suddenly and took a deep breath as if she realised she was speaking out of turn with a servant. She turned to look out of the window, lifting her hands to her face.

'What can I do?'

You have an idea. A knot of anxious excitement is in you. Also, desperation as you fear making a mistake. You see another woman, finely dressed, hair golden and a genuine smile. You wonder.

'Is there anyone at court who might give you information, my lady?'

A jerk of the head and the eyes widened. 'You must be reading my mind, Margaretta.' Mildred looked at the door again. 'Can I trust you?'

'Yes.'

Her voice dropped to a whisper. 'My sister, Ann Bacon, is a lady-in-waiting to the queen.' She paused. 'If there is something about yellow sheep which links to court, she just might be able to help.' Another hesitation. 'She is only days away from birthing her first child. Then I will have reason to visit.'

There was a knock on the door and Father Thomas entered, bowing his head in a greeting. 'May I speak with you alone, Lady Cecil?' He looked pointedly at Margaretta and smiled. 'A private discussion. Nothing of help to our friend, John Dee.'

Lady Mildred pointed to the door. 'Off you go, Margaretta, and say nothing of our conversation.'

Chapter Thirty-Six

'Leaving again?' Goodwife Barker's voice was raised in indignation. 'You are more pest than presence in this kitchen, girl.'

Lottie did her usual squeak when alarmed but Margaretta stood still, her gaze level. 'I'm sorry, Goodwife. But it's on the orders of Lord Cecil.'

The older woman scowled and transferred her anger to Lottie, who was peering over Margaretta's shoulder. 'What are you looking at like a dote? Back to your chores before you are put in the stables with the mice for company.'

With a yelp, Lottie ran across the kitchen and skidded into a pail of carrots, which only caused Goodwife to shout at her that she was 'a clumsy dolt at that'.

The child sniffled and huddled down to her paring. Margaretta sat next to her. 'Come, Lottie. I have a few minutes before I must go. We'll soon get these all clean.' She was rewarded by a watery smile and more sniffing. 'When I go, I'll ask Sam to be my wherryman. Can you come to the river?'

In an instant, Lottie was bright eyed. 'Oh, Margaretta. Can you ask for me? Please?'

The carrots cleaned, Margaretta risked approaching Goodwife. 'Goodwife Barker, please may Lottie come to the river with me?'

The sneer was all over Goodwife Barker's face before she

even spoke. 'And why would I let a foolish dolt go running about for no reason?'

'I'll get a wherry with Sam, Master Tovey's apprentice. He may have word for you.'

The housekeeper's hand fluttered to her suddenly mottling neck.

Excitement. You feel like a young maid but are too frightened to even think about the possibilities. You've not felt this for many a year.

The voice wavered like the hands. 'Well, I would not want Master Tovey to think us rude.'

There was no need for further discussion. Lottie was already pulling on her woollen shawl and preening her hair back into her coif.

They had nearly a quarter of an hour to wait after sending a street lad along the riverbank to find Sam. Every minute was filled with excited chatter from Lottie and endless questions about Sam for which she never waited for an answer. When he came into view, he was hailed with a loud squeak and that twisting of the hips.

'Two maids awaiting me. Must be my lucky day,' he called up the steps.

There was no need for an invitation. Lottie was already bounding down the stone stairs, asking if she could ride in the ship once more. Margaretta sighed and put down her bag. This was going to be a long wait. She must have spent twenty minutes watching Lottie throw up her hands in mock terror and grab at Sam's knees as if clutching the side of a cliff-edge, which only encouraged him to wheel and tip his wherry all the more. Eventually, she hailed them back and could see the disappointment in Lottie's face as they approached the steps.

'I really must get back to St Dunstan's.' She stepped down to the bottom step. 'We hoped your master might have a message that he'll return.'

Sam's eyes lit up. 'Well, no words. But he did arrive back in the boatyard like a dog with two pricks.'

Margaretta flapped her hand to sign he should watch his language in front of Lottie, but the girl was already doubled over in mirth. 'I cannot send Lottie back to say that.'

Sam looked more serious, winked at Lottie and put on a serious voice. 'You may say, missy, that my master did arrive home with warm words of his visit and I hope he will be welcome again.'

Margaretta bent over to look into the eyes of the other girl. 'Did you get that, Lottie?'

'Why, yes. He did go home like a dog with two –'

'No,' shouted Margaretta and Sam in unison, sending Lottie into further chortling.

Margaretta held up her finger like a stern mother. 'What are you going to say?'

'That he spoke warm words and Sam hopes he would be welcome again.'

'You are not so silly, are you, Lottie?'

'No, Margaretta.' The child winked, turned to give an elaborate curtsey to Sam and scampered up the steps.

They were halfway down the river before Sam broke the silence. 'You seem to be in a dream.'

'What? Yes. There is much to tell my master.'

'He is a strange one, I hear. The wherrymen – well, the Spanish wherrymen – have been asking questions. Asking who you are, too. And I overheard some of what your master said on the way to the Savoy then I did hear of that man dying badly.' He leaned forward. 'You be careful, missy.'

Oh God, if only I could tell you my worries and fears. For you are a better man than I could ever have thought to exist.

Sam frowned. 'But I don't think you want my advice or protection, do you?'

Margaretta smiled and nodded back towards the steps where they had left Lottie. 'Maybe you need a girl you can laugh with? A maid who would gaze into your eyes all day? A maid with no family, who needs to be cared for by a strong boy…and will love him for it.'

Sam pulled up his shoulders and looked away over the water. 'Good thoughts, missy.'

Strange. I felt a pang when you looked so eager.

Then Sam turned back to her. 'When you saw Sniffer Simeon the other day, did he say he was going anywhere?'

'Huh. There was no polite conversation before he set his hound at me. Why?'

'Disappeared. The hound too. Found the other dogs in the street howling at his door.' Sam shrugged. 'Strange. He never leaves that hovel of his.'

Oh, God. Please not another one.

CHAPTER THIRTY-SEVEN

The house was quiet. Margaretta went to their sleeping room and found Mam swaddled in blankets, her face to the wall.

'Mam. Are you awake?'

'Praying for my boy,' was the low wail. Mam Morgan pushed a crumpled piece of paper over her shoulder. 'Susan is in fear.'

The ink on the paper was smeared with tears, but the words came through sufficiently to make Margaretta reach for the wall to steady herself.

We are finding ourselves watched since Huw arrived. Huw must leave in the morrow and render our house safe.

Susan

'Susan is being ridiculous. She's always been prone to fancies. Probably just had enough of tending Huw.' Margaretta tugged at the blanket only to feel her mother clutch it closer. 'I need your help in the kitchen. Get up now.'

Her mother gave a sniff and said: 'The ache in my heart has reached my legs. Cannot move, not I.' Another moan.

'It's been many a year since that heart was big enough to reach your legs, Mam.' She slammed the door shut and leaned against it, whispering: 'Oh, Dada. Where are you now?'

There was a clatter in the hallway. She ran to find Doctor Dee calling her to his office, dropping some of the books burdening his arms. She stooped to pick one up. '*The Divine Language of Angels?*'

'Yes. More powerful than the cards. My new passion.' He frowned. 'Bring them into the office and hide them in the large cupboard. I had them sent from the Low Countries to my mother's house. No one will venture there.' He patted the side of his nose. 'Tell no one.'

'Why?'

'Would be seen as…well, un-biblical. More conjuring than Christian.'

'Why do you take such risks? You know that Lord Englefield is seeking out players of magic as heretics. Are you mad, doctor?'

He growled. 'Cecil will protect me. He is in too deep.'

Inside the office, the books well hidden, he sat at the desk and smiled. 'So what news do you bring?'

'Cecil has no connection to a yellow sheep and is disturbed. They insist the priest has spoken to no man of anything. He has Cecil's full trust. Oh, and he told me to tell you he had started your path to court as it was his idea to set you conjuring for the Lady Elizabeth.'

Dee leaned back. 'Did he indeed?' Suddenly he narrowed his eyes. 'Why are you so anxious, child? You sit on that chair as if the fires of hell will start below it.'

Margaretta pulled her sister's note from her pocket. 'This arrived from Susan.' She bit her lip. 'I am frightened, doctor.'

He leaned over and peered at it, holding a candle close. It seemed an age before he raised his head, suddenly looking kind.

'How many staff does Susan have?'

'At least ten. She needs an army to manage her easy life.'

Dee chuckled. 'Less anger, Margaretta. When we get back to court, Susan will be asking to hold your hem.' He assumed a serious tone. 'I know about the stupid husband, but are there strong men in the kitchens and gardens?'

'Oh, yes. Susan likes to be surrounded by them.'

'While people watch Susan's house they do not watch us.' He smiled. 'I would lose this note *accidentally on purpose*, as they say in Wales.'

Through the hallway came the sound of knocking on the outer door. Margaretta jumped to her feet and went to open it. On the doorstep was Christopher Careye, his fair hair matted to his skull in the evening mist and shoulders hunched. He had a haunted look on his face. 'I n-need to see John Dee.'

A minute later he was standing before Dee's desk, his hands trembling. 'They are closing in, doctor. I don't know what you've brought us into, but the crucified man arrived at my house this morning. He told me to beware and left this.'

Christopher reached into his satchel and pulled out a ball of yellow wool with four plaits dangling and another ball shaped into a head, but blackened with dried blood.

CHAPTER THIRTY-EIGHT

The morning was dark and the skies full of threatened rain. Collecting logs for the kitchen fire had chilled Margaretta to the bone, though she knew it was made worse by a night of lying in the dark imagining every terrible outcome. *Why is the black of the night such a lonely place?*

Inside, the hounds whined and the kitten was mewing like a child for attention. The table was still littered with the cups and plates she had used when Christopher had followed her to the kitchen. It had been past midnight before she had nudged him towards the door, ignoring the way he lingered on the step hoping for a small signal that he might kiss her cheek. But she had stayed back, smiling, thinking what a good man he was.

But my life is about caring for Mam and Huw. No point in thinking of love. That's for others.

Dogs pushed into the corner and the kitten put on a shelf with a lump of cheese to clamp its teeth, she set about the normal morning routine. Mam was refusing to leave her bed, so at least there was a little more room by the fire. As the smell of baking bread started to waft through the house there was a creak of the door and a grunt. She looked round to see two red eyes and a bloated face, the bristles of an unshaven chin and a mouth of pure misery. Master Constable had evidently been on the port the night before.

'Good morning, Master Constable. Can I get you some small beer, and maybe a slice of yesterday's bread with cheese to line your stomach for the day?'

He peered through rheumy eyes. 'What is John Dee up to now? They are saying in the market that he is being sought by Spanish ne'er-do-wells. You too.'

Oh, sweet Jesus. They are circling, and cleverly. They know any questions will pass back through the gossip trails of Leadenhall Market.

'I don't understand.' *And Jesus forgive me for speaking false.*

Master Constable grunted. 'They say he is working in secret for Lord Cecil. That evil deeds are happening, designed to replace the queen.'

Oh, no. 'What nonsense. Doctor Dee would never be involved in anything so cunning. Certainly not in your house.' *My second lie. I must do an extra prayer tonight.*

Constable shook his head. 'He is blinded by ambition and the desire to recreate his father's status and be a man of court.' A long sigh. 'All I want to do is help my old friend's boy with a roof and a bed.' He winced. 'But I am much disturbed by the attention of those Spanish villains.'

Margaretta stood, wringing a cloth, not knowing what to say. Master Constable heaved himself up and stated he must away and make money for his wife's new brocades. He grunted and left.

Minutes later she was hailed by a call from John Dee's office. He was sitting well upright, his eyes bright. Already piles of parchment littered the desk and a volume had been pulled from a shelf. She noticed the copper globes had been moved – the precious equipment given by his friend Doctor Mercator in Louvain. 'Monday. It needs to be Monday.'

'Doctor?'

'Scrying, of course. We need to test my theory that evil cannot defy the voices of angels. Sit, sit.' He wagged a hand at the chair before the desk, then tapped hard on the book. 'I have made the calculations. Monday the twentieth day of May is a new moon and there is a partial eclipse. That is when the air is thin. The voices may better come through.'

'Voices?'

'My new theory.' He pushed a stone that looked like clear glass towards her. 'See this? So pure it can attract and channel the spirit of angels and refract them into words. Just like a prism on the boat takes a single light and spreads it into the hull.'

'But how will you understand the angels?'

Dee smiled. 'Good questions, Margaretta.' He stretched sideways and pulled another book towards him and smiled as he fingered the fine tooling on the leather cover. '*Voarchadumia Contra Alchimiam*. The writing of Johannes Pantheus.' Dee opened the book to a page covered with strange symbols. 'This is the Prophet Enoch's script written in the language of angels. All we need to do is decipher and we will hear their voice.' He snapped the book shut and eyed her, his eyes glassy and bright. 'Go to Christopher Careye and tell him to attend here on Monday evening at seven of the clock.' He turned to the window. 'When the new moon will be shining through that glass.'

She leaned forward to look straight into his eyes. 'Rumours are flying in Leadenhall Market that you are somehow involved in Cecil's plot to replace the queen. It has reached Master Constable's ears. He is concerned about Spanish villains asking about you…and me. Sam said the same.'

Dee stared, his face inscrutable. Then he looked back to the window. 'The wagging of fishwives' tongues will not stop me seeking what I am duly deserving.' He did not turn back. 'Go and tell Christopher I expect him here on Monday.'

CHAPTER THIRTY-NINE

The market thronged with merchants and hawkers racing to get their best patch for the day. Richer men, dressed in black and maroon, pushed people aside with sticks and harsh words. The only women were the market fishwives, gutting the catch with blades which would slice through steel, their fingers bandaged in bloody rags to cover the cuts and nicks. Today, being Friday, was the busiest of their week.

Outside the taverns, pot-men threw buckets of filthy water to slew down the pavement where last night's drinkers had fallen over and emptied their stomachs. It stank of fish-guts, vomit and old beer. Margaretta covered her nose with a linen and pressed on.

Christopher was not long awake, his hair still sticking up from his sleep. As soon as Margaretta entered the kitchen where he was supping pottage, he coloured and began to stammer. 'G…good morning, Miss Margaretta. Yes, g…good morning.'

You may have been up late, Christopher Careye. But you are also a slugabed. Doctor Dee always speaks of sleeping only four hours a night when he was early in his learning. He will not approve of this.

'And to you, Master Careye.' She gave a small curtsey. 'My master asks that you attend his office on Monday evening at seven bells.'

Christopher looked immediately perplexed. 'W-why Monday?'

Margaretta looked around quickly to see if his landlords were listening. The plump goodwife was pretending to knead bread. *So you are the biddy who calls my people sheep. Interest. Suspicion. Straining to hear. You are wondering who I am to make him blush. You have a daughter.* She turned back and pointed to the sky and only mouthed, 'The moon.'

The words made every pink of embarrassment in Careye's face pale to white. 'Oh, Lord. I…I…I…think that is foolhardy.' He dropped his voice to a whisper and stepped closer. 'I fear we have already stepped too far into danger.'

'He is quite insistent, sir.' She dropped her voice further. 'So is Lord Cecil.'

'Enough of your secreting,' snapped the woman at the bread table. They both jumped and turned to her. She was reddening with anger. 'I'll not have whispering in my house.' She nodded at Margaretta. 'I don't know your connection to my tenant, miss. But I'll not abide a lack of manners.'

Worry. You think of your daughter. I am a threat.

Margaretta curtseyed. 'Forgive me, mistress. My master has asked Master Careye to do important work and told me to be discreet in talking of the reward.'

An instant change. The woman smiled, making her soft cheeks balloon out. *Money. Prospects. Worry has turned to excitement.* 'Very well. We cannot hold Master Careye back from a good living.' She set back on the dough with determined kneading.

Seconds later, a girl arrived at the door. She was a younger version of the landlady, except with twice her girth. *How could any woman be so fat-covered in these times of want?* She glared. Christopher sighed. *You feel pressed.* 'I must go, Master Careye. Could you give me direction?'

In a second, he was reaching for his cloak. 'Let me w… walk you to Leadenhall.' Behind him the fat girl glowered.

Outside, Christopher took her arm. 'Margaretta, that man was outside the house again last night. Staring at my window. I fear for you – and John Dee.'

John Dee was hard at work when Margaretta arrived back. He listened intently to what Christopher had said. 'So the Spaniards are circling. But who links Spanish wherrymen to court?' He paused, then tapped his temple. 'Someone directs them.'

'A shepherd directs a flock,' whispered Margaretta.

'Exactly. We have to identify this Shepherd.' He hastily scribbled a note. 'Our scrying will assist.' He smiled. 'And you must attend and learn.'

'I have been away from the Cecil residence so much, doctor. Goodwife Barker will be raising a terrible fuss.'

He thought, frowned and nodded. 'Yes. Return in the morning and stay until I call for you. I will read my angelmancy books while you are away.' Then he looked up. 'On your way, call at the Savoy and enquire about the funeral of Robert Meldrew. We need to attend.' He looked down again as his attention went back to his books. 'Pay that young man of yours to come back and tell me the time and date. I shall see you there if you are not back here in the meantime. There are pennies in my purse by the door.'

'He is not my young man.'

No answer. She was forgotten.

Back in the kitchen, Mam had roused herself and was hunched in her chair, pulling apart a slice of bread and nibbling it through. She raised weary eyes to her daughter. 'Have you been to see Huw? Is he dead?'

'No, Mam. And if I do go, Susan will only insist that he is brought back here. I have to go to Lord Cecil's tomorrow. So you would have to tend to him.'

With the speed of an arrow, Mam's hand flew to her back.

'Not able. Would do my old bones more damage.'

'It might do you good to think of someone else for a change,' snapped Margaretta, stepping past to get her bag, ignoring her mother's sulky scowl. She banged open the door to their sleeping room and sighed to find the bed unmade and clothes on the floor. 'So you can bend to get into the bed but cannot bend to make it.'

The only response was a groan.

How are you, my little brother? I try to feel what you are thinking but you are too far away. It only works when people are close. Our sister's note is bothering me. For all Mam's love for you she is too lost in her bleakness to care for you. So I must leave you with Susan. I think of the fears of Christopher Careye. My heart goes cold.

CHAPTER FORTY

In the grey dawn of Saturday, Margaretta waited on the bank for Sam, having paid yet another half a penny to a street urchin to have him found. She scanned the water looking for the flash of a crucifix. But nothing. She looked over her shoulder. Maybe they watched from the land now. Still nothing to be seen. Just as in the night when she had woken every hour and peeped out of the window to see if there was a spying villain. She shivered and prayed for the wherry to come quickly.

'So only one pretty maid today, missy.' Sam grinned from the boat.

'Lottie lives upriver as you well know,' snapped his customer as he threw her bag in the back of the bobbing craft. Sam's face fell. *Damn my quick tongue.* 'Sorry, Sam. My mood is as black as the sky above us.'

He looked up. 'I would call that blue in comparison.' He winked to soften the words and managed to get a small smile in reward. 'What upsets you, missy?'

'My brother has been hurt. You saw Mam's distress. He's with my hell-sent sister who now says he must come back here. But I can't look after him for a while.' *Oh God, I wish I could tell you everything. But with talk of plots and intrigue, I dare not either trust you or put you at risk.*

'First time I have seen you close to tears, missy. You must love that brother of yours.'

She could only nod. Sam leaned forward and patted her

knee, kindly this time, not as a flirtation. 'Do you want me to visit and enquire over his health?'

'You're a good man, Sam. But no. My dear sister would pull you into her web and start her yapping. You'd carry Huw home on your back just to get a little peace.' Margaretta laughed at her own words.

Sam bowed from the waist. 'I am grateful you speak of me as a "good man", missy. Honoured indeed I am.' Suddenly he looked sad. 'But I don't think you'll ever think more of me.'

'As I said yesterday, you need a young woman who only has eyes for you.' She forced a smile. 'A girl who loves ships.' She leaned forward, raising her hand and pointing a finger of warning. 'And you be as good to her as you've been to me.'

Sam flushed, pretended he did not understand, then stared over the water smiling as he pulled on the oars and dreamed.

Margaretta wondered if she dared ask, but the question was burning. 'Have they found old Simeon yet?'

Sam barely emerged from his dreaming and shook his head. 'Still no sign of him or the big hound. They think he's gone visiting someone.'

I fear he's dead and there's yellow wool around him.

With the tide going out it took over thirty minutes to reach the bank of the Savoy. Sam passed his painter around a post and promised to wait.

The elderly nurse who answered the door had one milky eye, though the other was kind enough. 'Master Meldrew's funeral is arranged for Sunday.' She shook her head. 'Never a better master or a better man.' She gave Margaretta a small piece of parchment and a pen to send a note to her master, who would want to attend to pay respects. Ten minutes later, Sam was taking instructions on how to get to John Dee's lodgings, a penny pressed to his hands for the trouble. He kept glancing out onto the water.

'What are you looking for, Sam?'

'Thought I saw that Spaniard again.' He winked. 'Think your dark mood has given me the jitters, missy. Let's get you to Freny Bredge and I will away direct to your master.'

'What time is this? Half the day is gone already.' Goodwife Barker was at her desk and the look severe, but not as angry as usual.

'I am truly sorry, Goodwife,' insisted Margaretta, fingers crossed behind her back. 'I had an errand for my master, on account of his work for Lord Cecil, and so I was really working for this household and not for him.' She paused, picked up courage and continued. 'And he asks if you would indulge him in allowing me to attend a funeral tomorrow afternoon, Goodwife.'

The other woman huffed and snapped at her: 'Find Lottie and help with the cleaning. We can make the most of the house being empty to spring clean.'

'Empty?'

Barker flapped her hands as if batting away a fly. 'Not your concern, girl. Lord and Lady Cecil have departed. We will use the time to have this house gleaming like a state carriage.'

Upstairs, Lottie was struggling to fold a large sheet. Her eyes lit up when her friend entered the room and hugged her hello. 'Oh, Margaretta. It's felt like such a long time since you left.'

'It's only a day or so.'

'But such busy days. I had to get up special early yesterday morning to help Lady Cecil do her hair and then...' She sat down heavily and sighed. But then a smile. 'But good news, too.' She ran to the door to check they could not be heard. 'A note did arrive from Master Tovey, asking if he might walk with Dogwife after church tomorrow.' Lottie's excitement made her face flush and her breath run out.

'Slow down, Lottie. Tell me why the house is empty.' Margaretta picked up the sheet so they could work as they talked.

'Oh, a great man with a long name.' She frowned. 'I don't recall it, but he arrived in a carriage that could hold all this household. Met with Lord Cecil, he did.'

The child took a deep breath as she tugged on the sheet to pull the creases. 'Since then it's been all a flurry getting cases packed and the horses ready for the leaving.' She looked puzzled. 'I cannot understand the rush.'

'So where have they gone?'

'Lady Cecil to Wimbledon and Lord Cecil another place…I don't know where.' Then there came the harsh sound of Goodwife's voice calling up the stairs that she could hear more chatter than toil. Margaretta and Lottie worked away in silence with only whispers between them for hours.

At four o' clock, they were called down for bread and milk. On the first floor, Margaretta told Lottie to go ahead and say she was just sweeping a little patch of soot that fell from a chimney. The child looked confused but nodded. As soon as she had rounded the bend in the stairs, Margaretta crept to the library. It took only seconds to scan the shelves. The red book and green were as they had been. The white spine of Lady Elizabeth's notebook was gone.

In the kitchen, Father Thomas was at the table talking to a man Margaretta had not met. He was of middle age, swarthy and square.

Father Thomas smiled that strange smile. 'And how is the good doctor? Has he progressed his searching at all?'

Concern again. What worries you, priest? Now it changes. A feeling of irritation. Your eyes narrow when you look at me. You suspect I hold back information. You are right. How can I tell a man of the cloth that my master is arranging to conjure? You might be of the mind that this is against religion. I dare not trust.

'I don't know, sir. I only ever pass messages. None today.'

The new man looks at me like a cat looking at a mouse. I don't like the way his eyes move to my waist and then up. I glare but it makes no difference.

The servants' meal was a quiet affair. Goodwife Barker was away in a dream, only breaking it to gently scold Lottie for fidgeting with her cutlery. At the far end of the table, Father Thomas talked in low tones to the new man. Whatever he was saying, the man glanced up at Margaretta and made a slow, sickly smile.

Goodwife Barker sent Margaretta and Lottie to bed early. She pointed to a pile of white linens in the corner. 'You will need to press them before church tomorrow.' Lottie groaned and was pulled up with a sharp word, though not the usual berating.

Up in their room, there was time to talk. 'Who's the new man, Lottie?'

Those blue eyes shone brightly. 'Ooh, I don't like him one little bit, Margaretta. Keeps staring at my person, he does.' She went to the door and looked out, then came back and snuggled onto the bed. 'Father Thomas brought him to replace Luke. But I think he's not the good man that Father Thomas thinks he is.'

'Have you remembered the name of the great man who came in the carriage?'

Lottie stared up at the ceiling, her mouth making little twitches. 'Well, I think I heard the name Engle...Engle... something.'

'Englefield?'

'Yes. Oh, you're truly clever, Margaretta.' She jumped into bed. 'Let's speak of nicer things. Tell me about your ship ride.'

'It's a wherry, Lottie, and I spoke well of you to Sam.'

The girl reddened, then her eyes went sad. 'Oh, I can't think of being sweet on your boy, Margaretta.'

'He's not "my boy", Lottie. Now go to sleep so you look pretty for church tomorrow. Sam will be there.'

With a squeak, Lottie blew out the candle, curled up and closed her eyes, leaving Margaretta to stare into the dark. Something felt dark and foreboding. She closed her eyes and prayed to take away the lies she had uttered to Master Constable.

Chapter Forty-One

J ust as before, Lottie refused to wash as it was a church day. Not even Margaretta's insistence that she should try to smell sweet for Sam would shake her fear of water on Sundays.

'Come, Lottie. We have spent all of Friday and Saturday in toil cleaning this house. You will be grey with dust.'

Lottie folded her arms and shook her head.

Downstairs they worked until eight o'clock pressing the linens, Lottie so excited that she prattled like the green birds sailors brought from the far lands. Goodwife Barker was little to be seen, staying at the far end of the kitchen and seeing to her ledgers. At nine, she called to them to make ready for church and disappeared into her room, commanding all to be ready in thirty minutes.

'Oh, Goodwife Barker, you do look lovely.' Lottie was wide-eyed. The rest of the kitchen was open-mouthed when the woman emerged from her room, dressed in a sky-blue dress, topped with a white linen collar and her hair in a blue silk coif. The normally hard face was flushed in the cheeks and even broke into a grateful smile.

Lottie prattled, 'We would never have known your face could be so…' Then a loud squeak as Margaretta elbowed her in the ribs and took over '…so well framed in a pretty hat. You look as pretty as a picture, Goodwife.'

Barker flapped her hands and insisted they stop their talk and that this was only an old dress and that it was simply respect for the church and the good weather which caused her to bring out more colour. Everyone looked at her. Even cook sniffed her disbelief and a blushing Goodwife shooed them all to the door.

As ever, the rich filed in first, followed by the merchants, leaving the servants to trail in and try to find seats at the back of the church where only those of wealthy households would be afforded a pew. Margaretta looked ahead and could see the back of Sam's master, listing to the side as he clicked ahead on his wooden leg, his arm on Sam's shoulder. Next to her, she was aware of Goodwife Barker standing a little taller as she noticed them too. But they seemed to be progressing slowly. Maybe Master Tovey's stump was hurting him today.

The service was long and dreary. Every Latin word caused the wealthy to nod, the merchants to listen and the servants to sit and wonder what was being said. They were back to the old ways where the priest was the mouthpiece of God.

At last, the service finished and congregants processed, led by the priest in robes of rich fabric and shining jewels. *I feel the wonder of the poor sots around me and also my bitter resentment. Why does money make you closer to God? You poor fools, believing that, if only you had the price of an indulgence, you would be heaven-sent. As if paradise is found in a purse. As if . . .* Suddenly there was a cry from Lottie and the girl gripped Margaretta's arm. 'Oh, my Lord. Sam.'

Dear God. Walking towards them was Sam and Master Tovey, both serious and silent. Sam's face was black with bruises, one eye was shut with swelling and his upper lip bulging and cut. The arm that supported his master was bandaged tight from the hand up and the other in a sling. He glowered at Margaretta.

Before Margaretta could stand, Lottie had pushed past and run to Sam. As if oblivious to the niceties of church, she lifted her hand to his face and looked up in tears. 'What did they do to you, Sam? Your poor hands. Your...' Rivulets of fury ran down her face.

Sam attempted a smile. 'Don't worry, missy. I'm strong.'

Margaretta arrived quickly, followed by Goodwife Barker. 'Who did this to you, boy?'

'Seems I delivered a message that was much in demand,' was the bitter reply as Sam glared at Margaretta.

Master Tovey spoke. 'Was a terrible shock when my boy arrived home all shook-up.' He looked to Goodwife. 'I bandaged him best I could, but I have no woman's touch.'

Goodwife Barker gave a small smile. 'Why, sir, you are not built to have a woman's touch.' She reached out to pat Sam's arm. 'I have salves aplenty and good cotton for bandages. We will soon have you mending.' She looked back to Master Tovey. 'Maybe our walk should wait, sir. We should attend to your lad's wounds first.'

Lottie and Margaretta could only gawp at the softness in her voice and the tenderness of Master Tovey, who bowed and declared her 'a true angel in blue'.

They walked back to Lord Cecil's house, Goodwife Barker and Master Tovey ahead, and the other three bringing up the rear. Lottie was fussing Sam, patting his back. Margaretta was silent at first, waiting for the couple to be out of earshot. Then, 'What happened, Sam?'

He shot a hard look at her. 'Seems your note was of interest. Interesting enough to earn me a battering with their wherry oar.'

'I'm truly sorry, Sam. I had no idea at all that you would come to harm. I would never have –'

Sam snapped, 'But why were they so determined to stop that note being delivered?'

Margaretta ignored his question and Lottie's protests and questioned the boy. She learned that he had been followed when he rowed back with the note for John Dee. At Dycekey Steps he was rammed onto the riverbank and beaten. Sam puffed up and winked at Lottie. 'Fought like a lion, I did. Refused to hand over the note and got the knife out of my boot to stick the bastard.' He bowed to Lottie. ''Scuse my language, missy.'

Lottie patted him again.

'Got him in the arm. That'll stop him rowing a while. Then I managed to get up the steps and run to the house of Margaretta's master. He couldn't catch me, despite my injuries. Spanish bastard. Sorry, missy.'

'Spanish?' Margaretta grabbed his arm and made him yelp, earning her a scowl from Lottie.

'Yes. The bastard with the crucifix around his neck who was following.' Sam's eyes narrowed. 'What are you messing with, Miss Margaretta?'

She stepped back and shook her head.

Sam stepped forward. 'Seems you bring bad luck. Your note has me beaten and your visit with Simeon was soon followed with his death. They buried him this morning. Found in the river near the Savoy, he was. Tied to his hound.'

Margaretta tried to quell the tremor in her hand. 'Tied?'

'Yes. Some bastard tied them together with yellow wool and threw them in the water.'

CHAPTER FORTY-TWO

Goodwife, having salved and bandaged Sam's cuts with the gentleness of a real nurse, went for a walk around the gardens with Master Tovey. For well over two hours, she tinkled like a bell and the usual harsh tones were softened to the voice of a young girl.

Inside, Lottie and Margaretta worked on the linens while Sam, his feet up on a bench to keep blood in his arms, as instructed by Goodwife, enjoyed himself with a stream of teasing encouraged by Lottie chortling at every word, cooing admiration for his bravery and running to get him a small beer as soon as his beaker was empty.

'You is very quiet, missy. Not like your pretty friend.'

'I cannot get a word in edgeways with you two,' answered Margaretta, smiling.

God forgive me, but I feel a little jealous.

Suddenly there was a gasp from Lottie. 'Quick, Margaretta. Look.'

Through the window they could see Goodwife Barker walking slowly, holding the arm of Master Tovey and a smile on her face that would melt the hardest of hearts.

The funeral was to start at three in the afternoon. The small church was packed. Doctor Dee was waiting by the back wall. 'What news, Margaretta?'

'Well other than the poor wherryboy being battered for

having a note telling you of this, the Cecils have departed.'

'Yes. The lad was sorely beaten, though he is a tough scamp.' The frown deepened. 'Where has Cecil gone?'

'I don't know. But it was quickly organised after a visit by Lord Englefield.'

Dee frowned. 'Why would Englefield be visiting Cecil? And why send him away?'

Margaretta shuddered. 'There is something else. Simeon. The man I went to ask about making a false seal. He was found dead near the Savoy. Tied to his hound with yellow wool.'

'Where is the body?'

'Buried already.'

John Dee groaned.

The bell tolled and people started to move into the church. John Dee and Margaretta took a pew towards the back, next to the aisle. At the front, members of Robert Meldrew's family sat, heads bent.

At exactly three bells, the choir started to sing a low lament and the funeral procession began their slow progress towards the altar. The priest held a cross aloft while four young men carried the coffin on their shoulders. Behind them was a woman, her face covered in a veil, holding the hands of two small, weeping children – a boy of about eight and a younger girl. Just as they came abreast of Dee and his servant, the mother bent over and whispered to him: 'Be brave like your father. You can cry later.' She patted his head. 'Remember you have my Spanish blood which gives you strength, my darling.'

Margaretta looked to Doctor Dee, whose eyes were wide. He mouthed, 'A Spanish wife?' Then he leaned over to whisper, 'Get close to her and see what she feels.'

The funeral was long and mournful. The little boy could not staunch his tears and his little sister kept asking her mother, '*Que pasa? Que pasa?*' At the end of the service, the family trailed out behind the coffin into the graveyard. Friends kept a respectful distance while the coffin was lowered and handfuls of earth tossed onto it with plaintive calls to God to take up the soul of Robert Meldrew.

Margaretta made her way towards Widow Meldrew. 'Please know how sad we are today, mistress.' She nodded to John Dee. 'My master and I visited him recently at the hospital and found him a good man.'

'Thank you, miss.' Her accent was strong and the vowels long. She made a half-smile as if she did not know what else to say.

Fear. Anger. You think of a dark face and feel the horror of what was said. You can still hear your husband arguing with someone, saying he wanted no part of their deeds. He would do no more. A deep voice rings in your ears. A threat. An insistence. Oh, God. You know who was behind your husband's beating. Your husband was killed by someone close. Very close.

Suddenly, Margaretta was aware of a man at her shoulder. The widow was staring at him, her eyes filling with tears. She bit into her lip as if to stop the words from coming out. Then the voice from behind. '*Vamos, hermana.* We must away from prying eyes.'

Margaretta spun round to a tall man, his face covered by the rim of a large hat, but the light on his chin showed he was badly pock-scarred. He quickly twisted to put his back to her and took the other woman's arm, guiding her towards the church gate, the two children loping after them. As she left, Margaretta had an intense feeling rise inside. *Hate. And why does that man not want to be seen?*

John Dee was waiting by the wall. 'What did you feel?'

'She knows her husband's killer. He was close. She hates the man who led her away. He used the word "*hermana*".'

John Dee nodded. 'I think it means sister.' He frowned.

'But that can be used as a term of friendship.'

'Oh, there's no friendship there, doctor. No friendship at all.'

Mourners trailed from the graveyard, all heads down and eyes sad. A few women dabbed at their eyes. John Dee stopped one and asked if he knew the man who was accompanying the widow. With a small shrug, he offered, 'I think he may be her brother, sir.'

John Dee tensed and whispered to Margaretta, 'Did Robert not say his brother-in-law works for Englefield?'

Chapter Forty-Three

Monday evening was bright and clear as Margaretta said a prayer of thanks to Master Tovey. For the first time, Goodwife Barker had not sniped at her having to return to St Dunstan's for an evening. With Sam still recovering, she had taken the first boat she could get, making sure the wherryman was local. No dark skin, no accent, no crucifix.

The house was quiet and cold. Margaretta walked into the kitchen to find Mam huddled over a cold grate, the grey shawl up to her ears. 'We will catch the death of cold in this place,' came the moan before she even looked up.

'Dear God, Mam. The doctor has visitors tonight. Could you not even put a twig on the fire?'

Another moan and her mother's hand flew to her back. Then an accusing glare. 'You've not been to see Huw, have you? You're leaving him in danger. Bad girl, you are.'

Margaretta slammed the bag of flour she was pulling from the cupboard onto the table and shouted: 'Dear God, Mam. I care for him as much as you do. But I cannot bring Huw here to fester in a bed with no one to tend to him.' She clattered a bowl and a jug of water onto the table and started to put flour in the bowl. 'You are not going to nurse him. So my dear sister will have to get her hands dirty for once in her damned life.'

'But the baby needs all her care. Little Jack will start to wither away if she neglects him.'

'Wither away? That child is like a stuffed piglet.' She put

the yeast into the flour and started to agitate as if it had insulted her. 'And he has an army of maids who fret if he even passes wind.' She cursed as she put in too much water and banged the spoon on the side of the bowl, making her mother wince.

'Wither away,' muttered old Mother Morgan. With a stifled scream, her daughter left the kitchen and went to see what was wanted for the evening meal. Even the gloom of Mistress Constable was preferable to her mother's insistent misery.

Christopher Careye arrived on time. As ever he blushed and stammered his words as Margaretta guided him to John Dee's room. At the office door, he held back. 'P...please, Margaretta. May we walk a little when this is done?'

Oh, Lord. Don't get sweet on me, Christopher. I don't want to cause pain. 'I think Mistress Constable would not allow it, Master Careye. Though I thank you for the thought.' *If I turn quickly I'll not see the hurt in your eyes.*

When they went in, Dee was deep in concentration. On his desk were two parchments, both with squares penned on them, divided into sections by the drawing of another square and then a third. In each section were symbols and numbers. Each one was being checked against a table of figures. Each confirmation was signalled with, 'Yes. Yes.'

Christopher Careye paled. 'I thought you left these with Mistress ap Harri at Woodstock, doctor.'

'I made copies for tonight,' muttered Dee. 'We will need them.' He looked up. 'Were you careful not to be followed?'

Christopher nodded. 'I took the back lanes.' Then he pointed at the paper. 'But I feel that is more of a threat, doctor.'

John Dee growled and wagged a hand in irritation before turning to Margaretta. 'Go and make sure our landlords are content. We want no interruptions.'

Only Katherine was home, trying to make a listless DeeDee

sit on command using titbits of cheese. 'Is Doctor Dee wanting company tonight?' was the hopeful question.

'He has visitors at the moment, madam. I think he is doing a lesson.'

Katherine Constable made a huffing sound and plumped up her breasts. 'I will give Doctor Dee some company when his teaching is over.' With that, she turned away and put the kitten on a cushion with a high-pitched command to 'be a good girl'.

Back in the hallway, Margaretta heard Dee at the top of the stairs, his whisper low and urgent. 'Come along quickly, Margaretta. We need to start.'

Back in the office, Christopher was tetchy and kept asking Dee if he was quite sure this was safe. The atmosphere chilled when the doctor barked at him that 'the pursuit of knowledge cannot be stopped by a fucking Spaniard or your fear of the other side'. They all jumped and fell silent, for John Dee was not one for cussing.

He started giving orders in quick succession. Margaretta was to stand and hold the convex glass; Christopher Careye was given parchment and the task of scribing any sounds or thoughts which came to anyone. Then John Dee used his copper rod to carefully measure and adjust the stones so that they were perfectly placed.

Suddenly the light in the room shifted as moonlight started to come through the glass.

'Quickly,' ordered Dee. 'Everyone concentrate. Breathe yourselves into a state of listening.' He nodded to Careye. 'Are you ready?'

The young man nodded and gulped.

In seconds, the light of the moon hit the glass and the crystals began to glow. Dee raised his hands and began to speak in Welsh. '*Dewch atom, angylion.*' Come to us, angels. '*Gadewch i ni glywed eich lleisiau.*' Let us hear your voices. Dee tensed and looked around.

'Do you hear anything?' All shook their heads. He pushed one of the crystals so that a different side was lit. Nothing. Then Margaretta began to shake. 'Keep the glass still, girl.'

'I cannot. There's a tremble going through me.'

In seconds, Dee was across the room. He took the glass from her hands and pushed it into those of Christopher, commanding him to capture the rays. Margaretta was pulled across the office and put into a chair. 'Put your hands into the centre of the crystal triangle. Lean forward so that the light of the crystals hits your face.' Margaretta leaned forward and her eyes were dazzled by the colours. 'Just feel. Listen. Tell me what you hear,' instructed Dee.

The sound was distant, as if coming up a tunnel. 'I hear something. Like singing.'

'Lean in further. Listen. Tell us what you hear. We have only minutes of the moon left within the windowpane.'

Margaretta closed her eyes. 'It's louder now. But I don't hear words.'

'You will not.' John Dee's voice was cracking with excitement. 'Give me the sounds.'

Suddenly Christopher called out: 'Stop this. You know the language of angels is dangerous. It is not for our mortal ears. You are wrong to –'

'Shut up, boy,' was the sharp retort. 'What do you hear, Margaretta?'

Margaretta shook as the sounds kept coming, urged on by Dee. Then a loud crack and a cry from Christopher. The convex glass had split in two. Margaretta slumped back in her chair. 'I feel sick. What happened to me?'

John Dee grasped her shoulders. 'What words are in your mind?'

'Three faces.'

Chapter Forty-Four

Dawn arrived and, as ever, Mam refused to rise and help. Margaretta dragged herself out of the damp bed and made her way to the kitchen. It was cold and grey, and seemed all the bleaker as the memories of the previous night filtered back into her mind.

Christopher Careye's anger had not abated as he warned John Dee not to put Margaretta in danger by meddling with angels. He also spoke with increasing concern about the commission of Lord Englefield. 'They say in the streets that a list of suspect conjurors has been written up by his spies,' he insisted. His words were dismissed.

At the door, Christopher had put his hand on Margaretta's shoulder. 'Tell no one of this. Nor tell anyone about your gifts. In these times they are more of a danger to your life than an enhancement.' He tipped his head forward as if to plant a peck on her cheek, but as she flinched he bit his lip and looked away, then sprinted off. As Margaretta closed the door, she thought she saw a glint in the moonlight at about the height of a man's neck.

Margaretta opened the door to Dee's office. He was bent over a parchment, eyes narrow, brow furrowed in concentration, penning quickly. He looked up for a second and nodded to the seat on the other side of his desk. 'Sit.' He made a few more scratches on his parchment of circles, then tapped on one circle.

'That child in Southwark spoke of a "turn face". The angels spoke of three faces. The wherrymen who circle come from Southwark. They are the Flock.' He looked up, eyes bright. 'I think the Shepherd is in Southwark and has many faces.' He grinned. 'We are getting closer. I need you to go back and see what else you can get from the child.'

'No, doctor. The little child was frightened, her mother felt terror and an old man died.'

'All the more reason to go. Fear is a good tongue-loosener.' He pointed to the door. 'Come back and report. While you are away, I will do a horoscope for Cecil. It might reveal something.'

Margaretta sighed and went to the door. Then she turned. 'Doctor, I am frightened.'

He looked up, face hard. 'Failure is what we should fear, girl. Failure means a chance lost and money withheld.' He looked down and started writing.

She was in the wherry within the hour, her hand to her belly to try to stop the churning. *What if I am recognised? What if someone accuses me of killing Sniffer Simeon? What if I cannot find Tilly? What if I do and her mother attacks me? What if I find the Shepherd and he kills me? What will happen to Mam and Huw?*

'You look like you are going to be sick, young lady. Want to stop?' The wherryman was pointing to the shore.

'I just don't like Southwark,' she responded with a wan smile.

He shrugged. 'No surprise. All kinds of rumours going around there these days. The word is to see nothing, say nothing and repeat nothing.' He grimaced. 'Any loose words will be met with the death of the yellow beast.'

Margaretta could not repress her jolt. 'What?'

The man sliced his finger across his throat then pointed to

the water. 'All bound in the wool of a yellow beast.' He bit his lip and looked around. 'I'll say not a word more'.

The steps were a slime of weed and filth. Already the stench was assaulting her nose. Hardly was her second foot out of the boat than the man had hauled away.

The main street was the usual thrum of hawkers and men pulling carts. On every corner, a pretty girl looked hopeful and the older ones desperate. She sensed their hostility as she pushed through, lifting her skirt to keep it from soaking up the piss and the mulch of rotting vegetables. It took a few minutes to reach the Tabard Inn. There was no sign of Harriet. The stocks were filled today with two old men begging mercy as young louts made sport of pelting them with rotting rubbish.

Suddenly she spotted a head of glossy hair. It was Tilly holding a stick, drawing pictures in the mud. 'Tilly. Come here.'

The child looked up and stared across the street, shook her head and ran. Margaretta followed, pushing people aside and ignoring the foul-mouthed objections. But Tilly was as quick as a whippet and wound between the legs. Halfway up the street she stopped, pushed a door and went inside. By the time Margaretta caught up Harriet was coming out, eyes filled with fury. 'What the hell are you doing here?' she spat.

'I am sorry, Harriet. I just...' Margaretta stopped and stared at the woman's chest. 'Oh my God, where did you get that?' She pointed at the crucifix mark on the woman's white skin, just above the curve of her breast. The exact mark found on every victim.

You have a look of fury. But it is fear. Beyond fear. Terror. I might as well be a guard come to take you to prison.

Harriet leaned forward, grabbed Margaretta's chin and pinched. Her breath reeked of stale ale. 'Some clients just like it rough, dearie. Now shove off.'

'It's the wherryman with a crucifix, isn't it? He's dangerous, Harriet.'

Harriet darted a look up the street then snarled, 'He ain't as dangerous as a goosehead asking questions. It was your questions which had another in the river.' She shook Margaretta's chin harshly. 'Get away from me and Tilly. You don't know what you're meddling in.'

'I know something bad is happening. People are dying… being killed.'

Now Harriet dug in the thumbnail, making Margaretta wince. 'The evil doesn't start in Southwark, luvvie. It just hides it.'

'Who's the turn-face shepherd, Harriet?'

The nail dug deeper, making Margaretta cry out. But Harriet's face had turned from fury to fear. 'Get away from me, d'you hear? You ain't putting me and Tilly in way of the palace flames. Piss off.' With a final shove, Margaretta was pushed back, almost landing on her backside in the dirt, and the door slammed. She looked around. No one appeared to be taking any notice.

What if the crucifixed killer is peeping around the corner? Dear God. If I had known what faced me, I would never have exposed my gifts to John Dee.

Dee was just finishing his horoscope when she arrived back in his office. He barely looked up. 'Worrying.' He looked back to his tables and calculations again. 'Duplicity.'

'Doctor?'

The frown deepened. 'This shows a period of living a lie. He has Mercury, the planet of messengers and commerce, rising in his chart. It means the pursuit of money. But Pluto is strengthening, which is a sign of secrecy and hidden acts.' Dee leaned forward and stared into Margaretta's eyes. 'Are you sure nobody mentioned why he was away?'

'No, doctor.' She paused as he sighed over the scribbles and squares before him.

'He has great power in his future. We need to stay close.' Then Dee seemed to shake himself into the present. 'What did the child say?'

'Tilly ran away. But I saw Harriet. She has a mark on her chest like the dead men. Caused by a…well a…'

'Ha. So the crucifixed Spaniard is a customer. Go on.'

'When I said he was dangerous she shouted that Southwark only covers the danger and if I meddled, I would be putting her in the "palace flames". I am sorry…'

'No. This is good. She confirms.' Dee tapped on another paper. 'As I have shown, the thread goes all the way to the palace.' He sat back and put a hand to his chin, stroking the beard as if it were a cat. 'I think this goes to the king, Prince Philip of Spain. The tarot shows Philip's uncle, the Holy Roman Emperor, who is an ambitious man and would like England as a useful base for his wars in Europe. Elizabeth is the only block to Philip of Spain becoming king if – when – the queen dies.' He looked up at Margaretta. 'I think we have the plot. But we do not have the plotters.' He wagged a hand at her. 'My report to Cecil will be ready in minutes. You can take it to him.' He pointed a finger. 'Put this letter in his desk where no other man can see it until he returns. This is for his eyes only.'

Goodwife was still in a calm mood. Not happy, but not spiteful. Lottie was back to chattering, telling Margaretta three times before their midday beer that Sam and his master were due back the following day so that Goodwife could salve and bandage the wounds again. Goodwife had taken her bobbins out and had taken up her lace-making again. She had even offered to teach Lottie, though the child had wrinkled her nose and stated that so many sticks and threads made a muddle of her mind.

Father Thomas arrived, the red lead paint covering his scarred face more thickly than usual, and the patch had been polished to a gleam. He spoke quietly to Goodwife and then sat to drink with them, passing greetings to all. When he came to Margaretta he asked more questions. How fared her master? Had he any news to deliver? She answered in few words: 'Well, father. No, father.'

With every response, your irritation grows behind that milky smile but the eye stays cold. Suspicion. You don't believe me. Yet there is another feeling. Excitement. Satisfaction. Something is happening away from here.

Father Thomas bid them peace and went to the stable.

It was another hour before Margaretta was able to break away and creep up the stairs to Lord Cecil's office. She pushed open the door. Everything was gleaming and the soft smell of beeswax filled the air. She made her way to the desk and opened the drawer. The seal was still there.

The door opened. It was Father Thomas, staring at her, not moving. 'What are you doing here, Margaretta?'

Suspicion. Stronger than before. Oh, God. Have you seen the letter in my hand? No. But I am like a rabbit in a trap. How do I distract you? I look over your shoulder and frown as if seeing someone. It works. You turn and, in a split second, I have slipped the letter into the desk and silently pushed the drawer closed. You turn back and I smile. 'I…I came to polish, father.' *Oh, God. You know I am lying. I must keep my eyes directly on yours and try to smile again. I feel your anger.* 'But it seems Lottie has done it all.'

He walked towards her slowly, all the time that one beady eye on hers. His voice dropped to a coarse whisper. 'Are you quite sure, Margaretta, that Doctor Dee does not send any word?'

'No, sir. But…'

He smiled. 'I thought so. Tell me.' The voice was milky again.

'Simeon. The old man in Southwark is dead...killed...with his hound. And there was yellow wool. I did not say downstairs for I could cause fear.'

Father Thomas bent forward and put his head in his hands. 'Oh, God help us. When will this evil end?' He looked up. 'And what did you find at the funeral of Robert Meldrew?'

'Only that the poor widow was Spanish, father. And I think she hates a man who calls her sister.'

The priest winced and tutted, then pointed to the desk. 'I will sit there, Margaretta. I have a letter to write.'

She nodded and moved quickly to the door. Her stomach churned as she heard the slide of a drawer being opened. Spinning around she could see that he had opened the other drawer. He looked up and smiled.

Suspicion.

Chapter Forty-Five

Wednesday came and went with no word from the Cecils. Goodwife kept everyone busy and polishing every inch of wood and stone. By the end of the day, Lottie was moaning that it would be easier to polish Westminster Abbey.

The following morning both Goodwife and Lottie were bright-eyed and smiling. Cook was asked to bake some cakes ready for visitors and fresh beer was put in the jugs. The only blot on the morning was the presence of the new man from the stables. For a still man, he had busy eyes. He watched everything. But, in particular, he watched Margaretta. It was over forty minutes of being eyed before she spoke up. 'You seem to have a great interest in what I do, stableman.'

There was no response. Only a grunt and he looked away.

Goodwife Barker looked up from her ledger, beckoned Margaretta over and whispered: 'Do not be alone with the new man. And never leave Lottie with him.' She shot a glare across the room towards him. He did not move.

Margaretta gave a grateful smile and returned to her duties. As she passed by him the reek of manure was strong. *Interest. Not just my looks and body. More than that. When you see me you feel some satisfaction. What is your game?*

At eleven of the clock, there was a knocking on the back door sending Lottie into a frazzle of excitement. Goodwife stood, smoothed her skirts and walked with calm elegance to open the door.

Master Tovey and Sam were standing tall and Sam was looking better already. His black eye was less swollen and the cuts to his face dried to dark lines. They both gave a little bow. Master Tovey pulled a bunch of flowers from under his coat and looked crestfallen, for they were as bedraggled as a dog in the rain. 'I was trying to keep them from prying eyes,' he explained with an apologetic shrug.

Goodwife tinkled yet again and took the flowers with a delighted smile, saying they would soon revive with a little water and attention. She touched his arm and bid him sit. As she walked to the water basin, she shot a look at Lottie, who was wide-eyed, looking at Sam. 'Stop swinging like that, child. Your legs will fall off.' Lottie stilled herself with a squeak.

Sam was soon re-salved and bandaged. He gave a grateful bow to Goodwife Barker and then earned a cuff from Master Tovey when he said that to feel so good was even worth being forced to wash that morning and brush his hair. Margaretta watched from a distance, not sure that Sam had forgiven her. Then Goodwife's face caught her eye. A mix of gladness and sadness.

You feel the tenderness of a young woman but also that of a mother. You look at Sam and feel care. Also, sadness that you never had your own to hold and love. There is a deep hole in your soul. You look at Master Tovey and feel surprised that the feelings you thought had gone for ever are still there deep inside. But it's mixed with fear. What if he is not true? You look again at Sam and think of the child you had once talked of having.

Master Tovey leaned forward, his brow furrowing. 'Why the sudden sad face, mistress? With the skill you have shown in mending my apprentice, you should be full of joy.' Then he leaned back with a wink. 'And a lucky boy Sam is to have those hands upon him.'

Goodwife showed the girl inside her as hands fluttered to

her blushing face and she told Master Tovey to mind his words. But the tone and laughing said she wanted the very opposite. A walk in the garden was suggested to cool his mind.

With them gone, Lottie bounded to Sam and demanded tales of daring on the sea. Margaretta worked on cleaning the dishes. All was happy until Father Thomas appeared at the door. He pointed at her and sneered, 'So, Lottie, you will lift your skirts to another poor boy and get him in trouble, will you?'

Lottie shrieked and put her hands to her face. 'No, father. I did not –'

Sam turned to look at the young girl. 'You have a boy already?'

'No. I…'

'Harlot,' whispered Father Thomas.

Dear God. You are enjoying this. You thrill at her pain and fear. You want to destroy any happiness. The more she weeps, the more your satisfaction grows. You feel warmth in your loins as she crumples. 'You are wrong, father. And unkind.'

He turned to glare at Margaretta. 'You dare to contradict me?'

'Yes.' She took a deep breath. 'Lottie has told me all about Jonas and she did no wrong other than being friendly.'

Your nostrils are flaring. You are angry. Very angry. You feel confused. No one ever speaks up to you.

Father Thomas left, leaving them in shocked silence, only broken when Lottie started to sob. Sam stood, evidently not knowing what to do. Margaretta gathered the younger girl into her arms and cooed comfort into her ears.

'But why did he change so?' the girl blurted between her tears. 'He's always been so kind with us.'

'Because his mask slipped.' Margaretta turned to Sam. 'I hope you don't listen to false words, Sam. That man was being cruel, not godly.'

But Sam just shrugged and said it was nothing to him anyway. Lottie hung her head and said she would go and clean her face. As soon as she was out of the door, Sam stood and announced he must be away.

'Please don't go, Sam.'

He was already at the door, calling over his shoulder that he was back on the wherry tomorrow if she needed any assistance. But his tone was distant, disappointed, dull.

Margaretta crept up the stairs and across the landing as the clock struck four in the afternoon. She pushed open the door of Lord Cecil's office and stepped quietly to the desk. The letter from John Dee was still where she had placed it. The seal was intact. But the air was heavy with the smell of melted wax.

CHAPTER FORTY-SIX

The priest did not appear for days. Master Tovey arrived every day with good excuses, but never with Sam. On Friday, he arrived with two good fish; Saturday he came with a flower basket, made of beautifully planed new wood; on Sunday, he offered an arm to walk to church. As Goodwife smiled, Lottie saddened. She was quiet, eating little and nibbling at the side of her nails even when Goodwife threatened to soak them in vinegar. At night she cried into her pillow.

Sunday evening was time for Margaretta to go back to John Dee's lodgings. She had been away longer than usual and was given leave to stay until Tuesday. Lottie sighed and sloped away to their room without a goodbye.

The Constables' house was in an uproar as the mistress wailed her kitten was missing and the master dragged furniture to see if it was behind it. In the kitchen, Mam was huddled over a dead fire, her shawl over her head. Margaretta cooed that kittens were apt to go wandering and coaxed Master Constable from heaving the great china cabinet with the promise of spiced wine. Peace was restored.

Margaretta went to Dee's room and found him scribbling onto a parchment. He raised his head, eyes bright. 'At last, you are back. What did Cecil say to my note?'

'They are still not returned, doctor, and no word when they will. The note is hidden in his desk.'

Dee looked crestfallen and muttered that with no new evidence and no word from Cecil, he was unable to progress.

Later in the evening, Margaretta sat by the kitchen fire, trying to quell her fear. Suddenly the dog growled and turned to lick something behind him. There was a woeful cry. The kitten.

The creature was hot but limp, its little belly blown out. When she picked it up, another pitiful mew. The eyes opened for a second and blinked shut. 'Mam. What do I do?'

Mam rested her gaze on the little animal. 'Too much rich food. Die it will.'

Fear turned to fury. 'Damn it, Mam. I remember you saving the farm runts. You knew what to do.' She stamped over to her mother. 'Help this little thing, if only for the old times.'

Slowly the wizened hand came from below the shawl. 'Give it to me.' Then she rubbed its belly in gentle clockwise circles, whispering words of comfort in the old tongue. The kitten went quiet. 'Get me a cloth,' whispered the old woman.

Margaretta watched her mother roll it around her little finger and then rub the pink button of flesh at the base of the kitten's tail. 'Taken from your mam too early, you were. She would empty your little belly like this.' Seconds later the kitten gave a loud mew and squitted a stream of excrement and a trumpet of odorous wind. 'Now a wet linen,' commanded Mam. The kitten was cleaned and kissed a welcome back to life.

'You saved it.'

There was no response, but Mam, a small smile on her face, was watching the kitten race around the kitchen in the delight of an empty belly. Suddenly Margaretta was back in her childhood when Mam was soft and kind. 'There's still goodness in you, Mam.'

The old woman handed her daughter the shit-filled linen.

John Dee did not even hear the door open. He jumped when Margaretta cleared her throat to tell him of her presence. 'It gets worse,' he muttered. 'Look.'

There was a spread of the strange cards in an arc. At either end were two of the crystal stones and below them the parchments with the squares and symbols. Dee tapped on the cards. 'The prophesies darken every time I ask for guidance.'

Margaretta shuddered and bent over to look. Some were the same cards as had been pulled before. On the far right the empress, sitting stern on her throne. But the card was upside down. Far to the left was the emperor on his throne of sheep's heads. But between them a new card. It depicted a tall man looking over fields, though his head turned away, a crook in his hand and a lantern hanging on it. Below him was the card with the woman in a bed, weeping under a bedspread of Tudor roses. Margaretta pointed to the new card, showing the sad man. 'What does this mean?'

'It is the hermit card. Often called the shepherd card. Always seeking destiny.'

'But what is the destiny?'

'Another lesson for you, Margaretta. When you look at the cards you must go beyond their immediate symbols and look at the patterns. Look at where each card sits against another card. Dee tapped on the empress, his finger trembling. 'He leads away from this.'

He gulped. 'The empress upside down means emptiness, no insight, no view of the future. Miserable ignorance.' He turned to look at his helper. 'This tells me that destiny is leading away from the queen and towards the king. And under his feet is Elizabeth.'

'What does it all mean?'

He turned slowly to look at her. 'No prince will be born to Mary. The shepherd card leads to the emperor and walks over Elizabeth. He is seeking to stamp out the Tudor line.'

Chapter Forty-Seven

M onday dawned on another drizzling, grey day. Outside stinking paths were greasy and people miserable. Even the Leadenhall dogs looked as if scraps were not worth growling for.

It was mid-morning when a rattle at the door resounded through the quiet house. Margaretta ran and opened the door onto a shower of rain and a man standing, his bent head covered in a wide brim hat. He looked up. It was Father Thomas. 'Take me to John Dee.' His foot was already inside.

John Dee looked up bleary-eyed. 'What brings you here, father?'

Without a word, the visitor pulled a package from under his long black cloak. He turned to look at Margaretta. 'Maybe some small beer, girl?'

As she left, the feeling started to tingle. *Excitement. Anticipation. But also some anxiety. Do you worry that I have told my master about your cruelty to Lottie? No. Why would you care?*

She was on the way back through the hall with the brimming mug when she heard the shout.

'Damn that bastard. May hell rise up and take his soul.'

Inside the office, Dee was pacing like a tormented tiger in a cage, smacking the letter into his palm. Seeing Margaretta, he shook it at her. 'Calais. That explains the silence.' Dee jabbed at the letter. 'Gone for weeks.'

'What news makes you so very angry, doctor?' In the corner

of her eye, she watched Father Thomas lean back against the wall, watching.

Dee shook the paper again. 'Cecil has gone to Calais. On the instruction of Lord Francis Englefield, he says. And the reason? The fucking reason? To accompany Cardinal Legate Reginald Pole!' spat Dee. 'That mad would-be-pope, so adored by our queen. He will bring this country to an incense-reeking, Latin-chanting pit of papism.'

Margaretta glanced at the priest then back to Dee. 'Quiet your voice. You'll have us all in the stocks at Southwark...or worse.'

Dee grunted and slumped into his chair. 'Cecil is as wily as a fox. This whole sorry business centres on his link to Elizabeth, a Protestant princess, and so a moral enemy to our Catholic-crazed queen. Anyone who stinks of supporting Elizabeth and her right to the throne lives under the threat of being accused of treason or heresy,' he growled. 'So what better way is there to deny your support of a Protestant princess than by befriending the very man who would put that princess in the Tower or on the scaffold?'

'Would he really do that?'

'Oh, Cecil will squirm his way out of any sniff of danger. Why was he the only privy councillor to escape punishment when he put Lady Jane Grey on the throne instead of Mary?'

Margaretta shrugged.

'Because he fawned and fussed and used soft words to convince our queen that he only signed his witnessing of wrong and not his support of wrongdoing. Liar. He wanted a Protestant queen and not this Spanish-maddened woman who will sell us to Emperor Charles for his empire.'

'Hush yourself, doctor.' Margaretta was alarmed now, but Father Thomas still leaned against the wall, showing no emotion. John Dee flung the letter on the floor. Margaretta stepped forward and tapped on his desk. 'So the man who employed Robert Meldrew now employs Lord Cecil?'

Dee frowned. 'Well connected. Interesting.' He made a scribbled note.

At this, the priest leaned forward to look straight at John Dee. 'Good doctor, I must speak with you.' He glanced at Margaretta. 'In private.'

Dee wagged a hand irritably. 'The maid holds her tongue. Continue.'

Father Thomas pressed his lips together, irritated. 'Very well. I was at Lord Cecil's when Englefield came. He talked of arrest warrants being prepared in connection with his commission to root out conjurors.' He cleared his throat. 'Lord Cecil was asked about you, sir.'

Dee jumped like a startled hen. 'But I am no conjuror. Just an honest mathematician. A philosopher.' He jabbed a finger towards Mercator's globes. 'I work with the most learned of men. I have taught in the great universities of Europe and you call me a conjuror?' his voice had risen to a high pitch and the eyes glistened with anger.

The priest raised a placatory hand. 'Not me, doctor.' He smiled. 'I come as a friend, just to alert you.' Then a wink of the good eye. 'We Welshmen must help each other.'

This seemed to calm Dee, who sat back looking thoughtful. 'I thank you, father.' Then an annoyed grunt. 'But I have done nothing of which to be concerned.' But his cheek twitched, betraying that this was not true. 'That said, our protection is gone.'

Relief. I feel it. It must be you, father. For I cannot feel John Dee. Are you relieved he has listened? Or is there something else? Is it because he cannot take your place with Cecil?

Father Thomas rose and tipped his hat. 'I bid you farewell, sir.' He nodded at Margaretta. 'Lady Cecil returns tomorrow to arrange the move of all staff to Wimbledon. Goodwife Barker asks you to assist.' He left without another word.

'Well, it's down to you and me, doctor. We still need to find out why people have died.' Margaretta gave a weak smile. 'We can do it.'

Dee just stared at the desk, his wincing giving away his fury. 'See what you can find out from Lady Mildred.'

They heard the front door close and the house was quiet again. Back in the kitchen Mam was petting the kitten and cooing it to calm, though she put it down swiftly when her daughter entered. Not for long. The kitten simply clawed back up her shawl and nestled in.

All seemed quiet until early afternoon, when another messenger came to the door. 'Is you Miss Morgan?'

'Yes.'

'This is for you.' He thrust the package into Margaretta's hand and gave a hopeful smile for a ha'penny.

The letter was short and insistent.

Sister
Come to get our brother from this house.
His presence is encouraging the visitation of
vagabonds who do threaten our staff. Your
sister Susan in the presence of her husband,
Angus McFadden

It was not far to the Vintry, where the unsavoury Angus would surely be filling his head with wine with the French merchants. The smell of rotting fish assaulted her as she pushed past Billingsgate into Thames Street, which was slowing down in the late afternoon with the hawkers shouting at each other about another bad day in the rain. A few drunks took a crooked path between the alehouses. Past the steelyards, she reached Three Cranes Lane.

Sure enough, Angus was poised on a barrel, in his grasp a good measure of red wine, which slopped over the brim of an expensive beaker. The doxy on his knee giggled loudly as he fondled her breasts with his free hand and slurred filthy words into her ear.

'Is business good today, brother-in-law?'

There was a shriek and a splurge of curses as Angus jumped up, tumbling his plaything to the ground. Her loud demands for sixpence were ignored as Angus tried to insist he was being harassed by the 'foul harlot'.

Margaretta stood, arms folded. Eventually, the girl stomped off, shouting over her shoulder that his 'little prick was not worth a penny anyway', leaving them in uncomfortable silence, broken only by the sniggering of the wine traders. 'My sister has demanded I take Huw away. What is amiss?'

Angus sniffed and stepped forward. 'Indeed, she has. You need to get dog-boy out of our house.' A spray of wine-stinking spittle hit Margaretta's face. 'And don't you wrinkle your pretty nose at me, girl.' Immediately his eyes went to her body and the usual leer arrived on his face. 'I don't want Spanish villains stalking my house.'

'What do you mean?'

'Every day there is one watching, following.' Angus pointed a finger close to her face and jabbed at her. 'Dog-boy brought trouble. Now get him away from my wife and child.'

With that, he turned away, calling back over his shoulder. 'And don't open your mouth about my enjoyments.'

Margaretta shouted after him. 'My silence for one answer, Angus.'

The man stopped and turned.

'Does that Spaniard wear a crucifix and have a bandaged arm?'

Angus frowned and growled. 'He does.'

Chapter Forty-Eight

Huw scowled. 'Left me with bad Susan.'

'I'm sorry, Huw.' She went to pat his arm but the boy flinched away. 'Has she been kind to you?'

'For two days only. Then…snip-tongue.' He nodded satisfaction when his sister laughed out loud.

'It's about time you were here,' came the harsh rebuke.

Margaretta jumped and turned to see Susan at the door, her face reddening with fury. 'And what did you say to Grace, the kitchen maid? I heard her laughing with the other servants. Something about not knowing a pig from a sheep and asking for a blanket of pig-wool. Who were you talking about?'

Margaretta feigned innocence and glared at Huw who was rocking and chortling in delight. Susan pointed at Huw. 'We cannot keep him any longer.'

'So, your milk of human kindness has soured already, sister?'

'You did not tell me that our house would be watched. He will be out there now, those dark, foreign eyes following every movement.'

'Then you need to help us. I want a good dress, a cloak and your carriage.' Margaretta looked at Huw. 'And you will wear my clothes.' She ignored the shaking of his head.

Susan shook her head. 'My dresses are expensive. Not for dragging through the midden in the gutters of St Dunstan's.'

Margaretta stepped across the room and grabbed her sister by the shoulders. 'Damn you. Our brother is in danger. Now

squeeze the last drop of kindness from your stone of a heart.'
Minutes later Susan thrust a dress into her sister's arms.

The sun was just falling behind the trees as two women walked
across the yard towards a waiting carriage, one dressed in a fine
dress of blue silk and a bonnet in the Spanish style. The other
in a plain servant's dress and a coif covering the head, walking
with small steps as he had been taught inside the house.

As the carriage moved away a figure stepped out of the
trees. The sun caught the silver of the crucifix around his neck.

CHAPTER FORTY-NINE

Tuesday morning dawned brighter than the previous day. Margaretta raced through her chores and readied her bag for the journey back to the house of Cecil. Mam's initial relief at Huw returning home soon descended into the usual litany of woes. She had now decided that the beating had made his affliction worse. Not true. The boy was bravely ignoring his pain and had spent hours in the yard chopping wood to re-ignite his imaginary merchant practice.

A street boy was not long finding Sam, who rowed up to the steps with a nod but no smile. 'Back in your service, missy. But I think I'll stick to the rowing.'

'It's good to see you, Sam.'

He simply nodded and pulled away at the oars.

Embarrassed. Thought you had a chance at having a girl to care for and now you feel we are laughing at you. She leaned forward to look straight into his eyes. 'Are you a man or a mouse?'

He bridled and opened his mouth to put her straight. As he did, he lost concentration and his bad arm failed to dig the oar into the water. Margaretta was rewarded with a slop of filthy water off the blade, straight into her face. Sam smiled. 'Better than words, missy.'

She glowered. 'That water is less vile than the lies that half-hidden priest spoke of Lottie.' She swiped at the drips on her nose.

Sam shrugged, but his eyes showed interest. 'But he said

your friend had another boy. More than *had* him, it seems.'

Margaretta shook her head. 'There was a stable boy called Jonas who was sweet on Lottie.' She pointed at his face. 'You cannot blame him for that. The boy is dead and my master is investigating. That's why I go between the houses.'

Sam looked perplexed. 'Is that why I was beaten black and blue?'

'Yes. Thank God you were not found dead in yellow wool.'

The boy's head jerked. 'Yellow wool?'

You are remembering something. Surprise. There is a connection. I hear a voice loud and bawdy, then soft to the child. She holds the little one close. There is yellow in their hair. 'Have you seen Harriet lately?'

Sam reacted again. 'How did you know I was thinking of her?' He leaned forward. 'You is a strange one, missy. It was your talk of the yellow wool.'

'Go on.'

'I saw Harriet yesterday with new ribbons in her hair. Plaited from yellow wool.' Then he frowned. 'And old Simeon was bound by the same, wasn't he?'

Chapter Fifty

As Margaretta stood at the side of the kitchen waiting for Goodwife to return and list her duties, the new stableman entered and quickly skirted across the floor to Goodwife's desk. He opened her ledger and flicked through the pages, muttering. Then the words, '*Qué ocurre en esta casa?*' Margaretta stepped forward. 'So you are a Spanish man.'

He twisted towards her, his face creased into a look of fury. 'No.'

'What goes on here?' Father Thomas appeared in the doorway. He told the man to go, then turned his eye on Margaretta. 'What did you do to annoy him?'

'Nothing, father, except hear him speak Spanish.'

'Rubbish.'

'But I heard –'

The priest rounded on her, his voice lowering to a snarl. 'Contradicting me again?' The eye narrowed. 'Get back to your duties.'

Lottie was trying to heave a wooden trunk across Lord Cecil's sleeping room. 'Oh, Margaretta. Seems I must go without Sam ever knowing the truth.'

Margaretta patted her arm. 'I have told Sam you are a good girl. Have faith, Lottie.'

The other girl brightened and launched into her usual chatter.

At midday, all were called for small beer and bread. It was Margaretta's chance. She sent Lottie ahead and crept to the office. Everything was already packed in boxes. She slid open the desk drawer. *Oh God.* Empty. No letter.

Lady Cecil arrived early afternoon to oversee the removal to Wimbledon. An hour later Goodwife, her face back to sour, told Margaretta to attend to her.

Mildred Cecil was in the window seat of her room, staring down into the street. She turned slowly when Margaretta entered, pointing to a stool. 'Sit, child.' The command obeyed, she smiled weakly. 'So our friend Doctor Dee must have received the letter from my husband by now.'

'Yes, my lady.'

The older woman batted her hands in frustration. 'Enough of this hesitancy, Margaretta. What was his mood?'

'Angry, my lady. He feels abandoned.'

Mildred clasped her hands together and bent her head.

Guilt. Also shame, but you will not betray your husband. You are thinking what you can say to me which might calm John Dee. There is a tinge of embarrassment. But stronger than that is the need to escape. You feel fear.

Mildred lowered her voice to a whisper. 'Tell John that my husband had little choice. Lord Englefield insisted that William go as an envoy.' She straightened up and looked back through the window. 'There is much concern at court and our queen needs the support of good friends.'

'Concern, my lady?'

'Yes…yes,' was the slow reply. 'The future may not be filled with joy…or a prince.' She suddenly turned as if realising she had said too much. 'We depart for our manor in Wimbledon much liked by Cardinal Legate Reginald Pole. We need to show the manor in his bishopric is well looked after.' She gave a weak smile. 'Please tell John Dee I did not abandon him. I will help as I can but cannot go against my husband.'

Margaretta rose and curtsied. 'I'll tell him so.' She walked to the door then turned. 'I put a letter in your husband's desk from the doctor. It is gone.'

Mildred Cecil frowned. 'I know nothing of it but it will be safely packed.' She smiled. 'Father Thomas oversaw the office removal.'

'What of the book secreted away for Lady Elizabeth?'

'Taken by my husband.' Lady Mildred sighed. 'And flung into the briny sea if he has any wit in his head.'

I hope so. But something else disturbs you. Your brow makes little frowns and your eyes are distant. 'Is there anything else causing you concern, my lady?'

Mildred Cecil seemed surprised. 'Reading my mind again, Margaretta. I worry for my sister.' She looked towards the window. 'Her child is still not born.' Her brow creased. 'She feels no movement.'

'I'll surely pray for her.' There was no response and so Margaretta crept from the room.

CHAPTER FIFTY-ONE

Lottie sobbed when Margaretta left to get the wherry back to St Dunstan's, despite an assurance that her friend could visit Wimbledon. Goodwife scolded the girl for being a flimsy but then patted her arm and led her to the table for a glass of warm milk.

Sam was faster to arrive this time and seemed a little warmer. He asked after 'the other missy' and was told: 'She's feeling sore at your coldness. Have you thought on my words?'

The boy scowled. 'Who am I to argue with a man of God?'

'With one eye gone, and the other one blind.'

Sam laughed and pulled on the oars as he blushed.

'You'd better move quickly. They move to Wimbledon.'

The boy tried to feign disinterest. 'I'll call to say goodbye if I have time.'

And I feel regret.

The sense of something wrong was in the air as soon as Margaretta opened the door. Mam was on her feet, holding the kitten; Huw was pacing the kitchen, placing each foot squarely in the centre of every flagstone.

'What has happened?' demanded Margaretta.

Before they answered, Katherine Constable stormed through the door. 'They have taken him.' She flew across the floor at her servant and grasped her arms. 'Terrible it was. All shouting and screaming of dark deeds.'

'Please calm, mistress. Who came?'

A man called Lord Englefield and his men. They pulled John Dee from his office. Then the swarthy servant came and boarded up the office door. It is like a barricade before a battle.'

'Where's the doctor now, mistress?'

'They took him away to Hatfield House.'

'What is the accusation?'

'Conjuring the life of Queen Mary and her sister.'

CHAPTER FIFTY-TWO

It had been an early start, and still the Great North Road seemed to stretch on and on. Margaretta held tight to the door of the carriage, looking out to stop her stomach turning from the lurching. It was not working. The plump woman on the opposite seat tried to distract her with a torrent of tales about her sons and daughters, and the sons and daughters of her third husband. A twenty-mile stream of noise.

It was early afternoon when the carriage halted outside an inn and the horseman shouted: 'Bells Inn. All out.'

Margaretta jumped down, grateful to be out of the chattering. 'How far to Hatfield House?' she called up to the driver.

'A good two miles, miss,' He looked down, his face kind and also concerned.

Something about him made her feel like a child. It was his eyes. Just like Dada's. Suddenly she felt the tears start to rise and looked away. 'You get up here, miss,' called the man. 'I can take you.' He patted the seat next to him.

Within a quarter of an hour Margaretta was taking a deep breath before pulling an iron bell-pull. A cross-looking woman eventually tugged the oak door open. 'Who are you?' was the rude demand.

'I think my master is here. Doctor John Dee. May I see him?'

The woman gave a harsh laugh. 'He'll not be needing a

servant while he's here. A lawyer, more like.'

It took a few minutes of bargaining before she was told to wait while the woman disappeared along a corridor. A few kitchen staff busied themselves and looked sideways in suspicion. Eventually, the woman returned. 'You're lucky. Lord Englefield will see you.'

Lord Francis Englefield sat behind his desk. Thick curling hair and a beard covered a craggy face with a deep-furrowed brow. Dark eyes surveyed her with no hint of warmth.

'So. You are our prisoner's servant?' The voice was thick, harsh and heavily accented. This man sounded like a Berkshire farmer. He leaned forward, pushed aside the papers he had been reading and a sickly smile spread beneath the whiskers. 'We know of you. So you can tell me all about your master's work of conjuring.'

Satisfaction. Like a fox in a hen house. You are thinking of how to use me through terror. 'I am only the kitchen maid, sir.'

A sly hiss through his teeth. 'And why would a kitchen maid travel over twenty miles to see her master?' He leaned back to peer at her down his nose while he twirled the end of his beard. 'No. I think you must be the Margaretta who he told that squawking woman to find.'

You are beginning to feel the excitement of a kill. I'll put on Lottie's voice. 'Margaretta? That bobolyn? She went a-running as soon as Mistress Katherine said our master was arrested. That little skitter-mouse has probably –'

Englefield rapped his fingers on the desk. 'Enough gabbling, girl. Why are you here?'

'To tell him the Constables say they can keep his room but only for two weeks.' *It's working. You are irritated now. Disappointed but tinged with anger.* 'I think they're surely unkind, sir. Terrible if you ask me. You see –'

'For pity's sake, stop.' He waved at the door. 'You may have a few minutes to give him the message. Tell the guard I sent you.' With that, he pulled back the papers and gave her no more attention.

John Dee was sitting rigidly on a chair. There was nothing else in the room save a cot bed with a rough blanket and a pail for his pissing. She put an urgent finger to her mouth and waited for the door to slam shut. 'They think I'm just a kitchen maid,' she whispered. 'Englefield was going to use me for information. I felt it.'

'Oh, God help me.' John Dee slumped back on the chair. He was a poor sight. His usually pristine gown was ripped and splattered with mud, as was his face. Above his eye a deep scratch and a blooming bruise. His lips were tense and the cheeks drawn in by anxiety. 'They took some papers. They have arrested Christopher too. Conjuring. Sorcery, they say.' He gulped.

'But who would accuse you?'

Dee got up and began to pace, though with a pronounced limp. 'George Ferrers and someone called Thomas Prideaux.'

'Do you know these men?'

'Ferrers, yes. A fool of a man. The lord of misrule.' He turned to see Margaretta staring. 'You may well look confused. He leads the court foolery and high drinking at Christmas. Only ever asked of a real fool and they always think it is a compliment.' Dee snarled: 'He is nothing but a debtor and a dramatist and dishonest to his bones. He hates me for speaking against him when a wax effigy was found in the churchyard of St Dunstan's. But that was years ago.'

'And Thomas Prideaux?'

Dee shrugged and started pacing again. 'I do not know him, but…' John Dee stopped in his tracks. 'Englefield must know him well. He uses his first name, but with George Ferrers, it is the full name.'

'But why would they accuse you of sorcery?'

Dee gave a harsh and cynical laugh. 'Probably they are puppets of court. They want my downfall.' He put his hands to his face, the tremble evident. 'My lands and pension granted by King Edward are revoked.' There was a long groan. 'I will be even more penniless than before.'

The door opened and the rough guard glared through the gap, pointing at Margaretta. 'Time to leave.'

Margaretta trilled that she would be but a minute more and waited for the door to close. 'We can think of money another time. Tell me what to do.'

He seemed to come back to some sense. 'You need to get into that room and remove anything which could be used against me. The crystals, the cards, any paper with a horoscope on it. Burn the false letter with Elizabeth's name.' He put his head in his hands. 'If they find the tarot, the new books on angels and the horoscopes, I will be dead in a week. No court will find me innocent.'

Margaretta nodded. 'They've boarded your room, but there'll be a way.'

John Dee took her hand. 'Knowledge hides knowledge. Hide them, girl.'

'You need to think how to answer their questions, doctor.'

Dee began to shake. 'Tomorrow they bring John Bourne.'

Margaretta raised her eyebrows in question.

'Queen Mary's principal secretary and a man with a love of inflicting great pain.' He gave a little mew. 'Pray for me.'

Chapter Fifty-Three

Katherine Constable looked alarmed. 'Break into the room? But Lord Englefield himself commanded it boarded up.' She began to mottle about the throat and dabbed at her face with a linen. 'He said they would return tonight to search it.'

'The doctor's enemies will use what they find in that room.' Margaretta reached for the other woman's arm. 'They'll kill him, mistress.'

Katherine Constable gave a little cry and looked away.

Fear. It's more than the fear for a stranger. The feelings a woman has for a man she loves. My God. You do more than flirt with the doctor. You feel desperation and live torn between your love for him and the duties of a wife. 'You could be no better friend to the doctor by helping me. And I promise no one will ever know.'

It worked. Katherine nodded. 'But how can we hide our doings?'

'We have Huw.'

Huw stood at the door, Margaretta at his shoulder. He twisted his head away from her gaze.

'Every plank removed as if it were silk and every single one put back where it was found, the nails in exactly the same place – after we have been in the room. Can you do that Huw?'

'Yes.'

Margaretta patted his shoulder, ignoring the shudder, and

left him alone. He hated being watched as much as he hated being touched.

In the kitchen, Mam was teaching the kitten to run for a pom-pom of wool and bring it back for a treat.

'Mistress Katherine will be very sore if you take her kitten, Mam. Don't get too fond of it.'

The old woman ignored her and picked up the kitten to plant a kiss on its head. Margaretta looked on as memories of being a child flooded back. Of being held, and loved, and patted when she cried; her father swinging her in his arms; Susan mithering and Dada laughing at her; Huw standing at the side, Dada not understanding and shouting at him to be a man. She recalled how Mam would take her husband's arm, speaking soft words to calm his concern, saying that Huw was special, God-loved, angel-kissed. *Dear God, Mam. What happened? Where did the kindness go? Did it die with Dada? I was so sad and bereft myself, I did not notice you turn. Just one day I woke up and you hated me. Not Susan. Not Huw. Just me.*

It was a long hour before Huw arrived back in the kitchen, staring at the wall and shuffling. 'All done. Huw good. No hurt.' Then he jumped sideways as his sister reached out to pat his arm.

The office was in disarray. Chairs upturned, papers scattered, the precious globes thrown in the corner, the ink-well upturned and Dee's cap on the floor. *Damn you, court men. You think you can bring my master to his knees with your accusations. Not if I can help it.*

'I fear we are doing much wrong.' Katherine Constable's tone was high pitched with fear.

'Go to your sitting room, mistress. What you don't see you can't speak about.'

Margaretta shut the door, lit a candle and started her search with the bookshelves. The cards were somewhere deep in their shadows. She pulled out every book. No sign. She checked the desk, the corners, inside his trunk, behind, inside and also under the bed; the carpet was lifted and all boards checked. The ledgers on the desk held only his diary and in that there was nothing of importance other than the news of the day and what time he ate. Maybe a note of a child being born or someone coming with sickness and seeking advice. Nothing dark. She looked at the clock. An hour gone.

What were his words? Evening sun began to stream through the window and a ray of light was cast across the books. 'Knowledge hides knowledge,' she whispered.

She started with the thickest book, and there it was. This was not a book, but a wooden box, lined with silk and bound in leather. Inside was the garnet crystal and the white quartz. She looked up at the shelves which covered three walls of the room. She ran to the door and shouted down the stairs. 'Mistress Katherine? I need your help.'

It took the two women over an hour to check every tome for hidden artefacts and papers. By dusk, John Dee's desk was piled with crystals, horoscopes, small books showing the movement of the moon and other stars, notes on the character of people at court, the books he ordered from abroad, the scroll of his angelic language and, in the middle, the cards. Katherine Constable looked at them in confusion. 'What are all these strange things?'

'Simply his wisdom which his enemies will render as evil,' answered Margaretta. She turned to the other woman. 'Can you give me a sack to take these away?' She nodded at the globes. 'We will leave these as the men would have seen them.'

Katherine simply nodded and left, her face twitching with anxiety. As she shut the door, Margaretta's eyes moved to the box holding the cards. Slowly, she opened it and took out the deck, spread the cards on the table in an arc with the pictures down. She passed her hand over the cards. 'What do we face?' The card ten from the right felt different, warm, like a tingle through her hand. She turned it over and shuddered.

It was the moon card. Two dogs, one red, the other yellow, howled up at the globe. In the distance two towers with no doors and one window. Between them, a road stretched into bleak hills going nowhere. Beneath the dogs a dark pool, full of currents and out of the water was climbing a clawed creature, its pincers raised as if spurring the dogs on in their anger. The face of the moon was twisted in fury and despair.

Then she realised there was another card stuck to the moon card. She pulled them apart. 'Two of pentangles. A man juggles two coins and, behind him, ships on a stormy sea.'

Hearing Katherine on the stairs, Margaretta snatched up the cards and put them back in their casket, clenched her hand to stop the tremble, and tried to put the image of the dogs from her mind.

The women had the desk cleared in minutes and carefully placed the furniture as it had been. Huw was recalled and told to do his magic. They left saying nothing. The only sign of the secret they shared was a brief nod before they parted at the kitchen door.

It did not take long for Huw to knit back the wooden boards into the barricade. Then he helped disperse the books, cards, crystals, parchments, and scrying equipment into his woodpile. By evening meal no one would know John Dee had ever seen the light through a crystal in this house. Burning in the bread oven was the false letter with Elizabeth's name, and three horoscopes.

At eight in the evening, two armed men arrived at the door and insisted on searching John Dee's room. They found nothing and left angry. Katherine Constable demanded a large beaker of French brandy.

But relief was short-lived. As they ate their evening pottage, there was a loud knock at the kitchen door. Mam scooped up the kitten and muttered about bad tidings. Outside was a messenger. 'Please attend Lady Cecil in the morning, miss. There is concerning news.'

CHAPTER FIFTY-FOUR

Goodwife was irritable. 'So, you grace us with your presence again, Margaretta.'

The girl bobbed a curtsey and tried a small smile. 'I was summoned by Lady Cecil.'

The other woman sniffed. 'This is a strange business. Servants going and returning, my lord departing in the night. Now the rush to Wimbledon.' She pulled at her fingers. 'Seems we will not see London this summer.'

Sadness. You fear losing the attention of Master Tovey. What if his eyes fall on another woman in the church? Wimbledon feels like another country. Here there is the delicious possibility that you might bump into him on your daily walk. 'But Wimbledon is a nice place to visit and the air is sweet, Goodwife. A few more strokes on the wherry-oar will do much to heal Sam's bruises.'

Goodwife blushed, smiled, then realised her reaction. The scowl was pressed back onto her face and she dismissed Margaretta with a flick of her hand and a command to go direct to Lady Cecil and not to interrupt Lottie's chores.

But Lottie was waiting at the top of the stairs. The hallway was almost empty now – just the large dresser but no clock. 'Oh, Margaretta. You're back.' The child clutched her friend's hands. 'I thought I would never see you again.' The child bit her lip and then pinched them together.

You are abashed, little Lottie. You fear I'll be angry about something. 'What worries you, my friend?'

Another bite of her bottom lip and her face pinked. 'Well… it's just that…Sam did come here,' she blurted out. 'He did say he was sore and sorry for walking away when the paint-faced priest was so cruel to me. And, well, he…' Tears started in her eyes. 'He's asked me to walk out with him. Just a little walk.'

'So, why the tears?'

'Well, he's really your boy, Margaretta. He saw you first. And I think you may like him…just a little.' Her voice rose to a squeak of distress.

Something lost before it is even touched. Sadness and a feeling of being totally alone. But it's not you, Lottie. No. These are my feelings. And I am the builder of them. For I cannot allow any boy to take my eye off Mam and Huw. 'Oh, Lottie. You speak like a silly-thing. The moment he saw you on those steps he was only for you.'

The younger girl gasped. 'You're sure, Margaretta? You mean it?'

'Yes, of course. Now, where is Lady Cecil?'

After Lottie had thrown her arms around her neck, declaring her a 'true sister', Margaretta was pointed towards the door of Lord Cecil's office. She smiled to hide her sadness.

Mildred Cecil turned from her seat at the window and carefully closed her book, taking care to place a silk ribbon to mark her page.

'Your messenger stated there was some concern, my lady.'

Mildred nodded. 'Indeed.' She shifted in her seat and sighed. 'So, John Dee is taken to Hatfield and accused of conjuring.'

'Yes, my lady. He has been roughly treated.' She raised her hands in disbelief.

Lady Cecil closed her eyes and sighed. 'As a woman of no

standing, you cannot assist. Better you left London and never turned back. It would be safer.'

Discomfort. You know you are asking me to do what you would not. Just over a week ago, you said you would assist. Now you are frightened. You know something. 'No, my lady. He is a good and honest man who has worked to help Lord Cecil and now finds himself a prisoner.' She took a breath to calm her nerves in the face of Mildred's look of angry surprise. 'I'll not walk away from him.'

Mildred Cecil stood abruptly. 'Margaretta.' Her voice was harsh. 'I was genuine in my offer to assist when I go to tend to my sister's birthing but I cannot be associated with John Dee while at court.' Margaretta stood and stayed in silence, knowing it usually brought more words. It worked. 'These developments may put us all into the glare of his accusers.'

'What developments?'

'The children of George Ferrers were struck down yesterday by a mysterious affliction. One lies dead. The other lies blind.' She put her hands to her face. 'John Dee will be accused of both sorcery and witchcraft.'

CHAPTER FIFTY-FIVE

The North Road stretched out again. The kind man was driving and had given a few warm words, but nothing was enough to keep out the chill of fear. Margaretta held fast and looked out of the window as ever, trying to calm her stomach. This time the man took her to the gate of Hatfield House.

The same servant opened the kitchen door to her, 'Back again?'

'I bring fresh clothes for my master. I'll tarry only a few hours.'

The sour-faced woman just shrugged and let her in, gesturing to a side room and telling her she could wait there. Minutes later she returned. 'You'll have to wait. Your master is being seen by Lord Englefield and his men.' She raised her eyebrows to indicate this was not good news.

After waiting for over an hour, Margaretta could sit no longer. She was blocked from all feelings within the room. She ventured into the kitchen. 'May I help? I can work while I wait.'

The woman pointed to the scullery. 'If you've a good stomach there's laundry aplenty for you.'

Margaretta walked into the scullery and was hit by the acrid smell of vomit, blood and piss. In the corner was a bundle of sheets, shirts and braies all in various soakings of human mess. She filled a copper pan with water and began to heat it. On the shelf was a bowl of soapwort, which would help, and vinegar for the stains. So began the grim task of cleaning the proceeds of whatever was happening in this house.

She had been pummelling the linens in hot water for some time when a lad put his head around the door. 'I heard you're the servant of the strange one.' He giggled. 'The one who's put spells on the queen and king.'

Margaretta spun round. 'That's a stupid lie. My master would do no such thing.'

The boy shrugged. 'Only saying what I hear.' He looked Margaretta up and down. 'You're a pretty one.'

And you are gormless enough to be useful. 'Well see if you can keep me interested in the comings and goings of this house.'

He settled himself on an upturned pail. 'They have three now. Man called Benger and a fair one called Christopher. Beat 'im like a carpet, they did.' He made a gap-toothed grin.

Oh God help us. Thomas Benger and Christopher Careye. They are rounding up the people who were present in horoscoping Lady Elizabeth. How would they know of that? I feel as bilious as the person who wore these clothes. 'So what else, handsome man?' She gave a little wink and hid her distaste.

She learned that Doctor Dee had been under interrogation for over five hours each day. They used parchments that he was forced to look at; they used fists when required and he could scream louder than a pig facing the axe. 'So what do you think they'll do with my master?'

'Master Bourne says it depends on whether the lord can put sense into him.'

'They think God will make him speak?'

'No,' sniggered the lad, sidling up. 'They're bringing Lord Pembroke today. Your master will need God then.'

'My master used to work for him.'

'So he'll know that Lord Pembroke is not a man to say "no" to.'

As the lad sidled even closer, the woman looked around the

door. She beckoned to Margaretta. 'Your master is back in his
room. Be quick.'

The dark room smelled of sweat. Not the sweat of hard work,
but the sweet, cloying musk of fear. 'Doctor Dee?'

There was a groan from the corner and a shape moved on
the trestle bed. 'I am dead.'

Margaretta stepped across the flags and pulled John Dee to
sitting, ignoring the moans and protestations of pain.

His face was ashen white. More bruises were emerging and
his upper lip was swollen. She looked at his hands, which were
grazed across the knuckles and shaking. 'They know all. How
can they know so much?' He glanced at the door and dropped
his voice to a whisper. 'They know we went to Woodstock to
calculate Elizabeth's and Mary's horoscope, who attended, even
the predictions.' He looked up at Margaretta with fearful eyes.
'But it is worse.'

'What?'

'They accuse me of the murders.' He gulped. 'They have
all the details – the seals, the wool, the strange baubles, the way
they died, the tides I calculated. They know of the false letter
from Elizabeth. Also the letter in Spanish. The book hidden by
Cecil. Everything. They are calling it sorcery.' He gave a low
moan and put his head in his hands.

'They say it is the perfect disguise – the killer investigating
his own killings.'

'Would any of your students betray you?'

Dee shook his head, wincing. 'No. Christopher is no back-
biter and Thomas Benger was the organiser. Why would he
incriminate himself?'

He turned, his face even paler. 'They are rounding us up.'
Then he pulled up straight. 'Let them. I will not speak. I have
told them nothing.'

'Which is why they're bringing your old master here – Lord Herbert of Pembroke.'

Her master's head rocked back. 'Another animal of a man who will stop at nothing to get what he wants – whether it is the truth or not.' He clenched his hands. Then Dee stood and began to pace. 'But not even Pembroke can knit this together into sorcery. There is no connection between my horoscope for Elizabeth and the murders.'

'But there are certainly connections, doctor. Both Lord Cecil and Father Thomas recommended you to do the horoscopes, and the murders link to the Cecil house.'

Fear grew in his face. 'Did you hide my equipment?'

'Yes. Every book emptied. Mistress Katherine has been a good friend to you and Huw too. There was nothing left to find when the officers arrived.'

'Good, good. Then there is no evidence.'

'But there have been dark developments, doctor. The children of George Ferrers have been blighted. One is gone to heaven and the other left blind.'

Dee crumpled like a puppet whose strings have been cut. 'Dear God. I would never hurt a child. Even a child from Ferrers' loins.' He bent forward and put his head in his hands.

The guard rattled on the door. 'Time you went. One minute.' He slammed the door.

'One last thing, doctor. I pulled two cards from the pack.'

He turned slowly. 'You should never do such things alone.' He faltered. 'What did you pull?'

'The moon.'

Dee howled and sank to his knees. 'The worst card. Hidden enemies, deception, betrayal.' He turned to her with wild eyes. 'Did you see the creature coming from the lake?'

'Yes.'

'That signifies a hidden and vicious enemy who hides

behind a shell.' He gasped. 'We are being hunted by someone hidden. What was the second?'

'The two of pentangles.'

Dee gave a harsh laugh. 'George Ferrers. A fool juggling for money and raising a storm behind. How true.'

Chapter Fifty-Six

The sour woman softened further when Margaretta helped wash and stack the eating plates, and gave her a bowl of lavender water and a linen for John Dee's bruising. The surly guard believed her lie of having Bourne's permission to return.

Dee was back in the cot bed, his hands over his face. 'Let me bathe that cut, doctor.'

He sat up slowly with a groan and shook his head. 'I cannot even think.'

'Let us go through this step by step. What was the start?'

'Over a month ago, Christopher and I did the conjuring at Woodstock, though Lady Elizabeth was at Hampton Court to attend the queen in her lying in.'

'Father Thomas had recommended you to Cecil who advised Thomas Benger and Cousin Blanche to approach you. What next?'

'Ritualised deaths of Cecil's servants, Meldrew and the seal-maker. A false letter incriminating Elizabeth. There is a Spanish thread – the crucifixed wherryman, the thieving maid, Meldrew's wife, the letters.'

'And a new man in Cecil's house is Spanish, I am sure of it. He watches me.'

Dee turned, eyes bright. 'So the Flock is Spanish, but they are organised by someone. Someone who has sight of us.'

Margaretta chimed in. 'That takes us to Southwark. Tilly spoke of the bad wherrymen and the turn-faced shepherd.

Harriet has the mark of the crucifix on her skin, which she says is from a customer. And now Sam has said she has new yellow ribbons in her hair.'

Dee was jabbing at the air as the thoughts came together. 'Jonas went to Southwark, made friends...or enemies...and was secreting letters. The letter introducing the Spanish maid, the letter setting out Cecil's movements and the false letter from Lady Elizabeth are written by the same hand of a Spanish speaker. Someone who has sight in Cecil's house.' He stopped dead and stared at the window. 'You pulled the moon card. Someone hidden beneath the surface who can move unseen beneath the waters of life.' He turned to look at her. 'And my cards showed that all lead back to court.'

'So the unseen person can walk between Lord Cecil's house and court – and Southwark?'

Dee turned with a self-satisfied smile and came close, dropping his voice to a whisper. 'Everyone threatened here has helped and supported the Lady Elizabeth. I did her horoscope, as did Christopher, and Thomas Benger. William Cecil is her secret advisor and agent of her lands. He also secreted her book of thoughts on being king. If we break, she can be accused of plotting to become queen. She is the target.' He sighed loudly. 'Such treason means death and the end of the Tudor line – and all our chances go with her.'

'But what is the connection to Robert Meldrew?'

'I suspect it is through his Spanish wife.' Dee pointed at her. 'Go to the Savoy and see what you can find out.'

'Yes, doctor.'

Then a trumpeter heralded an arrival, followed by the clatter of many hooves on the cobbles. Dee turned to look at Margaretta, brows raised in alarm. 'Pembroke.'

Chapter Fifty-Seven

If it was not for the fine clothes, William Herbert, Lord Pembroke would be taken for a forest villain. Dark eyes, a strong but much battle-scarred face under a thatch of thick hair only receding slightly over his temples, which made him look more severe. He slammed through the door, closely followed by a small dog that stank as if it had been rolling in the piggery. They say dogs and their masters share looks and mind. The dog raised its hackles and bared sharp teeth.

John Dee stood his ground, giving only a short bow. 'My Lord. It has been many years.'

'Two years, Dee. Not long enough to distance your name from mine.' Lord Pembroke slammed the door shut, making the dog yap and growl. 'What the fuck have you done now?'

Dee pulled his hands behind his back and stood tall. 'I have done no wrong.'

'That's not what I'm told.' Pembroke started to walk around Dee in a circle, like a wolf circling a sheep, the cur-dog at his ankle. 'Conjuring horoscopes for the queen's sister. Conjuring the queen herself. Involvement in terrible murders with signs of witchcraft.' He stopped in front of Dee and thrust his face forward to be no more than inches away from the doctor. 'What strange plot are you involved in?'

'There is no plot. I was invited to cast a horoscope and then asked to investigate the murders. There is no connection.' Dee was digging his nails into the back of one hand behind his back in an attempt to stop shaking.

Suddenly the churlish dog trotted over to where Margaretta was hiding in the shadows, and started to bark. Pembroke looked up. 'Who the fuck is that? You have a doxy in here?'

She stepped forward, mouth set straight. 'I'm no doxy, sir. I'm the doctor's servant.'

Pembroke mumbled that it is a strange world where prisoners have servants, and turned back to Dee. 'No connection? That's not the story we're hearing. We're told that you're plotting the rise of the Lady Elizabeth.'

'How so?' yelped Dee.

'We're told that you first conjured her destiny then found a willing servant to take her notes. The boy Jonas. Being a servant of Elizabeth's closest friend, my Lord Cecil, he was the obvious choice.' The words 'my Lord Cecil' had a bite of sarcasm. 'When the boy became loose-tongued, he was dispatched in the Thames.' He leaned forward, lowering his voice to a growl. 'Is that true?'

'No,' croaked John Dee, his voice almost strangled. 'And how would that explain the other killings?'

'The man Luke – he was looking for Jonas's murderer: you. Robert Meldrew, the poor bastard, had seen you put the bodies in the water. The Southwark man had made your false seals.'

'What? Who the devil has made up this fancy tale? None of this is true.'

'Jonas indeed had a letter on him, did he not?'

'Yes, but I found it when I inspected the body.'

'No, Dee. You knew where to look for it.' Pembroke made a little cackle. 'You're shaking, man, and your voice squeaks like a mouse in a trap of its own making.'

'Who says this?'

'Thomas Prideaux and Ferrers. And now you extend your lewd practices.' He jabbed a finger towards Dee's eyes, making him blink. 'Blighting and blinding children. Low even for you, Dee. Is your thirst for court so strong?'

Dee swallowed and spoke slowly, evidently trying to quell the terror. 'I have done no harm to any person. I mean no harm to our queen. I only sought to help Lord Cecil in investigating the demise of his staff. I would not, could not, hurt any child. As for this man Prideaux. Who is he? I do not know him, nor him me.'

'Oh, he knows all about you, Dee. It is he who gives all the detail.'

Fear. Anger mixed with fear. You fear reputation. It must be you, sir, for I cannot feel my master's mind. You think of your money and power.

Pembroke snarled. 'Frankly, I care little for who has left this mortal coil. But it does little for my standing if a former person of my staff faces a treasonable end.' He made a slicing motion across his throat, making Dee step back in alarm. 'I want this stopped.' Pembroke jabbed the finger in Dee's face again. 'This has gone as high as Bishop Bonner. You'll likely face the Court of Star Chamber. I suggest you weep on the cross and get his favour. That might save all of us connected to you.'

'But I have done nothing –'

'I care not!' screamed the other man, spittle flying from his lips into the face of John Dee. 'I tell you now. Seek Bonner's sanctuary by saying anything you need to.' He hissed his last words. 'And keep my name clean of this.'

Pembroke turned on his heel and wrenched open the door, commanding the dog to follow. He walked out, slammed the oak shut and left them in silence. Dee gave a long wail and sank to his knees.

John Dee sat on the cot, rocking like a terrified child, repeating over and over that he would die.

Margaretta took his shoulders and shook him. 'Stop this, doctor. We have to think quickly. Lord Pembroke will say I'm here.'

He looked up, tears in his eyes. 'I cannot think. No thought will come. The tale presented by Pembroke all threads together, but it is a web of lies.' He gulped. 'Somebody can see into everything. They are close and yet hidden.'

'What can we do to uncover them?'

He sighed. 'Nothing from here. I have none of my equipment.' He looked up, eyes bright. 'Can you secret it here? Can you bring my cards and the red crystal?'

She gulped. 'That is dangerous, doctor.' He stared at her, his eyes pleading.

I cannot leave you in this fear, though I feel my heart quake at the thought. God help me. 'Yes. I'll return tomorrow and go to the Savoy on the way.' She squeezed his arm. 'We'll find your creature from the lake, doctor.'

But the door opened. They turned to see Francis Englefield in the door, his shoulders filling the gap. He looked Margaretta up and down, his eyes staying too long on her breasts. He raised a finger and pointed at her. 'I told you only five minutes yesterday. Why are you back?' The voice was cold and threatening.

Anger. You feel foolish. You fear losing control and looking as if you are not in command.

'I was just –'

'Enough,' was the shout. 'Get out of here. Go home. And do not return.' The finger swivelled towards Dee. 'Your master is my business now. And you have no business here.'

Back at the Constables' house, Katherine was waiting up and in agitation. 'What has happened to John?'

'Troubling news, mistress. He is accused of conjuring,

sorcery and even the killing of men and children. But it's all lies.'

Katherine gave a little cry and sat down heavily, her hand going to her throat. 'What will become of him?' Her lower lip began to tremble. 'My poor John.'

'I can think of only one person. I'll go to Lady Cecil in the morning. Ask for help. She must go to court to assist her sister. One accuser is a court man, Thomas Prideaux.'

Katherine frowned. 'I know that name.' Her eyes went to the ceiling as she tried to recall. 'Why, yes. The man sent to board up John's office.' She nodded excitedly. 'He said, "I am Thomas Prideaux, come to seal the lair of John Dee." The rough beast. Calling it a lair indeed.'

'Did he say anything else?'

'Not much I understood.' She crossed her arms in indignation. 'Rummaged through the desk he did and then upturned the brass globes like a ruffian. Shouted something strange. Then the hammering started.'

'Something strange?'

'Indeed,' said Katherine. 'I understand none of these swarthy Spaniards.'

Chapter Fifty-Eight

Sam pulled into the bank and winked. 'I knew you couldn't ignore me for long.' Then he looked serious. 'You look terrible tired, missy.'

Margaretta clambered aboard. 'My master is in trouble, Sam. Arrested.'

Sam grimaced. 'Can I help?'

Margaretta gave a cynical smile. 'Better you use your energy to step out with Lottie.'

'You was right about her sweet nature, missy.'

Margaretta leaned forward. 'If you dare take advantage of it, I'll put a Welsh spell on you.'

His eyes opened wide. 'What will it do?'

'Make you so seasick that you could not row the width of the river to see her.'

He looked puzzled then brightened. 'No matter. Master Tovey is taking a carriage to Wimbledon this very Sunday.' He grinned. 'I can ride there.' He leaned forward conspiratorially. 'Goodwife has told him that no man has ever shown her the countryside in a carriage.' Sam rolled his eyes. 'I have been up since the break of day polishing every corner. Then I had to put cushions in it. Good enough for Queen Mary, it is.'

I feel your warmth. Your feelings are as if for a father. 'Do you have a family in Bristol, Sam?'

She regretted asking as his eyes clouded. 'No, missy. Fire. I rose in the morning, helped my father from his bed to his spindle, kissed my mam and little sister goodbye and by evening I was all alone.' The boy looked away, biting at his bottom lip.

'I'm sorry, Sam. I didn't mean to make you recall sadness.'

Sam straightened up and sniffed, forcing himself to smile. 'Lottie and I are much alike. For she is all alone too.'

Oh, that pain in my heart again.

Sam pointed behind her. 'Here we are, missy. The Savoy.' He wrinkled his forehead. 'Why are you stopping here?'

'Clues, Sam.' She jumped out. 'Will you wait to take me on to Wimbledon?'

He nodded and scudded down to the bottom of the boat. 'Time to catch up on the sleep I lost polishing.'

The door opened, revealing the face of the nurse who had told Margaretta about the funeral. 'You again, child?'

As if God was trying to help, the heavens opened, and fat drops of rain began to fall. The old nurse beckoned her in and slammed the door to stop the wet from getting onto her wooden floor. She pointed down the corridor. 'Down there, child. Come warm yourself.'

'My master borrowed two books from the office here and wonders if they should be returned to Mistress Meldrew.'

'That's surely thoughtful.' The nurse sat and sighed. 'Maybe we should wait a while before asking her to make any decision. The poor woman is surely in distress.'

Margaretta affected an innocent voice. 'I noticed she was Spanish – very beautiful.'

'Yes, indeed. A beautiful nature too. Just like the children.'

'But now she's alone in a strange country. I wonder what she'll do.'

'I'm sure her brother will take care of them. Thomas has a good position at court.'

'Thomas?'

The nurse gave a start. 'Why the surprise, child? It's a common name.'

Margaretta feigned self-depreciation. 'I'm a fool. It's just not a Spanish name.'

'No, but the family name is surely not of these parts.'

'Oh, I love Spanish names. What is it?'

The nurse faltered. 'I can't recall.' She looked up and knitted her brows as she searched her mind.

You are seeing his face. Dark, dark eyes. In your mind, you are working through the alphabet. A B C D. No it's more like a T. D. No. P. The name starts with a P.

'Prideaux?'

The nurse stared at her. 'How did you know that, child?'

Sam was soaked and scowling. 'What took so long?'

'I'm sorry, Sam.' She gave no explanation. He had already been hurt in this terrible mess. 'Now, row upriver to where I can get to Wimbledon.'

He looked up at the dark sky. 'It's going to fall again in buckets. Why not come Sunday when you can jump on the back of the carriage? Master Tovey will be willing.'

'I'm in a rush, Sam.' She smiled. 'Surely it's worth the extra fare so you can save to buy Lottie a ribbon.'

Sam grinned. 'Good thinking, missy.' Then he frowned. 'Don't look so sad.'

Putney Steps were slick with rain by the time they pulled in, and Margaretta was soaked to the skin. Sam looked concerned. 'You'll be as cold as ice by the time you arrive.' He pointed to the left. 'You'll find a small market down the road and men driving back to Wimbledon. They'll let you sit on a cart for nothing.' He winked. 'Especially if you smile at them.'

'Thank you, Sam.' She paused. 'Shall I tell Lottie you'll be on the carriage?'

'Nah. Let it be a surprise, missy.' He blushed. 'I love the way she squeaks when she's excited. Like a little mouse finding a truckle of cheese. Want to hear it myself.'

Margaretta smiled. 'She's a lucky girl, Sam.'

Oh, this hurts.

Wimbledon Manor was a strange place, obviously built in sections with different types of windows and roofs. Margaretta stopped in the wide front courtyard, trying to see the servants' door.

'Who are you?' The voice was harsh, unkind.

Margaretta spun round to a youth, maybe thirteen years old. Yet his manner was much older as he stared down his nose at her. There was something familiar about him. The eyes were grey, face thin, hands long and elegant.

She gave a small curtsey. 'Margaretta Morgan. I've come to see Lady Cecil.'

The youth gave a harsh laugh. 'Good luck.'

'Are you of the household?'

He glared at her. 'I *am* the household.' He emphasised the word 'am' with a bark in his voice. 'I am Tommy Cecil.'

'Forgive me. I forgot Lord Cecil had a son.'

Tommy snorted through his nose and made a cynical smile. 'So has Lord Cecil.' He turned away and walked into the copse of trees at the side of the house, calling over his shoulder, 'Servants' doors are on the left side of the house.'

What terrible pain you feel. Anger at the world, even God. Yet you have all this. But something is missing. You are an unloved child. And there can be no deeper pain. I know it myself.

Lottie raced across the kitchen and threw her skinny arms

around Margaretta, ignoring Goodwife's barking to stay at her chores. 'Oh, Margaretta I thought I wouldn't see you again.' The child clung tight and Margaretta held her back. *You poor child. You so fear being left.*

Goodwife raised her eyebrows. 'You grace us with your presence again, Margaretta.'

'I've been sent by my master to speak with Lady Cecil.'

The older woman frowned. 'Then you have wasted your journey, girl. Lady Cecil is at court with her sister.' Goodwife's face clouded. 'The poor woman.'

Sadness, Grief. You feel the sadness of another woman. You cannot find the energy to be angry, such is your preoccupation with someone's sadness. It reminds you of what you've never had.

'What's happened?'

Goodwife's lips were pulled tight and straight, leaking her sadness. 'The poor woman gave birth to a girl…and held her just minutes before the Lord took her back.'

The kitchen went quiet. *Sad memories here.* 'I think Lady Cecil also lost a baby girl.'

Goodwife nodded. Were those tears in her eyes? 'Yes, but loyalty to her sister helps her overcome the memories.' The woman turned away. 'We all pray that God will smile on her again.' She sighed. 'May he smile on both of them.'

'When is Lady Cecil due back?'

Goodwife bridled. 'We do not question, girl.' Then a softening. 'She is gone some days. Your message must wait.'

It was well after dark when Margaretta crept through the door of the Constables' house in St Dunstan's. There was no cart going back into London, it being a Friday and people going home for their fish supper. She had walked all seven miles and was weary to her bones. Goodwife had set her to work sorting linens with Lottie and then dusting every corner of the bedrooms. Lottie had chirruped for hours. She learned the house was being upgraded by Lord Cecil's son, Tommy, a miserable boy, soured by the disdain of his father. Lottie had looked sad. 'I think he's just mourning the fact that his father is so cold to him when he is warm to others. Even Goodwife has said he might be a good boy inside. But he is all shut away.' Then there was talk of Sam. Margaretta's news that he had rowed her to Putney brought a squeak of delight which quickly subsided to worry she would not see him again. Margaretta had bitten her lip and smiled to herself, imagining Lottie's reaction when Master Tovey's carriage arrived in the courtyard. But Lottie had said something else. 'Lady Cecil was surely glad to go to court, no matter the sadness. She will seek to say that Lord Cecil is clean of any bad rumour.'

So Mildred Cecil was as much a politician as her husband.

CHAPTER FIFTY-NINE

Saturday morning and Mam shambled into the kitchen, the kitten under her arm. 'For pity's sake, Mam. You cannot keep secreting that cat away from Mistress Katherine.'

Her mother scowled and sat down with a 'huh' sound before pulling the grey shawl around herself and the kitten. 'I showed her how to make its belly empty.' A small smile spread across Mam's face. 'Screamed at the stink, she did.'

Margaretta stood with her hands on her hips. 'So, you've frightened Mistress Katherine with her own pet.'

Mam scowled, shrugged, kissed the kitten on its head and mumbled, 'Cadi needs caring for.'

'Cadi? The kitten is called DeeDee.'

'Foolish name. Cadi didn't like it.'

There was relief when Huw came in. He was stepping side to side, shaking his head. 'Bad man here. Hurt Huw.' The boy pointed to the door. 'Same man Susan's house. Bad arm.'

Margaretta ran to the door. No one. She went out into the street. Empty. She sensed Huw at her shoulder and turned. 'Where did you see him, Huw?'

He pointed across the street. 'Went to river. Wherry.'

Back in the house, Margaretta tried to quell her nerves. She was alone in all this. When she took the newly baked bread, cheese and small beer to the Constables for their breakfast, there was an icy atmosphere in the solar room. Katherine was staring out of the window, her mouth pursed into a red button. Master Constable was slumped in his chair, his hair dishevelled. He raised rheumy eyes and a loud belch of stale wine escaped him, making his wife tut and flap her hands.

He pointed a finger. 'I am hearing more rumours about our house guest. People are saying John Dee and his pupil are sorcerers.' He shook his head. 'They say he practised his dark arts here in this house.'

Oh, God. You are full of concern. So is the mistress. But the feelings are different. She feels for Doctor Dee. You feel concern that your business will go down. You think of the doctor's father. You recall the fall from money to disgrace. It makes your gut churn. 'Those rumours are foolish, master.' She looked at Katherine.

The other woman took her cue and joined the conversation. 'Indeed, the girl is right. There is nothing in John's office to incriminate him.'

Master Constable's eyes widened. 'You went in after the court men boarded the door?' His voice betrayed alarm. Katherine looked at Margaretta, anxious.

'I spend much time there, sir. I assured Mistress Katherine.' She gave a small smile to hide the lie.

The man was satisfied and turned his attention to the bread, breaking it roughly and stuffing it into his mouth with no attention to manners. Between mouthfuls, as Margaretta poured the beer and sliced some cheese for Katherine, he announced: 'They say the Privy Council has sent a list of questions. Set by Bishop Bonner, they say. If they don't like the answers then John and his companions face the Star Chamber.' He shook his head. 'God help my old friend's son. I fear he has little time left on this earth.'

Katherine gave a little cry and put her hand across her mouth. Then there was only silence.

And so began days of rumour and fear.

Every evening Master Constable returned with ever-worsening tales of John Dee's demise and Katherine went deeper into despair. He seemed not to notice that his wife was crying for love and not a concern for the reputation of her house.

When Margaretta went for provisions, she faced the calls of the hawkers and fishwives. 'Heard from the devil today? How's the sorcerer?' Children would ask if she could fly on a broom and older, more moneyed merchants turned their backs as she walked by. No one wanted to be seen selling their wares to a condemned man's maid, especially when that man was under the glare of Bishop Bonner. 'That's the way to the pyre,' said one man. 'And Bonner likes your friends to fry with you.'

Soon, the Leadenhall Market hummed with rumours that John Dee had confessed. People went quiet and stared at her as she walked past the stalls, but she could hear the muttered gossip and felt their mix of pity and disdain. Sometimes a call would come from the crowd. 'It's the warlock's maid. Don't meet her eye if you want to keep your soul.' The rougher of the fishwives would spit at the ground as she passed by.

The worst day was Sunday. Margaretta was already tired after a night of black thoughts and Mam snoring. Huw was agitated again, saying the man was back. She did not know if it was true or his fear making magic in his mind, for each time she ran to the street, there was no flash of a silver crucifix.

But that morning, the atmosphere was different. Now they parted and moved away from her. One child shouted that the witch was coming and threw a stone before scampering away between the legs of the adults. Some people glared, others made the sign of the cross. Only one person looked at her. It was Master Constable. He walked across the square holding a parchment which he pressed into her hand as he growled, 'John Dee will leave my house even if he escapes the pyre.' His face was dark with fury.

The pamphlet was roughly written and obviously one of those hastily prepared overnight in secret rooms with illicit printing machines. She looked at it and her heart sank.

Found this day in the churchyard of St Dunstan's, a horrible effigy of our sovereign with belly large and pricked with pins.

Evile spells are abounded. The great ambassador of the French is today proclaiming that all evile emanates from the Englishman John Dee and his vile conspirators who control the devil.

God save our Queen from the hand of evile and magick.

She looked up to see that a crowd had gathered in a circle. 'It's not true. He's done nothing.'

'So why is there an effigy of the queen found in a church, witch?' challenged a young man.

A woman shouted out of the crowd: 'He magicked it here from Hatfield. Only a warlock could do such a thing.' She pointed at Margaretta. 'Or did you put it there for him?'

In seconds they were baying and a fish head flew through the air, hitting her on the cheek.

Hate and fear. Hate and fear. Oh, God. They are readying to move.

Margaretta ran. As she did a man stepped aside. She saw a grin of rotten teeth and a flash of silver from his neck before she disappeared beyond the crowd.

CHAPTER SIXTY

Monday morning and the urchin demanded an extra ha'penny for running to find Sam, declaring, 'Witches have to pay more.'

At last, he arrived, smiling and in good cheer. But his face changed as he pulled into the bank. 'You look sad, missy.'

Margaretta sat heavily. 'Things get worse for my master – and so for me, Sam.' She sniffed and sniffed and swiped away the tears. 'People think I am part of his ill-doing, not that he has done any wrong. I need to look for a new home.'

Sam leaned forward and patted her knee, his face softening in sympathy.

Dada would do that when I was little. He would pat me and tell me to talk to God and ask for better times. I would believe him. But I have done that and it only gets worse. It seemed that such little acts of kindness died with him. I want my dada. I want you, Sam.

'God's teeth, missy. Where are these tears coming from?'

Margaretta swiped at the salty rivulets falling down her cheeks and sniffed loudly. 'Take no notice. I'm being a baby.' She took in a deep breath and regretted it. The Thames was reeking this morning as the breweries in Southwark emptied their vats of old hops ready for a new week of brewing. 'Tell me about the carriage ride.'

Instantly Sam was back to grinning and his chest swelled. 'I drove the carriage, missy. Reckon I could have a second job doing that. I had the horse well driven and the carriage steady.'

'Was Lady Cecil back from court?'

The boy frowned. 'I thought you would be more interested in what a nice day we had.' Getting no response except a hopeful face, he nodded. 'Yesterday evening.'

He started to tell her about his walk in the lanes with Lottie, but Margaretta was too concerned with getting help.

'Take me to Putney Steps, Sam. Quick as you can.'

It was after midday by the time Margaretta jumped off a cart, on which she had inveigled a ride from Putney Market. She offered the carter a ha'penny but he refused, saying he could not take money from a woman who weeps.

Was that you, Dada? Coming through the veil to make me feel a little better?

Tommy Cecil was in the garden again, this time talking to a man with a sheaf of drawings, and pointing at the house turrets. As she drew closer, she could hear the hard tones of the young man. 'The new part is mine. I want no connecting doors.'

Hearing footsteps on the gravel he turned abruptly. 'You again?'

She gave a little curtsey. 'I come to speak with your stepmother.'

His face clouded. 'You mean Lady Cecil.' He chewed at his bottom lip. 'She is no mother to me.'

Sadness again. Pain. You've never known the kindness of a mother. Only the harshness of a bitter parent who seems not to like you. We are so far apart, you and I. You rich, me poor. Yet we share much.

As if he felt her sympathy, Tommy Cecil blushed, nodded to the servant's door and turned back to the architect without another word to Margaretta.

The kitchen was like a beehive. Servants flying around, cook sweating over her pots and Goodwife barking orders. Seeing Margaretta at the door she gave a little frown, but no glower. 'Back again, Margaretta?'

Lottie shrieked and flew across the room to clasp her friend and chatter about her Sunday walk. Goodwife shook her head, though there was a hint of a smile.

Excitement. You think of yesterday. Your heart flutters like a young girl's. Even Lottie amuses you today.

She nodded to Margaretta. 'You look as if you have had a hard few days, child. You may eat here with us.'

Margaretta decided to bide her time before asking to see Lady Cecil. She settled at the table, with Lottie snuggling up. The walk with Sam was covered in great detail, even to the number of late lambs in the field.

'For Sam can count,' she announced proudly. Then she leaned closer. 'And there was a miracle yesterday, Margaretta. Something I never would have even dared pray for.'

'What?'

They were silenced by Goodwife's look and set back to their pottage, but little Lottie could not hold her tongue. 'Master Tovey kissed Goodwife on the cheek.'

A sudden quip from Goodwife rattled along the table. 'You look as if Lottie has put a pin in your leg, Margaretta. What does she say that is such a surprise?'

Lottie gave a squeak but Goodwife simply smiled and looked away. Lottie was not a quiet whisperer and Goodwife had good ears.

'Has Father Thomas visited Wimbledon, Goodwife?' Margaretta enquired.

The older woman looked thoughtful. 'Actually, no. We have not seen the good Father for days.' She made a little frown and muttered, 'Strange.'

The dishes away, Margaretta carefully made her plea. 'May I speak with Lady Cecil? It's about my master.'

'No, child.' Goodwife started to walk away. 'Such sadness takes a toll on the body and the mind. This is no time for discussing other people's woes.'

So Goodwife had heard of the doctor's arrest.

Oh my Lord. What now? Lady Cecil is my only hope. And even that is slim.

After saying her goodbyes and hugging Lottie with a promise to come back soon, Margaretta closed the door behind her. The garden was empty, yet she sensed someone.

Frustration. Anger. Where are you?

There he was. Tommy Cecil, sitting on a fallen trunk in the copse, hunched over his papers. Margaretta stepped across the grass. 'Master Cecil, would you please help me?'

The cold grey eyes looked up slowly. 'Why?'

'I came here to see your...I mean Lady Cecil.' She gave a little smile in an attempt to show him some warmth, but his face remained unreadable. 'But Goodwife Barker says she's not to be disturbed.'

'Then that is your answer,' he snapped and looked back to his drawings.

'Please. I have no one who can help me. I am quite alone.'

He looked up, slowly.

She did not give him time to think of another rejection. 'It's business concerning a friend of your father.'

Instant anger. But also sadness. You can never please him. Never get a word of praise. That is why you are working so hard on this house. Maybe he will say you've done well. Just once. 'I think your father would be pleased to have his friend aided.'

Tommy Cecil sighed and put his papers under a stone. 'Sit on that seat under the oak tree,' he commanded, pointing to a tree in the middle of the lawn. 'If she looks out of the window, happens to see you, and calls you in, then you cannot be in trouble with Dogwife.' He walked towards the house, apparently ignoring her call of gratitude. But the feeling changed. *Hope.*

Minutes later, a window was pushed open and Mildred Cecil looked out. 'Margaretta? Come in, child. Tommy will let you through the front door.' She put her finger to her lips.

Lady Cecil's eyes were dull and dark circles showed beneath them. Her face was paler than before and her usual energy muted. She sat. 'I suppose you come about John.'

'Yes, my lady. He's much troubled. I have not been able to see him since Lord Englefield sent me away with a command not to return. It is days now.'

Mildred Cecil rose and moved to the door. 'Well, John will be even more troubled now.' She turned, her eyes sad. 'Court is full of the news. The Privy Council is not satisfied with the answers to their questions.'

Margaretta stood. 'I need to find the yellow sheep. 'You once said that you would help. Will you do that?'

Mildred turned away. 'I cannot get involved, Margaretta. My husband's name cannot be associated with treason.'

'There has been no treason.'

'That is not the view of the Privy Council, Margaretta.' She shuddered and her hand flew to her throat. 'They have given licence for torture. John goes to the Tower tomorrow.'

Chapter Sixty-One

Dawn broke on a new June day. Margaretta must have looked terrible. Even Mam offered to stir a pot and Huw kept stepping from foot to foot and looking at her face with concern. Katherine Constable was in her sitting room, picking at an embroidery, tutting at her mistakes. Her face fell when she saw Margaretta's expression.

'What has happened? You look so tired.'

'They have given orders to torture Doctor Dee.'

Katherine gave a sharp cry and dropped her linen, the needle making a tiny rattle on the wooden floor. 'For why?'

'Because torture makes men speak of what they have not done and don't know, mistress. They are trying to make him confess to a falsity.'

Katherine's hand went to her ample bosom. 'What can we do?' Then she looked alarmed. 'Without my husband knowing.'

'I'll go to the Tower.'

Katherine gasped and clasped her hands to her throat. 'But it is a terrible place. They say you never come out alive.'

'That's not true. Merchants come and go every day. So do men of court. Anyway, I have to help the doctor.'

Katherine gulped. 'Do you need more money?'

'Yes…and a petticoat onto which I can sew a secret pocket to put under my sister's dress.'

At the Tower, the guard stared at his ledger. 'I have no note that visitors are to be admitted.'

'But Lord Englefield told me to attend to cousin John and bring him to his senses.' She copied the voice of Lady Cecil – piety mixed with unquestioned confidence. 'Are you suggesting I am to be turned away?'

My, what a difference a dress makes. If I were here in my kitchen brown, you would be kicking my backside out of your door with a stream of abuse to carry me further. But a bit of blue silk, a Spanish hood and a purse of coin, helped by a confident tongue and you are flustering like a chicken facing a fox.

'Er, no. Your name please, my lady?' The guard scratched at his chin, still staring at his ledger.

'As I said. Cousin to Doctor John Dee.' She tapped her toe to show impatience. 'How many times do we need to go around this circus ring?'

It worked. The gates were opened with a terrible clang of bars being raised. A man was called. 'Take the lady to prisoner nought nought seven. He's in the Salt Tower.' They walked along the cobble path towards the tower, rising grey and terrifying into the blue sky. Above them, soldiers walked the battlements, pikes ready to pierce any escapee. She was walked through a dark door and into a small round room with arched slit windows. The man muttered his apologies for the rank smell. 'It's always bad in summer, lady. I think the heat does make the stench of fear grow.'

She was led up spiral stairs of granite and waited, trembling as the man sorted through a ring of keys. The door was opened and the cell guard gestured her in. 'We allow only half of an hour a visit, lady.'

Margaretta turned her eye on the man who was evidently an old soldier from the broken nose and scars across his face. He stank of wine and chicken fat. 'I will require an hour. See Lord

Englefield if you need confirmation.' She almost laughed at the voice she used.

But amusement lasted only a second as he snarled back: 'I don't give a rat's arse if Jesus Christ sent you, lady. You have only half of an hour.'

The cell was dark and dank. One candle burned on a small table in the middle of the cell, casting a low light. Canvas was hanging over the slit windows, blotting out the light of day. An acrid, musty smell rose from the floor. Rats. John Dee was at the far side of the room, on a low cot bed. As she approached, Margaretta could smell mould from the paltry hay mattress. A cough from behind made her spin round. There was a crouched figure on the floor, face in the shadows. 'I apologise if I frightened you,' came a croaked voice.

She looked back to John Dee, who pointed at the man across the cell. 'This is Barthelet Green. Detained for heresy. It appears they group prisoners by accusation.' He shook his head. 'Cannot stand because of what they have done to him.'

Margaretta walked towards the man in the corner, picking up the candle. As she approached her stomach lurched. He was broken. Arms hung loose and the legs protruded out at a strange angle. He just about managed to raise his head from a body slumped against the damp wall. He gave a wan smile.

'What did they do to you, sir?'

'The rack, child.'

As he tried to raise his hand, the door crashed open and the guard shouted, 'Calling Barthelet Green for interrogation.' Then a sneering laugh. 'It's the scavenger's daughter today, heretic. Your eyes and ears will be bleeding in an hour.'

The man moaned. More the moan of a tortured animal than a man, followed by the sound and smell of his bladder giving way in panic. Margaretta turned away to hide her horror. Two men hauled him upright, ignoring the scream. One complained that he would be soaked and then they started to drag their prey towards the door. Another scream and the door slammed shut.

In the other corner, John Dee began to cry. 'What if they do the same to me?'

'Come now, doctor, there is no time for weeping.' Margaretta pulled his shoulders up and looked straight into his eyes. 'We have to work quickly. Only half an hour.'

She turned away and pulled up her skirts. From Katherine's pocketed petticoat she pulled the crystals and the cards. 'Here. Now let us seek answers.'

With trembling hands, Dee pointed to the candle. 'We will need that.' Then he placed the crystals on the floor, putting the candle between them. Slowly, he opened the box of cards and muttered a prayer in the old language, their language, and raised his eyes to the ceiling as if imploring God, or maybe the gods, to come and give answers. With a deep breath he spread the cards in a wide arc, the picture sides down. 'Tell me of my enemies,' he rasped, and started to select the cards.

One by one he pulled them from the arc, picture side up, until he had created a cross. When five were chosen, he groaned. 'God help us.'

'What do they tell you, doctor?'

He pointed to the central card. It depicted a young man, a magician, conjuring with arms open, a double halo above his head, vines growing at his feet, and a wary smile on his face. 'This is me. It is the card of looking forward, new beginnings, and most of all, hoping for a miracle.'

He moved to the card to the left. The high priestess. 'She has the scythe at her feet, pomegranates at her head, the cross of faith at her heart, the TORA in her hands. She understands everything and nothing. Intuition and always seeing.' He looked up at Margaretta. 'This is you.'

'But that card on the other side of you? The devil?'

John Dee made a little whimper, then controlled himself and straightened his back. 'This means entrapment, others having the upper hand, bad faith and bad speaking against truth. Intended evil.' Dee sighed. 'This is the current condition.'

'So, look to the card below. What is that?'

John Dee traced down. 'The emperor again. A man bent on power. Whoever this depicts is the centre of this.' He tapped the sheep heads on the throne. 'Yellow wool.'

'And the lowest card.'

'The hermit. It supports the other cards. This is the keystone in the cross. He is the hidden man, only half seen. He shines a light and yet you cannot see his face. This card often means the final stage of an endeavour.' John Dee swayed back and looked to Margaretta. 'The other name for this card is the shepherd and he is the root and foundation of this mess.'

Margaretta started to pace. 'The turn-face shepherd again.' She stopped. 'I need to go back to Southwark and find that face.'

John Dee was about to answer when footsteps came from the stairs. Margaretta grabbed the cards and crystal and secreted them in her petticoat just as the door crashed open and the guard yelled, 'Time up!'

She nodded and turned to leave, hearing Dee's whisper of, 'Help me.'

She held up the penny to glint in the candlelight. 'I wish to see the prisoner Christopher Careye.'

A sneer. 'Tuppence a visit. One minute.'

'*Mochyn.*' Pig.

'He's over in the Beauchamp Tower, even though he's no noble. Keep 'em well distant, we do.' He grinned, revealing a row of rotting teeth. The smell hit her.

'*Mochyn drewi,*' she muttered. Stinking pig.

'What you saying?'

'I'm saying what a good man you are.'

She was only allowed to speak through the grille on the door. Christopher looked through, his face cut and dirt on his cheeks. 'You are k-kind to come, Margaretta.'

She crooked her finger to tell him to listen closely and whispered: 'Have faith. The doctor is pulling together clues. I go to Southwark now to find the face of the person behind this. Say nothing. No matter what they do.'

The man nodded miserably and pushed his fingers through the bars. 'Will you take my hand, Margaretta?' Tears came into his eyes. 'If I never see you again, p-please know my feelings are warm. I will say nothing to harm you.'

She wound her fingers into his and tried to smile. 'You're a good man, Christopher. Have trust.'

The gaoler yelled and their grasp broke.

Chapter Sixty-Two

'Please, Harriet. Don't walk away. I need your help.'

The woman turned, her hare lip curling to a vicious snarl. 'I told you to stay away.'

'People are about to lose their lives. You're in danger too – and Tilly.'

Harriet huffed and started marching away. 'I can look after meself and Tilly. See this yellow ribbon? It makes me safe. That's what they say.' She jabbed her finger over her shoulder. 'Now be away before you 'ave me in trouble.'

'But more will die, Harriet.'

There was nothing to lose except her teeth if Harriet decided to pelt her one. And so Margaretta trotted after the other woman, pulling at her arm. Harriet was speeding up as she turned into Foul Lane and past the Tabard Inn. She hissed, 'Go away,' through the side of her mouth but not another word. She swerved sideways and through the door of the doxy house and tried to slam it shut, but Margaretta was too fast and shoved the closing wood so hard it went back hard on Harriet's arm and led to a stream of cussing. But Margaretta was in. The smell of stale wine and cheap perfume was overwhelming.

'Please, Harriet. My master will die and he is a good man. He's only ever tried to find out why Jonas and Luke were killed.'

'Then he's a fool!' shouted Harriet.

'Why is you shouting, Mammie?' It was Tilly standing in a doorway halfway along the dark corridor, which led to the back of the house. Her big eyes shone bright and a smile lit her face as she ran to her mother to be picked up and kissed. 'Madge made me a dolly.' She turned to stare at Margaretta. 'Hello. You said I was pretty.'

'That's right, Tilly. Like a princess.'

The child smiled, shyly. 'Mammie said I'm never to speak of the turn-face shepherd again.' Her little face fell as her mother snapped at her to hold her tongue. She was bounced back on her feet and told to go back to Madge.

'Harriet, I know you're frightened. So am I. Please will you just listen to me?'

The woman sighed in resignation. 'I need a beaker of wine. You can tell us all if you can lower yourself to our company.' With that, she marched ahead.

The room was filled with three other women, two lying on cot beds looking as if they had been knocked out. They reeked of wine. The third was in a chair, rocking Tilly, who was sniffing back her tears and clutching a rag doll. It had yellow wool as hair. This woman was older and terribly scarred by the pox. Much of her nose was eaten away and one eye half-closed and blind. She raised her eyebrows as Margaretta walked in.

'Not sure we have room for more business in this house, dearie. Better you go down to Bessie's. She needs a new girl to replace the one who ran off with the Dutchman.'

Harriet laughed and pushed the other woman's arm, before picking up Tilly and hugging her tight. 'She's no doxy, Madge. Come for information, she has. Thinks she can save her master by putting us in line of trouble.' She picked up a cup of coins and rattled it. 'Not much business today then, old girl?'

'Nah, but he were old and grateful,' cackled Madge. She nodded at the two sleeping women. 'They've had a hard morning. Ship of Frenchies moored up at dawn.' She looked back at Margaretta. "Scuse us talking business, miss.' She cackled again.

You speak like this to cover your embarrassment. You think I look down on you. You laugh at yourself to cover the pain. 'No matter, Mistress Madge. I'm grateful to be let in to speak with you.'

Madge took in a sharp breath as if shocked at the respect, nodded to the seat, and offered a glass of cheap wine in a filthy beaker, only to down it in one when it was refused. 'So, what do you want?'

Margaretta nodded at Tilly who was immediately put down and shooed out to play in the back yard.

'Go on then,' snapped Harriet. 'But the answer is no.'

'My master is facing death in the Tower because he tried to find the killer of Jonas and Luke. The same people killed a good man called Robert Meldrew at the Savoy, then Sniffer Simeon, and they also beat my brother.' She looked at Harriet. 'I think the man who hurt your chest with his crucifix had a wounded arm.' Harriet nodded silently.

Margaretta continued. 'Everyone killed died terribly and was bound with yellow wool and a woollen bauble that looks like a sheep.'

Harriet and Madge looked at each other. 'That is how Simeon and his hound were found,' murmured Harriet.

'Because he had helped the killers by making false seals. We know there is a Spanish connection, and it all goes back to a man who is some kind of shepherd.' She nodded towards the door through which Tilly had run. 'Your little girl spoke of a turn-face shepherd.' Then she took a risk of saying too much. 'We think he means harm to the Lady Elizabeth and that those men died for knowing too much.'

The atmosphere chilled as Harriet and Madge looked at each other. 'What's it got to do with us? We know no plot,' insisted Madge, her voice going high with anxiety.

'Of course not, but if you could get me into the inn and point out the turn-face shepherd, then I know who to describe to my master. That's all I want.' She leaned forward. 'Would you not do that to help the Lady Elizabeth?'

The two women stared. Then Harriet seemed to soften. 'I do truly love that Lady Elizabeth. Not one good soul has burned on a pyre due to her word. They say she's a good princess.' She nodded at Margaretta. 'Well, you can't go in looking like that. You will be the shame of me.'

'I can't breathe,' Margaretta gasped.

'Stop your mithering,' snapped Harriet. 'Men likes tight dresses. Makes our bubbies go higher.' She stopped at the door of the Tabard. 'Sit at the back with your face to the wall. I'll say when you can look round.'

They stepped into the inn. It was two storeys around a central courtyard full of rubbish and a few dead rats. In every corner, there were patches of drying vomit and a strong smell of urine. Margaretta put her hand over her nose, only to have it slapped down by Harriet, who hissed that a good doxy never showed weakness. They walked into the bar room, which was in a fug from the brazier in the middle belching smoke from damp twigs. Around the side of the room were wooden trestles and benches, occupied by men in various states of drunkenness. A few whistles went up as Harriet walked in and then a volley of drunken calls to ask if today was a good day for business. She flicked her nose at them and shoved Margaretta towards the bench at the back. Leery eyes watched as she sat down facing the wall.

They had been there ten minutes, making awkward conversation about the inn and Southwark while Harriet slapped away the hands of a drunk sitting near. Then her eyes opened wider and she nodded at Margaretta. 'They're here. Down from their rooms. Turn when I say.'

A minute later she nodded again. The first face Margaretta recognised was the dark-faced, rotten-mouthed wherryman. Around his neck a silver crucifix, and his arm bandaged. She turned back quickly and whispered. 'Which one is the Shepherd?'

'End of the table, wearing a hat.'

Margaretta turned again. He was medium height, dark-haired, and with the skin of the Spanish. A hat was pulled down over his forehead, putting his eyes in shadow. But she could see his skin was pocked. And under the left eye, a long scar. A yellow bauble in the shape of the sheep hung from his sleeve, exactly like the one they'd found on Jonas. Margaretta realised the man was looking back. He had seen her. She spun round to look again at the wall.

When I looked at you, I felt concern – deep concern. So strong it blots the din of other thoughts and feelings around me. Even a little fear in you. Slight panic. I feel you staring at me. Anger.

Harriet stiffened. 'He's coming this way. Time we went.' She pushed Margaretta towards the door. The man called her to wait, his accent Spanish, but not strong. Harriet called back that she would return soon and gave Margaretta another shove. 'I have to get this one a bit of business before evening,' she called.

Outside they ran, swerving into the lane and towards the doxy house where Madge was downing another beaker of cheap wine. 'Get what you wanted, dearie?' she slurred.

'More than I wanted,' answered Margaretta. She turned to Harriet. 'I can't thank you enough. But for your own sake and Tilly's, stay away from that man.'

Chapter Sixty-Three

'Back again, my lady?' The Tower guard was leering and stank of brandy.

'To see my cousin. To try to make him see sense.'

The man sighed, shook his head and wrote in the ledger. 'Not sure you will get any sense today. They've already tried.' He looked up. 'You've gone pale, lady.'

'Have they, have they…?'

'Ah, no, lady. Not yet.' He looked back at the ledger, running a gnarled finger down the list of visitors. 'Though Master John Bourne was here today. That don't bode well for your relative.'

John Dee was back on his cot, rocking. He did not seem to hear Margaretta come in and she had to grasp his shoulder again to get his attention. The bruising around his eye was deepening into a blueish purple.

'Thomas Benger was questioned yesterday. Christopher, too. They showed me the torture chamber.' He leaned forward and retched, making Margaretta jump back to save her skirt, but only a little water escaped his mouth. 'Bourne took me down for what he calls "advance warning". The animal. He was laughing.'

Margaretta crouched down so she could look into his face. 'Then we have to work more quickly.'

He ignored her and kept rambling. They say the Star

Chamber is being set up for me. Bonner is creating his questions to assess heresy.' He shuddered convulsively. 'There is only one road out of there and it leads to the pyre.'

'Doctor, listen to me,' snapped Margaretta. 'I've found the Shepherd.'

Hearing this, John Dee jerked upright, eyes widening. 'Tell me all.' He listened carefully to the description, the strange bow with the woollen bauble and the company of the crucified killer. How Margaretta had felt his concern.

'Did he see you?'

'I'm not sure. But he came towards us and spoke to Harriet. He's Spanish.'

Dee tutted. 'You must be careful, girl. Stay hidden. That is your strength.' Then he leaned forward. 'Do you bring the cards again?'

She nodded and pulled them from under her skirt. John Dee, hands trembling muttered a prayer and pulled a card. 'The emperor again. The shepherd supports the emperor. An emperor sits in a court. My accusers come from court. You said the doxy said "the palace flames". Find the link to court.'

'Leave it to me.'

Chapter Sixty-Four

'Tommy should not have let you in again.' Mildred Cecil was looking out of the window, her back to Margaretta. 'I told him after your last visit that I had made my position clear. I cannot help you.'

'I think he saw my distress and took pity, my lady.' *Guilt. Good. That is what I want. I want you to feel shame, for your piety will only amplify the feeling. The more you feel guilt, the better my chances.* 'I think he saw how desperate I am. I told him John Dee is a friend of his father. A good friend who had only tried to help Lord Cecil.'

'Enough, Margaretta,' snapped Mildred. 'I do not need to be reminded of John's great efforts.'

'So must I beg, my lady? I'll go down on my knees if you would only…'

'Stop!' The older woman turned around, her face drawn. 'What if Lord Cecil finds out?'

'That you returned to see your grieving sister? That only you could comfort her as you have trodden that path yourself?' Margaretta raised her hands in question. 'Would he really object?'

'You overstep your station, girl.' The voice was high with emotion.

'I'll risk that to save a good man, my lady.'

A pause and then a deep sigh. 'Be ready early in the morning. I will collect you from the Putney Steps at eight.' She paused. 'And you will never tell my husband of this.'

Dawn was bright but bitter cold.

'Where are you going so early?' asked Sam, yawning. 'I was pulled from me bed.'

'On an errand with Lady Cecil. Don't ask questions.' She smiled. 'Lottie was full of your cleverness. Told me five times how you can count lambs even when they skip and jump.'

Sam grinned and she was sure his chest puffed. 'I reckon Master Tovey will be heading down again this Sunday. I'm asked to drive the carriage.'

Then from the bank the voice of a crier. 'Body in the Thames! Murder most foul!'

Margaretta shuddered and tried to hear more, but Sam was chattering and she could not make out the words. Did she hear the word Savoy?

At exactly eight o'clock, the Cecil carriage trundled up the road. The door opened and Lady Cecil beckoned her in.

Hampton Court Palace loomed up as they progressed along the long drive. Margaretta stared at the beauty of the red brick, soaring into the sky as huge chimneys. The gate was higher than three men and made of huge planks of oak, braced with iron and guarded by a line of soldiers in purple livery, each one holding a pikestaff with blades glinting in the morning sun.

Lady Mildred leaned out of the carriage window and beckoned to the nearest guard who came over and nodded a greeting. 'I am Lady Cecil and have business with Lady Ann Bacon, the queen's lady-in-waiting.' She pointed to Margaretta. 'I would like my maid to meet with Beatrice ap Rhys in the laundry. She misses speaking her own tongue.'

Beatrice was a big woman with an ample bosom, bound tight to keep it off her belly. Grey, curly hair sprang from under her coif and the smell of lavender drifted around her. She grinned at Margaretta and spoke only in Welsh.

'So, missing home, are you?'

'I am.'

They fell into easy conversation about their home towns and who they might both know, who was the local priest and the names of their fathers' brothers and cousins. Beatrice winked. 'Would you like to maid today? You can see inside the palace.'

'What do I do?'

'Hold the linens in your arms and follow me. If I stop and bow my head, you do the same. If I curtsey, you do the same.' She put her hands on her hips. 'Can you curtsey, girl?'

Five curtseys later, Margaretta was deemed ready to follow as a laundry maid. Her arms were loaded with five folded sheets and two petticoats. Beatrice heaved a pile of pillow covers into the crook of her arm and nodded to the door. 'Stay close behind and copy all I do.'

They made their way along a cobble path, through the outer door into a stone-floored corridor. Men decked in red braes and white shirts bustled everywhere, carrying joints of meat, vegetables, pots, pans and dishes. The smell of roasting beef was in the air and the clang of metal on metal and shouts came from a door ahead of them. 'The great kitchen,' called Beatrice over her shoulder. 'If a red-liveried man comes out with plates, stop and let him go ahead. Nothing can allow the queen's food to cool before she eats it and they have to keep a constant flow of food up to the great hall to feed the men of Court.'

One of the lads whistled at Margaretta and his friends started whooping their encouragement, only to get a bark from Beatrice. They scuttled on and the older woman turned to Margaretta. 'Ignore the kitchen lads. They're all rougher than the beasts they butcher.' She gave a little laugh. 'The upstairs servants are better mannered. Sons of merchants and seeking favour at court.'

'How would I know one from the other?' asked Margaretta.

'They wear black upstairs and don't charge around like red-bottomed ruffians.' Beatrice winked. 'Come on.'

Margaretta nodded and trotted along behind Beatrice, turning into a well-lit corridor. A sudden clatter and a barrel rolled out of a side door followed by a dozy-looking boy. Margaretta looked around as Beatrice snapped at the lad to keep his wine smoothly handled, then a sharp command to Margaretta to 'stop dreaming and follow'.

Near the end of the corridor, a set of stone steps curled up. Beatrice paused. 'This brings us to the procession gallery. If you see anyone well dressed, stop and curtsey.'

At the top of the stairs, they stepped into a wide gallery blazing with colour, glazed windows on one side and tapestries on the other. Then a door opened at the end and a flurry of men flowed through. Beatrice wagged her hand behind her in a warning to Margaretta. 'Knees down, eyes down,' she hissed in a low whisper. They both dropped to the floor.

The men walked towards them, oblivious to their presence. In the front was a dark-haired young man, dressed in black and his hair oiled. His thin face was the colour of the Spanish, but his eyes a strange blue.

Unease. Irritation. A sense of shame. Something is happening here which is causing you great embarrassment. You fear they are laughing at you and so demand they follow and listen. You want control.

As he drew closer, Margaretta glanced up through her lashes and swallowed a gasp. There was no colour to his clothes but the bauble around his neck was yellow: a golden sheep, hanging as if dead on a chain. Behind him were more than ten young men all talking in the tongue of the Spanish, hands dancing and arms flailing. At the very back walked a man also dressed in black. He was in deep conversation with an Englishman much older than he. They bent their heads together and seemed concerned. Margaretta looked up again.

Then she saw the bow of yellow wool on the button of his sleeve and a bauble shaped like a sheep. As he came level, she dared to catch a look at his face and she stifled a cry. He was pocked, with a scar under his eye. It was the Shepherd.

'Well, did you ever think you would be in the presence of a king, girl?'

'The short, pale one.'

Beatrice hissed then softened when remembering that only Spanish, French and English were common parlance in these corridors. She winked. 'Yes, the small, pale one.' Then she stiffened up and tried to look stern. 'And you watch your tongue.' With that, she turned and bustled ahead along the wooden floor and round a corner. Up ahead the sound of church chanting started.

Margaretta trotted after her. 'What's he so worried about?'

Beatrice's eyes narrowed. 'You've not been reading those damned pamphlets, have you?'

Margaretta shook her head. 'He just looked worried, and his hands were wagging as if they were trying to escape flames.'

'We are all in fear for our queen. Every day that passes and the child does not come, she falls deeper into despair,' whispered the older woman, her eyes filling with tears. 'Poor love. She has only known sorrow and fear since a little child. She wants this so very much.' She sniffed and cleared her throat. 'But no gossiping. Come.'

Damn. I will hold my questions back awhile.

Along another gallery, also richly adorned in tapestries,

they came to an elaborate door painted and inset with Tudor roses. Beatrice turned. 'You'll wait here while I go in with the linens. Keep your head down and eyes to the floor.' Beatrice knocked. The door was opened.

Oh God, what is happening in there? Despair. Fear. Terrible pain. And the smell. It is thick with dust and sweat and the sweet smell of illness. Not even a dog would thrive in such heat and darkness.

'Ah, Beattie. The woman of the washtub. Do you come to wash our sheets or our feet?' A sharp laugh. 'For our feet are surely foul with pacing the floor of this tomb all night.'

'I bring clean linens, Jane Foole,' answered Beatrice with a hint of irritation.

Margaretta used her long lashes to spy the door-opener. She was thin, short and pale. Large round eyes made her look somewhere between mad and alarmed. And under her cap, her head was shaven quite bald. Another woman stepped forward. 'Jane, you are letting in cold air. Step aside and let Beatrice in.'

'Frideswide Knight, always right,' sang Jane Foole, tripping a little dance before skipping back into the darkness.

The other woman tutted and opened the door wider to let Beatrice pass. With the door left open Margaretta could spy inside the gloom. *It grows. Despair is like an iron grip on someone's soul. Everything seems dark and terrible.* She looked up for just a second and the sight was desperate. In the middle of the room, curled up on the floor was a small, frail woman, her legs pulled up to her belly like a babe. She had her hands over her face and was weeping, every sob wracking her shoulders. Behind her a woman kneeled on the floor and stroked her head, sadness etched across her face. Further back in the shadows, another looked upon the tragedy. She was young, in a plain dress and headdress from under which flowed a cascade of copper hair, her face quite impassive, as if watching a play.

Then Beatrice came back with Frideswide Knight who

stepped outside and spoke in a low voice. 'We all pray that you will be called for birthing linens soon, Beatrice. But hope is waning. Make sure there is no gossip in the kitchens or laundry.'

'Yes, Mistress Frideswide. Leave it to me.'

With no more conversation, the door was closed and Beatrice bustled Margaretta back towards the stairs, shaking her head with sadness.

'What terrible events go on in there?' asked Margaretta in Welsh.

Beatrice turned, her face stern. 'That is your queen, Margaretta. Wracked with fear for her desperately wanted prince.' Tears came to the woman's eyes. 'I have known her since she was just a child. I have seen every pain and fear she has endured. But this is surely the worst.' She sniffed and straightened up, her voice dropped to stern. 'And keep your mouth well buttoned. Do you understand?'

Margaretta sped up to keep pace. 'I promise.' She paused. 'Who was the lady with copper hair?'

Beatrice turned and raised her finger. 'I told you not to look.' She smiled. 'That is the Lady Elizabeth, come to attend to her sister as they wait for the child.'

But there is no child. We both know it. That was not a pregnant woman on the floor. It was a very sick woman. Margaretta nodded and followed in silence until they reached the laundry and could speak more openly. 'I cannot believe what this day has brought, Beatrice.'

Beatrice laughed and patted her arm. 'I am glad to have given such pleasure to one of our own. If you worked here, you would see more. Maybe even the Lady Elizabeth would share a few words in our tongue with you.'

'She speaks Welsh?'

'Yes. Taught from a child by Blanche ap Harri, who is determined to remind us all that the Tudors are a Welsh dynasty.'

Beatrice winked. 'But they keep it quiet in the company of these English nobles. It would only add to the suspicion of her.'

'I noticed another thing.' Margaretta smiled. 'The king had a great gold chain and bauble. What was that?'

Her new friend put her finger to her lips. 'Follow me.' She picked up an armful of large table covers and put a few in Margaretta's arms. 'I'll take you to the great Watching Tower. His majesty and his men will be at Mass for at least another hour. We can change their table covers.'

Beatrice pointed at the portrait. It was Philip of Spain, looking sideways at the artist, his face looking younger than the man she had seen earlier. In this portrait, he was fair, full-lipped and wearing a look of muted interest or maybe boredom. He was dressed in armour, decorative and gilded – more ceremonial than for fighting. He did not look like a fighting man with a face so soft. But Margaretta's eyes were drawn to the gold chain around his neck and from it dangled a bauble of gold, fashioned to look like a sheep being hung from its belly. 'A yellow sheep,' whispered Margaretta. 'And the Shepherd was in your flock of young men.'

'What was that, dear?' asked Beatrice who had busied herself putting a cloth on each table ready for spreading by the hall servants.

'I said, he wears a yellow sheep.'

Beatrice chortled. 'I think they call it a golden fleece.' She raised a brow. 'Princes don't wear sheep, pet.' She pointed to the door. 'We should go.'

'One more thing, Beatrice.'

The older woman turned.

'There was another man at the back of the king's party. I saw a yellow bow on his sleeve.' She smiled innocently. 'Who was that?'

Beatrice huffed. 'A bad one if ever there was. Works for Lord Englefield, who he was talking to. His name is Thomas Prideaux. A bad one.'

Chapter Sixty-Five

Margaretta stepped down from the carriage at Putney Steps and bid thanks and farewell to Lady Cecil. It had been a quiet homeward journey with both women avoiding any talk about troubles. Mildred asked only one question: 'Did you find what you sought, Margaretta?'

'I found something which might assist, my lady.'

The only other talk was of the heavy air of the evening. They needed a storm.

Margaretta was lucky, there was already a wherry, the oarsman on the bank looking out over the river. 'Hello, wherryman. Are you for hire?'

He turned.

'Sam. How did you know to be here?'

The boy flew up the steps, face red and mouth turned down in fury. 'I've waited hours, knowing you would return this way,' he shouted. 'What kind of evil are you meddling in?' He did not wait for a reply. 'You keep Lottie out of this, d'you hear?'

Margaretta stepped back. 'What's happened, Sam?'

'They found her drowned at the Savoy. You went to see her yesterday. Today she's dead. Killed.'

'Harriet?'

He nodded and his voice went to a hoarse snarl. 'She was bound up like a trussed chicken. She had...' He went pale and looked away.

'A mouth full of a yellow wool. Probably a seal around her neck.'

He nodded and swiped at a tear. 'She were a good sort. Did no one any harm.' He stopped and stared. 'How did you know about the wool and stuff?'

'It's the pattern my master is investigating.' Margaretta struggled and failed to stop herself from weeping. She sniffled and insisted she had no idea it would come to this. Sam turned his back on her, shaking his head in exaggerated disdain until suddenly she cried: 'Tilly. They'll know that she knows the turn-face shepherd. She was heard saying it. Oh, God, Sam. Would they hurt a child? *Yes.* 'Jonas, the first to die for speaking, was a child. They will silence Tilly too!'

Sam had no air to speak, he rowed so hard. By the time they arrived at Southwark Stairs, he knew the whole story. With the painter rope through an iron ring, they ran to Foul Lane and up a back alley. It stank of rotting vegetables and something that had died. Sam stopped to get his breath.

'Tilly will be with the other girls. They all love the little pet. We have to move fast. Whoever seeks her will know where she would have been taken. Are you ready?'

Margaretta nodded.

'I'll go first as if I am a customer, and I'll leave the door ajar. Count to ten and run along the road and in.' Sam signalled. Margaretta pressed her back to the wall and started to count. At the count of ten, she was off, running along the road towards the doxy house. She could see the door open. But then a movement on the opposite side and a shout. She looked sideways. That dark, angry face, mouth open in another shout. And the flash of a silver crucifix.

'Bar the door. They saw me.'

Sam cursed and pulled a wooden box across the floor to

brace the door while Margaretta ran to the back room. The three women turned to stare at her, their faces twisted in fury. One was holding a bottle. It was clear all had been crying. Tilly was clinging to Madge, her face buried in the old woman's neck. She was sobbing and calling for her mammie.

Madge pointed a gnarled finger and spoke through toothless gums. 'What did you do to visit this on our Harriet?'

Hate. You all hate me. Blame me. One of you is thinking she will hit me, throw me to the floor. She can already feel the rage rising. 'I had no idea they would kill an innocent. It's my master they want to harm,' stuttered Margaretta, but trailed off as she faced a wall of angry silence. She nodded at Tilly. 'We have to get her away.'

One of the younger women stepped forward, thrusting her face into Margaretta's. 'Well she ain't going with you. We're not putting our Tilly in line of evil.' As she spoke the hammering started on the door.

Sam appeared round the door. 'The girl's right. We have to get out of here.' He looked at Tilly and paled. 'God love her.' Then at Madge. 'Help us, Madge. Those Spanish knows she knows them.'

The three women looked at each other. The hammering was getting louder. Someone was using metal against the wood. Margaretta stepped forward, her voice rising in panic. 'I'll take her to the house of Lord Cecil. No one will get her there.'

They stared open-mouthed as Margaretta assured them that it was true. Then a crash as the metal broke through and an accented voice shouting. 'Give us the child, whores.' There was no time to wait. Madge pushed Tilly towards Margaretta, ignoring the little girl's attempt to cling to her and the screams.

'Out the back,' ordered the woman with the bottle. 'You can escape down the back lane.'

'Give me a sack,' insisted Sam. 'We have to hide her.'

Five minutes later, Sam gently placed the heavy sack into the stern of his wherry and jumped in. Close behind was Margaretta who hunkered down in the scuppers and put her arms around the bundle, cooing at little Tilly to keep as quiet as a mouse. Sam pulled hard on the oars and whispered thanks to God that the tide was in their favour. But he rounded the bend at Westminster before he nodded to Margaretta to let the child out.

Dark was descending as they ran up the drive to Wimbledon Manor, Margaretta having spent two more of her pennies on a bad-tempered carter to drive them from Putney Steps. They knocked on the door. Goodwife answered and peered out into the gloom, a candle in her hand. 'Sam? Margaretta?' Her hand went to her mouth. 'Is all well with Master Tovey?'

Sam nodded. 'Yes, mistress. But we need your help.' He pointed down at Tilly who stood head down and snuffling.

Goodwife looked puzzled and beckoned them in, then sniffed. 'The child is filthy. Where did you find her? She cannot stay here.' Tilly looked up, her big eyes red and damp with tears. 'They killed my mammie, missus. What will happen to me?' She started to sob with desperate little gasps.

Lottie arrived in the kitchen and after an initial squeak of excitement, felt the sadness and stared at the bedraggled group.

Goodwife looked down her nose. 'The child needs a wash and some food.' Was that a crack in her voice? She held out a hand. 'Come with me.'

A bewildered Tilly took her hand and followed, to be put up on a chair by Goodwife's desk where she continued to sob. The woman returned with a damp linen and knelt in front of her, dabbing gently at the tears. Then she stopped, held out her arms, scooped Tilly up and held her tight like her mother would have done.

Chapter Sixty-Six

Sam was still surly when they arrived back at the Dycekey Steps near St Dunstan's, though Lottie's insistence that 'Margaretta would never do any harm – it's the bad men who hurt that little girl's mother,' had softened him a little. When they left, Tilly had been curled up in Goodwife's lap, her belly full of warm milk and a clean nightgown keeping her warm. Goodwife had insisted she would have to work for her keep the next day. Then she cuddled the child closer.

'Here you are.' He nodded up the steps. Huge drops of rain had been falling most of their journey and, in the distance, thunder rumbled. Each rumble had been closer and now they could see flashes of light in the sky to the north. 'It's dark, missy. Shall I walk you to the door?'

'Better you were around tomorrow, Sam. If I may send a boy to hire you.'

'Suppose,' he mumbled. He pulled away. Then a call from the water. 'Take care, missy. Wouldn't want to see you hurt.'

Yes. But you are Lottie's boy now. What would I give to change that? I have learned that love is something not to be pushed away.

The kitchen was dark, but it was only seconds before Katherine Constable walked in, her face full of concern. 'What news, Margaretta?' she looked over her shoulder. 'My husband is to his cups in wine. He will not hear us.'

'I reached court, mistress. And I found the man who came

here to board the doctor's door. I also know he manages a band of wretched wherrymen in Southwark. He is central to the troubles in this house.'

'What is there to do?'

'Tomorrow I return to the Tower and pull on the doctor's great wisdom.' She made a small smile. 'I am sure he can put together the pieces.'

Katherine made a watery smile then turned to leave. She paused and pulled some pennies from her pocket. 'Take these to help my John.'

Margaretta turned to make her way to the bedroom, her legs aching with weariness. There was a clap of thunder and a flash of lightning lit the kitchen. The figure in the corner made her cry out. 'Huw? What are you doing in the shadows?'

'The bad man with Christ at his throat has been back. Staring at the house.'

CHAPTER SIXTY-SEVEN

The morning was crisp and everything washed after the storm that had crashed through the city overnight. The roads and paths were pooled with puddles and mud made the way both sticky and slippy.

The wet walls of the Tower were even greyer than before, and the slitted windows blacker. Inside the main door, the ledger man growled, 'Back again, lady?'

She affected the voice of Lady Cecil again and was shown along the path to the Salt Tower and the cell of John Dee. The air was thick and the smell of vomit and sweat was rank. A moan from the shadows told her that Barthelet Green still lived – just. The jailer gave his common command of, 'half an hour', and trudged back into the dark.

Dee was in his usual place, standing up, but stooped. He was looking pale and drawn, but his voice was stronger as he asked the details. 'Describe the sheep again.' As she did, he began to nod. 'Of course. That is the symbol of the Order of the Golden Fleece. A secretive Catholic order bent on the supremacy of the papist faith. More than that. All members are deemed answerable only to a court of their own and not the laws of any land.'

'Who says so?'

'The emperor. Charles the Fifth. The man who wants his son to be king and not Elizabeth if Queen Mary dies.' Dee wagged a finger at Margaretta. 'So if King Philip is part of this, then he cannot be accused of treason. Clever.'

'There's more, doctor. I have found the Shepherd. Thomas Prideaux moves between the honours of court and the horrors of the Tabard Inn in Southwark where he controls the Spanish wherrymen. In court, he wears the same yellow bow and bauble like a sheep we found on Jonas's button.'

Dee jumped up and peered at her. 'You have been crying. What has happened?'

Margaretta gave way to tears. 'Harriet was killed yesterday. Found at the Savoy, drowned, and bound and gagged with yellow wool.'

Dee seemed to crumple with a long moan. 'They will kill anyone who knows them.' He looked up, eyes wide. 'You are in danger, child. And it is all my fault.'

She raised her hands to stop his talking. 'Too late to worry, doctor. We need answers.' She turned, lifted her skirt and pulled out the cards and the red garnet crystal. 'Quickly, we have less than half an hour before that oaf of a jailer returns.'

Hurriedly, Dee moved to the small table and moved it to the window so that a shaft of morning light fell on its centre. Again, he spread the cards, face down, and placed the red crystal in the centre of the arc. Then he pulled the clear crystal from his shirt and held it to the light, muttering his question. 'There is only one question. How does the Shepherd know what happens in the houses of Dee and Cecil?'

Slowly he moved his hand over the arc, stopping and hovering five times. Each time he stopped, he picked the card under his palm and turned it over. The first card turned was the hermit. 'There he is again,' muttered Dee. The next card was the emperor. 'And again. The cards are telling us a story.'

The next card was the empress, but Dee gave a sharp intake of breath. 'It is upside down again. It means the reverse of fertility and abundance. It means emptiness.'

'I glimpsed the queen. That woman is not with child,' whispered Margaretta. 'It was pitiful to see.'

As she finished speaking Dee turned the next card. 'The Tower.' He looked sideways at his visitor. 'Signifying terrible change and destruction. A bleak fate awaits our majesty.'

Margaretta glanced at the door. 'Be careful, doctor. This is getting close to the treason they accuse you of.' He ignored her and turned again. 'The queen of swords.'

'The Lady Elizabeth?'

He nodded. 'See, her card comes to the position below the others. They seek supremacy over her. They seek to crush or cover her.' He turned to Margaretta. 'It all makes sense. They know the queen is barren and want to ensure Elizabeth never becomes our monarch.'

Dee placed the clear crystal on the hermit. 'Tell me who you are?' He looked back at Margaretta. 'What did you feel when you were in the company of the Shepherd, or Prideaux, at court?'

'Concern. Alarm. As if he knew my face, but a man of court could not know me.'

The sun came through the window and the room seemed a little lighter. Dee asked more questions. Could he have seen her the first time she went to Southwark? She thought no. Suddenly there was a smell of burning. They spun round to look at the cards. A thin line of light was reflecting through the crystal onto the queen of swords which was smouldering and curling brown at the edges. Dee snatched it up and blew out the flame. Then he looked back to Margaretta. 'The hermit: the Shepherd seeks the death of Elizabeth. We have to uncover the hermit. A man with a hidden face.'

'Time up!' yelled the jailer as Dee hastily gathered the cards and crystals and stuffed them into Margaretta's hands. She secreted them into her petticoat just as the door banged open. 'Time up, I said,' snarled the man, breath heavy with stale beer and onions.

Margaretta held up a penny to shine in the light of the window. 'A few minutes, sir?'

He walked across, snatched the coin and retreated, growling, 'Two minutes. No more.'

Dee was on his cot, head in hands. 'There is a connection I am not making. How could he see inside our houses; inside our business, inside what we know? How?'

Margaretta kneeled in front of him. 'Tilly called the Shepherd "the turn-face shepherd". That is when Harriet first showed her fear. Could there be something in that?'

Dee jerked his head up. 'The hermit only shows half a face. The other side is always hidden. Someone has been hiding their identity.' He frowned. 'The angels said –'

'Three faces and we have found only two.'

The door slammed open. 'Time up!'

John Dee took her hand and nodded for her to go. For the first time, she felt his thoughts. Like a voice in her head. *Go to Southwark, girl. Find how the face turns. It is my only hope. I need to know the true face of my persecutor.*

Chapter Sixty-Eight

'You want to go back? Those doxies won't let you out alive, missy.' Sam shook his head. 'I'll not take you to your death.'

Margaretta pointed downriver to the Tower. 'There's a good man facing his death in there, because of the same man who we think had Harriet killed. I won't let that happen. Nor will I let Harriet's killer go free for fear of a few women with loose kirtles.'

Sam suppressed a smile and shrugged. 'Don't ever say I didn't warn you.' It was only a few minutes across the river to the Southwark Steps. 'I'll wait for you here, missy.' He grinned. 'You can outpace old Madge, but the other two will give you a run for your money.'

The battered door of the doxy house was already open, probably to make it easier for customers to fall over the threshold after a few hours in the inn. Margaretta stepped inside and walked towards the back room, which was already spewing a strong smell of cheap wine. Hearing footsteps one of the women called out: "Ave your money ready, sir. It's money up-front these hard days.'

When a woman rounded the door, they fell silent. Then one flew at her. Only a bark from Madge saved their visitor from a pummelling. The pock-marked woman stood. 'What you doing bringing your backside back here, gobermouch?'

Margaretta gulped. 'I think I know who killed Harriet.'

The older woman flapped her hand as if Margaretta was an odious smell. 'So you're a dalcop as well as a pest.'

'I am trying to bring justice, Mistress Madge. Justice for Harriet and for the man who lies in the Tower for seeking the killers.'

All three cackled, though the one holding the wine bottle did mumble that Jonas had been a sweet boy and Luke was like a father seeking revenge.

'Tilly spoke of a turn-face shepherd. What did she mean?'

'That was a child making up stories,' snapped the youngest of the women, a pretty girl with old eyes. 'She used to say that he went in with one face and came out with another. But children always say such things for attention.'

'I think that child told the truth. And only by checking will we get justice.'

Madge batted her hand again. 'There is no such thing as *justice* in Southwark, dearie.' She hardened the word justice to a cynical sneer.

'That's because everyone is frightened. Harriet was afeared, so was Jonas, so was Robert Meldrew. They use fear and that way will hurt Lady Elizabeth.' She pulled the purse from her pocket. 'Will this make you brave enough to help me get justice? There are five pennies left. All I need is to get to the lodging rooms of the Tabard Inn.'

Guilt, alarm. Fear. But one of you likes me. Which one? The only woman not scowling is you, Madge. I remind you of someone. Yourself. All those years ago, before the pox took your face. You were brave. You fought for life. Now all is gone, even self-respect. 'Will you help me, Mistress Madge? For Tilly's sake?'

For a moment that felt like an eternity, there was total silence. Then Madge rose and looked at the others. 'Well if I die there is little loss.' She made a small sigh. 'Get ready, girls. I am going to tell the Spanish wherrymen that today is Spanish ha'penny day.' They looked back at her confused as she held up her hands in incredulity. 'Gawd. Just lift your skirts for a ha'penny and do your bit for our Harriet.'

Margaretta hid around the corner and waited. Sure enough a trail of beer-stinking Spanish wherrymen, all talking in their own tongue and evidently telling bawdy jokes, headed out of the front door of the Tabard Inn. Seconds later, a whistle told her the coast was clear.

Madge was at the bottom of the stairs. 'Third door on the right and be quick. They're so full of beer, they'll be back in ten minutes.'

Margaretta sped up the steps and found the door, turned the handle and pushed. It was locked. 'Madge, help me. Get Sam from the Southwark Steps.'

Minutes later, Sam appeared in the corridor followed by Madge, who was puffing and wheezing in her exertion. He did not need asking. It took three hits of his shoulder before there was a crack of splintering wood and they were in. There was little light inside, but enough to show a bed, a table and, under the window, a leather-bound trunk.

Margaretta pulled it open and let out a cry. Inside was a skein of yellow wool, a pot of red lead paint and an eye patch. Her hands flew to her mouth as she saw the priest's black cassock with a wide-brimmed hat at the bottom of the trunk.

Chapter Sixty-Nine

Margaretta sat in the window of John Dee's cell tracing her fingers over the letters of a name carved into the stone. Some poor sot who faced the axe trying to be remembered. The circles under her master's eyes were almost black with lack of sleep. In the past few days he had been pulled before the Star Council and interrogated for hours. They sat nervously waiting for Lord Pembroke to arrive. It had taken some days to arrange. First Margaretta had run to the Tower to tell John Dee that the hermit had not two faces but three. He bid her go straight to Mildred Cecil with a message to alert the doctor's old employer, as he was the only man who could intervene over Lord Englefield and the Privy Council. A day later a message arrived from Lord Pembroke to await his presence. The jailers had been suddenly less cruel in their jibes.

Margaretta and Dee heard the sound of heavy footsteps approaching the cell and the door opened. Lord Herbert Pembroke stood in the frame, hands on hips, shoulders squared, like a black statue against the light of a pitch-torch behind him, his dog at his ankle. The stinking cur growled as his master snarled, 'This had better be worth my while.'

John Dee rose. 'There is a plot to snatch this country into Spanish hands by fouling the reputation of the Lady Elizabeth and removing her from the succession.'

Shocked, Pembroke slammed the door behind him after

shouting for good wine and bread. He sat on the rickety chair. 'Go on.'

'Some months ago, a young priest, claiming Welsh birth and sympathy with the Protestant cause, arrived in the household of William Cecil. He was humble and shy, having been blinded and skin-blighted by the pox. He showed wisdom and smoothed the ripples when a Spanish maid stole a seal and then he prevented a stable lad, Jonas, being flogged for hawking pies to buy his sweetheart a ribbon. William Cecil could not know that this same priest would go to Southwark, take off his disguise and become a leader of a gang of Spanish wherrymen who would kill at his command. They call him the Shepherd and they gather at the Tabard Inn, where the sign is of a man with a lamb. They are called his Flock. They take the bodies to the bank of the Savoy where the Shepherd's brother-in-law – Robert Meldrew – was the architect responsible for renovating the hospital. He had been engaged by the office of Lord Englefield. He was forced to take in the bodies. Each body was a message bearer.'

Pembroke looked confused, 'What messages?'

'Young Jonas probably died too early because he became scared. He was tongue-stabbed as a message not to speak and his body carried a false letter, which looked as if it came from Lady Elizabeth, and Cecil's seal – also falsified. No doubt made from an impression of the seal stolen by the maid, as it was flawed. A crucifix had been pressed into his hand enough to break the skin.' Dee shifted and rubbed his shoulders again. 'Luke, his almost father, was killed for finding out who killed him. The message was increased by not only stabbing his tongue but also in the sewing up of his mouth. He also had the mark. Meldrew had his eyes smashed and his mouth stuffed with a yellow wool bauble like an animal, as a message to see and say nothing. Another false seal around his neck. The same pattern of an

The Conjuror's Apprentice

imprint on his forehead.' Dee pointed at Margaretta. 'Then the seal-maker was found in the water, drowned and bound in yellow wool, and Margaretta's brother was beaten and marked as a warning to me.'

Pembroke turned to her. 'What happened?'

'Beaten black and blue, sir. His attacker is one of the Flock and wears a large crucifix. The same man has followed and watched us – waiting outside our lodging house, the lodging of Christopher Careye and also my sister.'

Pembroke shook his head. 'Anyone else hurt?'

'The last was a doxy-girl called Harriet. Drowned with her mouth stuffed and legs bound because she helped me identify the Shepherd,' answered Margaretta.

Dee came in again. 'Every dead body had a false seal that linked them to Cecil. Every victim bore the yellow sheep.'

Pembroke leaned back in his seat. 'But why has Cecil gone if he has a reputation to protect?'

'Their game was to frighten Cecil and make him want to flee and to save his reputation. It meant he would run rather than stand by the Lady Elizabeth.' Dee huffed his indignation. 'Cecil left us all to face the horror alone.'

Pembroke leaned forward and rubbed his temples. 'I still see no reasoning.' He looked sharply at Dee. 'And how did you become implicated?'

'In April, I was asked to conjure the horoscope of the Lady Elizabeth. I thought Cecil had fashioned the idea with Blanche ap Harri, our cousin. But it was the suggestion of the priest, Father Thomas. It was also his suggestion that I was called to assist when the first body – young Jonas – was found. That priest, also known as the Shepherd, wound me into the web.'

'So who is this priest? This Shepherd? This is sounding more fantastical than your moving models, Dee. Are you conjuring fantasy?'

Dee raised his hands. 'No.' The voice was stronger now. 'The priest and the Shepherd have a third face. They are both really Thomas Prideaux, who is no man of God. He is a Spanish man of the king's entourage who works with Lord Englefield.'

A knock at the door silenced them and they sat tense as a man brought in wine, bread and cheese and loitered until Pembroke threw him a coin and a sharp instruction to go away and shut the door fast. He looked back to Dee. 'The man who accused you?'

'Yes. And as he had arranged evidence for my arrest, he had all the information to convince Lord Englefield and Bishop Bonner of my sorcery around Lady Elizabeth. He has sight inside Cecil's house and so sight of all my investigations. That is how he laid down all the clues. If I am found guilty, then all the evidence is laid out and the shadow of suspicion and sorcery will fall on her too – and end the Tudor line. She is unprotected.'

Pembroke narrowed his eyes. 'And where is Cecil now?'

Dee pressed his lips together. 'He is accompanying Bishop Pole in France at the request of Lord Englefield's office. I suspect it was suggested by Prideaux to remove my one ally.' Dee smiled mirthlessly. 'Naturally, Cecil agreed. What better way is there to distance yourself from Protestant trouble then by escorting the most Catholic bishop in the world and beloved of Queen Mary?'

'Wily bastard,' muttered Pembroke. 'Go on. From the look of you, there is more. It still makes no sense. Why the yellow wool?'

'The exact question, sir.' Dee smiled, though warily. 'As well as being bound by yellow wool, the bodies have been decorated with a strange woollen bauble. Yellow wool fashioned to look like a sheep. The same artefact was stuffed into the mouths of Robert Meldrew, the maid's brother and the doxy Harriet.

Lord Herbert stood and slammed his hand on the desk. 'God save us, man. What is the yellow wool telling us?'

'That the plot starts in court and is designed to advance the king, sir, should our dear queen not have a child, or die.'

Pembroke stared, took a long draft of wine and looked at the door. 'Go on.'

'The only decoration worn by King Philip is the necklace of the Order of the Golden Fleece. An order bent on the supremacy of the Catholic faith and Catholic rule. I believe the yellow wool and the strange decoration attached to each body, are indicating that these foul deeds are done to further the aspirations of the Order.'

Pembroke was on his feet, stamping towards John Dee, who flinched. 'Are you trying to say that King Philip is behind this?'

'That I cannot say. But I will say that the only person in the way of him becoming king, and making England fully Catholic by church and rule, is Elizabeth. If she is implicated in the sorcery of which I am accused and may burn for and if she is linked to the ritual deaths associated with her greatest supporter – Cecil – then she will follow her mother to the block.'

Pembroke slumped back on his chair and reached for the flagon. 'Dear God. Save us.' He turned to Margaretta. 'You are quiet, maid. What do you have to say?'

'All my master says is true, sir. I have seen the faces of the Shepherd and Thomas Prideaux and can confirm they are one and the same. And I found these in the trunk of the Shepherd in his rooms in the Tabard Inn.' She put the patch, the red paint and the priest's garb on the floor in front of Pembroke. 'I have followed the doctor's instructions and found that Thomas Prideaux, disguised as Father Thomas, was close to Jonas and advised Lord Cecil to contact Doctor Dee. I hid a letter from the doctor to Lord Cecil. It disappeared and could only have been taken by him.' She noted his look of suspicion.

You wonder why a maid is so close and so informed. Suspicion grows. This does not sit well with you. 'As a mere maid, sir, I could get titbits and give them to my master for his mind to put all parts together.'

It seemed to work. Pembroke nodded and looked back to Dee. 'Two parts of your theory don't make sense. How can a Spaniard present as a Welshman and why George Ferrers? He accused you too.'

Dee nodded with assurance. 'It is the skill of a spy to disguise all. Face, body and voice. He also claimed to have left Wales many years ago. It was a skilled excuse.' Dee gave a hard laugh. 'It is the lack of skill which gets men into debt and make them seek immoral reward. Hence, they could easily recruit Ferrers as an informant.'

Pembroke chuckled. 'I need to think.' He was quiet for minutes then looked up. Dee was tense. 'You are being interrogated by Bishop Bonner.'

'Yes. And roughly. Another eighteen questions have been delivered for answering.'

'He thinks himself the great shaper of this land and the highest of all authorities – even above Mary. If he can burn people by the dozen, then what is a princess, even if she is the daughter of Harry Tudor?' He stamped his frustration and turned to Dee. 'I told you before to get close to Bonner.'

'You did but…'

Pembroke growled. 'And I say it again… Listen to me.'

Dee stood. 'But what about justice? I demand to go to court and expose my accusers.'

Pembroke leaned back, closed his eyes and groaned. 'You are a gifted mathematician, John, but you are an innocent fool when it comes to the calculation of politics.' He gestured to Dee to sit. 'If you think you would survive standing before

Philip of Spain and his entourage to accuse them of bringing down the English monarchy and subjugating our country to the Holy Roman Empire, then you are beyond foolery.'

'But the queen must know of this and –'

'And what? Do you think she will look on you with favour?' Another growl. 'The woman is maddened by grief for her never-to-be child and her desperate love for Philip.' Pembroke pointed at Dee. 'Your search for justice will take you to the block and all of us associated with you and your tale will follow. This hornet's nest is too big.'

'But –'

'There is no "but".' Pembroke gave a wry smile. 'Trust me, John. The Tabard Inn will be raided this night and a flock of wherrymen will swing – one by his own crucifix. That will send a sufficient message to Thomas Prideaux to stop his plotting.'

Dee's voice rose in indignation. 'So I get no reward or payment? Or satisfaction?'

'Your reward, John, is protection and life.' Pembroke raised his hand to silence the prisoner. 'I repeat my suggestion. You will go to the house of Bishop Bonner and satisfy his Catholic zeal. That will render you safe in the eyes of court and the Catholic Church. Get humble, get close, get inside his house and this time, Elizabeth will have a hidden friend.' He walked to the door and opened it, then paused. 'You are prisoner nought nought seven.' He turned back to Dee. 'They say it is a helpful number. Remember that as your sign, John.'

As the door slammed, Dee slumped on his bed with a sigh. 'Well we did it, Margaretta. Your senses, my science.' He looked up with a weak smile. 'Maybe next time we will be smiled upon by Court.'

On Wednesday, 18 July 1555, Margaretta Morgan received a note from her master telling her that he would be the guest of Bishop Bonner for the foreseeable future. Christopher Careye was also free. Inside the letter was another closely folded and sealed parchment to be handed to Katherine Constable. The lady never mentioned the content, but she wept and spent that evening convincing her wary husband to give Margaretta and her family a position as servants until John Dee was able to come and collect his belongings. That night, even Mam gave a small smile of relief as she cuddled the kitten, which was already toileting in the yard. Huw confirmed no crucifixed man had watched the house in over a week and opened his bag of letters to spell '*Diolch i Duw*' – thanks to God – over and over again.

In August 1555, John Dee was released from his imprisonment in the house of Bishop Bonner. He had already been made a doctor of divinity in the Catholic faith.

The following April, one year after the plot of the Golden Fleece, Margaretta, wearing her sister's dress, accompanied John Dee, William Cecil and Lady Mildred Cecil, along with hand-clasped Lottie and Sam, to St Margaret's church. There they celebrated the wedding of Mistress Barker to Master George Tovey of Somerset, gentleman boat-builder. At the end of the service, the priest rose and asked for additional thanks to God. For Master and Mistress Tovey were to take and raise as their very own daughter Matilda Hern, known to all as Tilly.

As all cheered in the churchyard and the couple came out into a warm spring sun, Lady Mildred Cecil whispered to Margaretta that she believed she was with child. The following December, baby Ann Cecil, called Tannakin by her doting parents, was born and sadness began to subside.

HISTORICAL NOTES

This is a book of fiction, though many of the characters existed and events did happen.

In April 1555, John Dee was called to Woodstock to conjure the horoscope of the Lady Elizabeth, her sister, Queen Mary and the queen's husband, Philip of Spain. At the time, there were many rumours of plots to put Philip on the throne if his wife and child should perish. Sadly, Mary was not with child. It was a false pregnancy, probably caused by the condition that would kill her two years later. Her distress at not being pregnant was pitiful to see. Beatrice ap Rhys was her laundress all her life, Jane Foole her fool and Fridewide Knight her closest lady-in-waiting. William Cecil did escape execution after he supported the throning of Lady Jane Grey instead of the rightful heir, Mary. He spent years in exile from court, though remained a fierce protector and advisor to Lady Elizabeth, managing her estates in Lincolnshire and visiting regularly. He was cousin to Blanch ap Harri and would have known about the conjuring of the horoscope. He did, at the request of Lord Englefield, go to France on 20 May to accompany Reginald Pole, the queen's cousin and a Catholic Papal Legate. During his court exile, however, his wife Mildred continued to visit court to see her sister, Ann Bacon, lady-in-waiting to Mary Tudor. Ann Bacon lost her baby girl soon after birth in the early summer of 1555. She grieved with Mildred, who had also lost a baby girl, Francisca, the previous year, though joy came to the Cecils when Ann was born in December 1556.

Englefield was already heading the investigation into conjuring, and on 28 May, eight days after Cecil's departure, John Dee was arrested on suspicion of conjuring and magick. He was sent to Hatfield (though some records say Hampton) and then the Tower, where he was interrogated by John Bourne. He had been accused by George Ferrers and Thomas Prideaux, the latter of whom was employed in Englefield's office at court. Suspicion about Dee was further fired when the children of George Ferrers were struck down with a disease that killed one and blinded the other. Within days, a wax effigy was found in St Dunstan's churchyard.

John Dee faced the Star Chamber and was probably tortured, but in August 1554 was released to the house of Bishop Bonner, who was most indignant when his guest was called the Arch Conjuror. John Dee was made a doctor of divinity in the Catholic faith. We do not know if Dee was spying for Elizabeth's supporters, but he certainly used the code 007 on many documents throughout his life.

Years later, William Cecil, by then Queen Elizabeth's greatest spymaster and advisor, was given a list of spies living abroad. On that list was the name of spies still paid by Philip of Spain. On the list was Thomas Prideaux.

The Tabard Inn did exist in Southwark, as did the doxy houses of Foul Street and others. An influx of Spanish traders and workmen had followed Philip of Spain to England, and London would have been well populated with Catholic men speaking Spanish.

John Dee spent his life trying to get back to court and to get paid by Lord William Cecil. He never stopped trying to claw back the status his father had won and lost at court.

Acknowledgements

I am in debt to many people – my mam who taught me to read and bought every book I ever asked for; my dad who fired in me a love of history and adventure and my teacher, Mr Gerry Williams, who allowed me to use my imagination to create stories, plays and lessons for my schoolmates. I have been tutored by many but special thanks go to Alex Marwood, Mel McGrath, and Bill Ryan for the insights which helped me develop my craft. Then there are the friends who have always encouraged and spurred me on – Nicky, Mick, Ceri, Annie, Peter, and Liz Jenkins, who made me promise to never give up before she went through the veil. I hope she still sees this. Thanks also to anyone else who helped me on my journey to being published.

All authors need great editors. My sincere thanks go out to Laura Gerrard my first editor and great tutor, and then to Charlotte Chapman who copy-edited the final manuscript. All books need a great cover to invite people to turn the page and I have been blown away by the skill and responsiveness of Kari Brownlie.

Then there is my gratitude to Clare Christian and all at RedDoor Press – a dream team who have made a dream come true.

Thank you all.

Many thanks for reading my first novel, *The Conjuror's Apprentice*, the first in the Tudor Rose Murders series.

If you enjoyed reading it and have a moment to spare, I would really appreciate you leaving a review on Amazon and also through your Twitter account. Any help you can give in spreading the word is gratefully received.

If you are in a book club and would like some questions to guide your discussion, these can be found on the book club page of my website gjwilliamsauthor.com You will also find articles which give you more insight into the characters and events depicted in the book.

The next book in the series will involve a series of murders linked to the scandal which enveloped young Elizabeth. It starts when the body of Thomas Seymour is found hanging on the oak at Hatfield House. But how can this be when he was beheaded on Tower Hill exactly nine years previously to the day? Margaretta and John Dee must unpick the past and the growing body-count if they are to stop an old scandal preventing Elizabeth ascending to the throne.

If you would like notification of publication, alerts to new articles and any give-aways, please sign up to my mailing list on the website.

In the meantime, you can follow me on 🐦 gjwilliams92 or 📷 gjwilliams92.

About the author

Dr G J Williams, like John Dee, is Welsh but raised in England. After an idyllic childhood in Somerset, where history, storytelling and adventure were part of life, a career of psychology, first in academia and then international consulting beckoned. It was some years before the love of writing returned to the forefront of life.

G J Williams now lives between Somerset and London and is often found writing on the train next to a grumpy cat and a cup of tea.

When not writing, life is a muddle of researching, travelling to historic sites or plotting while sailing the blue seas on the beloved boat bequeathed by a father who always taught that history gives the gift of prediction.

G J Williams has one dream as a writer – to be chosen by readers who love the books of C J Samson, S J Parris, and Rory Clements, and to see John Dee and Margaretta enter the hearts of all who pick up *The Conjuror's Apprentice*.